JENNIFER M. WALDROP

Dedication

For anyone lost in the hellscape of modern dating.
And for those still trying to connect anyway.

A Note from the Author

Hello lovely reader!

Thank you so much for picking up my dark romcom, *CHOICElover.* This series grows progressively darker, and there are a few themes you should know about before diving in:

Content Warnings:

• Death & resurrection

• Suicide (atmospheric)

• Suicide (the MC's twin, off-page but a recurring theme)

• Mentions of abduction & human trafficking

• Medical experimentation

• Mentions of emotional neglect by a parent

• Violence (brief)

• Loss of autonomy

- Mentions of euthanasia / dead bodies
- Murder (kinda)

Please read safely—and I truly hope you have as much fun reading this world as I did writing it.

<3 Jennifer / @AuthorJMWaldrop

Prologue – A Brilliant Idea

Res6

November 14, 2299, before the events of this book.

When did it last rain? Res6 can't recall—months ago? Years, even? A full-face respirator muffles his bitter laugh. Of course, it had to rain today.

Droplets hit his exposed skin, the acid faintly stinging. He shakes off the mild discomfort, stuffing his bare hands into the pockets of his jumpsuit. A dull ache squeezes his chest as he stares at the barren spot on the pavement where Jerme, his twin brother, took his last breath exactly seven years ago. He's memorized every detail of the setting. The hundred-year-old manufactured stone cladding with the gouge resembling a lightning bolt that Jerme must have leaned on. The palm print pressed into the sidewalk when the concrete was fresh, next to the barely legible date he thinks reads "June 1, 2025." There's a storefront on the opposite side of the street, its supposedly impenetrable glass window acid-streaked but still clear enough to showcase an array of colorful garments. Clothes in various shades of bright blue hang in front of particle panes, which display a jungle setting with large spotted cats roaming through it.

Movement in the window catches his attention. A woman steps into the display, removing a scarf. He watches her slip back to the sales floor, and there's just enough of an opening to see her hand the scarf to a customer before they both step out of view. Had there been a salesperson there that day? Did they watch Jerme die? Did they even try to help? Or did they ignore him? He squeezes his eyes shut, turning back to the stone wall.

The ache that's been there since the day Jerme voluntarily left this world steals his breath. *He left me.*

Vivid memories of that day splash through his mind. Res6 sitting in the lab reviewing the data from the breakthrough that would define him as an up-and-coming researcher. The ping of his device. The notification. Back then, he was whole and blissfully naïve, but it took less than a second for the m-volt to initiate the series of synapses that would change the trajectory of his life forever with a single email.

From: MSP Coroner's Office. Subject: Death Report. Do you wish to continue?

A fresh wave of grief seizes him, nearly knocking him to his knees. His hand shoots out, clutching at the wall for support as the acid rain continues to fall.

He remembers thinking, *Death report? Someone I know died? But why would they be sending me a message unless . . .* His vision momentarily blurred. At 21, he was far too young to conceptualize death or associate it with himself or anyone in his peer group. Because humans had the technology to halt or even reverse aging, why would he? To his mind, death wasn't a topic to consider for a long time.

At the time, he was focused on the place in the scientific community he intended to carve out for himself. Since his youth, the science of human engineering fascinated him, and he was determined to be a part of the next wave of advancement. Jerme always said he was destined for great things. He said he would enjoy watching his older brother—older by a few minutes—spearhead humanity into a new and better future.

Aside from being physically identical, they were opposites in so many ways. Still, they had a deep fondness for each other. A soul-deep connection he couldn't explain—a twin thing. Which was why this couldn't be true. Because if Jerme were gone, wouldn't he have known? Wouldn't he have felt it?

The respirator's mask fogs, and his surroundings cloud over, almost like he's living in a dream. He draws in a deep breath of filtered air, shifting the mask enough to wipe away the tears collecting in the seams where the rubber meets his skin before putting it back in place. As he stands on the sidewalk amidst his grief, a few people with black umbrellas pass, not paying him any heed. What does he look like to them, having his annual meltdown in public?

Does it matter? He can't tamp down the memory bubbling up like it wants to be seen. Like it is Jerme himself who needs to be witnessed one last time. Res6 takes a deep breath, determined to let it take the space in his mind it demands, like a penance of sorts. He's memorized the body of the message.

Valued Citizen A-RES6-MSP-00022960:

As the emergency contact listed in the NHOS Citizen Database, we regret to inform you that the remains of Citizen JERME-MSP-00022961 was found outside of Tower F39 at 10:03 this morning. After reviewing the body, including DNA identification tests, along with footage from area surveillance cameras, the medical examiner was able to certify the citizen's identity and determine the cause of death to be atmosphere-assisted suicide. The coroner has processed the citizen's physical remains and conveyed them to the nearest morgue in Quadrant H for recycling.

Please accept our sincere condolences. If you are thinking about harming yourself or others, remember, the health and well-being of all NHOS citizens is our utmost priority. Operators at MSP's GoodGrief hotline are standing by to take your call.

There was more to the message, but when he first heard it, he got to that point and thought: Replay message. It took listening a dozen times before he finally understood what he was hearing. They'd taken Jerme to the biological remains processing plant before he could see him. Before he could do anything. *Say goodbye.*

He stares at the concrete, visualizing himself lying there at his feet, slumped over. Still. Lifeless. It's what Jerme would have looked like. He forces himself to conjure the image in his mind; does that somehow count as closure?

There's a window a few feet down from the spot. The year Jerme died, it was an anti-aging clinic with bright particle panes displaying an array of procedures promising customers an aesthetic that would surely lead to unparalleled happiness. The current occupants have replaced the particle panes with a reflective film, hiding the interior from the street's view.

He stares at the silver surface, at the man looking back at him. "I'm still really mad at you." He isn't sure if he's talking to himself or Jerme. His reflection doesn't answer. He does this sometimes when he sees his reflection. It's never the same as talking to his brother. The reflection that stares back at him doesn't have the playful quirk of Jerme's full lips. His honey-gold eyes hold pain where Jerme's were once filled with humor. The hollows under his cheekbones are prominent, whereas his brother's were fuller. Jerme was so full of life.

He steps toward the reflection, placing his hand on the glass. "What happened to you? What did I miss?"

There is only silence as he stands in the street, drizzle dripping off his thankfully water-repellent clothes. The space in his chest carved out by Jerme's absence expands. Inflates, as if someone stole his heart, put a balloon in its place, filled it to the point of bursting, and left it there to remind him of the terrible vacancy.

Why is he doing this to himself? Coming to this spot every year so he can do what . . . remember? It's torture. But the Res6 of seven years ago had to know the exact coordinates in the city where his twin took his final breath. What did he expect? Jerme was already gone. Grime-covered concrete and a dingy stone wall were all he found. Standing there didn't stop the grief that first day, and it doesn't stop it now.

Instead, it seems to unleash it. Amplify it. He could avoid that spot and keep pretending Jerme was in a different MSP quadrant, going on with his life—probably charming his next lover. But that feels wrong.

Aside from the self-inflicted torture, what is he seeking? Answers? An awakening? Direction? As if standing here is going to give him a jolt of inspiration, knocking out the heavy cloud hanging over him.

He should have done something. Been a better brother. Been freer with his love. Let Jerme know how much he meant to him. He could have been enough to give his twin a reason to live. But he wasn't.

He must look insane, glaring at his reflection the way he is now. The weight of his emotional deluge doubles him over. He grips his knees to keep from collapsing. No one is on the street anymore to judge him. But that's what he's doing, isn't it? Judging himself. *It's your fault. Jerme is dead because of your shortcomings.*

In a flash, his grief is replaced by an inwardly directed anger so strong his teeth clench. And there's something else too. Something akin to a white-hot pit burning deep in the center of his chest. Something gaping, hungry, and shameful that he's desperate to extinguish . . . or fuel like the self-loathing he's been feeding for the last seven years.

A sudden urge to rush to the lab momentarily distracts him, almost a compulsion. That's what he always does when his emotions are getting out of hand. But his work has been fruitless since his initial break-through—the discovery that nucleic acid memory, or NAM, a form of DNA-encoded data storage buried in a previously undetected neural layer housing experiential memory, could have instructions or data imprinted into it. Despite the countless hours he's devoted to pushing that science—the potential theoretical applications for programming NAM are compelling—he hasn't made any significant progress. No notable findings. When Jerme died, so did his inspiration.

"What am I doing with my life, Jerme? You thought I'd make the world a better place, but I've done nothing." No meaningful impact. He could have at least discovered a way to shield others from the acute pain he still lives with daily. Doesn't he owe that much to Jerme? Instead, he's letting him down. Again.

But how can he possibly be good enough to fix the entire world?

He has a strong urge to slide down the smooth cladding and lay there on the warm stones until the coroner comes for him too.

Res6, it wasn't your fault.

Those aren't his words. They're from the psychologist he worked with during the first year when his grief was winning. The man's belief remains in direct conflict with the one his mind can't seem to release.

I wasn't enough.

He wasn't even who Jerme left a letter for. An image of 3Zeez flashes through his mind. Though Res6 never saw the woman's appeal, Jerme became enamored, and their relationship progressed quickly.

It was just like Jerme to jump into things—like the one time he came home on a mission to invent more realistic simulation chamber props. Another time, Jerme decided to bring back private aviation, even though the world's two major governing bodies manage all air transportation through the official state airline Uni-Fly due to unfavorable climate conditions. He started an online group that continued even after he lost interest, going as far as petitioning the government—which rejected their petition, swiftly disbanding the group.

The point is, when Jerme said they were moving in together after only a few weeks, Res6 had no reason to be alarmed. He figured his relationship with 3Zeez was a passing fling, and he'd lose interest soon enough. But one day, it all unraveled. Jerme showed up at the lab, claiming 3Zeez had disappeared and left no way to contact her.

Res6 had never seen his brother so broken. Nothing was the same after that. He didn't hate 3Zeez, exactly. He hated how vulnerable she'd made Jerme and how disposable she'd found him. But if it weren't 3Zeez, it would have been someone else. People had too many options, Bored? Replace your partner. Move halfway across the globe and reinvent yourself. It's what 3Zeez did. What society needs is a disposable—no, a *replaceable*—companion. That way, people like Jerme wouldn't become collateral damage.

He straightens, giving his reflection a hard look. Is that the answer? A disposable companion?

Before he was born, ASI Personal Companions had been popular. They're banned now—along with most advanced artificial superintelligence. After The Great Equalizer, the world's governing bodies moved quickly to eliminate any tech they saw as a threat.

Surely he could come up with a biological solution—no ASI required, so less government scrutiny.

Res6 glances down the street in the direction of F Quadrant, toward his lab. Considering NAM's programming potential, would it be possible to develop an accelerated adult clone that would—wait! What is he thinking? The ethical concerns would present a challenge, not to mention logistics. The raw organic material alone would require substantial funding. But if he could develop the neural mesh incubation technology to synthesize certain safeguards in the RNA structure, he might get approval from the Consumer Rights Protection Agency. He already has access to a vast catalog of DNA samples.

His cheeks pinch, the respirator cutting into his skin. Zorg, is he smiling? The science itself is fascinating, but if he could provide an option for the disposable companion people want, it would protect people like Jerme—the people getting disposed of.

A virtual—no, *literal*—flesh and blood manufactured partner could be programmed to meet the needs of its owner, and when they were done, the *manupartner*—its organic material—could be recycled and reused.

A fresh wave of energy hums through him. It's been so long since he's felt this way. Too long.

There will be certain elements of the brain-body connection to work out. He'll need to make sure any old synaptic memory is severed, for one, which isn't something he specializes in, but he can develop a team. Perhaps he can get access to one of MSP's new NAM Wave Reconstructors used in rare cases for memory loss patients. It might take a few years to develop a prototype. With the current promise of advancements in the scientific community and the significance of his initial discovery, he'll have no trouble getting funding.

He can do it. Set this new mission in motion. The question is, will he?

The answer flickers in his mind before he forces it into a solid *Yes*.

Yes. This is exactly what he needs to do. It will be his company. His impact on the world. His way of saving all the other Jermes out there, the way he couldn't save his own twin. But now his brother can live on. This will be Jerme's legacy.

His heart hammers as he stares at the spot his GPS guides him to every year. From his pocket, he retrieves the preserved poppy, a flower symbolizing remembrance, that he had specially procured. He clutches the flower, needing to act before the moment is gone. Do something—no, say something.

He draws a deep breath in through his nose, seeking the right words for a long moment before they come to him. His voice is muffled but steady as he says, "Jerme, I couldn't save you, but with what I will invent, no one will ever suffer like you did again. This is what I will do for you. It will be our legacy, and I will call it . . ." He hesitates as insufficient word combinations flash through his mind.

He scans his surroundings, searching for inspiration. A couple carrying a bright pink umbrella dotted with rainbow-colored hearts walks near, glancing in his direction. Their heads incline together as they pass by, but they don't spare him a backward glance. It doesn't matter what they're saying or what they think they've observed.

This is the moment he's been waiting for. Why he comes to this site year after year, searching for a spark of inspiration. For a reason to keep going. A purpose. Now he has one, and he's going to cling to it like life itself.

He feels lighter, as if the cloud that's been following him since Jerme died has lifted. He must capture the moment and name it. Then he'll pour himself into a strategic plan. Petition NHOS for funding. Build a team.

But what will he call it? A name. He needs a name. What would express the sentiment of his mission? He thinks back to Jerme's lover, 3Zeez, who never gave his brother a choice about his fate. Without a word, she left him with his love and heartbreak.

Then it's on the tip of his tongue. He stands staring determinedly at the spot. "The company will be called CHOICElover, Jerme, and it will be my dedication to you."

He unwraps the poppy, kneels, and places it on the concrete, the vibrant red a shock against the cool gray. Within moments, the rain dissolves the dried petals, and all that is left on the pavement is a smear of red. If that had happened last year, it might have tipped him over the precipice, allowing his grief to take hold, but not today. Somehow, watching the flower melt away in the rain feels right. Like an ending and a beginning all at once.

1 – Dear Reader

Electra

October 1, 2390.

Dear Reader,

You will never believe what I'm about to tell you. Hell, I hardly believe it myself, and I'm living it. But you must indulge me. I promise I will make it worth your while.

Imagine that one day you are riding your bike down the rolling streets of San Francisco, minding your business. The year is 2027. You just got the news from your agent that a big-time publisher has picked up your first series — three alien romances that were already drafted. The six-figure deal is everything you've been working toward since you started writing fan fiction in spiral-bound notebooks as a teenager because your family was too poor to afford a computer. Ironically, you didn't spare any time for romance because you were too busy writing about it.

But at twenty-nine, after everything you've been through, everything that you've overcome, all your hard work has finally paid off. The world will read your stories, and the advance you got is enough that you can quit bartending and focus on writing full time. Or even better, cut back your hours and pad your savings account. Or put it all in savings because you never know what life has in store for you next. What really matters is that your words will make someone's day brighter or give someone hope that there's someone out there meant just for them. Sure, they're only romance novels, but to you, they mean everything. And a team of people agreed.

And if they're successful, who knows?! Maybe you'll have finally earned the right to carve out some space in your life for a book boyfriend of your own. A girl can dream.

But most importantly, that little seed that lives inside you that demands you do your part to make the world a better place, to contribute something beautiful through your unique gifts, has found fertile ground. Love is love, and what better way to show that than with smutty a.k.a. downright filthy interspecies alien romance? You're on cloud nine. Flying high, soaring down the hill, soaking up the glorious sunshine. It's better than any first kiss, you're sure of it.

Then—and make sure you're sitting down for this part—you wake up naked as the day you were born. Staring at you is the most aggressively handsome man you've ever seen. Like, puts every A-list male celebrity to shame hot. Wavy dirty blond hair, sharp jaw, piercing gold eyes that match his warm golden complexion. He's wearing a space commander-esque jumpsuit—all black. Beside him are two other men—attractive, but not quite the masterpieces as the first. One has a bright orange afro, cool mid-tone brown skin, and glasses, but without the lenses—so, for fashion. The other has crisp black hair cut neatly, pointy, delicate features dotted with several facial piercings, and a complexion so pale it's almost translucent. Both of them are wearing white lab coats. They hold what look like tablets, but are clear like glass, flashing with bright multicolored lights. Their eyes are trained on you, and it's obvious that they're assessing you.

At this point, you're trying not to freak out, so you assess your surroundings. You're standing on what your bare feet recognize as a glass scale with cool metal plates in a nondescript room that looks like a holding cell out of a futuristic movie. Gray walls, gray floor, bright glowing ceiling. No furniture except a shiny metal table, which holds a dozen bottles of water lined up like obedient soldiers. It's antiseptic. And small enough that you think if you lay down and stretch your arms overhead, you might span the width. There's only enough space for the four of you to take a few steps each without colliding.

Then the man says to you, *and I'm not shitting you when I say he actually, literally,* turns to the orange-haired man and says, "Another excellent specimen, Lextr." You're trying to keep your mouth from falling open as he proceeds to rake his gaze up and down your naked body. He's not even subtle about it. Or suave or alpha, like you might guess—Reader, we both know the type. It is a little awkward, despite how unfairly gorgeous the man is. That only means one thing: he's a serial killer.

If you haven't figured it out yet, this is *me* we're talking about. This shit actually happened to me today.

Naturally, I freak the fuck out. My heartbeat ricochets out of control and I'm pretty sure my palms sweat. But here's the catch. I can't move, so I can't be sure. I'm completely paralyzed. Except that I discover I can talk. So I say, "The fuck you are!" Then I'm pretty sure I screamed something at him about *Who are you?* And *Let me go!*

Now, here's where it gets weird. Instead of getting aggressive or telling me to shut up, the man's brows furrow in concern. As if my outburst somehow confuses him. Like I'm not supposed to be acting this way.

He says, "Please remain calm," then runs a hand over his dark blond stubble. He seems to calculate something while the two lab coats jot things down in their tablets.

So I try again. "Hello?! Are you going to unfreeze me or what?" I've read way too many books to know that if I'm not a take-charge heroine, readers will think I'm whiny, annoying, or worse, self-involved. Hell, I've written those books. And right now, I'm playing a starring role in my own misadventure. Or having a really messed-up dream. Either way, might as well make it count and hope the heroine doesn't die in this one.

He gives me his attention. Thick brows furrow over his intense gold eyes. Then he asks me a question that rumbles the foundation of my existence. "What year do you think it is?"

I know what you're thinking. What the ever-loving fuck? Me too. I mean, this suggests I'm in the future, right? "2027," I answer, even though I'm already guessing it is not 2027 anymore. Why else would he ask? He lets out an exasperated sigh, as if this is somehow my fault. Indignant, I ask, "What year is it now?"

In my head, I formulate a plausible story. I was in an accident, went into a coma, and now it's ten years later. I've woken up, and this man is my strange miracle doctor. But my body feels strong, and I don't feel older. A quantum time jump then? Oh, he's an alien in human form. And I've not only jumped time, I've jumped space too. Or, again, this is a really weird dream.

What did I eat last? That's right. I ordered my ramen extra spicy, so that must be it. The most boring option, a dream. Does it make me strange, this pang of regret that hits me as I stare at the handsome man my mind has created, wishing that perhaps it wasn't a dream? What a shame that my life didn't just get more interesting. Like when a character discovers they have magic or their grandmother's locket is a powerful relic.

"2390," he says to me. Then to himself, "Damn it. I knew this could happen. So fucking stupid. We should have just taken them out of the program, but I had to ..."

The orange-haired lab coat says, "We knew this was a calculated risk. She's easily decommissioned, and at least now we understand the volatility of samples—"

I stop listening as my mind whirls, failing to connect to the word *decommission,* which I see clearly now. I'm busy thinking about the implications of year 2390. Three hundred and sixty-eight years in the future. No way. This can't be a dream. I'm completely lucid and it feels too real. I scan the space for a hidden camera like in one of those prank reality shows. I refuse to be one of those idiots who don't realize the joke until they've already made a fool of themselves. But the walls appear smooth except for a single metal door.

And why would I need to be naked for a prank show? I'm not sure why, but that single glaring fact makes me suspect he might not be lying. Crazier things have happened. Well, not to me. Or anyone I've ever known. Just fictional characters. Scratch all that. I've definitely read too many books. That's what my problem is.

Before I know what's happening, the lab coat men are slowly creeping forward as if not to alarm me. One has something in his hand that I can't see. Oh God, it's a needle. Probably a drug to put me to sleep or kill me? My blood runs cold. I've had the realization too late. Now the word *decommission* shines in my mind as blinding as fog light at close range. But I can't move. I feel a sharp prick on my wrist. The world goes fuzzy for a moment before it fades away completely.

The next time I wake up—and thank God, I wake up—I'm standing on the same glass scale thing, still unable to move, but my surroundings have changed. This new space is also stark, with concrete walls and floors, but less science lab aesthetic and more contemporary living room. Within my field of vision, I can see an ultramodern couch, three shiny round tables, and one large geometric area rug. The lab coat men are gone, and the gorgeous serial killer man is standing with his back to me, facing a huge floor-to-ceiling window which looks out on the most beautiful beach I've ever seen. Crystal clear water washes up onto white sand a dozen yards outside of the window. My first thought is how remote we are. What does he do that affords such a beautiful beach view? Do neighboring structures sit adjacent to this one? Is this the Caribbean or South Pacific? I see no people or foliage to suggest a location. And what about climate change? Considering the pristine scenery, I guess the climate deniers were right. The thought makes my stomach turn, though I think, yay Earth!

The tense set of the man's shoulders has my nerves firing. Still, I clear my throat. He turns around slowly, as if he's reluctant to.

"What was all that?" I demand. "Where am I? And who were those men?"

He doesn't answer. He only stares at me, reinforcing the murder-y vibes. I wish he would speak.

"Umm . . . hello? How did I end up in the future? And who are you?" A million other questions rocket through my mind. Why can't I move? Why am I naked? Are there flying cars? Has AI taken over the world? Can I go back? Are you going to murder me? Is everyone I know dead? That one almost doubles me over, but I'm still frozen. I don't ask any of these questions because he seems a bit overwhelmed. And on the off chance he isn't a serial killer, I don't want to increase my chances of the answer to the murder one being Yes! Perhaps he's just a nice man with a time machine and this is all some sort of accident.

Ignoring my questions, he comes to squat at my feet. Then he looks up at me between my exposed breasts. I can only catch his eye if I look down at the edge of my field of vision. My two pert nipples frame his handsome face. "Name?" he asks, as if whatever I say is guaranteed to annoy him.

"Electra Lynch," I say. And yes, *Dear Reader*, I know my name is PERFECT for a futuristic time travel novel. My hippie parents narrowed it down to Electra, Lily Breeze and Kilenya Rain, so I think I'll count my blessings. Not that I didn't appreciate my father trying to pick a tribal name to honor our heritage, thus mine, but Kilenya, while beautiful, literally means "coughing fish." Imagine explaining that on a first date.

"What's yours?" I ask him, thinking maybe this is something he'll answer.

"Ressix," I think he says. Then he spells out, "A," pause, "R-E-S-6-MSP-00022960," like that means anything to me.

"So, Ressix, then? I assume the rest of that is some type of identifier," I say. "And you spell it R-E-S and the number six, is that right?"

From his position at my feet where he's punching buttons on the scale thing, he releases an exasperated groan. "In a moment, you'll have full motor control of your limbs."

"Okay, then." I remember the way he looked at me earlier. I figure I better double check in case I need to come out of this paralysis state with swinging fists. "You're not going to hurt me, right?"

I mean, I was having such a good day. Three hundred years ago, I guess. And I really don't want to get tortured. This is what I was actually thinking in the moment, which as I write this now, I realize might seem a little too casual. Like, shouldn't I be more alarmed? Looking back, yes, but to give myself credit, I am probably experiencing some major shock and denial at this point. Remember, the mind is a powerful machine and, in the moment, my narration cannot be trusted.

"I'm going to press this button and you'll feel a flash of pain, but it will be over soon. Then you'll be released. Please don't freak out on me," he says, an unfeeling, aloof edge to his voice.

A beep sounds, then blistering pain the likes of which I've never known flashes across the soles of my feet. I jump-step across the room, howling in agony. "Fuck!" I finally manage.

I brace my hands on the back of the couch and work to steady my breathing. By now, my brain starts to fire again. "2390, huh? That's wild."

And it is wild. Like really, really wild. The million questions start back up. I want to shout all of them at his retreating back.

"Indeed," is all he says as he goes into another room. I cover my breasts with my hands, though it's pretty pointless, and wait for him to come back.

He returns, holding out a button-down shirt toward me as if he's trying to keep as much space between us as possible. As if he might catch something from me, like lice or empathy. "Put this on," he says.

I take it. It's his. It smells like him. Not that I know what he smells like. Only that I am guessing this glorious, woodsy citrus scent belongs to him.

After sliding it on, I take care not to miss a single button. Then I pull my tumble of black hair from the collar, so it falls down my back.

Res6 hasn't stopped watching me since he handed me the shirt. He blurts, "How is that so unbelievably sexy?"

This is what he says to me. Now imagine, after the last ten minutes I've had—waking up in the alleged future, getting drugged, feeling the most acute pain of my life, not knowing how I got here or what happened to anyone from my time, my friends, my family—he's thinking about how sexy I look in his shirt. His gold eyes darken slightly and I can tell he means it. Has this man never been around a woman before?

Still, like in every idiotic romance novel, my stupid stomach dips with the way he's looking at me because evidently my inner cavewoman likes the attention. He bites his lip and releases a forlorn sigh, as if it's a tragedy.

Thank goodness for my actual brain, though. Because fuck this guy. I cross my arms over my chest and make eye contact with him so hard I think he might be a little taken aback. "Tell me what is happening."

He glances away and walks over to a computer desk, which holds what I guess are 2390 computers. I assume I'm meant to follow, so I do. Three little metal stands with horizontal bars on top rest on a utilitarian gray desk. An electronic pad sits in the center of the arrangement. Some type of computer screen? There is a slit at the top of each bar. Right as I'm leaning over the desk to inspect them, light flickers from the openings and then

I'm looking at what appear to be completely solid screens. I reach out to touch one, but my fingertips only poke a hole through the screen, which fills in when they retreat. "Weird."

"It's probably easier if I show you." He motions to the desk chair. "Sit."

He seems to have some idea of what has happened, which is a relief, *I think*. But wait, whatever has happened was clearly not intentional. I'm torn between life-altering fear and morbid curiosity.

Curiosity wins out, and I take a seat. He hovers his hand over a little illuminated pad, moving his fingers. A red beam scans the space in front of the screens. He stares at the beam unblinking for a second. Must be some type of eye scanner. Then, without touching the electronic pad or anything, windows open. Letters appear across the screen, forming words in a search bar. Results populate.

Then the man, Res6, with some unseen technology, selects one. A page opens, and a video begins. I realize he must be telepathically communicating the commands to the computer. I'm momentarily fascinated until a man appears on the screen, facing the viewer.

He is slipping a thin strap off a woman's shoulder, the expression in his eye unmistakable. All we see is her from behind. Her beauty is implied. He kisses her bare skin, and she gives a little quiver. Then the man looks up at the camera. "When's the last time you found a partner who really desires to please you? Who wants the same things you do? Someone who recognizes and gives you what you need?"

Okay, so far, pretty innocent, right? Like a rich guy dating service. Or one of those sugar baby operations.

It gets weirder. And quickly.

The man puts his hand on the woman's shoulder and presses down. She slips below the camera's view, and we all know what she is meant to be doing next. At this point, I'm trying really hard to keep an open mind, though the feminist in me is raging. The man grins at the viewer. "Don't you think it's time to make the right choice?"

What misogynistic bullshit.

A logo pops up on the screen, CHOICElover, in block letters. Each letter of *CHOICE* matches the rainbow, minus violet, which is reserved for *lover.* The screen changes to a different man on a computer. He's on some type of shopping site, selecting checkboxes. I look closely at what he picks, and a voice says, "It's easy. First you select your CHOICElover's temperament. You can choose up to ten characteristics."

The man selects the following: agreeable, sexy, sweet, kindhearted, empathic, charming, caring, adventurous, sexual, and respectful.

Please join me with a collective eye roll. The more exaggerated the better.

Somehow, I know where this is going. I wonder what boxes Res6 selected for me. Because clearly this is what I was meant to be. A CHOICElover, which is some sort of futuristic sex doll for this man, hence his forward comments. This time when my stomach dips, it isn't in a cute, fluttery way. It's in an *I think I'm going to be sick* sort of way.

I keep watching. Because by the end of the video, I presume I'll have some answers.

The actor clicks NEXT.

A new screen pops up that looks like an online catalog. But instead of handbags or boat parts, it's people. A button at the top says FILTER. The man clicks it and the voiceover says, "This is the fun part. Just click Filter, and choose your ideal partner. CHOICElover will do the rest!"

The man clicks female, blonde, 5'3" – 5'7", blue eyes, soft curves (the other choices are voluptuous, athletic and androgynous). There are other criteria to narrow down, but the man leaves those alone. He presses search and the field of people to choose from narrows. He scrolls for a while until he finds the blonde-haired, blue-eyed woman he wants. When he clicks on her headshot, a new window pops up with the same woman but her full body. And guess what? She's nude.

At this point I give Res6 a *this can't be for real* look.

"Keep watching," he says, as if he doesn't think this the least bit insane.

Apparently, during my brief interchange with Res6, the man has checked out because he's begun a new scene. The man is collecting a package from an oversized mailbox. The label reads "Fully Customized CHOICElover Kit." Then there are a bunch of letters and numbers that don't mean anything to me. Almost like a mailing label.

The scene changes again, and the man is in a bedroom plugging the little scale-like thing into a wall. Then ... *oh God*. He unwraps what looks like a giant patty of Spam, all pink and gelatinous. It quivers as he sets it on the scale. He takes a bottle of water and pours it into a little slot. Green lights come on and the little meat patty gives a jolt.

I can't peel my eyes away from the time-lapse video that plays next. Every few seconds, the man comes back and speed-pours water into the slot when the lights turn red. He goes away and the meat patty morphs into ... I don't even know how to describe it. It's a pink blob that, with each bottle of water, becomes even more gelatinous. And bigger.

They say the human body is 60 percent water ...

Eventually, the thing goes from looking like a phallic blob to Gumby if he were made of canned dog food. Then it becomes more humanoid, and skin appears. I assume that inside the creature, the loaf of wet dog food is transmuting into organs and blood, etc. Hairs sprout. Eyelashes and fingernails. The definition of lips and nipples. Her clit and labia form before the pubic hair fills in. The last thing to gain LifeLike color are her irises. The man comes in with a final bottle of water and surveys the creation. His grin as he assesses her turns my stomach.

Suddenly, all I want to do is take a scalding hot shower. To scrub every single inch of my skin until it's raw.

Now the woman is blinking. The man sets the unused bottle aside and leans down to the scale thing. He punches a few buttons, and, unlike me, the woman doesn't react. He stands and offers her a hand, which she takes. She steps off the scale, giving him the sweetest trusting grin.

"Hello, darling," he says to her, and her grin becomes toothy. "What would you like to do today?"

Even though I know what's coming, I still brace.

In the most compliant Stepford wife voice, she says, "Anything you like."

The video ends with the man from the beginning giving the rest of his spiel about how with a small down payment, a CHOICElover, the premium manupartner of our time, can be yours. "So, what are you waiting for? Make the right CHOICE today!"

I stare at the BUY NOW button, a little dumbfounded. The implication is that this is what Res6 and his lab coat buddies did to get me. But how? This is too elaborate to be fake or a joke. I spin the chair to face him. I'm shocked and angry and in desperate need of an outlet.

"That is the most horrific, disgusting, and pathetic thing I've ever seen in my entire life. You …" I get to my feet, my words staggering like the rest of me. "You thought, what? That I was going to be some type of sex toy for you? Is that it? Can't get an actual woman to spread her legs for you? So you needed one of those things … what was it called?"

Res6, for his part, remains calm. "A manupartner," he supplies.

"So creeps like you just pull women from the past to be their sex slaves. Is that it?"

His expression clears. "CHOICElover is not just for men. In my opinion, the commercial geared toward cis straight women is even more graphic."

Is he offended? Never mind. I don't care. I don't want to imagine a woman speaking to the camera while simultaneously pushing a man's head down, out of view. I think back over the video. I'm missing a few key details, like the significance of the woman morphing into existence from a meat patty. But I'm freaking out. Palms sweating, bile churning, I'm-going-to-vomit freaking out.

I jab a stiff finger into his chest. "If that's what you think you're going to get with me, you clicked the wrong buttons, asshole. There is no way

I'm having sex with you, and if you try to force me, I'll fight you the entire time. I promise it won't be fun for you."

My blood runs cold. So very, very cold. Frigid and icy and bone-chilling. If he tries to force me ... Is that what he wants? Did he pick me and my traits because he knew I'd be more likely to fight him? And he gets off on that? I take several quick steps back, scanning the room for the exit. I have to run away. I remember the beach outside. Surely there's a resort somewhere nearby with security.

He slowly lifts his hand like I might startle if he moves too quickly. "Easy. I'm not going to force you. There is more you need to know. Please come sit back down." He looks like every word he speaks is an effort.

Reluctantly, I follow him to the couches and take a seat on the opposite side of the space from him. The one nearest what might be a door that leads outside.

He takes a measured breath, gripping his knees. "See, manupartners are the standard form of companionship now. For *all people*. Ever since we brought them onto the market, nearly everyone gets one. Easier to get just what you want from a relationship and so on. The thing is, manupartners aren't actually meant to be people from the past. You are supposed to be a blank slate. A programmable partner."

"Like a sex robot," I interject. "That is the most messed-up thing I've ever heard."

How far has society regressed if this is what humans are reduced to? My liberal hippie parents would be horrified. At this point, I am refusing to consider that they are likely dead. That they *are* dead. A knot builds in the back of my throat, but I swallow it down. This has to be a dream. My subconscious is incredibly imaginative.

"Yes, precisely. But more like a clone, so real. Made with human DNA from the past that has been collected and traded over the years." He says the word *real* as if it doesn't have the same meaning it did during my time.

As if its new meaning is more like "real, but not really real." Real-like. Or real-ish. Faux-real.

"Okay," I say, urging him to go on.

"There were rumors about manupartners retaining the identity of the DNA's original vector. I had my assistant Tommy search BLACKOUT, the dark web of our time, for anyone claiming to have a manupartner who thinks they're from the past. Of the handful he's identified, so far they're all from pre-2050 and linked to our competitor GROW who recently released a Realer Than Real update."

"What is so special about this period?"

He shrugs. "It's not that the humans from the period themselves are special. It's just that around 2050, the birthing industry took off. Prospective parents could select their offspring's genetic traits: eye color, height, nose shape, and so on. It became common practice. Since then, our DNA has been altered, if you will. Streamlined, even."

"So basically, people from your time like us because we're mutts?"

He frowns. "People from your time have a more authentic feel, which our more discerning clients appreciate. The point is, you are an unfortunate but necessary consequence of an experiment to test the DNA from that time period. Aside from you, CHOICElover, the premium manupartner, hasn't reported a single mishap."

I can't help but grin, since this asshole's pride is about to be shattered. "Until now." I hold my arms wide for emphasis.

"Thank Zorg it happened during our trials. But at least we can reasonably guess that there is a link between the purity of the DNA from that time period and the volatility of NAM expression." He pulls a device from his pocket. A glass cell phone? He taps the screen a few times, then he holds up a finger to silence me.

Someone must pick up because he says, "Listen, Brix, let's pull the line pre-2050." A pause. "No, nothing wrong with the unit. Just not worth the risk of a malfunction." Another pause. "No, it isn't exhibiting any signs of NAM expression." Pause. "No." Pause. "No, just the standard embedded functional memory." The person must be convinced—relieved?—because the questions stop. "I'm going to hang onto this one. Get a little mileage out of it. We can always put the series back online if something changes."

He lied to a coworker about me. That might be the greatest revelation from his call. And mileage—how callous. My skin crawls.

My thoughts must show on my face because he says, "I didn't mean that. I only . . ." he trails off like he knows he can't win.

I'm beside myself. I want to scream and throw things. Now my questions mount in the millions. I add to the list *Why did you lie to your coworker?* I'm not sure I'm ready for the answer. "What happens when you're done with a manupartner?"

Res6 looks away, shaking his head. "They get recycled."

I jolt back.

"Don't worry. That won't happen to you."

"But . . . but if you hadn't lied, would that happen to me?"

"We are in unprecedented territory here—"

"Is that why you lied? To protect me or your employer?" I ask as I piece his motivations together.

"Is it a problem if I say both?"

Great. He's only a borderline psychopath. I know the look I'm giving him is dripping with disgust. I don't need to answer.

"It's not what it seems. It's an ethical dilemma we haven't faced. And with the company, I have a duty to the workers. Do you know how many people CHOICElover employs? If NHOS got involved or shut us down, it would be bad for more than just me. I have a responsibility—"

"NHOS?" I interject to ask.

"Northern Hemisphere Organizational System, the governing body of half of the continent." He leans back in his seat, rubbing his eyelids.

"Oh," I say. "Well, I don't see why you feel so responsible. I appreciate you protecting me from your corporate overlords, though. I can't imagine the type of greedy pervert that would invent a *manupartner* would be so accepting of someone in my situation." I make air quotes around the strange word.

I guess something I said struck a chord because he groans, loudly. It is the most significant display of emotion I've gotten out of him. "I wish this weren't happening," he says. "But hopefully you're the only one, and now Brix, my product line manager, will take care of it before it happens again."

"What about those other two men that were in the room when I first woke up?" I ask.

He lets out another long-suffering sigh. "Don't worry about them. Lextr is my lead scientist and Tommy, as you know, is my personal assistant. They each have signed a nondisclosure agreement. Knowledge of your *nature* is limited to the three of us."

"Excellent," I say, but my terror has numbed me by this point. I don't even know what to think. How is a person supposed to process all this information in—how long has it been? Two hours?

There are more questions. More things I need to know. My subconscious pushes me to ask. But right now, I have enough to digest. Res6 seems to hold some regard for others, demonstrated by his concern for his employees. I feel it's safe to say I'm not in imminent danger.

Wait—*his* employees? My next question is on the tip of my tongue, but I don't think I can handle any more surprises right now.

I stand up, knowing exactly what I need. I can feel this wellspring of words I'm sharing with you, Dear Reader, searching for a way out. Searching for a page to tumble onto.

So I say, "I need a minute to process all of this. And a notebook or something if you have one." If my thoughts don't find an outlet, I'll implode. I've always been this way. I've filled hundreds of journals throughout my life. He hands me a tablet, directs me to a program called Scrawl, then just stands there staring at me. I scan the room quickly. "Is there a bedroom I can use?" I wiggle the tablet at him. "I need a minute. *In private.*"

His eyes narrow, as if what I'm requesting makes no sense to him. Still, he directs me through a door to an adjoining room, then leaves me.

That brings us to the present. I now sit in a minimal but luxurious bedroom that I assume must be his. The massive bed draped with dark silken bedding and olive-gray walls lend an overall masculine and cave-like feel to the space. I have a tablet in hand and am writing with a sleek metal stylus. I've gotten it all out of my head and onto the page, so it no longer has to rattle around in my mind. A lightness settles over me. I still have questions, like what am I supposed to do now? But I'm alive and I'm fairly certain this isn't a dream.

Feeling centered, I'm convinced I'm ready to tackle what's next. Thanks in part to you, Dear Reader. I'm in the future, and it's going to be okay.

Cautiously hopeful,

Electra

Electra glances up from the tablet, clutching her precious words to her chest as the door cracks open.

"Hello?" Gold eyes peek in at her. "Is everything okay?"

Something about Res6's concerned frown sends all the cautious optimism Electra spent the last hour nurturing flying out the window. She's in the future. What is she going to do now?

2 – An Actual Woman

Res6

Why is there a real human woman in his bedroom potentially having a mental breakdown? That's right. Because after a brief argument with Lextr about the ethics of recycling her, he decided to bring her to his unit. His reasoning: keeping her in his lab is out of the question. His staff would quickly realize that his latest experiment illegally brought back a woman from the past. The rumors about GROW's mishaps that Tommy found on BLACKOUT are already making the rounds in the scientific community—evidently, he isn't the only one who heard a rumor and went searching. Soon NHOS will catch one of these mishaps. There will be headlines. Public trust regarding the safety of his product will be questioned. He must secure CHOICElover's public image—his life's work, his passion, and his brother's legacy. To do that, no one can know about the woman in the bedroom.

Therefore, since it's his company he's protecting, she's his responsibility. So he did what any normal person would do in such a situation. He brought her home, stuck her in the corner of his living room like a floor lamp, and waited for her to wake up.

If he really believed she might have retained her memories, he'd have activated her in the privacy of his unit to begin with. Disregard that. He wouldn't have activated her at all. But doing it in his unit would have saved him and Tommy from the cramped ride in his private sealed air transport, or SAT. Plus the dozen strange looks as they carried her through the halls to the private elevator reserved for the penthouse units in his tower. Yet activating her in his unit wouldn't have saved him from the horrendously uncomfortable conversation he just had and the painful cocktail of panic and dread he's now experiencing. What is he going to do with her? It's not like she can stay in his unit forever. He wipes the sweat rapidly collecting on his forehead.

Shit, shit, shit. Get it together, Res6. She'll be out at any moment, and she can't catch you crawling the walls like a caged animal. She's already wary of you.

He should have made Tommy stay as a buffer.

I can't imagine the type of greedy pervert that would invent a manupartner, she said. No, better Tommy didn't stay and accidentally reveal that Res6 is in fact the greedy pervert in question. *No wonder she's hiding from you in your own bedroom.*

The rays of sunshine from the particle panes, which illuminate the room in bright cheery light, aren't helping his disposition. He thinks the command: Update particle pane. Play Drizzle. The sunny beach scene morphs into a custom rain aesthetic. Hidden speakers in the corner of each window mimic the soothing sound of fat raindrops pattering against the glass. He takes a seat at his desk, inhaling deeply, and allows the scene to soothe him.

Just approach the situation logically. Methodically. His several mini-meltdowns were entirely unnecessary. The rain façade is coming down in sheets, beating against the particle panes—or it would if it were real. He thinks the command: Increase volume. A moment later, the melodic drumming surrounds him. Water sounds, particularly rainstorms, ease something inside him.

He glances at the door, contemplating the woman on the other side. She came from the year 2027. A time before acid rain and oceanic dead zones. A pang of envy strikes him in the gut. What would it be like to feel the sun warm your skin as a wave rushes over your feet? The simulation chambers are great, but they can't come close to the real thing.

During her time, they probably had other things that only exist as replicas now. Her presence in his life might give him an opportunity to hear a firsthand account of those things—but his curiosity will have to remain unsatiated for the time being. Forever, because he has no intention of discussing her experiences or anything else remotely personal with her. Not who she was, not what she likes or dislikes. Nothing that might build a connection. Getting to know her feels like a bad idea. Dangerous. Look what happened to Jerme because of 3Zeez. He should get a manupartner as insulation, but the woman thinks they're horrific, so a manupartner would only add to his problems.

He paces past the closed door, shooting it a glare as if it caused the offense. Wait—when did he stand back up? No matter. Trying to sit still is a fruitless endeavor. His priority is figuring out what to do with her while simultaneously keeping her identity a secret.

That feels only slightly monumental. Fuck me.

The trials that led to her existence seemed reasonable at the time. Prudent even. Clearly, he needs to reframe it as a mistake. A colossal mistake that is his responsibility.

How could he be so stupid? He and Lextr knew this was a possibility—GROW, it seems, proved that. But instead of just pulling CHOICElover's pre-2050 line, he approved the trial. Now there is a real human woman on the other side of his bedroom door grappling with her fate. He hasn't even told her the worst part—how she ended up in the DNA pool.

She died. They all did. They weeded out the famous ones, like movie stars and political figures, or vectors with telomeres so aged, the DNA wouldn't survive the replication process without mutations that would corrupt the integrity of the specimen. Outside of that, DNA from anyone in the past is fair game. Soon, he'll have to tell her.

The thought makes his stomach clench. Perhaps he can delegate the task to Tommy. *No, she's your responsibility.* Zorgdamn his curiosity. It pushed him to get CHOICElover off the ground—well, his curiosity and the guilt, his constant companion. *Not dwelling on that.*

Motivations aside, his curiosity has been a benefit more often than not. It led him to experiment until he developed a nearly flawless product, and when his research direction became public, the competition to get a product on the market exploded. He won. CHOICElover was the first and the best. When kept in check, curiosity is a good thing, especially for a scientist. So, sure, he was curious.

Restless.

The word pops into his mind, unwelcome. Is he restless? Is that why he allowed the trial? Is running CHOICElover not enough anymore? Did he get bored, or worse, complacent?

He shakes off the concerning thoughts, finding himself hovering outside her door. *Her* door . . . Having her in his space, a real woman right on the other side of the door, makes his blood pressure spike. He keeps pacing. She's a liability. An existential threat, one he's terribly physically attracted to—*which normally wouldn't be an issue*—who is primed to disrupt the stable life he's cultivated.

He should have pulled the line and kept on . . . living, or whatever this is that he is doing.

That's it. He needs something to do, or he's going to drive himself mad overthinking. Maybe Lextr has pinpointed the biochemical synapse relay stage responsible for triggering memory activation.

The DNA samples GROW inadvertently used, which resulted in solvent NAM expression, probably originated from the brain tissue of the vector. Though why GROW would have used physical samples instead of the industry standard synthesized DNA was anyone's guess. For the experiment, Lextr selected hundreds of DNA samples from vectors with perfectly preserved prefrontal cortex tissue along with samples from various areas of the body as the control group. As the experiment got underway, the vectors from the control group showed failure markers early in each trial. On average, the brain matter group made it much deeper in the grow period before failing, until the final successful vector made it all the way to activation.

That brings him full circle to the beautiful, real woman in his bedroom. He glances at the door for the twelfth time. What is she recording on the tablet? He can't even guess, because that woman, Electra Lynch . . . She's so *alive* . . . and those freckles . . . they're something else entirely. If he is being honest, a very small—*infinitesimally small*—part of him finds her utterly—

The point is, he needs to go to the lab and speak with Lextr.

He marches toward the bedroom door and pushes it open. "Hello?" Poking his head inside, he eyes the inconvenient woman. "Is everything okay?"

Electra absently glances up from her tablet. Her eyes widen as they land on him.

"I need to run back to the lab," he says. "Will you be okay here while I'm gone?"

She gives him a subtle nod.

He narrows his gaze. She looks so small sitting there on his bed, as though whatever bravery she drew upon earlier has run out. Did her bottom lip just quiver, or is that his imagination? Where's the spunky woman who marched into the bedroom with the tablet? Strike that. It doesn't matter. Her new reality is shocking, so if she cries, it is perfectly natural. Excellent. He'll leave her to it, then.

"I'll bring back food," he states crisply. "Shouldn't be long. A few hours." With that, he spins out and flees his unit.

Res6 studies the dozen 3D DNA models Lextr has pulled up on the center panel of the Spot-Gene Interface. The enormous set of screens spans the entire wall of the conference room on the R&D floor of CHOICElover's main operations hub. "You're saying a key gene sequence didn't get spliced correctly, causing her embedded memory expression to be solvent?"

Sure, they couldn't erase the memory data, which his early research proved nearly a century ago. So, his team developed an effective strategy to make sure the original vector's NAM stayed repressed while also accepting their programming since it accessed the same gene sequences as for memory suppression. Isolating the necessary genes, psion-splicing in their proprietary LifeLike™ programming, and ensuring only their programming's expression during activation proved to be his team's biggest hurdles.

They used AI simulations to run thousands of experiments before they ever brought the experiments into the real world. Fortunately, they were able to decommission the clones the moment the failure markers appeared—*before the vector ever opened its eyes and it became an ethical dilemma.* When his team finally tried a live activation, they were confident that the vector's memory was repressed. The clone opened its eyes a blank slate. They'd succeeded!

The next challenge was depositing actual information, like language, into the human genome, and even trait expression if, say, the customer didn't prefer the original vector's eye color. Truly, the applications were endless. Sharing that bit of genetic engineering with the government was part of what got him the final approvals he needed to take CHOICElover to market. His work had ultimately benefited humanity. Not only did CHOICElover pave the way for an entire new industry, it outshone every other competitor in every way, from its innovative technology to its rigorous testing—a large part of why he found the woman's existence so concerning.

He clears his throat, waiting for an answer. Lextr and Tommy share a glance.

"I synthesized the damage, yes," Lextr says. "I hypothesized that the old plasmid storage vectors from that period might have stability issues. They maintained integrity during the replication process, but during the accelerated protein compounding phase, the specification period to be exact, a slight increase in the electrical transmission caused our LifeLike protocols to be overridden by the sample's original code expression." Lextr shrugs as if what he's saying isn't startling. "We knew sending varying electrical synapses to an unstable DNA source might have unintended consequences. This was all in the experiment design you approved."

"Could you try a bio-gel substrate next time?" Tommy asks.

"Wait, I thought the DNA purity of the pre-2050 line was the variable?" Res6 asks, pointedly ignoring the interjection from his assistant.

Lextr sighs. "It is. One of the several factors listed. Maintaining NAM solvency seems to require a perfect storm of factors."

"No more experiments." Res6 sighs. "As best we can tell, if during the specification phase, the sample doesn't remain stable during a variable electrical load, it may cause our programming to fail and lead to the expression of the sample's stored NAM?"

"Pretty much," Lextr confirms. "I ran a comparison using a random sample of CHOICElover units from the past few decades and the sample we extracted from your unit. They're identical except for this area here where you can clearly see our LifeLike sequence. Our mRNA instructions appear to be dormant, giving the subject access to their retained NAM data, causing memory expression. I'm adding these data points to our catalogue of failure markers should it become relevant at some point."

Lextr points to two of the samples on the screen, which enlarge, and he takes a section of each, comparing them side by side. Beneath, a series of nucleotide codes appear. "I reviewed your early research since your trials never brought back a vector . . . wholly restored."

It's true that his failures in the early days never pointed to a true NAM expression—like Electra, where the subject wakes up believing they're still the same person they were in the past. Just enough NAM expression that the subject might have some lingering memory resonance—which would have been problematic for his product design. They needed complete control, and with what essentially amounted to an echo of the original vector's memories, that wasn't possible.

Lextr toggles through different windows until the experiment design is displayed on the screen. "I had some ideas about how we might achieve a complete restoration—"

"Hold on," Res6 says, scraping his nails across his scalp. "I wasn't trying to resurrect someone!"

Tommy frowns. "I thought you said testing the hypothesis was prudent—I can check my notes."

"Not now, Tommy," he says, keeping his focus trained on Lextr. "Couldn't we have proved it with an AI model? Now I have a real human woman from the past in my unit having a mental breakdown as we speak!" If he isn't careful, he'll be the one having a mental collapse.

He should have read Lextr's experiment design more thoroughly. He signed off on it thinking his head scientist might pinpoint a genetic alteration that would allow CHOICElover to produce manupartners exhibiting manneristic idiosyncrasies that defined generations and cultures past, giving users a more realistic, unique, and customizable experience. It's what GROW was doing with their Realer Than Real line that evidently led to their mishaps. Naturally, he assumed he'd succeed where GROW failed.

You couldn't just be satisfied with your success. He covers his eyes as if his hand might block out his stupid decision.

Lextr frowns, his gaze flicking past the glass doors to the cabinets where the medical supplies are kept. "This is precisely why I suggested decommissioning her. The more time passes from her activation, the harder it is going to be."

Tommy gasps. "She's a real person, Lextr. Sometimes you frighten me."

Is it possible Lextr has a point? Could he decommission her? Put her out of her misery? He thought about her trembling lip on the ride to his lab—he's sure those were tears welling in her eyes when he left. It would probably be better for all of them if he just gave the order and let Lextr go to his unit and deal with the woman. She doesn't belong in this time anyway. Decommissioning her will save him so much trouble. What they did is wrong on so many levels. What right do they have to resurrect the dead?

The scientific implications, though . . . The what-ifs . . . Time stills and his heart thumps out a set of insistent beats. He feels a little heavier than he did a moment ago. Like he's swimming through liquid mercury. That's what they did. They brought back a woman who'd been dead for hundreds of years using a DNA sample. A dead person.

Jerme.

Though he hasn't thought of his brother's name in weeks, it flashes in his mind like a lightning strike across a clear blue sky. *Jerme, Jerme, Jerme.* It eclipses all other rational thoughts. Was his subconscious guiding him all this time, leading to the invention that would give his brother a second chance? Was bringing Jerme back possible?

No, that's insane. Scientifically unethical. He already has one person from the past who shouldn't be here to deal with.

But it's his brother.

Slow down, Res6. Think rationally. Jerme is gone. But he's never fully rational about the people he cares about. Well, the person. The one person Res6 had, who is now dead and gone. Has been for nearly a century.

With a mind of their own, his feet carry him out of the conference room into the larger open laboratory, Lextr and Tommy behind him. He scans the room, glaring at the dozen lab technicians who share the space with him and Lextr. "Everybody out!" Lextr and Tommy jump but move to follow the other employees out the door, halting when he barks, "Not you two."

After the lab finally goes quiet, he turns to them. "Based on our successful experiment, we have the power to resurrect the dead. Is that what I'm gathering?" Because if that is what Lextr is telling him . . . what if he brought Jerme back? Would it be ethical? Legal? Obviously not. But he already has one person from the past to hide from NHOS. What's one more?

But to really go through with it . . . Are ethical limitations or man-made rules really enough to stop him if it means seeing Jerme again? He could do things differently. Be the brother Jerme needs. Fix everything. His heart squeezes, and there's a little voice inside his head that feels like it's trying to tell him something. *Bad idea, Res6.* He resolutely ignores it.

"You okay, sir?" Tommy asks. "You've gone ashen."

He feels like he's floating. The prospect of another chance with his brother is causing a not altogether unpleasant dizzy sensation. He'd thought inventing CHOICElover would be enough to atone, but with each passing day inching closer to another anniversary of his brother's death, he isn't sure. What if he brings Jerme back, then focuses all his attention on getting Jerme the help he needs so he won't leave him again?

He turns his attention to Lextr. "Answer me. Can we bring people back from the dead?"

Lextr has no trouble meeting his eye. "Not reliably."

Res6 slumps back against the counter, the brief glimpse of joy leaking out of him. It's not possible—he got his hopes up. Electra was a fluke. Jerme is still lost to him, which only emphasizes how alone he's been.

"But . . ." Lextr says, which Tommy responds to with a disapproving frown. "But with a few more experiments, it might be possible."

He perks up. There's still the issue of the perfect storm Lextr mentioned since Jerme's DNA is from the modern era, unlike Electra's unaltered sample. "What about someone from our lifetime?"

Lextr scratches his chin. "I suppose if the conditions were just right—"

"This has to violate countless NHOS laws, not to mention the ethical implications of playing Zorg." Tommy's lips press together in a disapproving line.

Is that what he's doing? Playing Zorg?

"Oh, Tommy, don't be so moral. Just think, studying Res6's faulty unit for this special project will give us a perfect excuse not to decommission it," Lextr offers.

Tommy groans, running his hand over his face, grumbling, "I don't want to be a part of this."

At Lextr's suggestion, Res6, or at least his conscience, perks up. "Agreed then, we'll keep the woman." Within moments, he's at his station. His screen illuminates and a series of system access points populate. He clicks the double helix-shaped icon that calls up the DNA database. Behind him, the door clicks shut. He glances back to find Lextr peering over his shoulder.

"Don't worry about Tommy. He'll come around. Or you can fire him and find a new assistant," Lextr offers, nodding to the screen and the ominously flashing cursor. "Who are we bringing back?"

Res6 ignores his guilt and the nagging voice as he types the identifier into the database. In a flash, the file populates. The screen displays Jerme's bright, grinning face, a perfect mirror to his own.

Beside him, Lextr gasps, "Good Zorg, sir. I didn't know you had a twin."

3 – A Startling Realization

Electra

October 8, 2390.

Electra sits up in the center of the huge bed, blinking at Res6 in disbelief. "Everyone I know is dead!" she screams. "And you want to bring me to the lab with you for a few tests?"

"A few quick tests," Res6 repeats. "Shouldn't take long. I just need to confirm a few things."

Electra groans, rolling over into the sanctuary of the charcoal-colored blankets cocooning her. "Go away!"

A few days have passed, or maybe a week, since she woke up in this hellscape called the future. She has only enough energy to wallow in misery and yell at the man whose bedroom she's taken over as her own personal cave. A bedroom with a plush yet masculine warmth that is in direct contrast with its owner, from the excessive pile of pillows to the artwork filling two of the four walls. The large square canvases depict hazy landscapes, the dark, muted colors and soft focus creating a deeply soothing effect. Actual paintings, she guesses, though she's only emerged from her cocoon to eat and for quick jaunts to the bathroom.

The covers shift. Is he tugging on them? She buries her head in the pillow, gripping the blankets tighter. Her voice comes out muffled as she says, "I told you, I'm not leaving this room. Ever," she adds for emphasis.

"Ever?" he asks, tugging more insistently.

Grumbling, she throws the blankets back, instantly inhaling something that smells like food. Her stomach emits a pained rumble. Res6 takes a step back, holding out a takeout container to her like he's trying to tempt a hungry bear that might swipe at any moment.

"I brought you something to eat and a pick-me-UP nourishment packet," he offers tentatively. His gaze sweeps over her hair, then down his rumpled shirt that she still wears. "Maybe a shower first?"

"Not so sexy now, am I?" she mutters under her breath, which earns her a wince.

He sighs, heading toward the door, but stops to throw a concerned glance over his shoulder. "Listen, this cannot continue. We've been going back and forth like this for a week now, and it isn't normal."

She shrugs, eyeing the container. "What's the point?"

"The point of the shower? To get clean. Did you not have them during your time?" He frowns, head tilting as he studies her. When she only answers with a glare, he suggests, "I could decommission you. That is an alternative to consider."

That has her sluggish pulse firing. She shoots up, swinging her legs off the bed. "No." It's all she can think to say, because since she's entered her sloth/depression era, there's no compelling reason to offer him for keeping her alive. "That would be murder?"

He chuckles. "What happened to the lively, clever woman from the day we activated you? I much prefer her to whatever this is." He waves his free hand in her general direction, his nose wrinkling.

The words are on her tongue before she can stop them, even as the bed feels like it might swallow her whole. "So sorry to disappoint. That woman hadn't realized that everyone she cares about is lost to time—that means dead, in case you haven't been following—and that she's trapped in some inescapable sci-fi plot completely alone. Actual people aren't meant to live those plots!"

He blinks, extending the food again as if the depth of what she's said is beyond his capacity for response.

She swings her legs off the bed. The concrete floor is cool against her feet, and the grounding sensation offers her a tremulous stability. His features pinch in a pained expression as she takes the meal from his outstretched hand. "Thanks," she says.

He's right. They've played out some semblance of this routine every day since she woke up in the future. He's still frowning as he turns to leave, and suddenly there is a part of her that is overwhelmed with guilt. Instinctively, she grabs his arm to stop him. He flinches but turns back.

"Look, I know this isn't what you planned either, right?" she asks, really hoping the answer is yes, because the first day is a bit of a blur now, and she's pretty sure she was an accident.

He nods. "You were an experiment, but I assure you, I did not intend for you to be real."

What a relief. "I appreciate your patience. This can't be easy for you either, having a strange woman from the past in your home who is so depressed she can't get out of bed. Who you're suddenly obligated to. So what now?"

He lets out a long sigh, pinching the bridge of his nose. "I see that you're struggling, but I am not adept at offering comfort."

Electra steps back, snorting. Does he mean compassion? "Yes, I noticed. I realize I gave you a hard time about lacking experience with an actual woman, but you're coming across as rather clueless. I mean, some of the things you say make my head spin. And you leave me alone here for hours with nothing to do but let my thoughts spiral. Haven't you ever had a girlfriend?"

He's so glaringly attractive, there must be dozens of women willing to overlook his less than stellar personality. But he doesn't reply, so she presses on. "What about your mother? Surely you saw another adult in her life offer her compassion when she became upset." When he still doesn't respond, she suggests, "Some other family member, then?"

He stiffens, his knuckles going white on the door handle. "There are factors you are not privy to. Factors I don't care to share."

Seems she hit a nerve. That's okay. She isn't happy either. Still, he wants lively. Some fight. Fine. "It appears we're stuck in this situation together. If I'm guessing correctly, I'm not a legal person, so it's not like I can just call up a therapist or go to a grief support group, right?"

"You would be difficult to explain," he says.

"So that means for now, you're all I have. Therefore," she continues, "you're going to get a crash course in being a compassionate human being. How does that sound? Because the alternative is me never leaving this bed, which you've already expressed your disapproval of."

"Electra, I appreciate your distress . . ." He trails a hand through his lustrous sandy blond hair. "But with everything I'm juggling . . . I have work."

His rejection is enough to shatter her brief attempt at strength.

Of course this is happening. You thrive on connecting with people, so here you are, in the future, with a—get out of your head, Electra.

Try explaining things. Communication is how connection is formed, after all.

Electra clears her throat. "When I was little, we lost my mom to a form of breast cancer that should have been curable." His brows raise slightly. Encouraged, she continues. "We didn't have money for the expensive treatments. After she died, my dad held me and told me stories of what she was like when they first met. We spent hours talking about her and a bunch of unimportant nonsense. Then when he became disabled through a work injury, my friends and my stepmom Janet, who is," she clears her throat, "who *was* a licensed therapist, sat with me and helped me process my grief and fear while Dad struggled through his physical therapy."

Somewhere during her monologue, his brows furrowed and—did he drift a few inches closer to the door? "I'm listening but unclear about what you are asking of me."

"Those are examples of how people support each other when life gets awful. I would count this unfortunate circumstance among my worst life moments. You claim you feel responsible for bringing me here. How about offering me some compassion? You could sit with me and listen as I talk through . . ." She trails off at the deer-in-the-headlights expression he now wears. Is it reasonable to expect help or compassion from this future man? Maybe she's the one being unrealistic. Too bad she didn't wake up in the future to a woman. Such is her luck. Granted, for all she knows, future women are just as emotionally constipated.

He's right, though. They can't go on like this. She can't stay locked away in his bedroom forever, as comforting as the dark walls are. "You can't just drop off food like I'm some sort of lab rat and expect me to crawl my way out of bed. People don't work like that. Isolation isn't healthy."

He stares at her unflinchingly. If only she had someone to call. One person she could talk to. To actually check on her, not just drop off food and tell her she needs a shower. Even growing up as poor as she did, she had community. When things went wrong, as they often did, people chipped in, and they got by.

"I can't," he says, and she notices the twitch in his clenched jaw before he once again turns away.

Calmly, she sits, placing the container in her lap. "Great," she says without lifting her stare from the meal he delivered. Her hands tremble as she opens the lid. "Then it's as I suspected. I'm perfectly fucking alone."

He said *I can't*, not *I won't*. Is that worse or better? Either way, it really fucking sucks. Unbidden, tears stream down her face. How embarrassing. He can't even sit with her and talk because he clearly finds her just as horrifying as she does his manupartners. Now she's crying in front of him. They're never going to get anywhere. Thankfully, the door clicks shut, and she is left alone with only a box of flavorless mush she's loath to waste and a spork for company.

October 9, 2390.

The next morning, she's halfway through choking down another box of bland noodles when a knock sounds at her door. Considering Res6 hasn't demonstrated that he understands the concept of knocking, she isn't certain why he's doing it now. Irritated, she barks, "Enter."

Instead of the startlingly attractive man whose bed she lives in, it is one of the lab coats. Tommy, the assistant, she thinks.

"Hello. May I come in?" he asks, inching his head inside the cracked door.

Her eyes narrow, and she glances at his empty hands—actually, it was the orange-haired lab coat who surprise-injected her with whatever drug knocked her out. Her attention drifts to his black hair, worn spiky today, and the oversized blue-and-white checked smock he wears. Does the absence of a uniform mean this is a personal visit?

"I guess," she says.

As he cautiously moves into the room, she shuffles back on the bed, tucking her knees to her chest and drawing the blankets protectively over them.

He approaches, gesturing to the bed. "I'll sit, if that's okay. I'm Tommy, Res6's personal assistant."

The bed shifts under his weight. Thankfully, he's chosen a spot as far on the opposite side as possible. Once comfortable, he releases a long exhale, like he's preparing for a tense conversation. "He says you're struggling to adjust."

Electra coughs. "Well, considering I'm grieving the loss of everyone I've ever known, I'm not doing so great." Based on Res6's unfeeling interactions, she never would have guessed he was concerned enough to delegate her problems to his PA.

She mentally replays their last conversation from the previous night. The one where they argued, in a roundabout sort of way, about her current depressive episode, her need for comfort, and his inability to be anything resembling an emotionally available human being. He'd gone as far as to suggest—

"I don't want to be decommissioned, if that's what this is about," she blurts out.

Tommy chuckles. "I stopped by to check on you."

"Oh," she says.

"Believe me, I know how Res6 can be. Perhaps leaving you alone with him was inadvisable." Her gaping stare must convey her shock, because he adds, "Rest assured, he takes his responsibilities very seriously."

"He suggested decommissioning me in lieu of—" She gestures, embarrassed, at the nest of blankets cocooning her.

Tommy's smile doesn't quite reach his eyes. "Don't worry. They've already agreed not to decommission you." When her look is questioning, he shrugs. "He and Lextr think studying you might be useful for their special project—don't ask. I'm not at liberty to tell you about it."

Her voice squeaks as she asks, "Study me how?"

"Just a few noninvasive scans. Nothing to be afraid of," he says.

Still, a shiver runs down her spine. "So why did he offer to decommission me then?"

He eyes her blanket fort. "It was probably his way of nudging you to extricate yourself from whatever it is you're doing in this room."

"What's the difference between being locked in here versus out there?" She points toward the ominous door and the man who she suspects, based on his rhythmic footfalls, is pacing on the other side of it. "I tried to explain how I am feeling and what I need, but he's incapable of offering it."

"How are you feeling?"

If she were to take his question seriously and marinate on it, how is she really feeling? "Abandoned," she decides.

Tommy clears his throat. "By whom?"

A huff escapes her lungs, and she gestures at no one and everything all at once. "I don't know. God. The universe? Whatever cosmic entity is supposed to give a shit about our measly little lives." Well, there goes her victim mentality flaring back to life. She can practically hear Janet in her best TV voice asking a morning show guest, *How have these thoughts helped you in the past?*

"Ah, you're thinking of the non-deities Zorg and Zephyr. I'm a devoted follower. It seems they have decided to shake things up by introducing people from the past to our timeline."

That's right. Res6 mentioned rumors of others like her on her first day here, but it got lost in the deluge of new information. Why hadn't she thought to ask? "You're sure there are more people like me?"

Tommy's gaze slides to the door, then back to her. Then he leans forward, lowering his voice conspiratorially. "Yes! Mishaps from a competitor called GROW. Perhaps, once you're acclimated, we can identify a few and arrange for you to meet them?" he offers. She instantly brightens. "I'd have to clear it with the boss, though. His word is law."

There is so much information to take in, her head is spinning. She needs to break things down into simple questions. "As in The Boss, not just your boss?"

"Oh shit! He specifically told me not to mention that little detail to you. I suppose now that you know . . ." He shrugs as if violating his employer's wishes is no big deal. "Res6 invented manupartners. CHOICElover is his prized creation. You can't tell him I let it slip."

An awful sinking sensation takes hold in her gut. "Shit."

Tommy's brows raise in question.

"I may have said quite a few disparaging things about his prized creation."

"For example?" Tommy urges, making her want to toss the blankets over her head and hide from the inevitable confrontation her words have earned her.

"I may have called the manupartners sex robots and said they were the most messed-up thing I've ever heard." She said other things too. None of which she is ready to confess to her potential ally.

"Oh my. Well, perhaps that is why he is reluctant to . . ." He waves a hand in her general direction.

"To offer me compassion?" Are all future people completely devoid of it? Because if so, how dismal.

"Yes, that's what I was saying." Tommy jumps to his feet, expression brightening like he's on to something. He taps a finger to his lips twice before announcing, "I think you two got off on the wrong foot. Try to understand how things are now. People in our society value their ability to choose their own experiences. It is the ultimate freedom. And with manupartners, they can—"

"Get exactly what they're looking for in a partner. Yes, he explained this to me."

"Then what is the problem?"

"I just think it's sad, don't you?"

Tommy shrugs, plopping back down on the bed. "Manupartners keep people happy. Just imagine, no messy breakups. No disagreements over what to have for dinner. In the mood for romance? Your CHOICElover will be ready and eager to please. It isn't sad at all. It's the ultimate freedom." He pats the bed like he's solidified his argument and thinks she should accept it so she can get onto acting happy now.

"That sounds incredibly vacant to me. But I suppose we're from different worlds." Different worlds, four hundred years apart. She hasn't even seen the outside world yet or met any other future people. She keeps telling herself it won't be that bad, but considering Res6, now Tommy is here, is there any reason to hope? Exasperation has her burying her head in her hands. "I knew something like this would happen."

"A prophecy?" He leans forward, excitement written clearly across his pointy features.

A prophecy? That's right. He said he was a devoted follower of some modern non-deities—whatever that means—so he would be apt to believe in prophecies. "No, nothing like that. I just . . ." A grumble escapes her throat. "Everything always goes wrong for me. I grew up dirt poor. My mom died of what should have been a treatable disease. We couldn't afford college for me. Then, when I was finally getting somewhere—I woke up here!"

He shifts uncomfortably. "Sounds like a fortunate twist of fate to me! So what do I need to do to get you out of bed and into the shower?"

She pinches the bridge of her nose. What she really needs is a friend, and if there are people from her time, that would be great motivation to shower. "How soon do you think I can meet one of the people from my time?"

Tommy taps his lip. "I don't know. Like I said, your main hurdle will be convincing Res6. He's determined to keep your identity a secret. The public can't find out about you. Who knows what NHOS would do."

"He thinks he's going to keep me hidden away? That I'm going to live the rest of my life only able to interact with the three people who know about my existence? That's unacceptable." And daunting. She'll go mad, if she isn't already a good portion of the way there.

"I'm not saying that at all. Lots of people use anonymous identities online. There are countless chat rooms for you to choose from. I'm sure you can meet people interested in compassion or whatever else you're looking for. The faster you acclimate, the better chance you'll have of convincing him to give you some freedom."

Res6 dishing out her freedom is borderline insulting, yet this is a whole new world to her, so she understands the need for caution. Plus, acclimating is a good suggestion, regardless. "Chat rooms?" She fishes her tablet out of the mountain of covers and hands it to him. "Can you show me how to work this?"

"Res6 didn't?"

She huffs. "He showed me the Scrawl app but otherwise he's just left me to figure it out on my own, which is proving impossible."

"Ah, well. That explains a lot. I will gladly rectify his mistake. There are lots of things online that will make you feel much happier. Let's see . . . chat rooms, online shopping." He leans forward. "Res6 is flush with unicoin. I'm sure he won't mind if you buy whatever makes you smile. There are more games than you can imagine, plus there are videos. Some educational and some that are just for entertainment."

"We had all that during my time," she says, seriously doubtful of the modern internet's ability to make her happy if the internet in her time was anything to go by. Not to mention, the thought of spending Res6's money makes her stomach twist uncomfortably. Because if she relies on someone besides herself, that means leaving her fate in their hands. And what if they can't handle it? What if they let her down?

It's just money, and your new friend says Res6 has a lot, Electra.

That's not the point, Janet.

Then what is the point?

Maybe it's this: If she can't support herself, she has to prove she's worth existing some other way.

Before she can solidify *the point*, Tommy scoffs. "You had nothing like we do now. I'll order you a VR headset. You'll see. Maybe you can even have an m-volt implanted when you come to the lab. It makes the experience so immersive, and there are programs for anything you can imagine."

"Ugh. I don't want a fake blast of endorphins or to get lost down some online rabbit hole." She studies him for a moment, assessing whether he might understand what she's saying.

"What do you want then, Electra? Try to explain it if you can." His lips purse like he's losing patience.

Closing her eyes, she envisions what might make her feel good in this moment. Or if not good, give her a little relief from this ache in her chest and the fear of what will become of her. "I want to go to the park with a friend, sit on a bench and feel the sun on my skin. I need to vent or talk about the people I miss desperately. I need a friend to tell me they're on my side and that everything's going to be okay. Or at least make me laugh with some quirky observation about the irony of my situation."

"Let me talk to Res6 and see if we can find some vents for you. In the meantime. . ." He takes the tablet and begins furiously tapping the screen. A few minutes later, he moves to sit beside her so they can both see. "See this app here?" He taps the icon of a dancing monkey. "I've added several videos to your queue that will explain how the world works now. Shortly after conception, citizens get a certain base knowledge implanted into their DNA along with a few language models, just like manupartners, so this is the best place for you to start." Implanted? Electra blinks, nods for Tommy to continue. "It will all be explained in more detail in the videos."

The next icon he clicks on shows a stylized, angry-looking frog's head. There is a feed in the center and dozens of categories to choose from on the left-hand side, like a combination of some of the more popular chatroom platforms from her time. "This app, FrogBlog, will give you an opportunity to connect with others in our municipality."

"What about books?" Surely people still read. If she sees what's trending, maybe she'll discover where she belongs.

"Physical books aren't really a thing anymore, a consequence of The Great Warming, which will be explained in video four, I believe." Before she can deflate completely, Tommy continues as he taps the screen, opening a new app. "Most people prefer to listen to books via the Intella-VoiceActs program because physical words can be so tedious, but I do occasionally derive entertainment from the Books app library. Of course, anyone can upload content, so you have to sift through it to find just what you're looking for. There are lots of short-form publications to consume as well."

Her cheeks burn with a smile she can't repress. Would this little tablet tour have been so difficult for Res6? It's amazing how such a little sprinkle of human decency can make all the difference. The loneliness she felt before Tommy arrived threatens to bubble up, but her buzzing excitement overrules it. Maybe she can immerse herself in a book or find an online book club. Surely there are people now who have similar interests.

Tommy huffs. "You seem to be in better spirits. Time for a shower," he announces. He doesn't hesitate to grab her hand and drag her off the bed, giving her a not-so-gentle nudge into the bathroom. A second later he's in there with her, pressing buttons, and the room fills with steam. "Just set the rumpled shirt outside the door so I can burn it!" he chirps, seeming pleased with his accomplishment of herding her into the shower. "I'll put the fresh clothes I brought right outside."

The door clicks shut, and Electra is alone again with her thoughts. She catches her reflection in the mirror, first noticing the tangled mess of her dark hair. God, she looks awful. Fine, she'll shower. As she pulls Res6's shirt over her head, the woodsy citrus aroma is decidedly overpowered by her own body odor that is now mixing with the steam and threatening to gag her. She steps into the pleasantly warm water, cheeks heating. No wonder they were so insistent on her bathing.

Hope kindles in her chest as she washes away the stench of wallowing in her own self-pity for a week. It's crazy how being alone made her so depressed. All it took was a single visit from a kind-ish human being to lift her spirits—granted, at the behest of his employer. Still.

Tommy urged her to understand how the world is now and how devoid-of-personality manupartners make people happy. But there's no way that can be true. Not with what she's experienced time and time again. People need people. Maybe even people like prickly, compassionless Res6.

She holds her hand beneath a spout labeled Hair Wash and waits patiently as a thimble-sized dollop drops onto her palm. Considering the bird's nest she's currently sporting, one dollop won't be enough. She waves her hand under the spout several more times. When she is satisfied with the glob in her palm, she massages the luxurious-smelling product into her hair.

It feels like she's lived a lifetime in the last week, and she almost forgot herself. Because there is one truth she always comes back to. The universe may have dealt her a shit hand, but that's never stopped her from picking up the pieces—no matter how shattered they are.

With the resources that Tommy shared with her, she now has so many possibilities. So many ways for her to find a niche and start over. She can write another book and try to find a publisher. Or if that isn't a thing anymore, publish it herself through the Books platform. Maybe if she builds up a big enough audience, she can see what it takes to hire a human narrator.

Excitement zings through her as she towels off. She slips into the baggy gray jumpsuit Tommy left for her and rifles through the drawers until she finds a comb for her hair.

It takes a bit of time to make herself look presentable. She can only use getting freshened up as an excuse to avoid Res6 for so long. Especially now that Tommy has likely shared his triumph about getting her in the shower. She's going to have to face Res6, which means she is going to have to admit, at least to herself, how awful she was to him about his company. Granted, she didn't know it was his company when she said those things. It's not like she feels any different about it, does she?

No. If people are masking their isolation with glorified sex clones, it is sad. No human should have to live like that. If only she could show people.

Throwing her hair in a quick braid and securing it with a piece of cloth she tore from Res6's soon-to-be-discarded shirt, she gives herself a once-over in the mirror. Much better.

An idea hits her. Tommy said he believed his non-deities were resurrecting people like her to shake things up. Maybe that's exactly what she'll do. Shaking things up will be her mission. *A mission whose success will finally, once and for all, give you the right to exist.*

Argh, why does her inner narrator do that? She knows her worth, right? She pictures her stepmother, San Francisco's own Ask Doctor Janet, frowning. *Electra, dear, you are worthy of good things exactly as you are. No amount of money or accomplishment is going to change that.*

Sadly, she remembers thinking it isn't that simple. If she were truly worthy, why did bad things keep happening to her?

4 – My Buddy and Me!

Res6

Does delegating the task of motivating Electra to shower make him a coward, or something worse? He's not exactly handling her well. So what if he needs reinforcements? Tommy's job is to support him. Plus, Tommy's referred to a sister multiple times over the years. That means he's more equipped to—he glances at the bedroom door, which has become an ominous, threatening thing—more equipped to do whatever it is he's doing in there. Hopefully, getting her to shower.

Then she'll come out and . . . well, that's where his plan loses traction. He has no clue, so he's going to improvise. Not that improvising is going well either, based on the evidence. Every interaction they've had since she woke up a week ago is playing on repeat in his mind as he paces outside the bedroom door. His brain is only offering him two choices: retread every syllable he uttered, or let his curiosity about what's going on in the bedroom drive him mad. He has plenty of other things to think about, like his first Jerme experiment, but he can't seem to redirect his mind. The first option—retread—is winning.

Another excellent specimen, Lextr.

Get a little mileage out of it.

How is that so unbelievably sexy?

That last one haunts him the most. She even grumbled something like *I'm not so sexy now* as he attempted to get her out of bed. The problem is, she put on his shirt and he gawked at her like a teenage boy. Even now, a week later, he can't get the image out of his mind—her pert nipples poking through the soft fabric, the hem grazing her upper thighs. She was naked during the entire trip from his office to his unit, then standing there in the corner attached to the activation pad while the drugs wore off. But for reasons unknown, he developed a forceful attraction to her at that moment.

Still, why did he let it tumble out of his mouth? While he meant it, there's no telling what he was thinking. If she were a manupartner, she might have giggled and coyly pawed at his chest. This woman, however, isn't a manupartner, and he couldn't pull his head out of his ass and act normal.

He spends too much time with lab techs and clones. This confirms it. He definitely shouldn't have grown a manupartner using his DNA—basically a body double—to send to his weekly FRIENDS appointments, mandated by the NHOS initiative Project: LEN, Loneliness Ends Now. *FRIENDS are a vital First Response to Isolation via Engagement with Networking as a Deterrent System.* When NHOS first rolled out the program, he scoffed. Why would people need FRIENDS when they could get a manupartner? Yet even he can see how his NHOS-issued FRIENDS might have prepared him to interact with the woman hiding in his bedroom.

Zorg, is he considering going to his FRIENDS appointments? Her presence is clearly arresting his brain function. Perhaps that's why he showed her the commercial. Was it insensitive of him? If one isn't used to the process of manupartner formation, it must seem grotesque. But that wasn't what alarmed her. *Pathetic* was the word she hurled at him.

Is he pathetic? He needs context.

He glances at the door—not his bedroom door this time. The one next to it. Before he can talk himself out of it, he turns the handle and slips inside, closing it securely behind him. Nothing wrong with a little chat to gain some necessary insight while Tommy works to get Electra out of bed and into the shower.

Against the far wall, in an ergonomic antigravity chair—he isn't a monster—sits a manupartner. Specifically, the manupartner body double he's been sending to his FRIENDS appointments for the last seven months. He's been doing this for decades, of course, but he recycles and replaces the units yearly to avoid glitches.

The unit's eyes brighten. "Oh, hi! Time for another FRIENDS visit?"

This is a horrible idea. He'd be better off going into the bathroom and talking to his reflection like normal . . . but unprecedented times and all . . . fuck it.

"I want to discuss something with you," he says, forcing the words out.

The unit sits up, angling its head as if it's truly concerned. "What's bothering you, buddy?"

He groans. He programmed this unit, like all his body doubles, to be especially perceptive, sensitive, moral, and intuitive. Then, upon activation, he gives them a tablet and instructs them to study the Respectful and Considerate Conduct Manual, so they're prepared for when he sends them to his FRIENDS appointments in place of himself. To solve the memory issue, since there is—or at least there *was*—no way to carry memories between manupartners, he always complains in his annual Project: LEN survey so they switch his group right before he gets a new body double. It only gets awkward when he bumps into someone in public from a previous FRIENDS group and he comes across more abruptly than his finely tuned unit. When someone appears momentarily surprised, he knows they've met a previous unit and not him. In those encounters, he quickly adjusts, slipping on his CHOICElover public figure persona to smooth things over. It always works.

He clears his throat, addressing the eager unit. "What do my FRIENDS think of you?"

The unit's eyes narrow as it considers. "I've done as you've instructed. They believe I'm you." It grins brightly, pleased with its own response.

He shakes his head. "No, I mean, what do they think of me? Of my company? How do they act toward you, thinking you're me?" Zorg that's convoluted.

The unit's smile is gentle. "I see. Two of the three FRIENDS are quite taken with you and often invite you to join them for unrequired FRIENDS appointments. The other is a little less interested, but still very respectful." The unit stands and approaches him. It places a warm hand on his shoulder. "As your manupartner, I don't want to overstep, but is something else bothering you?" Though it was made with his DNA, for a second it feels as if it is his brother standing before him, imploring. His heart squeezes, and suddenly, talking to the mirror seems entirely inadequate.

Perhaps that's why he says, "There's a woman." The unit nods encouragingly. "She thinks CHOICElover and our mission is horrific. She thinks I've been with manupartners so long that I can't . . ." Technically, she said, *Can't get an actual woman to spread her legs for you?* but he certainly isn't going to say that. ". . . she thinks I can't attract a real woman."

"And this woman's opinion bothers you because?" the unit asks.

He sighs. "I don't know why I care what she thinks. It . . ."

The truth is, her accusation stung—what, his male pride? Because it questioned his purpose for existing? Or was it her general disapproval of him that chafed? Why does he even care if some woman from four hundred years ago doesn't like him?

". . . it bothers me that she doesn't understand my reasons. It's my responsibility as owner to embody our mission, to demonstrate that *Your CHOICE for companionship has never been easier*. What's *easy* about dating a real person?"

The unit's features remain placid as it waits for him to continue. He clenches his fists as his agitation rises. Why is he expecting some type of reaction? Manupartners are programmed for unquestioning obedience and agreement. He shouldn't blame the thing for being a little stilted. Robotic, even. The unit perfectly illustrates why he allowed the experiment that led to Electra.

If they could select for individual idiosyncrasies, the units might feel more human without the complications of actually being human. Look at where it landed him: with a woman-shaped dilemma. A woman he's currently responsible for—because her existence is his fault—who doesn't believe he'd be able to attract a real human woman. Which brings him full circle and back to the manupartner staring at him.

"With every other aspect of life customizable to one's preferences, people shouldn't have to settle for less than a perfectly agreeable partner. CHOICElover stepped in and offered an ideal solution so they no longer had to. You see how people react to us. They think I'm a trailblazer. A modern-day hero who provides a valuable service to society. I could probably garner the attention of any number of real women."

"But you want her attention," the unit observes.

He runs a hand through his hair, starting to pace. "No."

"Then you want her to understand that other women will want you?"

Is that it? It doesn't feel right—not entirely. His brow furrows. He turns the accusation over in his mind. *Can't get an actual woman to spread her legs for you?* What is it about that question that bothers him?

Even by modern standards, he's an attractive, successful man, so he assumes the answer is yes. He could indeed get an actual woman to *spread her legs*, as she so vulgarly put it. But he hasn't even attempted anything, casual or not, with a real woman in . . . he can't remember. He's always had a manupartner—at least since they developed the first prototypes. He'd been 31, and while he'd never had a girlfriend like Jerme, he still had needs, so he fulfilled them as his body required. But that was almost a century ago. Does it even count?

"That's not it," he finally replies. Again, it's not like he cares. As far as he's concerned, her existence is only interesting because of the scientific insight she's uniquely poised to provide.

His device pings. There's a message from Tommy: *Where did you go?*

He nods to the manupartner. "We'll continue this discussion later. Your next FRIENDS appointment is tomorrow. How's your fuel supply?"

The unit opens the closet, which displays a dozen nutrition packets. With his m-volt, he shoots Tommy a quick message to order more before slipping out the door to meet him in the living room.

"Any luck?" he asks. The soundproofing in the unit is so good, he wouldn't be able to hear the shower. He only knows she hasn't taken one before today because of the water usage monitoring report all MSP citizens get in their inbox every morning. And her rumpled physical state.

"She's in the shower." Right as he's about to release a sigh of relief, Tommy continues. "As your personal assistant, I'm obligated to inform you that the poor woman in that room is *grieving the loss of everyone she's ever known.*" Tommy says that last part in a poor imitation of a woman's voice. "As she was speaking, I queried DumBot for a more detailed explanation. Trust me when I tell you the experience sounds ghastly! Imagine losing your favorite aesthetician!"

Res6 winces, directing his attention to the particle panes. She mentioned that. After the seemingly never-ending pain of losing Jerme, he wasn't too keen to ruminate on the concept of grief, much less to dwell on it. As far as he's concerned, he's done with grief for the duration, so she's going to have to deal with it on her own, much like he did. With a thought, the particle panes switch to a sun-kissed meadow with a gentle stream meandering through it. He takes a moment to observe the sway of the vegetation—

"How am I supposed to do my job if you aren't even listening to me?" Tommy asks.

The image on the particle panes dissolves abruptly, leaving a view of the roofs of the other A Quadrant towers. The smog is so dense he can only see a few structures beyond the adjacent building. The sight does nothing to settle his discomfort.

He turns to Tommy, who has picked up the remote. While Res6 could simply reanimate the panes with a thought, his assistant is holding the remote with a defiant look that says he is prepared to turn them back off just as quickly.

"I was enjoying that scene," Res6 says, wincing at the petulance in his voice.

"If you want to keep her *nature* a secret, you need to take this seriously. She said staying trapped in this unit will not make her happy, so that isn't an option. I think encouraging her adaptation is your best strategy." Tommy turns toward the empty particle panes, wearing a disapproving expression—likely aimed at him.

"If you're so concerned, I'll send her to wage a hostile takeover of *your* living quarters."

Tommy chuffs. "Absolutely not. As you've mentioned several times, she's your responsibility. As your assistant, I've done my part. You could have at least shown her how to use the tablet, which I did, along with giving her access to a few harmless chat rooms and some history lessons. Oh, and she asked about books, so that should keep her occupied for a while."

"How was I supposed to know she didn't know how to use it?"

"She's from almost four hundred years ago. Computers were a very recent invention back then. Imagine trying to operate your system without your m-volt." Tommy shakes his head, moving to take a seat at Res6's desk.

"So now you're some type of historian?" Res6 prods, only subtly derisive.

Tommy completes the retina scan, logging in to the system using his credentials. A new window pops up. "I'm informed about our history, as it is each NHOS citizen's responsibility to be."

He wants to grumble that he doesn't have time, but that isn't entirely true. He just isn't interested in history, and the last thing he needs is to get Tommy started on one of his political diatribes. "What do you suggest we do?" He steps behind the chair Tommy occupies.

Tommy points to the flashing cursor. "*You* need to do some research. Figure out who she was, so you'll know what she's missing. I've thought about it, and she's right. She's not an orangutan that you can keep caged as a pet. She can't stay in that room forever, so you're going to have to figure out how to help her integrate into our world. Get her some proper clothing to start."

"You thought about it in the last five minutes?" he prods, but Tommy only scowls. "She can't go out in public. We'll get caught."

Tommy shrugs. "You could let her be herself, and if anyone asks, tell them she's a new prototype." His pale skin stretches across his fine bone structure as a bright smile erupts. "Think of her as a marketing campaign! That's brilliant. I can't wait to see the sales figures after you've had her out on the town for a few months!"

"Fine. She's a marketing prototype. That isn't a terrible idea." Res6 flippantly waves a hand. "Anything else?"

Tommy rolls his eyes. "That's not all. She said she wants to go to the park to sit on a bench and feel the sun on her skin. She said something about vents and talking too."

"Vents?" he asks.

"How am I supposed to know? People were into strange things back then, like sun worship and home projects." Tommy holds up a hand like he does when he's using his m-volt. He's probably querying his limited AI assistant, DumBot, again. A minute later he says, "DumBot suggests taking her to a custom rooftop simulation since roofs have excellent sun exposure and various styles of vents. Request a park bench, safely attached of course, and then the two of you can sit. Perhaps plan some conversation topics for the talking aspect. That should make her happy!"

That all seems feasible . . . and if that's what she wants, he should be able to get her to the simulation chamber in his building without drawing too much attention. It's the talking part that gives him pause. "What am I supposed to talk about to a woman from four hundred years ago?"

"I feel that this is getting a little beyond the scope of my job." He must look so pitiful that Tommy says, "DumBot says try asking her questions and then let her direct the conversation."

He stops pacing abruptly. "What type of questions?"

Tommy gets up from the desk. "Seriously, sir, you have access to the same limited AI assistant as I do."

"You haven't been the one interacting with her. The prospect of talking to her is daunting. She asked me when my last girlfriend was."

"Why would you have a girlfriend?" Tommy scratches his nose as he inches his way to the exit. A ping emanates from his pocket, and he fishes out his device. "Oh, that's my time for today. You can handle this, right?" He points to the computer screens as he practically skips to the door. "Research!" he whisper-shouts.

The door shuts behind him, leaving Res6 standing alone in his living room, completely lost.

5 – A Reasonable Plan

Res6

"How long have you been standing there like that?" Electra asks, stepping out of his room. She comes to stand beside him and joins him in staring at the bleak image framed by the empty particle panes.

"Not long," he lies. It's been almost an hour since Tommy left.

She nods to the smog-filled Minneapolis–Saint Paul cityscape. "Is that the real outside?"

"Unfortunately," he says, trying to imagine what his world must look like to a woman who could walk outside without a respirator during her time.

She covers her mouth as tears well in her eyes. "How horrible. Was it gradual or all at once? Can you still go outside? What about the plants and animals?"

He shakes his head, glad he won't have to be the one to deliver such disappointing news. "Tommy said he downloaded some history videos for you to watch. They'll answer all your questions."

"He did. It would have been nice if you'd shown me how to work the tablet." She crosses her arms defensively.

"I've already been scolded by Tommy for my negligence."

Beside him, she huffs. "Are you sure you're not a robot?"

Some unknown gravity has him pivoting toward her. She turns to face him as well, and her freckles, considered a genetic defect by modern standards, draw his attention. They're so lovely, reminding him of the stars that dot the night ceiling in the simulation chamber.

"What?" she says, brushing fingers across her cheek.

"I'm no more of a robot than you are," he says.

Her lips quirk. "Well, considering I'm one of these resurrected manupartner people, that isn't as comforting as you think it is."

He takes a long inhale, releasing it slowly. "Do you feel hungry, Electra?"

"No, I do not," she says robotically. Her hands shoot up so her arms bend at a ninety-degree angle, and she starts walking around the room stiffly. "Do you feel hungry, Res6?"

A sudden burst of laughter surprises him as he realizes what she's doing. "Are you making fun of me? That is highly inconsiderate." Though he should be offended, the teasing evokes a distantly familiar lightness, reminding him of when Jerme was alive. No one has teased him since Jerme.

"Obviously. To answer your question, no, I'm not hungry. I'm not a houseplant you put in a sunny corner and water once a week."

He groans. What does she expect from him? He really needs to lay out a plan like Tommy suggested. She follows him to the kitchen. He grabs two bottles of Storm Brew from the refrigerator, pops the resealable caps, and hands one to her.

She inspects the blue and gray bottle. Its label displays bubble lettering being blown around by a cyclone. "What's this?"

"Alcohol. I rarely drink, but—"

"I'm driving you to it?" She grins at her own joke.

"Precisely."

Her nose wrinkles as she takes a tentative sip. She coughs, smacking her chest with her free hand. "This is bad," she chokes out.

"It's an acquired taste. You don't have to drink it."

She takes another sip that goes down better. "Don't worry. I'll acquire it."

He walks back to the living room, assuming she'll follow. She does a moment later, carrying the Storm Brew, a bottle of water, and a box of Crack Tacks. "I'm not hungry. I just can't drink without eating something. Bothers my stomach."

She sets everything down on his coffee table and opens the box, lifting it to her face. Her nose wrinkles as she sniffs. There is a part of him that could watch her all day, as unhealthy as that sounds. She's so unlike the people of his time. Expressive? Flawed? Definitely sarcastic. But she's funny. Her snappy way of speaking isn't remotely measured, and she most assuredly needs a Respectful and Considerate Conduct Course at some point. It reminds him of Jerme's easy demeanor and—

An exaggerated moan slips past her lips. "I don't know what this flavor is, but I love it." She hums in delight as she chews.

The sound is mesmerizing.

She finishes the crunchy snack and glances up, catching him staring at her. He lowers his gaze as heat crawls up his neck. A few beats of silence pass. Her brow furrows—shit, he's staring again. It's unsettling how his eyes keep gravitating toward her, but what is he expected to do? She's just so . . . different. *Real.*

But if he tells everyone they encounter that she's a prototype, it might just work. The potential publicity, if he considers it from that angle, is intriguing. Seems that an initial test is in order. Tommy said she needs clothes, so they'll go on a trial shopping outing. There. Two problems solved. "Since you're clean," he says, and she gives him a derisive snort, "and dressed, perhaps we should venture out to find you some clothing so we can begin your acclimation to the world now."

"I thought you said you were too busy with work."

He said that, didn't he? Technically it's true, considering the copious amount of time he's spent this week oscillating between what to do with her and the implications of resurrecting his twin. At least he came to a determination about one of his two issues. Now that he's officially decided to bring Jerme back—or attempt to—he's eager to get the first trial underway, but one task at a time. Once he has a solid plan for the woman in his unit, he'll redirect his full focus to his brother's resurrection. It's unrealistic to think he'll succeed on the first try. He considered accelerating the grow time, but that typically yields a higher failure rate. The experiment might carry on for a few weeks; therefore, his Electra problem is more immediate.

He shakes off the thought. "My work can wait. Tommy illuminated the error in my logic." He gestures toward the door. "Shall we?"

"Not that I'm not thrilled at the opportunity, but shouldn't I learn a little about the world so I know what to expect before you thrust me out into it?" she asks.

Ah, finally something he has a solution for. He clears his throat authoritatively. He needs to convey that he has everything under control. "No need to worry. I have a plan." She grins, buoying his resolve. "You can be one hundred percent yourself."

"What's the catch?" she asks, narrowing her eyes at him.

"No catch. If anyone notices anything off about you, we'll say you're a new manupartner prototype." *See, Electra. I can be a considerate human being.* He awaits her approval.

"Okay . . ." She's clearly still skeptical. "Sounds too easy. You aren't afraid of our being caught anymore?"

Not exactly, but Tommy's suggestion of saying she's a prototype seems like a rational middle ground. Maybe he's giving her too much credit. "I assume you have enough common sense not to mention that."

She nods, which is reassuring. "So, when someone is curious about me, we just tell them I'm a new prototype. Easy enough, I guess."

"Exactly. If Tommy is right, everyone is going to be curious about you, which will create interest in what is next from CHOICElover. I would expect to see a bump in sales next quarter." He motions toward the door. "Shall we?" Her mouth has fallen open, and he's unsure if he's said something wrong. "Electra?"

Abruptly she gets up, abandoning her drinks, and for a moment he thinks she's agreeing to venture out. But then she angles around his desk, heading not to the door which would lead out of his unit, but back to the bedroom. He's on his feet and marching toward her before he can consider his actions. "Electra, wait! What have I done now?"

She spins. "I stupidly thought maybe we were getting somewhere. But your big plan is to use me as advertising for your horrendous company?! I've never in my life—" She slams the door in his face.

He groans. Not this again. Her emotional outbursts are so like his brother's, it's uncanny.

Jerme. His blood runs cold. What if she harms herself? He hadn't been paying close enough attention, and he failed his brother. He can't let that happen to Electra. He needs her. Well, the data from her scans. Plus, she's his responsibility, so in a way, his conscience needs her alive. Considering she and Jerme seem to be similar, maybe having her around will be good for Jerme too—when Res6 gets him back. Connecting them isn't a terrible idea. Between her shower and Tommy's several excellent suggestions, this is really turning out to be a productive day!

"Electra," he calls through the door. "Please come out. I didn't mean to upset you. Doesn't shopping sound fun?"

The door flies open, and her head pokes out. "I loathe shopping. I don't want anything to do with you or your unicoin!"

"But how are you going to acclimatize? What are you going to wear? Tommy said—"

"I don't care what Tommy said! You know what, I think I'm going to go watch those history videos now so I can see what is wrong with you people. Then I'm going to figure out what I can do about it."

The door slams closed.

Well, that doesn't sound like she wants to harm herself. And why wouldn't she care what Tommy says? The man has been his and Lextr's voice of reason since he hired him ten years ago. If it were up to Lextr, she'd be decommissioned. So what now?

You need to do some research. Figure out who she was. Ah, yes. Research. It's annoying how often Tommy's right. He should write down his suggestions while they're still fresh in his mind.

Another Storm Brew is exactly what will make this task more pleasant. He shoots his closed bedroom door a final annoyed glance before going to the refrigerator. Beer in hand, he sits down at his computer and opens the Scrawl app. At the top of the list, there are a dozen new Brain Dump files, obviously from her. What could she possibly fill so many entries with? Maybe he'll read them later. No, terrible idea. Nothing of interest, to be sure, and certainly not worth his time.

He begins his own Brain Dump, saving it as "Res6's Top Secret Task List."

Acclimate Electra Lynch to the Future in Three Easy Steps.

1 – Research to figure out who she was before she died.

Previously considered a bad idea because of proximity-related d angers—i.e., look at what happened to Jerme—but reconsidered per Tommy's sound *she's not your pet orangutan* advice. Task seems relatively straightforward. Determining who she was might lead to discovering what entertains her. Then she'll feel happy. Then, she'll agree to go to the lab for a few scans. Ideally before the week is over so we can find out if there were any markers left in her mitochondria which might give us insight into what specifically happened that caused her retained memories, thus her identity at the time of her death, to be expressed so fully.

2 – Acquire her proper clothing since trial shopping outing invitation failed.

Get dimensions from her product data sheet. Bonus points: try to determine her personal style from historical data such as archived images, social media posts, etc. She doesn't want anything to do with me or my unicoin. Too bad.

Seems relatively simple so far. The next one will be the challenge.

3 – Ask Electra questions so she can . . .

What did Tommy say? He runs his hands through his hair, unable to remember what the point was. Well, it doesn't matter. Asking her questions is the important part. Perhaps he can utilize DumBot to compile a list of options.

Reviewing his plan, he congratulates himself on his excellent work. Might as well get started. He thinks the spelling of her name and the year of her death, watching as the characters populate in the search bar, then pauses. He's not sure why he hesitates. What could he possibly discover that he wouldn't want to know? The little flutter in his gut isn't anticipation. It's not like she would have been a licensed therapist too, like the stepmother she mentioned, therefore lending some credence to her scathing assessment of him. Right? What are the odds? Comfortably negligible. Bracing his hands on the armrests of his chair, he thinks the command to search. Instantly, results populate.

A posed headshot fills the top of the screen, along with her name in bold letters and the description "American Writer." She's wearing a broad grin. Well, that was easier than he expected. An image of a book cover is pictured beside it. A red-skinned man wearing a crown between two sets of horns holds a distressed yet beautiful woman. Across it are the words *Tempting the Alien King*. Beneath it, her name.

Pursued by the Alien Prince is another title. He's starting to rethink this Electra Lynch and what her Brain Dumps contain. She didn't put *Top Secret* in the file names . . .

No, he's nearly 100 percent certain they are still of no interest to him. Her books, on the other hand . . . He's been known to go to an occasional holoplay. He has the audiobook versions, which are surely similarly entertaining, downloaded before he even clicks on the descriptions. Typically, he prefers nonfiction, namely business and science titles, to keep up with the latest advancements, but this is relevant research to give him insight into her personality. Maybe even help him discover what she likes so he can provide it, thus fulfilling his obligation.

He skims her bio:

Electra Lynch was an American author known for writing the *Out of this World* series. Her books were a blend of sci-fi and romance, featuring sensual alien-human love stories. The stories revolved around sensitive and swoon-worthy heroes, who easily outshone human men, and fierce female leads, finding love in unexpected places. In agreement with Lynch's family, her publisher released all her titles posthumously after a tragic accident that took Lynch's life right as her career was poised to launch.

The family bequeathed all proceeds from her book sales to the nonprofits Making San Francisco's Streets Safe Again, First Nations' Food Bank, and Romance Books for Overworked Mommas.

Res6 blinks, a little dumbfounded. What a strange culture this woman came from. Why would someone overwork a parent? Didn't people from her time know how significant giving birth was? These days, getting selected by the Birthing Agency is highly coveted. NHOS even arranges for the person bearing the child to have five years paid leave from their employment, as it is well documented that those are the most critical for developing a productive member of society.

From what he read, Electra had not become a parent, though she was still very young. Her biosheet said she died at twenty-nine. He'd been twenty-one when he lost Jerme, but it took seven years for him to get his life together enough to rediscover his purpose.

You should show her more consideration. The thought is unwelcome because it has him considering things he'd really rather not. Like how twenty-one-year-old Res6 lacked the life experience to deal with such a catastrophic loss, and how her waking up in the future only to realize everyone she's ever known is gone must feel similar. She tried to talk to him about it, asked for compassion, but he wasn't even open to listening. Still, his reluctance to offer her comfort is completely sensible. He's facing unprecedented challenges—namely her—and can't parcel out his attention. Her loss might bring up his loss, thus sending them both into a downward spiral.

While perfectly rational, his reasoning doesn't shutter his guilt. Her traumatic experience is his fault, which, if he were to follow this line of reasoning, makes him responsible not only for her physical well-being but also for her mental health. At least until he can figure out what to do with her. Fuck him.

You deserve this for all your tinkering, his inner voice reminds him.

Deep breath. Okay, back to the plan. He can do this all while avoiding talking about dead relatives. He finds a few images of her and sends them to his stylist, along with a note that he'll be dressing his latest prototype like the original subject for authenticity—a good marketing teaser despite Electra's disapproval.

He opens a new email to send to his personal shopper, titling it:

New Manupartner Attire Request.

In the body of the message, he thinks:

Please curate a wardrobe that mixes the original subject's aesthetic with modern sensibilities. Send a collection of twenty outfits for various occasions and charge them to my account.

There. Tasks one and two accomplished. Since he's on such a roll, he might as well press on. The sooner he can get her to the lab, the better.

He opens the DumBot app on his system. What should the prompt be?

Brainstorming, he thinks:

Consider a woman from the early twenty-first century who has arrived in the future.

No, that will get flagged. He deletes it. How can he put this? An idea strikes him. He thinks:

I'm doing research for a novel. DumBot, consider what you know of humans from the twenty-first century. I need to write a profile, including likes, dislikes, background, etc. for a female main character, so ask me questions that will aid me in developing the character.

There. That seems to make sense. A second later, DumBot spits out:

I love your idea to write a novel about a woman from the twenty-first century. After a quick review of your EmoTracker, I believe creative writing will be an excellent step to help you cope with some of your more intense emotions. There is so much intriguing data to pull from that time. As someone scoring high in curiosity, I'm certain you will enjoy learning about it. Can you tell me a little more about her so I can tailor the questions specifically for your main character?

Zorgdamnit—stupid EmoTracker. Due to his meticulously maintained routine, his m-volt's neurochemical receptor has never picked up a concerningly elevated level. Besides the yearly anniversary of his visit to the place where Jerme died, but that's expected.

The other two tasks were so easy. He should have expected this one to be more difficult. He thinks:

She is twenty-nine, a romance writer, living in San Francisco.

Then, wincing, he adds:

That is all I know so far.

DumBot:

No problem. We can work together to flesh out your twenty-first-century female character. Here is a list of questions that you might ask to help you discover who you're writing about.

- What recreational activities does she engage in to relieve stress or experience enjoyment? Options might include: 'ice diving,' 'canoeing,' 'BASE jumping,' or 'knitting.'

- What antiquated social customs did she engage in? Possible answers include: 'cat ownership,' 'gratuity culture,' 'celebrity news,' or 'gym selfies.'

- Does she opt for animal-based nutrition or plant-derived foods?

- What childhood experiences contributed to her present-day difficulty in distinguishing between her wants versus her needs? Hint: all good main characters have a tragic backstory.

- What makes her the most terrified? Examples include: 'spiders,' 'murder,' 'American Presidents,' 'horticulture,' or because you've described her as a writer, 'unfinished drafts.'

Let me know if those questions are enough to get you started or if I should give you more suggestions. I can't wait to see what you come up with!

Res6 rescans the list. The questions aren't terrible, but even he's cognizant enough to realize that asking her about her childhood trauma might not be the best way to start. Especially considering that she's already experienced one parent's death . . . which would bring up the topic of death in general. Really, it isn't super relevant. He thinks:

Those are great options, but I want to discover things she liked that would have been relevant to her time.

DumBot:

Great thinking! Here are a few things from her time that she might be interested in:

- Ancient figures. Many people during the period immortalized such figures in paper posters, which they hung on their walls. Try 'Kardashian,' 'Winnie-the-Pooh,' 'Steve Urkel,' 'Florida Man,' or 'Henry Cavill.'

- Fandom. Did she personally experience phenomena like 'Poké-mon,' 'BTS Army,' 'Disney Adults' (a potentially aggressive fandom subsect), or 'The Virgin Mary'?

- Belief systems, social media, and global mind-control experiments. Suggestion: TikTok, a popular yet controversial religion from the period.

- Animals. Many people captured and kept animals such as dogs, pigs, sheep, and horses in their homes. Note: Cats were either revered or feared as gods as they are today.

- Music and dancing. Popular styles included 'Jazzercise,' 'disco,' 'mosh pit,' 'synthwave,' and 'instruments.'

I hope this list helps you home in on your main character. Let me know if you need more suggestions. With these options, you're sure to create a thrilling character.

Res6 groans, dropping his head onto the desk. From a conceptual standpoint, he understands the need to put limitations on AI. Irritated, he thinks:

I need questions I can ask her. Like what would a man like me ask a woman like her if she were real. Which she is not.

DumBot:

Great idea to develop your character's personality. Here is an exhaustive list of quick and easy questions a modern man might ask a woman from the past to get to know her if she were real, which she is not:

- What is your favorite color to hear?

- Would you rather be a Pegasus or ride one?

- On a scale of one to 10, is it possible to know your life's purpose?

- If you could do anything you wanted, what would it be?

- If you could spend an afternoon with anyone dead or alive, who would it be?

- Why didn't you do anything about global warming?

Res6 briefly scans the rest of the list. Not perfect, but good enough. He glances over his shoulder at the ominous door looming behind him. He can do this.

He'll do just what Tommy did: go in there and have a conversation like a completely normal person.

6 – Twenty Questions

Electra

. . . and the thing is, my lovely readers, it's like every time he opens his mouth, he puts his foot in it. It would be comical if it weren't so sad. If only I could block him, but it seems he's all I've got. Well, and you, of course. Once I find you, which I'm more determined than ever to do.

So, imagine that. Not only am I stuck alone in the future, but my only companion is a man who thought so little of human companionship, he invented sex clones. He makes me want to throw things. I looked him up, you know. His assistant Tommy's tablet lesson came in quite handy.

I know I've been hitting you with one unbelievable thing after the other, but you'll never believe this. Res6 is 119 years old. And he's not even considered old now. Isn't that insane? Well, it wouldn't be insane to you, would it? Because presumably anyone who's going to read anything I write now won't think that's out of the ordinary.

Oh well. Just another perspective I need to adjust.

There isn't much in the records of his life before his first notable discovery, but it seems he went quiet for a while after it, then came out with his next big breakout: manupartners. Within a few years of their coming on the market, nearly everyone had tried one. It changed everything across the globe. Apparently, my roommate is the future's version of a celebrity, which is another thing that blows my mind, but perhaps explains why he doesn't know how to behave normally. But again, maybe normal is something different now.

I probably need to take him up on his offer to go shopping, if only for the opportunity to observe future people in their natural environment. But what am I supposed to do if someone asks about me? Smile dumbly? Willingly agree to be his one-woman advertising campaign? He's delusional. What would I say? "Hi, I'm Electra, CHOICElover's latest prototype. Oh, you think I seem real? That's because I AM! Res6 isn't the hero you imagine him to be. He's an inept pervert."

Then there are the scans he keeps trying to talk me into. Perhaps they would be a good idea. The video explained that they can prevent any potential genetic issues like cancer before they start. Considering my family history . . .

Electra pauses, letting the cursor flash. *Not going to start crying or worrying about it. Deep breaths. I'm safe. I won't die of cancer like her. If I have the markers, they can fix it now. Deep breath. Okay, we're good. I am not a victim.*

She opens her eyes, returning to the Scrawl entry to finish the "Brain Dump." She shakes her head at the goofy name and chuckles, returning her attention to the tablet.

So, I figure it's time to stop resisting Res6's misguided attempts, stop feeling sorry for myself, and get back to being the badass heroine you deserve.

Whew! I'm never going to publish this, but I promise you it is incredibly therapeutic. And soon, Dear Reader, we will find each other again.

Not okay, but working on it,

Electra

Electra's fingers itch to open FrogBlog and start publishing her thoughts like a fire hydrant struck by a hit-and-run. Even cranking out a few short stories would give her somewhere to funnel all this energy she's built up wallowing in bed. She meant it when she wrote that she'd attempt to stop resisting his advances. Perhaps not today, but that doesn't mean that when the time comes, she'll approach him. He can come to her—

There's a sound outside the door, then it's opening. "Electra?" As though she summoned him, he sticks his head past the doorframe.

Damn it. "You really need to learn to knock."

He assesses the door as if it's the door's fault. "Apologies. I'm not used to knocking in my own unit."

Internally, she cringes. She isn't sure if his comment was intended as a gentle reminder that she is now inhabiting his space, but she takes it as one. His apartment, which upon further reflection is much nicer than the cramped studio she's used to. Still, she isn't willing or possibly able to give up the sanctuary just yet. Sheepishly, she says, "Next time, just knock. No problem."

He gives her a forced smile and eyes the corner of the bed like it might bite. "I think we need to start over. I assessed my schedule and can move some things around, so I have time for our interactions now."

"Okaaaaaay . . ." she says. He eyes the bed again. The poor man is clearly way out of his depth and needs mercy. Not that her merciful nature negates her irritation with him. "Sit if you like, Res6."

He does. Stiffly, placing his hands on his knees and squeezing, which reminds her of a grounding gesture.

"In an effort to provide you with an opportunity to talk, I came up with a list of questions to ask you. *Entirely on my own,*" he adds so quickly that she's pretty sure he's lying.

Tommy seems to have good intentions, but she needs to have a talk with him. Meddling is never a good idea. She learned that firsthand when she accidentally caused a breakup between her good friend and her longtime boyfriend, a.k.a. Brad the cheating pig. She'd given Jessica good advice, but her friend's execution was off. Electra meant she should slash his tires *metaphorically*. The bottom line is Res6 needs to figure out how to navigate his mess on his own. Otherwise, he will never learn and will remain socially inept. Which, if the universe forces her to endure his continued presence, she must do something about.

At least he's trying. "All right. Ask away."

He releases a breath, along with some of the tension he brought into the room with him.

"First, let's start with something relatively benign. You lived by the ocean, right?" She nods, realizing he must have researched her too. *Interesting.* What would the internet say about her now? Did her books get published? She had written the first three books in the series before it got picked up. And if they sold out their advances, who knows how many more she would have published during her lifetime.

"Electra?"

"Huh?" she asks.

"I asked, did you ever actually see a mermaid before they went extinct?"

She barks out a laugh. "You're joking?"

He fishes his phone out of his pocket, scrambling to open something. "No. That's what it says." He frowns, as if his screen has led him astray.

Her heart thuds in a way that feels an awful lot like sympathy or an affection like one might have for a child trying and failing to pronounce a difficult word, like *incomprehensibilities*. "Umm, no, I never saw a mermaid," she says. She's not lying because technically, she can't prove there were never mermaids. Dragons too, or aliens. "Next?"

He scans his phone. Under his breath, he murmurs, "What is your favorite sexual position? Too forward. Have you ever taken a 'blind date'? If so, which party was blind? DumBot indeed. Have you ever had your heart catastrophically broken? Too personal."

Well, that gives her some hope. And it confirms the lying bit.

"Oh, here's one," he says, clearing his throat. "On a scale of one to ten, is it possible to know your life's purpose?"

She shakes her head, unable to repress a grin. "You used AI to help you come up with a list of questions for me?"

"Yes," he says, shifting to stare guiltily at the dark green wall. "Are you more upset with me now?"

She leans forward, placing a hand on his knee, which causes him to jump. "You're trying, and I appreciate that. If you really want to know if I think it's possible to know your life's purpose"—he nods insistently—"well then I'd say, yes and no." He opens his mouth, but she holds up her hand to stop a rebuttal. "I know that I compulsively need to write. I know I feel an intrinsic desire to make the world a better place. I also think people, at least from my time, put too much stock in the word *purpose*. I think just pick something you enjoy and do it. If you can find joy in that, you've got it made. What about you? Was creating manupartners your life's purpose?"

"I see Tommy told you they were my invention." His expression is pained. "I know you don't approve."

"Don't get mad at Tommy. You should have told me it's your company. Besides, it doesn't matter what I think about it. I'm asking how you feel," she presses.

"I guess the answer is yes, then," he says, meeting her gaze.

She can see he means it, which makes her insults that much worse. If only she could keep her mouth shut. Granted, a part of her is curious about what made him think manupartners were a good idea because between that and his resistance to offering compassion, there's definitely some tragic character backstory going on here. But it probably isn't the time to indulge her writer brain, considering they've spoken for ten minutes now and neither of them has yelled or started crying. "Well, that's something, isn't it? How about another question?"

He references his phone again and chuckles to himself. "What risky behaviors do you like to engage in?

She chuckles too since they both know his AI wrote the questions. "Writing. You?"

His smile is genuine now. "Science."

"Good one," she says. "Next?"

"What form does your existential dread take?"

"Cockroaches?" she answers, attempting to keep the tone light-hearted and hoping he'll take the hint.

"That isn't a real answer."

"Pass, then. Next question." She gives him an encouraging grin.

"Since she is a romance author, how many pages does she prefer her sex scenes to be?"

A laugh bursts out. "Umm . . . at least two. You?"

"I've never read a romance book, but I'm definitely reading yours now."

She groans dramatically, leaning back into the pillows. "Please don't. Having people you know read your books, especially the sex scenes, is so embarrassing. Next question."

"If nothing really exists unless it is observed, who are you?" He offers her a challenging stare.

"God, the AI bot came up with that?"

He chuckles, and it is an entirely too-deep, too-pleasant sound, and she finds herself wishing he'll do it again. "Yes. We can skip it. Here are two. How do you like your coffee, and are you a morning person or do you like owls?"

She bites her lip, pretending like she's really having to think it over. His gaze flicks to the motion, his cheeks darkening as he quickly redirects his attention to his phone. "Let's see. Black and owls. You?"

"Tea and morning. Would that be roosters?"

"I think so."

"Did you ever see one?" he asks, making her think of the sad state of the world if the smog-filled image outside the windows is any indication. He thinks mermaids were real, and he's never seen a rooster. It must be worse than she's imagining. She needs to get started on those videos. Back to roosters.

"Of course. They're noisy and can be aggressive. On the other hand, chickens can be quite beautiful. We had several different breeds when I was little." He looks thoughtful for a moment, prompting her to ask, "Is this as effective as you were hoping?"

He scratches his forehead. "I'm terribly afraid to say the wrong thing, but yes, I think so."

Why does that make her feel guilty? His ineptness is his own fault—a result of choosing manupartners over humans for companionship, but he seems earnest. Plus, she shouldn't judge. It's not like she has any idea about the people now and their norms and customs. "Go on. Ask me another one. This is kind of fun."

His eyes brighten as he scans his phone. For a second, she's so overwhelmed by how handsome it makes him, she can almost see how he blurted out his comments that first day. Because with the way the lock of sandy blond hair is falling over his forehead, how the open collar of his shirt exposes the strong line of his throat, or how his lopsided grin makes a dimple appear on one side only, the only coherent word her inner narrator can manage is *beautiful.*

"Do you have a boyfriend?" His brow wrinkles as he stares at the screen, which makes her giggle.

"I had many. More than I could count," she says, which makes his eyes widen. There's a certain thrill in surprising him.

"How many, really?"

She raises a brow in challenge. "Hundreds."

"How did you have time?" he mutters.

"Book boyfriends, of course! You know, the men written by women in romance novels. That's what they're called. Now I guess people have manupartners."

"I suppose since this is going well, I won't point out your obvious hypocrisy," he says, smirking, to which she responds by chuffing and rolling her eyes. "However, I will ask, why not a real one, considering it was so common during your time?"

Because she never prioritized finding one. She was too busy making sure she had enough to get by on. Not that she didn't dream of one day meeting a tall, golden stranger who would blow into her world and sweep her off her feet. A stranger whose cool, impassive eyes would ignite only when they looked upon her—

What is wrong with her? Her inner narrator really needs to get a grip. She can't say any of that, so she says, "Timing was never right. We should probably move on."

He looks up, seeming to sense her momentary discomfort, and damn her if the gilded flecks in his eyes don't dance with mirth. "Oh, here's a good one. What recreational activities does she enjoy?"

"Reading, obviously."

"Besides that, then."

"I liked riding my bike—"

Res6 beams. "I know that!"

Her eyes narrow. "Wait, how do you know that?"

"It's how you . . ."

"How I what?" she asks, more than a little curious now about what he's discovered about what became of her life.

He hesitates. "Died?"

"Died?" She picks up a pillow and chunks it across the bed at him. "That's not funny! God, just when I thought you might be decent. You're the worst."

Her laughter starts to dwindle as his expression turns stricken. His hands fall back to his knees, squeezing. Self-soothing.

Shit.

"Res6, please tell me you're joking." A sudden knot of dread takes root in her stomach.

"I didn't know how to tell you, and you already seemed so upset. Honestly, since you learned how to use your tablet, I'm surprised you haven't looked yourself up."

She considered it, but she was too afraid of what she might find. Her entire purpose in life right now is to drag herself out of this victim mentality pattern and get out of bed. *Thanks for the extra dose of self-awareness, Janet.* She isn't sure if she could bear learning that she died young of cancer like her mom or something equally horrible. "Ignorance is bliss?" A lump is quickly building in her throat and tightening. Tightening. Tightening. "I died in a bike accident?"

He rubs his temples as if he's the one receiving the hostile news. "You were hit by one of the trolleys, actually."

"How old was I?" she asks, sensing where this is going.

"The same age as you are now. Twenty-nine."

She gasps. "Is that why my memories stop when they do?"

He clears his throat. "Yes."

"Oh God, my—my—"

"Don't worry. Your books were published posthumously. All the proceeds went to charitable foundations—"

"My family, you idiot," she cries. It's like the floor has dropped out from under her. The tears she managed to keep at bay for twenty-four hours are back. "My dad and Janet," she sobs, as if somehow saying it out loud might garner some impossible sympathy.

Her parents must have been devastated. After everything they invested in her—all their love, their hopes and dreams for her—what a waste to have died so young. Her blood hums in her ears as a wave of dizziness washes over her. She cannot have a panic attack in front of him.

Janet's grounding voice sounds in her mind. *Remember the steps.*

Sucking in a slow inhale through her nose, she concentrates on the sensation of filling her lungs. Hold for three seconds. And release. Focus on three things that are real. Her breath is an easy one, and at this point, she's going to need easy ones. Two is the plush yet sturdy weight of the bed supporting her, holding her. Grounding her. Three—her head snaps to Res6, then down to the light dusting of hair on his forearm, which must be soft and warm. He notices her observation, then scoots closer, reaching out his arm for her inspection.

Before she thinks better of it, she wraps her hand around his forearm. "You're real," she mutters.

Res6 stares at where her fingers grip his arm. "Electra?"

"It is a technique my stepmom Janet taught me." She sighs as the pang of loss strikes her anew. But it's too surreal because it doesn't feel real, hence the exercise. "Remember, I told you she was a psychologist? I learned so much from her. I already miss her like crazy."

He doesn't say anything, and she wonders what he's thinking. He's probably comparing her and her emotional outburst to one of his manupartners, cursing his luck.

She releases his arm, takes the tablet, and enters a quick search.

He leans forward and takes the device. "Are you sure you want to know?" She glances up, blinking through her tears. "You've already had a distressing week. Perhaps you should put this off until you're more mentally—"

"Stable?" she interjects, shaking her head. "Like that is going to happen. Maybe I did something in my past life to deserve this. I must have been a tax collector, or politician, or worse!"

He reaches forward, takes her hand, and places it back on his forearm. They both stare at it for an extended moment. "Nothing bad is going to happen to you anymore," he assures her.

She lets out an undignified huff. "How can you possibly say that?"

"Because I may not be your version of perfect, but I'm highly competent, and you are my responsibility."

"Are you sure you aren't my punishment from your non-deities?" she asks.

He moves his arm, letting her hand fall away. "Maybe we are each other's punishment."

7 – Ten Tries

Res6

Res6 is pacing again. He checks the time. 07:52. She chose owl, so it is anyone's guess how late she stayed up. Should he wake her and tell her he's leaving? Ten days in, and this unexpected woman has already thrown his schedule into disarray. *One of the many reasons people in the modern era prefer my creation.* Limited disruptions and easily met expectations, that's what people get with his product.

If she were a manupartner, he wouldn't be running late for his meeting with Lextr because he was hovering outside her door, reluctant to leave her alone.

Knock first, she instructed, so he taps on the door before pushing it open and popping his head inside. The lights are dim, having already begun their morning sequence. He can just make out a vaguely humanoid shape within the pile of blankets. "Electra," he whisper-shouts.

The bedding rustles, and she rolls over to face him, but she's still asleep. He steps closer, intending to nudge her awake, when she tugs the covers down and throws a bare leg over a bunched-up blanket. Only then does he notice she's wearing one of his T-shirts, which, though oversized on her, has risen so she's barely decent.

If he touched her, would his fingers leave a brand on her skin the way hers did when she touched his forearm? It takes him too long to tear his gaze away from her smooth thigh and refocus it on her face. But the view isn't any better. Her dark eyes, still lazy with sleep, blink up at him, and a wave of irrational desire barrels through him.

His voice is raspy as he says, "You're wearing my shirt again." All at once, his blood rushes south. *Unacceptable*, he chastises his body, which only somewhat listens. Thankfully, it's still relatively dark in the room.

She yawns as if she's completely unaware of the way she's affecting him. "You didn't get me any pajamas."

He shakes off the thoughts crowding his mind, noting with his m-volt, *Order Electra Pajamas*. "I'm leaving for work. Are you okay?" he asks, like he does every morning before he leaves, though he normally doesn't get quite the visual.

"Mmmhmm," she murmurs, stretching, and nestles more deeply into the blankets.

Good enough. He spins on his heel and retreats.

A few minutes later, he's entering a SAT in the private garage for the penthouse units of his tower. As the vehicle seals, the exterior door unlocks. Strips of green lights that encircle the room flash red. The SAT vibrates faintly as the magnets engage. Then he's rushing through the dense air into the depths of the city.

He takes out his device intending to catch up on messages, but the image of her in his bed, with the suggestion of her curves beneath the thin fabric of his T-shirt, gets lodged in his mind. Was she trying to seduce him? He felt seduced. She wrote books about people falling in love. According to DumBot, people during her time had deeply committed relationships called *marriages*.

The laughable concept of True Love was a prevalent yet misguided societal expectation as well back then. He almost feels sorry for people who held such archaic, impossible beliefs, but even Jerme was swayed into the trappings of love, and those two were similar enough. With Electra's likely outlook, is that what she wanted? Was she misinterpreting his effort to help her adjust to this world as romantic interest?

Surely not. Still, a buffer would be useful. Neither Lextr nor Tommy is willing to do it, and getting a manupartner is still a no-go. He already has too much on his plate, and Electra's distaste for them could undermine her acclimation. There's the body double to consider, but what if it accidentally slips up trying to help her and lets something from one of their conversations slip? He could give it careful instructions, but she would probably hate it even more than a regular manupartner since it looks like him. Better that she not know of its existence.

The SAT pulls into the garage, and he waits long minutes for the airlock interchange process. He continues contemplating the issue as he walks to his office. Who else would be a good buffer—wait. Why didn't he think of it before? He already considered connecting them. But now, when Jerme is back, he can be the buffer. He already suspects they'll like each other. And if they both want a romantic partnership, a human-human one, they'll have each other!

Initially, he planned to give Jerme a manupartner, but Electra needs someone too. Despite his efforts to build the company in his brother's honor, he suspects Jerme wouldn't like having a manupartner. Should his theory prove true, he can insert Electra as the easy solution. He and Electra appear to be mutually attracted to each other. Therefore, he can deduce that she'll find his twin equally attractive, and Electra is stunning—not that he noticed. Well, outside of that first day, and maybe a few other moments here and there—and that disconcerting image of her in his bed this morning. The point is, Jerme will find her attractive, because who wouldn't? Her complaints about his emotional unavailability are another problem easily solved by Jerme. Upon further consideration, they will be perfect for each other.

It's really shaping up to be an excellent plan.

He attends his weekly meeting with Lextr, and a few others with various department heads. By lunchtime, he's had plenty of time to contemplate the next step in his plan. He needs to figure out what to do with her in the meantime. Tommy was right; the questions appeared to help. She enjoys talking, and they even shared a moment of levity. Perhaps keeping her stable until his brother is back is within his capacity after all.

He settles in at his desk and logs into his system. First, he orders Electra the salad with sautéed tofu that she enjoyed a few days ago, setting the delivery time for 13:00, then he orders his own lunch to be delivered to his office. An unfortunate flash of Electra in his T-shirt reminds him to shoot a quick message over to the personal shopper for more appropriate bedtime attire. Then it's time to brainstorm a few outings to take her on. Maybe even consult DumBot for good measure, since the questions seemed to go over well.

He opens the application.

DumBot, I need to do more research for my novel.

He watches the words populate. DumBot:

I'm here and excited to help make your characters jump off the page! Should I ask you more questions about the female main character, who is not a real person?

He winces, thinking:

I need your help in learning more about her culture. Based on what you know so far, what are some ideas for outings that she might enjoy that would also help acclimatize her to the future? That is, I'm considering making the novel a time travel adventure, he adds quickly. Please update your memory.

DumBot:

What an interesting twist! This novel is already shaping up to be a bestseller! I can help you come up with outing ideas that she might enjoy and also find educational. Here are several options along with clips from source material should you wish to study the subjects' interactions more closely.

The application spits out a list of options along with citations and links to clips ranging from three to five minutes. Perfect. He clicks on the first one from a documentary called *50 First Outings*.

A frumpy-looking man in an egregiously striped shirt approaches a brightly dressed woman sitting at a table in some type of outdoor restaurant. A plate of pastries sits in front of her. She appears to be using them to create some sort of building. The man takes a tiny stick and presses it into the stack, an excellent idea, offering much-needed structure to the pastry building. His contribution seems to make the woman happy.

Res6 closes the video, confident he understands the gist of the clip. Build things with food. Sounds easy enough. He clicks on the next clip.

By the time he's finished lunch, he's armed with a handful of excellent outing ideas, along with a few which might be more challenging to execute. But perhaps with a custom simulation chamber—

Lextr pops his head inside his office door. "Did you see the alert?"

He glances up from the clip. "No, I . . ." Was he distracted planning outings for a woman he barely knows, instead of focusing on securing a second chance for his brother? "I got distracted," he finally admits.

"No problem, sir. That is what I'm here for. The DNA vector sample stabilized. It's ready to be synthesized with the bio-coagulase. If we start now, we should have a sample ready to adhere to an activation pad within the hour."

Within the hour . . . That means he could get to see his brother again after almost a century in less than a week.

"Do you want to run the activation here in the lab, or," Lextr leans forward conspiratorially, "from the privacy of your own home? If the experiment succeeds—you recall how startling waking up in the lab was for your current unit. Not to mention the issue of relocating a specimen that bears an identical resemblance to, with respect, *you*."

Res6 nods. He hadn't considered it much beyond the prospect of getting to see Jerme again, but Lextr raises a good point. "I'll do it at home."

"Of course, sir. Based on the notes you sent yesterday, I think we should program the updated electrical variances you detected in your review of the data from the initial trial into the activation pad prior to beginning stage one."

"Excellent. Proceed. The *initial trial's* name is Electra, by the way." He thinks the command to shut down his system, getting up to follow Lextr to the lab.

"What are you doing, sir?"

"I want to prepare the sample myself," he says.

Lextr pauses in the sleek corridor outside his door. The dip of his shoulders suggests Res6 is missing something.

"Is that a problem?"

"I . . . uhh. No, I suppose not," Lextr says.

Res6 narrows his eyes as he studies the other man. Does Lextr think that by overseeing the Jerme experiment, Res6 is going to take credit for his breakthrough? While the project began under his own direction at CHOICElover, Lextr would be owed the credit if it went public. It was Lextr's experiment design that led to Electra.

It occurs to him then: A breakthrough of this magnitude would be monumental—granted, their Jerme replication study must succeed first. Yet Lextr could never share it with the world, considering its problematic legality. In the collaborative spirit of science, the man merits praise for his efforts.

How did Res6 overlook that? *By getting so absorbed in your pursuits that you failed to observe your surroundings—again.* Losing Jerme should have taught him that lesson. He'll do better. *Starting now*, his conscience nudges. Fuck.

"Lextr, if this works, if we can really replicate your findings, it opens up a whole new field of memory science. Consider this: If we could effectively manipulate memory, we could potentially suppress or even replace a person's unpleasant experiences with a memory of their choosing. And that's only one possibility. Even if we can't share your work directly, the possibilities of where it can lead are endless."

Lextr's face lights up with a huge smile, his green lip stain contrasting against his bright white teeth. "It feels significant, doesn't it?"

Res6 nods, fondly recalling the day he brought Lextr onto his team nearly fifty years ago. CHOICElover had already established itself as the premium brand, but with Lextr's drive and uniquely analytical mind, together they pushed the science. The advancements came one after the other. "I appreciate you taking on this challenge," he says.

"Sure thing, sir." Lextr frowns slightly as they make their way to the small Neuronic Gene Infusion lab.

"What it is?" he asks.

"You're prepared that we may have to run through a few failed trials before we achieve success?"

As a scientist, he accepts that failure is a natural part of the work. As a brother, however, failure isn't something Res6 planned to think about. What will he do with a copy of his brother that is a compliant, programmed blank slate? Decommission him? A shiver racks him. Even if it wasn't the real Jerme, like it was the real Electra, could he do it? The thought makes the tightness in his chest that is always lingering below the surface constrict. "I'm aware failure's possible."

"Don't worry, sir. I'll be here should we need to deal with the *consequences*." Lextr means recycling failed half-grown Jermes. It's a horrifying thought. "Since we don't have the DNA purity factor on our side, I expect we'll run through a few synthesized DNA trials to establish a baseline and weed out conditions that lead to early failures before we use an organic sample from the original vector."

"Good thinking. What area of the brain did Electra's sample come from?" Res6's brow creases.

"I believe a preserved distal axon terminal from her prefrontal cortex. It's possible that a sample from any area of the brain would do." Lextr pauses his work, considering. "Maybe not any area, but considering the relative by-comparison sample collection date listed . . ." his shoulders tense because they both know it means the date of his brother's death. Lextr clears his throat, continuing. "There should be enough viable samples in the storage to run a few dozen trials, I would think."

"I'll confirm how many in case we need to use them," he says as he presses his palm to the palm scanner beside the door. When Res6 designated the space for the trials, he requested the security protocols be set up so that only he and Lextr had access. The pad lights up green, and the lock clicks open.

They enter the first room, strip out of their clothing, and pass through the Steri-Light into the staging chamber. Once the system has confirmed the elimination of potential contaminants, they slip on their biohazard containment suits. During sample preparation, it is critical that no foreign bodies that might inadvertently contaminate the selected vector's DNA enter the production lab. Once stable enough to grow, the sample is impervious to defects.

The workspace is considerably smaller than Res6's main lab. Two walls are lined with metal tables, regular and refrigerated supply cabinets, and particle panes. A third wall has a long table with built-in chambers and equipment for the different stages of synthesis, which resemble smaller versions of the large production lines in CHOICElover's main biomanufacturing facility.

The first sample using synthetically constructed DNA sits in his patented Tissue Tangler, the mRNA incubation oscillator he designed that led to his first notable discovery in the field of gene sculpting. The next step in the process is to transfer the sample to the bioprinting chamber for replication, the final phase to occur in the lab.

He carefully makes the transfer and seals the bioprinting chamber's door. As the lights come on, the sample quivers, growing infinitesimally with each passing second. In half an hour, the sample will have grown ten times its current size and be ready to package and take home for activation. "Should we go ahead and begin the next trial?"

Lextr is at the metal table with the activation pad, ready to input the updated electrical variation pattern. He nods, disconnecting the pad from the sensor. "We should. I'll get the next base started."

As Lextr powers up the DNA synthesizer, Res6 opens the DNA catalogue and calls up his brother's file. He scrolls to the bottom, clicking on Jerme's BioKey. The samples, many of which were taken within the hour after his death, are each labeled with the date and method of extraction, as well as a series of codes indicating purity and degradation status. There are hundreds of samples in various conditions. He filters the list for viable samples from the brain region and scans it.

Glial Tissue

Synaptic maintenance and pruning—no.

Myelin Sheath Remnants

Axon insulation and routing—possibly as a last resort. He flags the one viable sample.

Cerebellar Purkinje Cell

Motor memory—no. Oh, here's one.

Prefrontal Cortex Tissue

Possible identity-relevant NAM storage. He flags the identifier, noting three viable samples. That's it? He takes a deep breath. *Moving on.*

Enteric Nervous System Tissue

Gut brain—no, flagging for incorrect categorization.

Olfactory Bulb Tissue

No, for obvious reasons. His heart jolts as his eyes land on the next sample. Jackpot!

Hippocampal Tissue

If anything will work, it's the hub for memory formation. He flags the identifier—only two viable samples? Fuck. That can't be it. He keeps scanning until finally landing on the last sample.

Axonal Segment

It doesn't specify what brain region, but if that's what worked to bring Electra back, he'll pull the four listed samples.

The synthesized DNA will likely fail, but it's worth a shot. Then only ten viable samples? His stomach clenches. Experiments sometimes take hundreds of trials, or in rare cases, thousands. Electra woke up swearing on the first attempt using her DNA. Granted, that success only came after dozens of failures from both the control and experiment groups.

Lextr comes to stand behind him. On the particle pane is a materials request addressed to the lead technician Bexly, his organic assets custodian who's responsible for biological material preservation, including CHOICElover's entire DNA stores.

"Only ten samples. I thought there'd be more," Lextr says.

A knot is building in his throat. "Me too."

Ten tries. That's it—if he fails, Jerme will go back to being a memory. An idea that exists only in his mind. He needs Jerme. Life is becoming too much to navigate without him, and not just because of Electra. If he's being honest, he's been aimlessly wading through a monotonous existence for a while now. That's probably the real reason he approved Lextr's trial design. But what did he expect to happen? Was he thinking of Jerme all along? At least in his subconscious? That has to be it, because it can't be that he was looking for something to jolt him back to life. This is why he needs Jerme back—nothing is clear anymore without him. He has ten tries, and failure isn't an option.

8 – Let's Go Outing

Electra

"Oh good, you're up," Res6 says, blowing into the unit wearing a determined expression. He's outfitted in one of his space commander-esque jumpsuits, bronze this time, which only makes him more golden. One hand clutches a large, ominous-looking silver case. *Not giving serial killer vibes at all.*

"Well, hello to you too," she says, watching interestedly from the couch. "I don't sleep all day, you know."

"I'll just be a moment." He pauses, making a quick scan of her attire, including her feet, which are housed in the softest pink socks she's ever felt.

She holds them up for him to see, wiggling her toes. His nose wrinkles, which makes her grin. "Your personal shopper did a good job this time. DumBot?"

He laughs. "No, another actual woman."

She gasps theatrically, covering her mouth. "So scandalous."

She found the socks in one of the many packages addressed to her that were waiting beneath the smartwaiter delivery drawer this afternoon. Res6 must have got them out, setting them there so as not to interrupt her sleep. It's like the woman picking out the clothes for her understands her tastes perfectly. The assorted outfits are a perfect combination of items she recognizes, like a pair of butter-soft skintight jeans, several shift dresses, and some oversized sweaters, but with a funky future-world twist. Like the structured blue sweater with an extra-large circular cutout in the center, which would expose her completely without a bodysuit underneath. The garment seems pointless to her, but she'll figure out how to rock it if that's what's in style now.

It took her an embarrassing amount of time to come to terms with the fact that he was spending so much unicoin on all these clothes. *On her*. The internet, or network as they call it, says he's loaded, which Tommy confirmed, so she forced herself to move past it. She doesn't have to agree with his spending habits. She nearly had a panic attack cutting off tags—as a principle, she always wore secondhand—but on the bright side, hanging up the clothing in his sparsely filled closet gave her something to do this afternoon besides staring at the tablet all day.

He comes back into the living room, wrinkling his nose as he studies her. "I'd suggest changing into something a little lighter. It's warm where we're going."

"Excuse me?" she asks, pausing the educational video she was only half-interested in watching.

He marches into the kitchen and collects a bottle of water before pacing to the closed door of the spare room she has yet to venture into. Since he's let her sleep in his room while taking the couch for himself, she guessed it was a storage closet.

"We're going on our first outing. Wear whatever you like, but you may find those," he nods to the socks, "uncomfortably warm. Shoes would be ideal."

"Okaaaaay . . ." She sets down the tablet, grateful for the distraction. She's close to information overload anyway. While the history of banking may be riveting to some, there's only so much a woman can take. "Where are we going?"

"It's a surprise," he says, watching her get up and move toward her bedroom as if expecting more of an argument. "I'll be fifteen minutes. Then we'll go."

He steps into the spare room, and there's a click. Did he just lock the door? Now the door is no longer benign. What is inside that is worth locking away from her?

As much as The Room now piques her curiosity, she's even more interested in leaving this unit. For the first time in a while, she woke up feeling refreshed and able to confidently meet the day. Going on an outing is a welcome idea. Especially as Res6 appears to already have something in mind. As long as it isn't shopping, which would be far too stressful, she's game.

Of all the videos Tommy sent, the dissection of modern social customs was the most interesting one, but it was too short at a mere three hours. An outing where she gets to see and possibly meet other future people will be highly beneficial to her research. A tangible step in her quest to figure out what is wrong with people now so she can figure out how to help them. She is not—to repeat, NOT—interested in figuring out and fixing Res6. Just people in general. She takes a deep breath. Even seeing what they're like so she can write a story that might appeal to them would be a good step.

It takes her ten minutes to decide on an alternative outfit. Not knowing what they're doing, except that it will be warm, limits her. She selects a pair of white-and-silver striped culottes and a cropped white halter top that is woven with a reflective thread that glitters when she turns in the light. A low pair of clear tech sandals complements the ensemble.

She steps out of the bedroom right as Res6 is closing the door behind him. He notices her watching him, and if she's being honest, trying to get a glimpse of what's inside The Room.

He pointedly clears his throat. "This room is off limits. Understand?"

Now she's even more curious. If only she had some real heroine skills like lock picking.

"Electra," he urges.

"What?" she asks, still trying to figure out what is so important to keep hidden. Obviously, the first thought that pops into her mind is Sex Dungeon. "Oh yeah, off limits. Got it." Under her breath she mutters, "Not giving murder-y vibes at all."

He chuckles. "Does this mean you're feeling revived?"

She shoots him a taunting grin. "Today, anyway."

"All right, let's go."

She follows him into the hall and into an elevator. It takes them from floor 300, labeled Penthouse Suites, to 102 Simulation Chambers. There are only a dozen total buttons, including 220 Sports and Recreation, 000 Ground Floor, 290 Private Dinner Suites, 150 Main Commercial, and 100 Main Cafeteria. "This is like a rich people's private elevator."

He hums in agreement as the doors open. His hand darts forward, and he presses the doors-closed button. "I forgot to mention, I might have to touch you if we're to convince people you're my latest manu-partner."

"Okay." For whatever odd reason, the idea of him touching his latest manupartner sits uncomfortably in her mind. "Latest?"

He allows the doors to slide open. She jolts as a warm hand at the small of her back presses her forward. "Do you have difficulty hearing?"

She chuffs. "No."

"Hmm . . . I'm not convinced. This is another reason we need to take you to the lab for scans. Typically, manupartners have an unblemished health record or aren't in existence long enough for long-term health issues to manifest unless the DNA vector had them at the time of death. You're healthy now, but considering your nature, scans would be prudent."

"What about cancer?" she asks, not really sure if she wants to hear the answer.

"It is extremely unusual for a manupartner to be activated with the disease, but it has happened. Usually because a DNA sample accidentally slipped into the DNA database or the manupartner has been activated for a while and it manifests naturally. At that point, the customer can either have them fixed or turn them in for a replacement. It's nothing to worry about." He clears his throat. "Especially after the scans."

Before she can offer an excuse about her fear of discovering her genetic defects, they're at the front desk, having passed a handful of other future people, all of whom are staring as much at her and Res6 as she is at them. Probably because he's famous. In her periphery, Res6 steps up to the desk, speaking to the person behind it, but she doesn't hear what he says because she's too busy observing the blonde woman who's come to stand beside her and is studying her in return.

"Hi," she says as the woman leans in to get a closer look. This draws the attention of her companion, a man with a very intricate white lace tattoo covering his neck and exposed shoulders. They are well inside the boundary of her personal space bubble, so she takes a step back, bumping into Res6. He glances down, then at the people inspecting her. His arm slides around her waist, and he pulls her to his side. Is he being protective?

"Please afford us adequate space," he says, turning back to the employee.

"Get a picture of her for your FrogBlog," the man says.

"Good thinking!" The woman pulls her phone out and snaps a few pictures.

Electra expects Res6's protective urges to doubly fire, but he leans down and whispers into her ear, "Smile."

She twitches, biting back irritation. A manupartner would comply. But he said, *Be yourself.* He adjusts her so they're angled toward the camera and uses his other hand to tilt her head up to him. He puts on a confident smirk, raising his brows like she's supposed to be doing something. That's right: smile. She gives her best *I don't hate this* impression.

"Perfect. Such a beautiful couple," the woman coos. "Do you mind if I ask you a few questions? It's not every day I have the opportunity to speak with someone so important."

Behind the woman, the man is fanning himself.

"I always have a few minutes to spare for a fan of CHOICElover." His voice is almost flirtatious.

Electra's lips part, and she has to consciously close her mouth to keep it from hanging open. Who is this open, funny guy? Where has he been? He can be jovial to strangers on the street, but not her?

"Is this your new manupartner?" the woman asks, and Res6 nods. "She seems special. Fresh. What can you tell us about her?"

Res6 releases a charming chuckle, moving his hand to the back of her neck. The firmness of his grip and the warmth of his palm shoot through her, and she has to fight her body's instinct to lean into his touch. "She's unique, isn't she?" He gives her an affectionate glance before turning back to address the woman.

As he explains some nonsense about the significant benefits of manupartners and the exciting things his company is working on, she can't help but feel a little dirty being a piece of advertisement for something she is so repulsed by. To each their own, and she's never been one to shame anyone, but the idea of a fake lover is just beyond her.

He squeezes her neck. "Did you hear the question?"

Her gaze snaps back to the woman. "No. Can you repeat it?"

"How do you like being the CHOICElover of MSP's most celebrated man?" The woman blinks eagerly as she holds up the phone to record Electra's answer.

She eyes the door as if it's an escape hatch. *Just be yourself.* Those were his words. She chuckles. Well, he asked for this. "It's not as exciting as one might think. So far, all we do is hang out at his unit, argue, and play this game he likes called 20 Questions." Looking up at Res6, she grins.

But instead of it ruffling him like she expects, he smoothly replies, "Impressive, isn't she? The fun question game is, of course, a series of tests we're running her through. Standard for each prototype trial. CHOICElover prides itself on making sure our products are held to the highest standards, including safety. Unlike some of our competitors."

"That's why CHOICElover is the best!" the woman agrees. "Tell me," she says, addressing Electra again, "if you could do something more exciting with your owner, what would it be? Besides sex, obviously."

The man behind her is fanning himself again. He's even blushing. Somehow the showiness of it seems superficial, though Electra can't pinpoint exactly how. Ignoring him, she considers the question. "If sex is off the table, we could test faulty parachutes."

"What's a parachute?" the woman asks.

Her friend answers, "I believe it's a massive sheet of fabric people used to avoid dying when they fell out of airplanes."

The woman coughs. "But then wouldn't testing the faulty ones be problematic?"

Her friend giggles. "I think she's being funny! What a great LifeLike innovation. What trait would I have to select to get that?"

"Sarcasm," Res6 answers, frowning.

In a moment of great fortune, the simulation chamber employee steps around the desk. "Sir, your chamber is ready. This way, please."

Electra steps in line with the woman, grateful when Res6's not entirely unpleasant hand falls away. Normally, she'd be an advocate for physical touch, but with him—

"Here we are," the employee says. "You have one hour of horseback riding followed by a prairie picnic, as requested. The basket with everything you need is in the supply bin."

Electra steps inside the room, which is nothing more than a large black box. There is a cubby to the side where a classic wicker basket sits, complete with a red and white blanket, presumably to spread out in the field.

"When you're ready, just press this button," the employee instructs, then slips out the door. Electra has no clue how this empty room is going to transform into a setting for horseback riding, and surely an actual horse won't appear. Were they on the extensive list of extinct species? She'll have to search that later. When she turns around to ask Res6 what exactly they're meant to be doing, he's putting on—"Are those chaps?"

His nose wrinkles as he assesses the bright orange overpants with a bedazzled strap that he buckles at his waist. "Whatever they are, they're a bit ostentatious for my taste."

"I guess that's something we can agree on."

He frowns. "Faulty parachutes. Really?"

She shrugs, trying and failing to hide her grin. "What? You told me to be myself."

He sighs, fishing around in a bin, and hands her a blue pair of chaps. She takes them along with a sleek pair of safety glasses, adding, "This is insane."

Five minutes later, to her utter shock and amazement, the room has been transformed into a vast plain surrounded by mountains that looks like it might be Montana, and she's sitting on something that resembles a mechanical bull but with a longer neck. The thing appeared from a hole in the floor after they watched a minute-long instructional video and Res6 pressed a button.

"Many of the simulations require VR headsets, but the more sophisticated rooms use an advanced holographic technology."

She glances around the golden, windswept field, then across the expansive blue sky, searching for the projectors. They're well disguised if they are there. "Where's your 'horse'?" she asks, using air quotes.

Her stomach sinks as he steps up beside her, first putting a foot into the stirrup and swinging a leg around like the video showed. "That wasn't difficult," he says, using her hips as leverage as he adjusts his position.

"Before we start, I have a question. Several, in fact."

"Oh, now you want to play my fun questions game?" He squeezes her hips for emphasis.

"I thought the purpose of these outings was to acclimate me to your world. How is this supposed to do that?"

"You said you don't enjoy shopping, so here we are," he says, as if that makes any sense. "Just try to get something out of this, okay? Enjoyment, perhaps. Or consider the technology it takes to recreate this experience. It's fascinating, really."

He points to a red switch at the top of the machine's "neck." She almost can't reach it, but she gets it flipped. Suddenly, the mechanical horse thing appears to have ears that twitch, plus fur. Amazed, she reaches forward, brushing her hand along its mane, meeting cool metal where the "animal's" coat ought to be.

"So weird," she says.

Behind her, Res6 kicks his heels into the "horse," nudging it into a trot. She lurches forward, grabbing hold of the saddle horn, a part she only knows because of the research she did for her *Out of this World* series. After the alien king saved Guinevere, he may or may not have used the horn *for her pleasure* on the long ride back to Outlandia. The thought makes her jump, which causes Res6 to grasp her hips again.

"You okay?" he asks, and she tries to focus on the gently rolling valley they're passing through.

Surely he doesn't think . . .

"Electra," he urges, squeezing to get her attention.

He knows about her books. Has he read them? Surely he doesn't think she's going to let him do that to her now. The woman out there assumed they were having, or at least would have, sex. That's the whole point of a manupartner. But Res6 doesn't seem interested in sex with her, though maybe he has a weird kink that he plans to use this poor horse for. Oh God, how many other people have had sex on the machine she's currently sitting on? Surely they sterilize the equipment after each customer.

"We're really going to need to have your hearing checked," he grumbles.

"I heard you fine." Now that she's used to the horse—and a little weirded out—she releases the horn, crossing her arms. "You didn't listen to my books, did you?"

He huffs like it's a stupid question. "No. I told you, I'm not interested in romance."

"Okay. Well, that's good." If he hasn't read them, he probably isn't entertaining erotic thoughts, so she can relax. Maybe enjoy this experience, like he suggested.

The horse whinnies, alerting them to an approaching dust storm—wait, are those cowboys galloping toward them? "What type of program is this?—Ahhh!" she screams as gunshots ring out.

The horse rears back, tossing her into Res6's chest. Metallic pings sound across the room—those can't be real bullets, right? Maybe she should have researched how future people entertain themselves before venturing out of Res6's apartment. If healing really is that advanced, maybe a minor gunshot wound is part of the fun. His arms snake around her waist, holding her firmly against him, which isn't entirely unpleasant. Well, it wouldn't be if the simulation hadn't turned into some type of western chase scene. "Is this safe?"

"Completely safe," he says.

They jostle in the saddle as the horse gallops up a small trail leading to—"Oh my God. That's a cliff."

"Looks that way. Fuck!" he shouts.

"Ouch! My leg! Something just hit me." She rubs the tender spot. Maybe the word *safe* has evolved and means something different than it did during her time. She should probably clarify. "The system won't actually hurt us, right? That's not something people do for thrills now?"

Something whizzes past her head, thudding right by her ear. Res6 yelps. "I don't think so."

"We've got you cornered! Give us the girl, or we'll shoot!" a rugged, disembodied voice calls out.

What in the Wild West is happening? "You're already shooting!" she shouts back. Another rubber-like projectile, like a paintball, hits her shoulder. "Damn it!"

"Thanks for catching that!" the voice says. "Let me try that again. Give us the girl, or we'll shoot you some more!"

A fake bullet pings off the metal horse. "Stop it!"

Behind her, Res6 grunts.

"We won't stop until we have the wee lass! Hand her over or we'll send you plummeting to your deaths!"

Did the system's voice just turn Scottish? This is too surreal. "End program!" she shouts. Nothing happens.

Res6 reaches forward, trying to hit the red switch between the horse's ears, but with each jarring stride, he misses it. "Can you help me?"

She reaches for it, but his one-armed grip limits her range of motion. "If you let me loose." She glances up. The cliff is getting nearer. "What do you think happens if they corner us?"

"Let's not find out." He squeezes her waist, pressing himself against her back as he attempts another pass at the switch. The horse jolts right as his fingers brush it. "Shit."

They're soaring past brambles, dust flying with each hoof strike. Though she knows—*well, she thinks*—it's all fake, her heart jumps. Their horse is running full speed toward the cliff edge, showing no signs of slowing down. At the last minute it brakes, sliding as it spins to face their attackers, throwing her and Res6 forward. Her hand darts toward the red switch, and she's just grazing it when the horse rears back, kicking at the attackers defensively.

They scream, sliding back. Before they fall off the machine, Res6 throws his arms around her and grabs the horn. The horse's hooves slam into the ground with such force that a fissure forms in the rock at its feet. At least the Scottish cowboys have stopped shooting.

The one sporting a bright rust handlebar mustache and matching rhinestone chaps slides off his horse and inches toward them. He holds his hand out. "Hand her over, partner. Nice and easy."

"Maybe if I go with him, the program will end?" she asks.

"I'll never give her up," Res6 shouts, out of nowhere.

Does he do these simulations often? If so, color her intrigued—just maybe next time, not a low-grade scary one. At least until she's used to them.

She shakes her head. "I can't believe you just did that."

He lifts his hand, pointing a finger gun at the leader. The others step up behind him, and she only now notices they're all wearing yellow star-shaped badges that say "Deputy Lawman."

A laugh bursts from her chest. "Wait, Res6—they think you're the bad guy."

Feeding into her amusement, he growls, "You'll have to kill me first!"

"Oh God, don't encourage them!"

The cowboys raise their six-shooters. "Look inta the black eye o' my pistol, for it'll be the last ye'll ever see, ye ken!"

Their horse prances nervously, its ears twitching. Beneath them, the ground shakes. The horse takes a few unsteady steps toward the cliff's edge.

Res6 squeezes her tighter. "This can't be good."

A shriek rips from her chest as the ground drops out from beneath them and they tumble. Her stomach lurches as rocks race down the cliff beside them, followed by a chorus of yeehaws that echoes over the distance.

"Hold on!" Res6 calls.

She throws herself forward, wrapping her arms around the horse's neck. The machine flops in the opposite direction. She slides up its neck, and the horn digs into her pelvis. Trying to ease the discomfort, she shimmies but slips. The side of her face slides against the cool metal, the safety glasses screeching as they dig into her skin. When her cheekbone brushes something knobby, there's a click.

Suddenly the horse stills, righting itself. She slumps back down its neck, the horn digging into her ass. "Oh my God, I think I stopped it." Her voice is unsteady but relieved. Res6 lifts her off the horn, settling her back into the saddle. The simulation dissolves into a benign prairie once again.

The system, in a cheery feminine tone, announces, "Guests are allotted ten minutes to disembark the animal and return to the staging area, at which time the room will rearrange for the picnic activity."

"I just need a second," she says, noting her mildly panicked breath. "I didn't expect that to feel so real."

He holds up one of the little squishy fake bullets so she can see. "In a way it was." He flicks the bullet to the ground, and she notes the dozens of others, plus a few clinging to her chaps. "I'm sorry . . ." He hesitates. "I didn't mean to cause you more trauma."

She huffs a laugh. "I'm fine. A little shaken, but it's all good. That was a great introduction to what the simulation chambers are capable of," she says, trying to make light of the mildly perilous situation. His intentions were good and she doesn't want him to feel bad or discouraged since he's trying. It's not like he put her in real danger.

"True," he says, shoulders trembling as if he's chuckling.

The warmth of his chest seeps into her back. He doesn't budge. Only releases a deep sigh, relaxes into their position, and slips an arm around her waist, which makes her feel . . . comforted? Is Res6, the inventor of the horrid manupartners, managing to comfort her? Impossible. He probably needs a minute, too. "That excitement was quite unexpected," she says.

His arm tightens, as if he doesn't want the moment to end. "Agree. I'll speak with—"

"No, don't get the nice woman at the front desk in trouble. We probably pushed the wrong button," she says, indulgently leaning her head back against his chest. When was the last time she leaned against anyone? Maybe her dad, when she was in middle school? It feels nice. Too nice. Ever since she woke up in this new world, all she's wanted is for someone to hug her and tell her everything will be okay. He doesn't stop her.

A few moments of comfortable silence pass before a big red digital clock appears in front of them, counting down from four minutes. "I guess we'd better disembark," she says.

He swings down from the saddle before reaching up to help her off. When they are safely back in the staging area, she peeks under the blanket covering the food. "What surprises do you think are in here?"

"I know what I asked for, but your guess is as good as mine," he says, removing his chaps. He folds them and replaces them in the bin, then turns her toward him and unbuckles her blue pair. The action is so surprising, she lets him do it. But that isn't him being caring, she reminds herself. He's used to having a manupartner. Maybe they can't undress themselves. That's it.

"Haggis sandwiches?" she asks, tossing the safety glasses into a bin labeled Discard Reusable Items Here. Surely the peril is over. "Oh, I know, cow tongue burgers? That matches the theme."

Res6's nose wrinkles. "That sounds incredibly unappealing. If we fish out any theme-related lunch items, we're reporting the woman at the front desk."

"Agreed." She takes the blanket and he follows her, carrying the basket to the center of the room. Once they have it set up, and the thankfully-not-gross veggie burgers plated, she settles onto the blanket, watching as he does the same.

The gold of the field brings out the gold of him: his eyes, the shiny blond of his hair, his warm skin, the stubble on his sharp jaw. He's truly, unfairly beautiful.

He ruins it by opening his mouth. "What?"

"Nothing. I was just wondering what you hoped to accomplish with this excursion. Is fake horseback riding a thing in the future? Or are we going to get chased by gun-toting bandits often?"

He takes a long breath and releases it dramatically. "Is it a cop-out if I repeat that your guess is as good as mine?"

"Yes," she says, taking a bite. "This is good, by the way. I'm ready for a real answer."

He frowns. "How about I read somewhere that horseback riding was de-stressing?"

"You mean distressing?"

"No, Electra." He waves a hand through the air as if he can bat away her comment. "Relaxing, or, I don't know . . ."

"Have you ever relaxed before? I hate to inform you, that's not what it feels like."

"Perhaps the narrative I read was referring to the calm state after an adrenaline spike—" His eyes go wide as a berry smacks his face.

"God, Res6. Do you always have to be so serious? I was teasing you."

He stares down at the uneaten part of his sandwich like it might contain answers. "You were teasing me."

She watches him for a minute. Has his skin become a shade paler? "Are you okay?"

"It's been a long time since someone did that."

"Oh." The safest thing she can think to ask is, "Who?"

Res6 nods to himself like he's come to some sort of conclusion. "Hopefully, you'll get to meet him soon. I think you'll like him."

She shakes her head. Maybe her hearing *is* a problem. "Res6, you didn't say who."

He glances off into the distance, and his voice is wistful when he says, "My brother."

9 – Accidental Dates

Res6

October 20, 2390.

Of all their daily outings over the past ten days, the boat ride was the most productive. After a little research, Res6 discovered that in the center of MSP, there's a large indoor holo-lake in a building that used to be a sports stadium. Citizens could go there and rent all sorts of equipment, from small roller-boats to artificial sunbathing rafts shaped like lily pads.

Future people, as she calls them, fascinate Electra, and there were tons of them for her to observe from her bench across from him in the roller-boat. So, they spent one afternoon with her "future people watching" and excitedly detailing her observations to him.

"Look at that man over there," she'd said. He followed her gaze. "Does that man have two manupartners?" The man in question did in fact have two CheapDate off-brand manupartners, if his guess was correct. "Look! Those people appear to be building some sort of shrine."

He looked as instructed to see MSP's famous feline cult assembling a five-foot-tall scratching post. "I believe they're trying to show the"—he cleared his throat—"cats they worship that the world is a safe and hospitable place for them to return to."

Her dark eyes went wide and full of wonder as she observed them. Fortunate, since his eyes remained glued to her. "Really?" she asked, and he nodded. "That is so messed up."

He actually agreed with her, though she seemed more intrigued than horrified. "Especially considering the atmosphere isn't remotely hospitable."

She nodded. "That's what I was thinking."

She was so elated from their experience, she didn't retreat to her—technically his—room until after dinner.

That bolstered his mood so much that instead of reviewing the sales report in his inbox the next morning, he planned their next excursion—the private food-building workshop. That didn't go quite as well, but she seemed amused.

What he really needs to do is figure out her thoughts about his efforts without her knowing.

He rolls over, trying to get comfortable. The new bed he ordered for his spare room isn't as inviting as the one in his room. When he finishes the Jerme project, he'll relocate her to this room and she and Jerme can share it. Or maybe he'll exchange it for a different bed and let them keep his bedroom. He doesn't entirely feel comfortable sleeping in his bed since her scent probably permeates his mattress the way it does his nostrils every time they're near.

Like during the horseback riding, how she leaned back into him. The smell that tantalized his olfactory receptors was torture—some sort of amber rose. Vanilla musk. He isn't a perfumer, and he didn't ask the shopgirl to add it to her items. Nor did he ask her to add the pink Electra had taken to wearing on her cheeks or that glossy stuff on her lips, either.

Honestly, who goes above and beyond in this day and age?

He flips over, burying his face in the pillow. This is precisely why he needs Jerme as a buffer. The ridiculous, teasing woman. Obviously, she wouldn't know the teasing reminds him of his brother, which gives him a warm feeling that he's problematically beginning to associate with her.

Jerme could make light of moments like their birth mother dropping them off for the year at Best Young Citizens School for the Especially Gifted and not returning for two years. Well, Jerme had handled it with levity at first, joking, *Mummy's gone mad!* But then she only stayed for a week before leaving again for another two years, and the reality of their situation set in.

If he recalls correctly, which due to him being ten at the time he may not, the note she sent said, *Raising two troublesome boys makes Mummy so sad, so Mummy needs a break.*

By the time her last note came, Res6 was in an advanced internship under MSP's leading bioengineer and supporting both himself and Jerme, who had followed him to the municipality. His brother had been between jobs at the time. He remembers getting home to their modest unit, finding Jerme passed out on the couch. Beside him was the tablet containing the note, still unlocked.

I hear my good boy Res6 is doing big things! So proud of you for taking care of your little brother and making it so Mummy can share her big news!

The next line said, *Be happy, Mummy is moving back to the isle of France!*

Res6 quit reading after that. He'd seen the medication bottles in the cabinet when they visited, though he was never really sure if they had been the cause of her instability or what kept her from toppling over the edge. Either way, he never really thought much about her after that.

Jerme, on the other hand, seemed to always be trying to fill his Mummy-shaped hole. Again, which is why delicious-smelling Electra will be the perfect companion for him. Once he connects them, he'll have two problems solved: Jerme's happiness and the Electra temptation. Then he'll get himself a manupartner and get on with being CHOICElover's owner and public representative. He flops to his opposite side.

"Is everything okay?" In the pitch dark of the spare room, he can't make out the manupartner in the chair in the corner.

"Shhh, go back to sleep." He turns back over to face the wall. Why can he still smell her? It's like an echo of her presence that his nose can't seem to let go of. Zorg, he needs to fumigate his unit and come up with a long-term solution. He can hardly spend the rest of his days with her prancing around his unit in too-big, shoulder-exposing sweaters smelling like that.

It could be worse. He could be fantasizing about how supple her hips felt in his hands.

He bolts upright. She's corrupting his mind.

The manupartner takes a sharp inhale. "What is it?" it whispers.

His device says it's 03:09. Surely there's something productive he can do if he can't sleep. Something to solve his Electra problem. He activates his device with a thought, trailing over the apps. DumBot—no. NewNews—no. DailyDataDump—no. Scrawl—

Scrawl? His finger hovers over the app. In the tablet's glow, he can see his manupartner body double staring at him.

Its eyes widen. "What happened? Did another one of your experiments fail?"

He winces. There was no way to run the activation in his unit while also keeping it secret from both his body double and Electra. He chose the simpler variable he could control. Plus Electra would judge him, which would ruin all their progress. It didn't matter what the overly moral manupartner thought.

"Not that. It's nothing." His response earns a frown, which is his fault for selecting intuitive. While he is on this third Jerme trial using the synthetic DNA, his failures aren't what's bothering him.

"Would scanning the unit in the closet help you sleep?" it asks, clearly not believing him.

The current Jerme trial is 62 percent through activation, with good markers according to his pre-bed scan. Sure, in ten days, he's already had two trials show early signs of DNA corruption. He expected as much, so he didn't allow himself to get overly upset. Science was a process. He'll succeed eventually.

"It's the woman again," he says, regretting ever having brought it up. "I've been taking her on outings to help her acclimate, and I think it's helping, but I want to know for sure."

"You could ask her," it suggests.

He shakes his head. "No. She can't know that I want to know."

"Why not?"

"It's complicated." Res6 groans at the manupartner's raised brow. "My brother will be here soon, and I'm going to set them up. I don't want her to get the wrong idea and think my interest is romantic."

"And you don't have romantic feelings toward her?" it prods.

"Absolutely not." His device goes to sleep, plunging the room into darkness.

"As your manupartner, it may not be my place, but I believe you're not evaluating yourself accurately."

"I'm perfectly clear about my feelings. The woman is completely off-limits to me." He taps the screen back on.

The manupartner blinks twice, and for a moment, he thinks it might be glitching. Finally, it says, "Why?"

He huffs out a breath. When two of the most important people in your life don't value you enough to stick around, it sends a message. You're not worth sticking around for. So they leave, and you have to pick up the pieces. Same thing happened to Jerme, which made one thing very clear: relationships aren't worth the risk. Hence manupartners. "We've been over this. I own CHOICElover. I can't be seen in public with a real human woman."

The unit sighs, and it's clear it doesn't fully buy his reasoning. "So how are you going to find out what she thinks of your outings, then?"

He pinches the bridge of his nose, debating. "She's been making entries in the Scrawl app daily. Maybe she wrote about it in one of them?"

It frowns accusingly. "I'm not sure reading them is a good idea."

"They aren't labeled Private or Journal Entry," he argues.

"How are they labeled?"

"Only the date and Dear Reader." He hovers his finger over the most recent entry and waits for . . . what, permission?

The manupartner grins. "Oh! Then that means she wants people to read it. You're in the clear."

Relieved, Res6 sits back against the pillows, taps the file, and starts reading.

"What seems to be the problem now, sir?" Tommy asks, glancing up from his workstation to address Res6 over his screen later that morning.

"I think I've been taking her on dates, not outings," he whispers, glancing around at the technicians going about their work in other parts of the lab.

He nods to his office, and Tommy follows. Lextr pokes his head out from around the corner, joining their march. "How do you know?" Lextr adds, also whispering.

When they're safely behind the closed door of his office, Res6 says, "She makes Brain Dumps in the Scrawl app to that effect. When I first saw them, I was curious, but I decided it was best to ignore them to keep a much-needed boundary between us. I'm not trying to get to know her."

Lextr snorts. "That's wise. You're just managing her livelihood until she can be re-homed."

"She's not a pet otter," Tommy interjects, shaking his head.

"Or a houseplant," he adds, repeating her chastising words. "I realize that. It occurred to me that the Brain Dumps might be useful in determining how effective my outing strategy was, but the entries are not flattering."

"Let us see," Tommy prompts.

When Res6 has the app pulled up on his large screen, he opens her most recent entry. Lextr and Tommy lean over his shoulder.

Dear Reader,

Help! SOS! Call in the troops.

Remember how I referred to Res6 as an inept pervert? I realize now that might have been a little harsh (though he might have a Red Room of Sex, *or Death*—that's a whole other story). The thing is, I don't know what I did to deserve this. Deserve what, you ask?

Dates! As in, I think I'm accidentally dating a future man.

He keeps taking me on these classically romantic excursions and calling them *outings*. I've read enough from this time to understand dates are still something people do, so he can't be confused. Well, not people/people dates, but ones with people/manupartner couples. Not that I would mind dates, under normal circumstances, and admittedly, they are doing a good job of cheering me up. Plus, I'm actively learning about future people. But this is the inventor of sex clones we're talking about! It makes no sense why he would try to date me. He doesn't like me, or real human women for that matter, and we're obviously not compatible.

Do you want to know what's worse? I think he watched a bunch of romcoms from my time and is trying to replicate the activities from them.

"DumBot?" Tommy asks.

"DumBot," Res6 confirms.

"Red Room of Sex?" Lextr asks.

"I believe she's referring to the spare room I'm using to conduct the Jerme trials in. I forbade her from entering."

"You should try locking it," Tommy suggests.

"Obviously. The problem is she's curious, so I explicitly stated the rule, which seems to have backfired because now she's more curious." He clears his throat. "Keep reading."

Thank heavens he's never read my books. Who knows what types of ideas that would fill his mind with? He's already taken me on a rowboat, which I'm pretty sure he got from *The Little Mermaid*, horseback riding, which I can't place in a specific romcom, and to a class where we learned to build structures with food. Again, I have no idea about that one, and I'm pretty sure the instructors were paid actors. I guess bonus points for creativity. You should have seen him when his tower of crispy potatoes toppled into the ketchup river, splashing a big red blob onto his pristine tan jumpsuit. Talk about controlled frustration. The poor man is clearly repressing some serious emotion—

Res6 closes the window. "Well, that's enough for you to get the point."

"Oh, I have an idea!" Tommy offers, perking up. "You told me she was a fiction author in her past life. Read her books. Surely that will give you insight into how to deal with her."

"They're alien romances," Res6 grumbles. Granted, it's not like he hasn't opened the audio files, hovering his thumb over the play button in a moment of insistent curiosity. "I think that will only reinforce her idea that I'm unsuccessfully trying to date her."

Lextr crosses his arms resolutely. "If you will recall, I recommended decommissioning her."

Tommy huffs, shaking his head disapprovingly. "But you agreed to keep her for the scans."

"Which have not happened yet," Lextr reminds him.

"They will, and she will be useful when we successfully activate Jerme." They both raise their brows. "She's a perfect companion for him. The exact thing he needs to . . ." Well, this he didn't plan on sharing. ". . . keep himself busy."

Lextr clears his throat. "I've reviewed the data from this morning's scan. It doesn't look promising. We should consider moving forward with an organic sample."

Res6's stomach sinks. "If we burn through the organic samples now, we eliminate the only guaranteed anchors to original NAM fidelity. We just need to optimize the sequencing pattern."

Lextr frowns, breezing past his weak argument. "Pull up the scan and I'll show you."

He thought the scan looked fine, so he opens it as requested. Lextr taps the particle pane. "See this overreplication signature?"

He squints, studying the nucleotide sequence. "I see what you're saying, but I'm not sure it's significant. Perhaps we should continue the activation just in case."

Lextr sighs, as if he's overcome with pity or exasperation. "If you insist."

Res6 shuts his eyes, inhaling. When he opens them, he rescans the replicated codon section, noting several loops. Lextr's right—it's enough of a mutation tied to cortical patterning and NAM retention that the unit might not even wake up. His hopefulness caused him to overlook it. "You're right. It's disappointing, but expected." *Stay positive, Res6. There's already a fourth trial ready to go.* No reason to tap into the organic stores yet. He plasters on a fake smile. "I'll consider what conditions need to be exhausted prior to moving to the organic samples."

He'll need to come up with some valid conditions or Lextr will think he's being emotional, which of course he is. He has a small, finite number of chances to get his brother back. They could burn through them in a matter of weeks, then he'll be back where he started, alone. Well, there's Lextr and Tommy, if they even count, and now Electra, who thinks he's an inept pervert. His stomach swirls, though he's not sure if it's fear or anticipation at the thought of seeing her in a few short hours.

"So, you're not going to attempt to activate the failed unit?" Lextr prods.

He clears his throat. "No, I'm not. I'm set to take Electra to the theater tonight. After that, we have a holographic tour of the Empire State Building, so my unit will be vacant for several hours."

Understanding, Tommy says, "I'll arrange for the specimen to be collected and decommissioned."

"Excellent," he says. "I'll take a new activation pad and start the fourth trial when I get back to my unit. Unfortunately, that extends my Electra problem another week." He gestures to the screen and her damning words. "Any suggestions?"

"I'm truly flabbergasted." Tommy tugs at the tips of his spiked hair. "You've never had an issue charming the manupartners or the public. What's different with her?

He's right. Part of the reason CHOICElover became as successful as it did stems from the ease with which he partook in social activities with a manupartner on his arm. It was excellent advertising. "I don't know."

"It's because she's from the past and not supposed to be here," Lextr says, crossing his arms.

Ignoring Lextr, Tommy grins encouragingly. "What techniques do you use when you do publicity, sir?"

Res6 presses his lips together in a tight frown as they await his answer. Finally, he offers, "I pretend whoever I'm talking to is a manupartner."

Tommy jumps, clapping his hands together. "There's your solution. Just pretend she isn't real. As far as you're concerned, she's a manupartner. And when you guys bring Jerme back—*don't take this as my approval*—you can pass your responsibility off to him! Then we can stop having these little Electra problem-solving sessions."

Res6 stares dazed at his screen. "Pretend like she's a manupartner. Easy enough." That, however, doesn't explain the sudden lump in his throat.

10 – Play Time

Electra

The lip gloss, the final touch to her look, smells like lavender and tastes like purple—a flavor not quite grape and a little blueberry. Res6 comes into the room, taking his position at the foot of the bed, something he's been doing since they started going on these "outings." It's like he's inexplicably drawn into the sphere of her presence, which only reinforces her belief about humanity's need for connection.

Once again, he's watching her through the open bathroom door from his perch on her bed as she finishes getting ready. Is this what it would be like to have a boyfriend? Especially since this seems to be the time little conversations blossom.

She glances over her shoulder. Her motion catches his eye, and he lifts his attention. Was he just staring at her ass? Considering his many awkward comments, he finds her attractive. Plus, it's possible he's trying to date her, which isn't horrible.

The corners of his eyes crease. His grin makes the butterflies in her stomach flutter wildly. She really should have dated more in the past. Her inexperience is clearly the reason for whatever is going on with her and her hormones.

"I was thinking of starting a blog." His grin dissolves. Still, she presses forward. "I can't not write. I need to put my words out there, and I thought that might be a way for me to contribute to"—she has to stop herself from waving a hand in his direction—"society."

"I'm not sure if people would be receptive. I'd hate for you to be disappointed on top of everything else you're dealing with." He's referring to her acclimation, as he calls it. "Don't misunderstand me. I think your writing is . . . *amusing*."

"You're reading my books?" Has he got to the sex scenes yet? Her work is definitely not slow burn. So, yes, he probably has. She groans. How embarrassing. Well, it could be worse. It's not like he's read her journal. Wait, has he? The entries appear to be in a file system they both have access to, as demonstrated by the several Brain Dumps that don't belong to her. Notably one labeled "Res6's Top Secret Task List." As if she would snoop. At least he seems to understand Brain Dumps are private.

"I, uh . . ." His eyes widen. She can almost see the calculations happening behind them. He nods once, almost to himself, and his demeanor changes. It's subtle, but she's been around him enough to notice the slightly straighter posture, the upturn to one corner of his mouth, even the way his eyes sparkle a little more than they did half a second earlier. The change feels similar to his shift while interacting with the woman at the simulation chamber asking him questions for her blog.

"I confess. I couldn't resist listening to your books. I was having trouble sleeping." He points to the couch, which he is no longer using; he's been sleeping in the forbidden room for days.

"But I told you, having people I know read my books weirds me out." She eyes him, planting her hands on her hips for emphasis.

"I already had them downloaded."

She chuffs. Is he really going to argue with her? "You could have found something else to download."

"I already spent the unicoin." He grins as if he's found her weakness.

Damn her for sharing that little tidbit about her childhood. "You're impossible."

He stands and steps toward her. "Electra, darling, they're available for anyone to read."

She isn't sure if it's his out-of-the-blue endearment or his clear disregard for her boundary, but her mouth drops open. "That's it. I'm starting an advice column. You people need serious help."

"A column is too risky," he grumbles, slipping back into his usual persona. "How can I protect you if you become well known? You can't tell people you're from the past. You don't have an identity."

"So you get to have your Room of Doom and Secrets, but I can't have my column? That's hardly fair. I can use a pen name," she offers brightly. "How does Dear Electra sound?" It actually has a good ring to it. Much better than Ask Doctor Janet.

"But that's your real name."

"No one knows that," she says, rolling her eyes.

After a minute, he adds, "It's not a good idea," which she pointedly ignores.

Clearly, he's only interested in protecting his company. Who cares that she needs an outlet, some way to cling to the identity she lost? Or that future people are hopeless and someone needs to show them that love isn't a scarce resource? The column will prove that she's still relevant, still capable, and has a place in this whacko future she's been thrust into. Plus, she wants to make Janet proud, or something like that. It definitely has nothing to do with figuring out what's wrong with the male model/duplicitous fiend she's roommates with and possibly dating. She can almost hear Janet say, *Don't drag me into your delusions, dear.*

Res6 lets her finish getting ready, quietly observing her as she slips on a delicate pair of gold heeled sandals. She gives herself a quick glance in the full-length mirror. Wow, these make her legs look killer. She rarely gets to dress up, given that her work as a bartender required a uniform. Then while she writes, she wears worn T-shirts and sweats, and weaves her hair into a messy braid. Definitely no makeup. There was a moment during their argument when she considered canceling, but decided it would be a shame to waste this dress. The way the fabric shimmers when she moves makes her feel like a Christmas ornament.

It obviously has nothing to do with the fact that she's enjoying their outings and how the amount of time he must have spent researching and planning makes her feel. She's never had anyone do that for her before. Granted, he's still claiming it's for her acclimation. She isn't sure that's the case though, mostly because of the lingering looks. It is almost like, if you could ignore the problematic stuff like his cluelessness or the manupartner thing, Res6 would be grade A book boyfriend material.

He's rich, successful, popular, and gorgeous, which of course aren't the most important qualities. He's protective, and he can be surprisingly thoughtful. But he's hiding things, which really should be a big enough red flag to arrest her wandering thoughts.

She takes a step and stumbles, not used to the shoes. He darts forward, grabbing her waist to steady her.

"Thanks," she says, hating how pleasant his hands feel after weeks of no hugs or barely anything resembling human contact. Why can't her life be simple?

"Are you still angry that I'm reading your books?" he asks.

"Kind of." Oh God. The implications! Considering he's read her kinky sex scenes, it's no wonder he doesn't know how to act around her.

He's still clinging to her waist as if he's unable to let go. "Electra, you look—"

The words seem to lodge in his throat. She eyes the door. "I'm ready. Let's go."

He sighs, defeated. "I didn't mean to upset you."

"Its fine. Amazingly, I believe that you genuinely don't have a clue, so I forgive you." They're just books, and since she put them out for public consumption, she can't really police who reads them. Her journal, however—she should probably mention that per the aforementioned cluelessness. "For future reference, you're not allowed to read my Brain Dumps. Understand?"

"Understood," he says, nodding earnestly.

What else does she need to explain to him? He seems to understand physical privacy besides the knocking thing, which she's corrected. There's probably something else, but she'll have to figure it out later. At least something good came of their conversation: he didn't push his opposition to her column. She just needs to give him time to come around to the idea—so he'll *give her some freedoms,* as Tommy insultingly put it. Res6 doesn't seem to see it that way; rather, he wants to keep her, and his company, from harm. That's why she needs to show him how well she's navigating the future.

They step out of the elevator and into a large glass box. A stunning blonde woman hops up from behind a desk. "I have your SAT ready, sir," she says, moving to a keypad on the wall. When her hand presses into it, it beeps, recognizing her, and she punches in a command.

Past the glass enclosure, centrally located within a much larger cement room, is a platform that does a one-eighty. His private SAT appears, its door sliding open. The vehicle is much nicer than the ones most MSP citizens use interchangeably. It keeps reminding her of a car from a movie she saw, but—"It's like Bladerunner!" she remembers.

The woman has stepped up to her and is inspecting her like a zoo animal. "What's a blade-runner?"

Res6 shrugs.

She raises her finger to Electra's face. "May I?" She directs her question to Res6.

The obvious answer is no, but he says, "Sure." Before Electra can smack the woman's hand away, she's running smooth fingertips over her cheeks. Oh God, hopefully this isn't another advertising opportunity. Of everything that's happened during the outings, future people's inspection of her freckles is the worst part.

"They're part of her skin?" she asks.

"Yes," he supplies.

The woman huffs, like she's confused.

Electra can only stand there dumbfounded. Why are people so fascinated with them? Though, come to think of it, has she seen a future person with her characteristic dusting of freckles?

"Why didn't you replace her? You own the company." As the woman says this, she runs a polished fingertip down Res6's lapel.

Before Electra can think better of it, she blurts, "Oh my God, are you flirting with him? In front of me, his manufactured lover, no less." She grabs his hand, lacing her fingers with his, and holds it up to the woman. "See."

The woman frowns, which is satisfying. Serves her right for insulting Electra's lovely freckles. It's not like she would lash out for any other reason.

"Are you sure she isn't malfunctioning? That happened with one of mine," the woman says.

Res6 chuckles, squeezing Electra's hand. "It wasn't a CHOICElover was it? Such terrible news would surely ruin my night."

There is hissing outside in the garage, and Electra gathers they're waiting on some process to finish, but she's laser focused on the woman. Blonde strands of hair fall into her face in an annoyingly sexy manner as she leans in, whispering, "If you want to recycle this one, I'd be happy to assist while you're activating your next unit."

She winks, and Electra is certain the future is melting her brain or she's come down with some sort of syndrome, because a flame of what feels dangerously close to jealousy flares like a blowtorch. More like one of those little crème brûlée torches, but still.

Before she can consider her actions, she reaches out, tearing the woman's hand away from Res6's chest. His eyes widen in response, but Electra ignores him, turning to the woman. "Res6 asked me to keep random women from pawing at him. He's very successful, so it happens a lot. Please behave."

He has no idea how extensively she's researched the strange phenomenon of the modern-day manupartner. She turns to him, saying, "You wanted me to do it just like that, right?" Then she beams at him. Why waste such a glorious moment to revel? That's what he gets for using her for advertising.

The woman gapes, so astonished that Electra doesn't need to fake her glee. She's really only doing herself a favor. The last thing she needs is for Res6 to screw this woman in their unit—well, *his unit*—while she sits there on the couch watching mind-numbing videos explaining late modern era government systems. Not that she would mind otherwise. The jealousy thing is irrational. She's misinterpreting her feelings since she's been having so many lately. The "outings" that are actually dates can't be helping.

Res6's brows pinch, and he's quiet for a beat too long. He seems to have an internal war with himself before finally coming to some determination, which makes her nervous. He nods to himself before reaching behind her to grab the end of her sleek ponytail. There's a gentle tug as he repositions her so she's staring up at him. Then he steps into her space. It feels like a challenge, which makes her pulse race like it does every time he is this near. It's startling but also—umm. Other things not worth mentioning. Who is this man?

"Just like that," he says, voice dropping an octave. *Oh God.* He leans down, and she has to swallow as his heat surrounds her. His nose brushes against hers and lingers there. "I adore her freckles. Otherwise, she'd be too polished. Too manufactured. And that would bore me."

He says *manufactured* like a dirty word, and she isn't sure whose benefit it's for since it almost undermines the entire point of his company. Her heart jumps to her throat, and things happen elsewhere in her body. When she swears he's about to kiss her—and she thinks she's either going to slap him or lean into it—he places a peck on her nose. She stands there stunned as he releases her hair. The same arm snakes around her shoulders, and he commands, "Come, darling, or we'll be late."

The woman lets out a swoony sigh as they walk away.

Well, that was something, wasn't it? The spot on her nose that his lips brushed burns, and for some odd reason, she's considering wearing a ponytail more often. How did he do that?

He leads her out of the glass box, tucks her into the humming SAT, and closes the door before going to his side. A minute later, they're in the smog-dense air, zipping between towering gray buildings past bright neon signs, and moving through MagTrack interchanges so fast her head is spinning. The SATs really are wondrous, efficient machines. She always thought they'd be more like hovercars, like in The Fifth Element. It takes a moment for her to catch her bearings. Then she notices Res6 is laughing. Like full belly-clutching, laughing.

"What?" she demands.

"The look on your face was priceless," he says.

She huffs indignantly. "I thought you were going to kiss me."

"I thought you were going to let me." He's still chuckling.

"God, no." She's only half lying. He doesn't need to know that a crazy part of her thought the same thing. Not only because she's pretending-ish to be a manupartner.

It's odd how quickly his awkwardness disappears, replaced by that sudden, panty-melting confidence. Talk about Dr. Jekyll and Mr. Hyde. But which one is the act, and which is the real man?

Refusing to join in his humor, definitely not pouting, she says, "I was trying not to slap you in front of that woman."

His laughing fit recharges. The rich sound is unfairly appealing. If she weren't a stupid romance author, she probably wouldn't even notice. Now she's thinking about how the next book boyfriend she crafts will have his exact laugh.

He wipes his eyes. "I can't remember the last time I found something so humorous. My brother is going to love you." He reaches over and pats her thigh. "Thanks, Electra."

She can only sigh before slumping back in her chair for the rest of the ride.

The play isn't like anything she expected when Res6 explained it would be their evening outing. An attendant welcomes them into a private, slightly cramped viewing box, giving them each a pair of virtual reality glasses. There is a large empty black stage before them, and the theater is so dark she can barely make out the audience. Wait. She leans forward, scanning as her eyes adjust. "Are we the only ones here?"

"Two Spiral Apples," Res6 orders, seeming not to hear her question.

As the server leaves to get their cocktails, she turns the VR headset over in her hands. "I thought you said this was a play, like with a set and actors."

"It's a private production. Just wait."

Great, another weird rich-people thing, like the private flying excursion. The seats suspended from sturdy-looking cables could only swing them in a circle like a children's carnival ride, though the simulation made it seem as if they were flying in a turbojet. Between the sparkling Vine and the turbulence, it was disorienting. Considering the government video claimed the future is more egalitarian, she thought there'd be less of this. Not more.

A moment later, the drinks show up and Res6 takes them, arranging them on little tables attached to their chairs. A chime goes off in the box. "That's the one-minute warning," he says. "You'll see the actors and the virtual set combined through your VR set. Here." He takes the glasses and helps her fit them comfortably. He must push a button because a sound test sequence takes place. "Is this okay?" he asks.

"Yes," she replies, though at this point she's only along for the ride.

"Okay, good. Just sit back and enjoy the show."

Another set of chimes sounds, this time in her headset.

"It's starting," he says.

As she settles back into her seat, an announcer begins to speak, giving the typical opening welcomes. The screen goes dark. Slowly, out of the right corner of her vision, a man emerges from a building like a medieval cottage that comes into view from a mist. He follows a forest trail, and soon she, the viewer, can sense he's following the soft, wordless singing she begins to hear. Stage left opens with a kelp-haired siren diving off a rock into the water.

At first, nothing she's witnessing is extraordinary. It's almost like watching a movie being shot in real life, but with the CGI already imposed onto it. But then it occurs to her that these people don't have a set with streams and cottages or nature scenes. She lowers the VR set to peer at the stage. Res6 was right. On stage, two actors wearing flesh-toned bodysuits navigate various black boxes and platforms. When she replaces the VR set, she sees the same thing, but with a computer-generated setting and costumes superimposed.

The siren swims until she comes to a larger body of water. Behind her, the man, now in a little rowboat, follows her. The clouds overhead turn gray as the siren glances back at her pursuer. Then she dives into the water, disappearing. The sound of the man frantically splashing as he fights the waves to get to her fills the space. The wind picks up, blowing the loose tendrils of her hair—her being Electra, not the siren who's still underwater.

"Not this again," she mutters, as very real water sounds surround her. Their little box quickly fills with water, so she's now sitting in a small tank. Her poor dress. The chair jolts, then falls into a gentle rocking pattern as if it too is in the water. She shakes her head, re-settling into her wet seat.

Finally, the siren pops back up, climbing into the man's boat.

"Don't do it!" Res6 shouts, startling her.

She can't help but laugh. He must be really into this; it's kind of endearing. She lingers on the man's face, trying to determine whether he's afraid yet, as he should be. The VR camera pans in automatically to give her a better view. She glances at the woman to see if the headset will do the same thing or if it was just a coincidence. Sure enough, as she holds steady on the woman, it zooms in so she can see tears streaming down the siren's face . . . or possibly leftover water droplets? She peeks outside her headset to see if the actors are wet too—she gasps, grabbing Res6's forearm. He peels off his headset.

The system says, "Pausing Program." The actors halt their motion.

"What's wrong?" he asks.

"Where's the water?" She gestures to the completely dry box.

He chuckles. "It's the HoloChair's electrotactile array." He puts his VR headset back on, saying, "Let's keep watching," like he's engrossed.

"Okay," she says, putting hers back on too. She reaches out, running her hand through the "water." It feels real. No wonder these future people can't perceive what is fake—nearly everything they experience is some type of imitation of the real thing. Yet, she's stuck in the future now, so she should keep an open mind.

The play ends with the original siren triumphantly climbing back out of the water in the same spot she entered, as if to signify her journey has come full circle. The narrative arc isn't the traditional hero's journey—the siren brutally sucked out the man's soul then threw him overboard, where a horde of hungry piranhas devoured his body, for no other reason than she's a siren and that's what sirens do. It adds another layer to the challenge of storytelling in the future. There's already so much she'll have to learn if she wants to publish again. It's daunting. Perhaps for now her Dear Electra advice column idea is the way to go. Another benefit would be the opportunity for her to get to know today's readers and develop an audience.

Electra is so consumed with her thoughts that she doesn't notice when he leads her into an empty room within the same complex of the theater. She glances around, taking in the 360-degree view of the New York City skyline. An artificial breeze lifts the lock of hair that's fallen across his brow as he steps toward her, holding out a blanket.

"Here, let me," he says, wrapping it around her shoulders.

She blinks, instantly recalling the scene from *Sleepless in Seattle*. This confirms it. He thinks they're dating. Still, for confirmation, she asks, "Is this the Empire State Building?"

11 – A Minor Disaster

Res6

"The observatory of the Empire State Building, in fact. How'd you guess?" he asks.

Her eyes sparkle as she scans her surroundings, and the grin on her face is so wide it seems permanent. "I saw this in a movie once."

There's something strangely heady about being the one to give her pleasure. He does his best to appear neutral. But this has to be the best outing—*not date*—he's planned thus far. That morning, he rewatched the clip from DumBot titled *Asleep in Seattle* and confirmed the visit to the simulated historical venue wasn't a date. The characters had clearly just met, as they spent a small eternity staring at each other before introducing themselves. There had even been a child in the scene. Therefore, there's no chance of her misinterpreting anything.

She shrugs, pulling the blanket tighter around herself, shielding him from the thin fabric of her dress—Zephyr, that dress. The slinky gold material has been calling to him all night. The blanket is a true blessing from the non-deities. Yet, if she's still cold, he could ask the system to raise the temperature, or if she were a manupartner, he might draw her into his chest and . . . He's reaching for her before he can think better of it. *She is not for you.* His fingers stop inches from her shoulder. He lets his hand fall away. Although his strategy involves imagining she's a manupartner, she is not. Embracing her for warmth or otherwise would be counterproductive.

There's a fine line between acting like she's a manupartner, who he'd normally have a certain physical proximity with, and the reality that she's a real woman. Perhaps Tommy's idea isn't so sound.

Thankfully, she's too consumed with staring out at the skyline to notice. "I always heard New York City was magical. I never got to go."

"My brother would have liked this too." He isn't sure why he says it. Only, being around her makes him think of Jerme more than he has in recent memory.

She turns, raising a brow. "Would have?"

His jaw tenses. If he keeps getting caught up in the moment, he's going to slip up, and she'll find out about his experiment. She already hates the idea of manupartners, so it stands to reason she won't understand about bringing Jerme back. Then she'll really think he's a monster. Not that he cares what she thinks. "Well, New York City isn't really accessible anymore."

"Right." She nods, offering him an easy smile.

"You remind me of Jerme," he says. "That's his name."

"I'm looking forward to meeting him. Does he live here in MSP?"

"He hasn't for a while," he answers, intentionally ambiguous. She'll eventually learn the truth, but it will be easier to explain with Jerme here to help smooth things over.

"Oh. I guess that means you don't get to see him often. That's too bad. I always wanted a sibling." She stares wistfully at the skyline.

He pauses, waiting for a painful wave of nostalgia to wash over him, but it never comes. "I think he'll like you."

She turns her smile on him. "You said that before. What will he like about me?"

He steps closer. "You're very beautiful, for one."

Her freckled cheeks tinge pink. "He's your brother. That doesn't count."

"Well, let's see." He reaches up, brushing his fingertips over her cheek. "I think he would like these."

She chuckles. "I gather that freckles have been selected out of the gene pool."

"They have, but they set you apart," he says. "Jerme liked unique things."

"Maybe I'll be the one to bring them back."

He lets his hand fall away. "If anyone could do it, it would be you."

"Well, I plan to shake things up."

He huffs, pointedly ignoring their earlier conversation about her starting a column. Now isn't the time to discuss it, and he doesn't want to ruin the moment. "You'll definitely do that."

She steps closer, and he can't bring himself to push her away. His nerves are firing with fear or anticipation. Maybe both? *Just pretend she's a manupartner and it will be fine.*

"What else do you think he'd like about me?" There's mischief in her dark stare as it meets his.

"You're quick-witted and playful. He was like that. Irritatingly stubborn, too."

Her brows knit so quickly, he wonders if he imagined it. "Too bad you don't appreciate my stubbornness. Your loss," she teases.

She moves to turn away, but he grasps her arm to keep her facing him. "Don't say that." *Bad idea, Res6. Let her go.* His hand doesn't budge.

"So you like me, then?" Her easygoing grin is enough to draw him a step closer.

I like everything about you. Oh Zorg. That's true, isn't it? He likes her. Fuck. This is bad. "Could be worse. You could have invented manupartners," he deflects, hoping his self-deprecation will . . . what? Make her think he's less of a monster so she'll like him back?

Right as she releases a tinkling laugh, fireworks burst overhead. She jumps, which puts them standing mere inches apart. They glance skyward in unison. Blue, white, green, and pink explosions fill the simulated sky. There's a red flash, and a crackling heart appears, eclipsing the other sprays of color.

Electra gasps, whipping her face back toward him. The reflection of the fireworks illuminates her skin, and she's glowing. Her hand presses against his chest, fisting in his shirt. He's helpless at the tiny point of contact. It's burning through his shirt, heating his skin, and melting his normally rational mind.

"Res6, are you trying to date me—"

Because he can't let her finish the question, he leans down, brushing his lips against hers. Her breath catches, and his skin prickles at the contact—at her reaction. At the way her lips tremble ever so slightly, as if she's as nervous as he is. Despite his normally logical mind, it feels like fate has genetically engineered this moment to lead to this kiss. The touch of his lips against hers is soft. Tentative. He savors the momentary contact, his heart thundering. When she doesn't respond, panic floods through him. Did he misjudge? This is exactly why he avoids—her lips move. Slowly at first, but then with more urgency. She's kissing him back.

Yes. Yes. Yes!

He cups her jaw, and her mouth parts. The relief that hits him is so sharp it weakens his knees. Maybe that's his desire, but fuck, it's so good. Moving closer, he explores, tasting the purple of her lip gloss and the mint from her cocktail. She's so unbelievably delicious, like he knew she would be the moment she first woke and her lips moved.

He slides his free hand around her waist and draws her against him. His cock takes notice, swelling. He definitely wants to fuck her—it's been years, but— *She's not for you. What are you thinking?* He doesn't care. He needs to be closer, yet he's terrified to do more. What if she comes to her senses and rejects him? This kiss is dangerous enough, though he can't seem to let her go.

The light from the fireworks display fades in the background, and she pulls away, leaving him dazed. Her lips are swollen from the kiss, and she grips the blanket protectively. His desire urges him to drag her back into his embrace, but she steps out of arm's reach. She touches her lips like she's . . . shocked.

Oh Zephyr, what have I done? His world—briefly lighter—falls out from beneath him. How can he tell Jerme he kissed the woman he wants to—fuck—hold—*possess. Get it together, Res6.* The woman he thought would be perfect for Jerme? This is bad. More so because she knows him and still kissed him back. *And she's already retreating.* Would she still be open to Jerme after this? Has he ruined everything? Yes, obviously.

"Res6, are you okay?" she asks.

"I . . . I can't believe I kissed you."

She gives him a shaky laugh. "Me either. But you did. And I'm not even a manupartner," she teases.

Getting involved with her is against his better judgment on too many levels. Does how much he liked the way her lips felt under his make him a hypocrite? Or that he planned to set her up with his brother for all of their sakes? Or that she's human? "If people knew I was doing this with a human woman, my reputation would be ruined." He runs his hands through his hair, resisting the urge to pace. Since he's already crossed the line, what's the harm in kissing her again? If he's honest, he desperately wants to. If his plan to connect her with Jerme is already ruined . . .

She looks as dazed as he is. "Excuse me?" A pretty shade of pink warms her cheeks as she stares at him.

Maybe he'll reconsider his stance on the inviting berry-flavored gloss on her lips and make sure she has a never-ending supply. He chuckles, stepping near and lifting her chin to kiss her again. "We're definitely going to check your hearing."

His lips brush hers. "Electra," he murmurs. Her name is so right on his tongue. Maybe the lip gloss isn't the only thing he'll need to reconsider his stance on—

"I can hear perfectly fine," she barks, pulling away. "What did you mean by that?" His mouth drops open, and she adds, "Not about my hearing. About your stupid reputation."

What did he say? His reputation. Right. A sinking feeling settles in his gut. He steps back. "I didn't mean anything by it." Her glare suggests she doesn't believe him. "I invented manupartners. Imagine what's at stake for me. How do you think people's perception of my company will shift if they knew I was kissing a real woman?"

She takes a few steps back. "Oh my God, I should have known you would do this. I am so stupid."

He reaches for her, but she jerks away. "Electra, please."

She lets out a comically exaggerated groan. "*You* kissed *me*. Did you forget that I'm a real woman? That you're you and I'm me?" She draws the blanket up to cover her eyes. "I would never even date you in real life. In fact, we aren't dating."

What does she mean by *real life*? This feels pretty real to him. "Look, I didn't mean it that way." She lowers the blanket, scowling. There has to be a plausible excuse. Something that doesn't get him into even more trouble. "I got lost in the moment pretending you were a manupartner." Shit. Why did he say that? That was before they stepped onto the observation deck. She'll definitely misconstrue—

"You were pretending I was a manupartner?!" she explodes, marching toward the doorway.

Why does he always say the wrong thing when it comes to her? Because she's a human woman. She's dangerous, and his self-preservation instincts are nonexistent. He replays their conversation in his mind. There has to be a way to backtrack. *Hold on.* "Not that I'm trying to date you, but why wouldn't you date me? What is wrong with me?"

She whirls, marching back toward him to jab her finger into his chest. "You think manupartners can provide human companionship, and I think that's whacko. This society has a serious superficiality problem. Like rotten candy."

"Rotten candy?"

"Yeah, everyone looks pretty—like perfectly manicured lawns, but people. You have access to all of this entertainment. Choices to suit every whim, but it's all a veneer. The entire experience is empty. Like rotten candy—it looks like it might taste good, so you have a lick, only for a foul taste to fill your mouth, but you're supposed to smile and act like you like it." She flings a hand in his direction. "Then you get cavities!"

"Cavities?" he asks. She definitely needs a scan. He has no idea what she's talking about. What are cavities? It's clear that his lust was misplaced.

She must sense he doesn't understand because she says, "Cavities are rotten teeth."

"But how would society rot your teeth?"

She throws her hands in the air, letting the blanket fall to the ground. "I meant it metaphorically!"

He gestures back at her emphatically. "You are precisely why I created manupartners. Real people are a colossal hassle!" Mentally, he shifts kissing Electra Lynch into the mistakes column. He also mentally decrees, *No more advice from Tommy*.

Res6 takes her hand and drags her out of the simulation chamber. She's welcome to spend the rest of her life in his Zorgdamn room for all he cares. Thankfully, for the first time since he's known her, she doesn't resist.

12 – Chryl

Res6

631,452—that's the number of steps Res6's m-volt has registered since Electra came into his life twenty-one days ago. That is over thirty thousand steps per day and 33.3 percent higher than his normal daily average. Electra Lynch is to blame. His pacing, mainly outside her door, can account for most of it. The rest are from the walking desk in his office, where he is now, still thinking about her. That maddening, tempting, irritating, beautiful woman.

Fuck. He runs his hand down his face, massaging his eyes as he does. The problem is getting worse.

Why did he have to kiss her?

He blurted out some poor excuse about getting caught up pretending she's a manupartner. The unfortunate truth is, no one's ever looked at him the way she does. Tease him like that. Her very presence seems to hold back the inevitable wave of grief that always comes when he thinks about Jerme. She was about to accuse him of trying to date her. So, in a move he's still trying to reconcile, he kissed her. And for Zorg's sake, she kissed him back.

Is a real woman what he's been missing this entire time? It goes against everything he stands for. Not to mention his plan with his brother, or that his customer base will think he's a hypocrite if they find out what she is, which would be terrible for his company. Considering she equated him and his world to rotten candy, plus said they would never date, it isn't worth it. She isn't worth it. How foolish of him to let his guard down, even for a moment.

He needs a manupartner to help him with these urges that are getting more insistent by the day. *Another great idea.*

He steps off the walking desk in his office and shuts down his system. He could select one and take the time to activate it, but that would extend his Electra problem another week. Unless the current Jerme trial succeeds, which is unlikely given how quickly the first ones failed. There's just no time to grow a manupartner. He's in crisis mode. He flings his office door open and marches through it straight to the bank of elevators that will take him downstairs to the recycle station. A lighted sign flashes above the sleek metal doors: Momentary Service Disruption.

He and Electra got caught up in something neither of them was prepared for. His stomach twists uncomfortably. *Jerme, is this what happened to you?*

He taps his foot, suppressing the urge to shout at something. Why did she have to make him feel so unmoored? He was perfectly fine before she appeared. Now, not only does he have to manage himself, but he also has to wade through the emotions of a real human woman. A nearly impossible task. He's obligated to share his space with her. Inconvenient. Therefore, he must interact with her, which leads to his unfortunate interest in her well-being. Inconvenient isn't the right word for that.

Dangerous.

Right. But he invented a solution to this problem. He's been stupid not to have used it. He rushes to the emergency exit, running down the stairs before he loses his nerve. Staff scatter as he throws open the doors to the M Quadrant recycling station. Some of the staff here have probably never seen him in real life, but they all know who he is. He barks at the first person he sees, "Where are the units waiting to be recycled?"

They jump at his brisk tone, but nod toward a door labeled Holding Rooms: Authorized Personnel Only. He approaches the door's locking panel, doing a quick retina scan. The door opens and he enters a room full of manupartners waiting for decommissioning. He scans the rows, looking for a suitable specimen. When he spots a woman with unblemished pale skin, big blonde hair and even bigger breasts—the exact opposite of Electra—he paces over to her. "What's your name?"

The unit blinks twice, as if coming out of a trance. Then she gives him a feral grin. "Chryl. What's yours, handsome?"

"Res6. I'm your new owner."

Her eyes brighten, and she loops her arm through his. "Looks like it's my lucky day!" she gushes.

As he escorts her into the SAT, he retreads the mental gymnastics it took to convince himself that a new manupartner as a buffer was a great idea. Anything to distract him from the temptation in his unit until his brother is back. But as Chryl rubs a burning hole in his thigh, and it takes everything in him not to rip her hand away, he's having second thoughts.

After a tense fifteen-minute SAT ride, he's ushering Chryl into his unit, having third and fourth thoughts. The third: with Chryl, the body double manupartner, and the actively growing Jerme, the spare room will be uncomfortably cramped. The fourth: the irate woman whose deadly stare might as well be a sparkler beam aimed at him.

"We kissed and had an argument, so you immediately get a manupartner?" Electra shouts as he guides Chryl into his unit. Given the frequency of Electra's shouting, she must get some enjoyment out of it. Perhaps he should hire a private tutor for a Respectful and Considerate Conduct Course.

He sits calmly on the couch, patting the spot next to him. Chryl plops down next to him. "This is Chryl. Chryl, Electra."

"Wow! She's pretty. Is this going to be a three-way thing? How kinky!" Chryl exclaims, patting the spot next to her.

"No, it is absolutely not," Electra snaps, planting her clenched fists on the back of the opposite L of the couch so she's facing them. She turns her laser-sharp gaze to him, hissing, "You. Are. Unbelievable."

"Please sit down so I can explain," he says.

"I'll stand, thanks." She stubbornly crosses her arms.

"Feisty one, isn't she?" Chryl says. "I bet the sex will be explosive!"

Res6 wipes his eyes. He really shouldn't have chosen a manupartner so indiscriminately, because whoever selected Chryl's traits clearly chose vivacious, Sexcitable™, and audacious—all traits he never would have chosen. "Chryl, please go wait in the spare room and remember what we talked about."

"Sure thing, handsome. I may have a little surprise for you when you're ready." Chryl mimes zipping her lips closed before winking and sauntering toward the door.

"The one on the left, and please, no surprises." He slumps back onto the cushions, defeated.

"Whatever you like, handsome," she says, slipping inside.

Electra points an accusatory finger at the door Chryl is safely ensconced behind. "So she's allowed to know what's in your supersecret room, but not me? The actual real person who lives with you, who might feel a little better knowing there isn't a gaggle of re-animated corpses behind that door."

His mouth falls open. The carefully thought-out words he hoped would smooth things over get lodged somewhere between his brain and his throat. *It seems you are throwing me off my carefully curated routine. I thought having a manupartner, which I often do, might help me resist your presence and regain a sense of security and personal space.*

Granted, it's been a few years since he turned his last unit in for recycling. Admitting the level of boredom he's reached in recent years would probably make him a hypocrite. Though it would explain his interest in the next wave of more LifeLike™ advancements. He sighs as a wave of emotional exhaustion rolls through him.

"Hello?" Electra presses. They stare at each other in a stalemate for a long moment. Her lip quivers, and a tear rolls down her cheek—a horrifying sight. "Fine. You don't owe me an explanation, I guess. I just really don't like this." More tears fall.

Though he has a strange urge to go to her, wipe the tears away, and wrap her in his arms, he roots himself to the couch. Getting involved was a mistake, and it will be best for both of them if she figures this out on her own.

Still, it would be considerate to explain his behavior, but now that he's facing her, his planned speech seems insufficient. "I don't mean to make you cry, but Chryl feels necessary."

"You made me believe you might give a shit about me." She looks down her nose at him. "As if you're capable."

"You said there's nothing between us."

"That isn't what I said." She resolutely plants her hands on her hips.

"Then what did you say?"

"It doesn't matter. Come to think of it, you're right. Chryl can be your advertising from now on."

"Electra!" he calls after her as she storms back into the bedroom.

It's obvious Res6 has misevaluated everything to do with Electra from the beginning. For instance, he now realizes how he might have misled her. He needs to convince her that their misunderstanding was purely accidental. Really, how could he develop an affection for a woman who respects his life purpose so little? Who rejected him after what he thought was a groundbreaking kiss. Not that he's developing an affection just because he admitted to himself that he likes her. At least the kiss and their subsequent misunderstanding reminded her that she does not, in fact, like him. So even if he is tempted, there's no concern.

Chryl pops her head out the door, glancing around, presumably for Electra. "Is the coast clear?"

He sighs, nodding.

"Good, because there's a half-formed man quivering in the closet and it's giving me the creeps."

She's referring to the fourth Jerme trial using synthesized DNA. It hasn't failed yet, thankfully, since Res6 is already dealing with so much inner turmoil as it is. He points to the cushion beside him. "You can sit here. I'm going to do some reading, so keep quiet." She perches on the spot, staring at him eagerly. Anticipation is evident in her bright blue eyes.

Since he's had years of practice with countless eager manupartners, ignoring her is easy. He leans back on the couch, determined to let his troublesome thoughts slip away. Now that Electra knows he's reading her books, he doesn't think she'll mind if he continues.

He reaches a chapter where the red-skinned, horned hero has the anti-damsel pinned against a wall in a cave on the outskirts of his kingdom. Vorack is growling something possessive in his native tongue into the heroine's ear, but he has yet to learn that Ella didn't run from him. The enemy clan kidnapped her, and she only just escaped before the tribe forced her into a marriage with their leader. While Res6 is keen to finish the scene, because he is fairly certain what comes next, it might be wise to save it for later. The couple's first encounter, which had only amounted to some heavy foreplay, was quite arousing, after all.

The last thing he needs is for Electra to emerge from the bedroom to find his pants tented with an erection and Chryl salivating over it.

Chryl leans against his shoulder. A wave of revulsion rushes through him, but he tamps it down. "Whatcha doing?"

"Still reading," he grumbles.

She leans over, scanning the text for a moment. "Oh là là. They're about to have sexy time." He jumps as her hand smacks his thigh and squeezes. "Anything I can help with?"

A chime sounds in his unit right as Chryl throws a leg over his waist, straddling him. "My last owner wanted me to call him Daddy. Is that what you want too, Daddy?"

"Please don't." He grasps her hips, about to hoist her bodily off him, when Electra's door opens.

"What was that noise—" she starts, but stops when she sees the precarious position he's landed himself in.

"Finally decided to join the fun, darlin'?" Chryl asks, winking as she gyrates as if she's riding the horse from the simulation chamber.

Though he should be glad that Chryl is serving her intended purpose—insulating him from Electra—he feels sick to his stomach. He never asked for this, so when he abruptly moves Chryl off himself, it is decidedly in frustration. "That's enough, Chryl."

By now, Electra has retreated once again, slamming the door behind her.

He and the manupartner stare at the bedroom door. He'll deal with that later.

"What's up her butt?" Chryl asks.

"Chryl, please go stand in the kitchen." Thankfully, she obeys.

At the front door, a delivery crew has arrived to swap the uncomfortable bed for a better and larger one since it seems he's going to be stuck with it for a while. He directs them to the spare room. Ten minutes later, they have the new bed set up, which is great because Res6 is ready to plant himself face down on the mattress and pretend, if only for a few hours, that this is only a dream.

13 – Idiots

Electra

Dear Reader,

It seems every time we talk, I've got another whammy to hit you with, and today is no different. Are you ready?!

Good. Because that idiot KISSED ME.

And this idiot (me) let him!

We're disregarding the fact that it may have been the single greatest kiss in the history of kisses, which, shudder to think, is likely a direct result of his hundred years of experience making out with manupartners. If we were to feign ignorance of that disturbing detail, however ... WOW! Can you imagine what it would be like to date a man who went to the effort of planning elaborate dates just to make you happy and kissed you so thoroughly you could have sworn he *cared*? The type of man who had things handled so all you had to do was sit back and revel in your wellspring of feminine power and be the inspiration of such devotion. For a moment there, it felt quite freeing, but I got ahead of myself.

The asshole opened his mouth, as men are apt to do. He got all concerned about what would happen to his precious reputation if people found out he was canoodling with an actual woman. That got me thinking. Can you imagine what would happen to his sacred reputation if I were to publish this? I could title the post "Discover what it's like to be kissed by MSP's most ineligible bachelor." Or what about "CHOICElover founder kissed me: A real woman's harrowing journey to darkness and beyond"?

That would only serve him right, as he is now in the living room with a manupartner in his lap! Not that I would do that to him. Unlike him, I'm a good human being and would never exploit his vulnerability.

Electra glances up from the tablet toward the door, wishing she could write away the little stab of betrayal currently gutting her, but journaling isn't helping like it normally would. Probably because she isn't actually connecting with any actual readers. Forgoing her normal sign off, she opens the FrogBlog app. A minute later, she has a new account created. Username: *Dear_Electra*. She grins at the screen.

Now, how does one start an advice column? She should research the columns from her time. Back on the home screen, her attention snags on an image of her and Res6 leaving the theater under a headline:

CHOICElover founder out and about with new prototype.

In the photo, her face is pinched in irritation while Res6 has a placid smile on his face, as if he had not just experienced the same argument she did. That gets under her skin more than anything. Even Chryl, because what he's doing by immediately getting a manupartner after their kiss is clear: He's dodging his feelings toward her.

Why is he like that? Why is he so averse to opening up to her, or anyone for that matter? She's pretty sure she isn't making things up. The question is, what happened to him to make him so closed off?

Her intense curiosity has her pulling up the CHOICElover website and going to the About Us section. She skims through the text but finds no new insights. Most of what she reads she already learned in one of the videos Tommy downloaded for her. CHOICElover was founded in 2302 by a young scientist, Res6, who'd already had an impressive career. They quote him saying, "I saw a problem, and I knew I could fix it." No one seemed to question what the problem was, or at least the website didn't. She runs a quick search. There are early critics of manupartners, but they tend to fall into two camps. First, the ethical considerations because of the source material, i.e., the consent of the people who existed once upon a time being used as sex clones. Then there's the safety of such technology, because of the AI wealth distribution event, The Great Equalizer, which led to many of the current regulations.

All interesting, but she's getting no closer to understanding him. Surely there is a way to discover more about a person's history, considering how much data is currently available on the network. She taps the DumBot app and issues the prompt:

Hi DumBot! If I wanted to discover everything there is to know about someone, including their early years, is that something you can help me with?

DumBot:

I can absolutely help you research someone. Is this person living or dead?

Electra scratches her head.

I'm just going to give you an identifier.

DumBot:

Great. I'm ready when you are!

She types:

A-RES6-MSP-00022960.

DumBot:

That's you! What an exciting way to gain insight into yourself. According to your EmoTracker, you've been experiencing concerning emotional spikes in recent weeks. We can work together to help you gain clarity on how to achieve optimal balance. Retracing your life milestones is one approach we can explore. Here are your milestones. Please let me know if I can provide any additional details on a particular memory that we can dissect in more depth together.

- (03/30/2271) A-Res6-MSP-00022960 is born at 19:58.

- (03/30/2271) /-Jerme-MSP-00022961 is born at 20:03.

Interesting. Res6 didn't mention his brother was his twin. And what does the slash mean? From what she recalls, the first letter refers to the quadrant and changes depending on where the citizen lives.

- (03/30/2281) Aptitude results notification received. NHOS Citizen's Career Specialization Agency recommends Res6 and Jerme for accelerated learning.

- (07/31/2281) First day of Best Young Citizens School for the Especially Gifted.

Electra scans the list, snagging on—oh God.

- (11/14/2292) Medical examiner lists cause of Jerme's death as atmosphere-assisted suicide.

Electra drops the tablet on the bed as her stomach clenches. Her mind quickly pieces together the little she knows about him. She picks up the tablet again and scans to see when he started CHOICElover.

- (11/14/2299) CHOICElover is founded.

- (11/14/2302) CHOICElover rolls out first manupartners to the public.

Those dates are exactly seven and ten years after his twin's suicide. It feels too significant to be a coincidence. Or is she jumping to conclusions again? A gut feeling tells her there is something to those dates. A loss that significant could explain his reluctance toward close relationships. Even some of why he might think manupartners would be a good idea.

She requests that DumBot remove its memory of the conversation and then deletes it for good measure. As she closes the app, her eyes snag on the date: October 21, 2390. That means the anniversary of his brother's death is less than a month away. No wonder he's so mixed up.

What is she supposed to do with this new information? It's not like it changes anything. Well, it explains why he keeps referring to Jerme in the past tense. A pang of melancholy hits her. He keeps suggesting Jerme will like her, even saying they'll meet soon. How sad is that? Her heart aches for him. She understands all too well what that feels like.

How long Jerme's been gone doesn't matter. She still mourns the loss of her mother, and it's been nearly twenty years. What now, though?

Be patient with him about Chryl, her inner narrator, who sounds a lot like Ask Doctor Janet, suggests. *Yeah, yeah.* Chryl is his shield, and it did seem like he was trying to push her off his lap when Electra walked in. It's hard to imagine a man as serious and emotionally constipated as Res6 being romantically involved with a bubbly, bodacious woman like that, albeit a fake one.

The urge to help him smacks her in the heart. *He isn't asking for your help*, the Janet in her mind reminds her. True, but it isn't just him. It's everyone! There is one thing this society is seriously lacking, aside from the ability to go outdoors, and it's partially because of his invention of manupartners: *human connection!*

Sure, she should be cautious—the world is a scary place—but the possible benefit outweighs the risk. The column could soak up her anxious energy and give her purpose. Maybe even prove she deserves a place here, instead of waiting for the world to remind her she doesn't belong.

With her experience of how things were before, she's the exact woman to show society how to reestablish real, meaningful relationships through her column. Not to mention she's a romance writer—she's basically a relationship expert!

And if Res6 grows as a by-product of her efforts, so be it. Not that she plans to use him as a test subject, or even tell him about the blog he's so disapproving of. Only influence him through the psychological concept of emotional contagion. *Take that, Janet!*

Grinning, she picks up her tablet and logs on to the FrogBlog app with her new account. It really is a perfect plan. What an excellent main character she's becoming.

14 – A Surprise Sparkler

Res6

October 30, 2390.

"Will you please act like a manupartner today?" Res6 asks as the SAT door opens. He jumps out, circles the vehicle quickly, and helps her out first, then Chryl.

"I thought I was allowed to be myself." She shoots him a snarky grin.

He stifles a groan. *Her existence is your fault, so you deserve this.* "I changed my mind."

Electra chuffs. "What does 'act like a manupartner' even mean?"

"Be agreeable. At least until we are alone, if you can manage that." He instinctively offers Electra his elbow. "Better yet, don't speak. That goes for you too, Chryl."

"Yes, Daddy!" Chryl says, earning a groan from both him and Electra. Chryl loops her arm through his offered one. "Don't be cranky, handsome."

He shakes Chryl's arm off, angling for Electra, who steps out of his reach.

"My not speaking wasn't part of our agreement," Electra says.

"Perhaps we can add it as a condition?"

"How about a second favor of my choosing?" She smiles at him smugly.

Zorg, give him strength. He shakes his head. "No."

It's not like his *attitude* is unwarranted, considering he spent fifteen minutes bargaining with Electra to get her out the door. Besides, he already heavily weighted the deal in her favor by granting her one request of her choice—at a time of her choosing—that he couldn't refuse, in exchange for agreeing to visit the lab with Chryl in tow, plus lunch for advertising.

It's a steep price, which feels a little ominous, if he's being honest. But after the sixth failed synthetic Jerme DNA attempt that morning, he was desperate to get her to the lab for some scans, so he gave in. Should the scans offer a path to bringing Jerme back, fulfilling her request will be well worth it. Then he won't have to use the organic samples as Lextr keeps pushing. It's getting harder to deny the soundness of his reasoning.

He takes Electra's arm, sliding down until he can entwine their fingers. She doesn't resist as he tugs her forward. They pass various staff members in the hallways, some of whom he recognizes. All recognize him and give the three of them a wide berth. When they are safely ensconced inside an elevator, she holds up their joined hands. "Considering we're at your company, is this necessary?"

"Yes."

"You aren't holding Chryl's hand," she points out.

"I don't have to worry about Chryl misbehaving." For her part, Chryl gleefully nods, pretending to zip her lips. He permits himself a bemused grin as he leads them into the hallway that connects the research and development laboratories.

"Good afternoon, sir," Lextr says. "We weren't expecting you this afternoon."

He pulls Electra forward. "Electra has agreed to a few scans."

Chryl starts, "You can scan me if you want—" but Res6 cuts her a warning look. She mouths *sorry* and re-zips her lips.

"Excellent. I can take care of it." Lextr holds out his hand in a gesture that says, *Just hand her over to me.*

Electra takes a wary step back, edging behind Res6. The fingertips of her free hand wrap around his arm, and an emotion he'd rather avoid swells in his chest. "I'll accompany her. We should do a full bio check while we're at it."

Lextr's brows rise, and he shoots an incredulous glance between them. "As you wish. Unit, please follow me." He leads them through the nearest double-paned glass door and down the long corridor that leads to the medical wing.

"Her name is Electra," Res6 repeats when they enter a large exam room.

"With respect, sir, I don't care what her name is. To me, she's an experiment. Fascinating, yes, but still an experiment." As Lextr collects the equipment, he shoots Chryl, who is shimmying with excitement, several wary glances. "Is she malfunctioning?"

"I'm not," Electra answers, busy eyeing the different pieces of medical and scientific equipment. He tries to see the blinking gadgets and human-sized chambers through her eyes: the shiny metal electro-regeneration scale, the transparent particle panes of the Spot-Gene Interface. His lab must be a strange place to her.

Chryl steps to Electra's side, shaking her bosom. "He means me, obviously, babes!"

"My mistake. Well, in that case . . ." Electra mutters, trailing off.

Ten minutes later, Lextr has collected a saliva and blood sample. They've come back normal. Res6 hovers nearby, trying not to fidget while Lextr takes the first of many scans. As the blue biowave makes a pass over her body, Electra is stiff.

The device beeps twice before lighting up green. "All internal systems are intact," Lextr says. He steps closer, inspecting her face. He lifts his hand, tapping her cheek. "I would suggest we remove these since you plan to keep her."

She flinches, and Res6 steps forward, forcing Lextr to take a step back. "Absolutely not."

"But they're a defect and will make her acclimatization in our society more difficult," Lextr pushes.

"I said no. The freckles stay," Res6 states.

"Fine." Lextr shakes his head, mumbling, "When was the last time you took good advice when I offered it to you?"

Lextr runs three more scans, each a different color of light. "Her long-term DNA malfunction prediction report will be emailed to you automatically as soon as it is finished processing." He glances up at the particle pane displaying the time, the indoor temperature, and the current light setting, and sets the scanner on the counter. "If that is all, I'm needed elsewhere."

Res6 narrows his eyes. Considering the scan results will be ready shortly, it surprises him that Lextr isn't eager to review them. Each failure bothers Lextr too. The man is as eager to succeed as he is, though his lead scientist is more interested in replicating the experiment, which will help them isolate the precise factor causing the NAM activation.

When the door closes behind Lextr, Electra lets out a long exhale. "That was exciting. Lextr seems like a real piece of work."

"I think he's kinda cute." Chryl twirls a lock of hair, but she jerks like she's surprised herself. "Don't be jealous, Daddy!"

"Chryl, please," he snaps, and turns to Electra. "Lextr means well, and he and Tommy balance each other out."

Before Electra, it never occurred to him that Lextr's behavior might be rude. Perhaps that means there is some value in attending his FRIENDS group after all. But if he showed up now, would anyone realize he's been sending a manupartner in his place the entire time? He could put in for a new group and within a week, NHOS would assign it, but it seems like a lot of trouble. Besides, he has her for human interaction now. Except he doesn't have her, given that he chose to avoid a long-term attachment, and she did too.

The woman is a disruption. Why did he do this to himself? His curiosity. Right. His thinking is growing increasingly repetitive, and his rationalizations are weakening by the moment, despite how desperately he's clinging to them. On the bright side, Electra's existence gave him the idea to bring back Jerme, so her presence will be worth it.

Electra groans. "Please tell me all future people aren't like him. What about the conduct classes you mentioned? He's probably due for one soon."

"I'll have to check his file. Then there are a few things I need to do in my office while we wait on your DNA malfunction prediction report. If anything comes up, we can stop by the corrections department to get a gene editing procedure while we're here."

Before she can pepper him with a million questions, he takes her hand and leads her out. Chryl follows, humming a tune he doesn't recognize, and he does his best to ignore her and the interested looks she and Electra are getting from his staff. Once the three of them are behind the closed door of his office, he waves his hand, gesturing for Electra to speak. "Go ahead."

"What?" she says.

"Ask away. I know you have questions." Res6 takes a seat at his desk. Electra and Chryl follow suit, plopping into the chairs opposite his desk. He checks his inbox and finds a few documents he can retina-sign while he supplies her with answers.

"Okay, questions then," she begins, but hesitates. "If the report says I'm likely to get the same cancer my mom had, what do I do?"

Res6 stops what he's doing, his attention drawn by the distressed wobble in her voice. What is with his visceral urge to draw her into his chest? That's not like him at all. *Be rational*, he scolds himself. He's about to offer her a logical reply when his inbox pings. "Oh, here it is now."

She moves to stand beside him, leaning over his shoulder to look at the screen. He scrolls down through the report, pausing momentarily on a couple of yellow-highlighted rows. "What are those?" she asks.

"Minor predictors. Those abnormalities are unlikely to manifest as an illness, but given the right circumstances, they could be triggered. Anything highlighted, regardless of the color, should be corrected."

"I see," she says.

He stops scrolling at the first green row. It reads:

Generalized Breast Cancer Risk 94%.

"Oh God," she whispers, putting a shaky hand over her chest. He stares at her hand for a long, unsettling moment.

"The report doesn't mean you have cancer. It is only a predictor based on a set of data points," he says, his voice admittedly robotic.

He's still staring at her hand. He's not sure what comes over him, but he takes it and cradles it in the space between them. It feels like the right thing to do, which only means her distress is doing things to him that cannot be explained with datasets.

"It says ninety-four percent." She draws in a few sharp, panicked breaths.

It takes everything in him not to pull her into his lap and promise to fight every battle that comes her way. He clenches his jaw so hard, his molars feel like they might crack. What was the exercise she showed him? Something about touching his forearm. Zorgdamnit, why can't he remember? *Because you were too busy enjoying her touch to be paying attention to what she was showing you, you idiot! Now she's panicking again, and your mind is blank.*

The twisted knot in his chest is deeply concerning. It has to be the romance novels—besides her, they're the only other variable he can think of. He needs to steel himself like he did in the years after Jerme died and figure out how deal with this very real woman—wait! That's it. He places her hand on his forearm. "R—"

Before he can finish, Chryl is there, wrapping her arms around Electra's middle from behind and squeezing—behaving more human than he is. Electra's eyes go wide, her hand falling away. For a moment, they're both frozen. Does she see the irony that a manupartner is the one attempting to comfort her too?

Chryl says, "Genetic engineering and gene therapy, in combination with advanced diagnostics, nanotechnology, and regenerative medicine, have effectively eliminated disease. I don't know how I know that, but I do. That means Daddy can fix you!" Chryl exuberantly bounces, which in turn rattles Electra.

"Thank you, Chryl." Electra extricates herself from Chryl's embrace and looks to him. "I must not be to that video yet. Is she right?"

He evaluates the manupartner for a moment, shaking his head. He doesn't recall that bit of data being encoded into the manupartner's base mRNA sequence. It's possible she learned it during her lease with her previous owner. He should check her file—

"Res6, am I going to die again?"

His gaze snaps to Electra. Her skin has lightened a shade, and her expression is stricken. "She's right. There is a solution. You'll be in the DNA modifier for no more than an hour. We have one here downstairs. We don't use it much anymore since our product is . . ." He can hear the company message he's about to repeat, along with her words concerning his company, so he starts again. "Occasionally, when we are working on advancements, we have to use it, so we keep it updated with the latest software package."

Her eyes are glistening now. He shoots up from his chair, determined to be the one to comfort her this time, but Chryl beats him to it.

Chryl ushers Electra back to her chair, pressing her shoulders until she plops into it. Chryl steps behind the chair, digging her fingers into Electra's hair, massaging. "There, there, honey cakes. It will all be better once you're recycled."

A sob bursts out of Electra. She jumps up, batting Chryl's hands away. "I hate the future," she cries, and darts out the door.

"Damn it, Chryl." Res6 glares at the manupartner. "Sit there and stay put." Then he runs to catch up with Electra, pulling her into the nearest vacant room.

"Hey, it's okay. Remember, you're safe now. I can take care of this." She blinks up at him, her lashes wet with tears. "In an hour, it will be as if you were born with perfectly scrubbed DNA."

"It won't change me, will it?" She reaches up, brushing her fingers over her cheek.

It strikes him that Electra wishes to preserve her appearance, despite being born in a time without the medical advancements to simply fix or even experiment with every nuance of one's aesthetic. He tracks the movement of her fingers, and the urge to kiss every single freckle barrels into him. "Only the things that may shorten your lifespan."

After a moment of deliberating, she nods. It's a quick ride down to the corrections department. He takes her hand and is guiding her down the hall, passing the refrigeration chambers where they store the DNA samples and other biological material, when a commotion from inside one room draws his attention.

"One second," he tells her before wrenching the door open.

An overturned table sits in the center of the room, and a material storage technician is cowering behind it. Two men hover over the frightened tech, their faces partially obscured by ID Scramble-Tech visors and black neckcloths pulled up over their noses. Their attention lands on him. The few inches in front of their faces flicker. Shit. The visor's scramble field will interfere with his building's surveillance. They hold silver cases similar to the ones he and Lextr are using for the Jerme experiments, but a little bulkier because they're equipped for temperature regulation.

Is this a robbery?

The electrical system hisses, and the overhead lights blink off. The building has been hacked. Only a slight glow from the residual phantom voltage illuminates the room.

"Res6?" Electra calls from the hallway.

"Its fine. Stay there," he shouts.

"That's our cue," one of the men shouts. "Time to go." They switch illumiboxes on, bathing the room in a soft violet light.

Res6 isn't sure what's in the cases, but he can't let them leave. What if they have Electra's DNA? Or Jerme's? Not to mention the woman in the hallway whose safety he just assured. Panic claws at his throat. He has to stop them!

He slams the door behind him, barricading them from her. The normally flashing lights on the retina scanner are dead, so he fumbles for the locking mechanism. It doesn't respond to his fingerprints. "Shit."

Two against one. No weapons. He can do it.

With his m-volt, he thinks the command: Message Security. *There's been a break-in. Two unarmed men, floor 78.* He glances at the dead panel where the room number is displayed. *Chamber 14.*

He gets an immediate reply. *Hold tight. We're on the way, sir.*

Just as he's about to go on the defensive, another man appears, walking backward out of one of the refrigeration chambers. He's pointing a sparkler, the automatic stun handpiece only the police are authorized to carry, at Bexly, his organic assets custodian, who is whimpering.

He thinks, *There's a third man with a sparkler. They've got Bexly.*

He hears, *Noted. We've called the police.*

With a quick glance, Res6 notes the sparkler's setting is midway between yellow and orange. Red, he guesses, is killing strength. Orange, the upper-level ion stun, temporarily blinds and disorients the target. Yellow—well, he isn't sure. Less than orange, logically. Still, with any of the settings, a direct hit would likely cause momentary physical impairment and possible residual effects requiring specialized healing.

Electra's in the hall. The man with the weapon isn't leaving the room. He'll just distract them until the police come. It's not like it's on kill mode.

Res6 darts forward. The other two techs shout a warning. In his periphery, several cases thud to the floor. Res6 grabs the man's weapon-holding arm. The sparkler fires, peppering three quick shots across the room. Bexly cries out as the final two shots hit the door and the operating panel of the refrigeration chamber.

He thinks, *Bexly's been hit, as* sparks spray across the room. Someone crashes into him and he loses his footing, slamming into the man with the sparkler. Bexly scrambles backward through the open door of the chamber, clutching his shoulder, and Res6 and the two men go down in a pile. The first man knocks his head against the wall, disorienting him. Res6 lunges forward, wrenching the weapon out of his hand. With his full weight, he throws himself back, elbowing the other man in the face.

Bone snaps, and the man jerks back in pain. Res6 rolls off him and jumps to his feet. He trains the weapon on the two lying on the floor, sweeping his gaze across the space in search of the third man. His stomach drops as the exterior door clicks closed.

Electra. It's possible they only have one black-market weapon, but—

Seizing the man with the broken, dripping nose by his collar, he drags him along, sparkler pointed at his head. He shouts over his shoulder to the man on the floor, who is rapidly recovering, "Red is kill, right?"

The man grunts something unintelligible. A second later, the back-up power source activates, and the refrigeration units kick back on, whirring. More blinking lights illuminate the dark space. Res6 presses forward, flinging the door open.

"Electra!" To his right, she whimpers.

He shoves the man out in the hall only to be met with the third man, who has dropped the cases at his feet. He's pressing a second sparkler to her temple.

"Easy," he urges.

"She's quite nice," the man says, brushing the tip of the weapon over her tear-streaked cheek. "Unusual. So LifeLike it almost makes me think she's real." He tilts the weapon so Res6 can see the settings. "You're right, red is kill."

He should have held her when he had the chance. No, he can't think like that. The police are on their way. Then when they're safe, he'll wrap his arms around her so tight he may never let go. "Please don't hurt her," he begs.

"Collect the cases," the robber holding Electra directs. The man from the refrigeration chamber complies, but the one with the blood seeping through his mask, who Res6 still holds at gunpoint, doesn't budge.

"Go on," the leader says. "He won't kill you. Not when we have his pretty little *manupartner* here."

The sarcasm in the man's voice sends a chill through Res6. Does he know Electra's real? How?

His lackey obeys, reluctantly moving one cautious step at a time until he's a few feet away from Res6. Free, he quickly gathers the remaining cases and sets them in the hallway.

"Sparkler on the floor," the leader demands. "If you take too long, my finger might slip."

When Electra whimpers again, he knows he doesn't have a choice. The sound of her distress is too much this time. He'd do anything to stop it, including letting the men take anything they want from this building, as long as it's not her. He slowly lowers the weapon to the floor. One of them picks it up. Res6 starts as it digs into his back.

"The layout shows a storage closet this way," the leader says. "Move." Then he shoots the locking mechanism, effectively locking the lab techs in.

He thinks, *Bexly seems to be okay, but needs medical attention. Where are the police?*

He hears *They'll be here any minute, sir. Hold on.*

Res6 glances at Electra, hoping his falsely calm expression is enough to ease her worry. If the criminals wanted to kill them, they would have done it already. They spared Bexly and the lab techs.

The robbers walk them to a nondescript door. The man behind him wrenches the door open, pushing him inside. As he stumbles forward, the sparkler clicks. A misfire? The man says, "Oops," as two green bolts hit the wall beside Res6. The third strikes the back of his thigh, and he yelps. His vision darkens, but he clings to the edges. "Electra! Give her to me." He staggers forward, grasping for the doorframe, as darkness overtakes his vision.

"Let me go," she cries, then she crashes into him.

He releases the doorframe and draws her into his arms. "If you're going to lock us in too, do it, then leave."

The larger man with the broken nose, presumably the shooter, shoves them back into the cramped space. As his back hits the wall, the door slams. There's another series of shots; the mechanism has been disabled, locking them inside.

Electra is finally in his arms. The taste he got after the horseback riding fiasco wasn't enough because this feels incredible. Addictive. So right, despite her trembling. Just knowing she's safe is enough for him to keep it together. "Shh." He tries to calm her quiet weeping, cradling her tighter into his chest. "The police are coming. Security will search the building. They'll see the blown locks and get us out. We're safe now."

"Is your leg okay?" she asks, sniffling.

"It's fine."

She must sense his lie because she tries to pull away, but he doesn't let her. *I'm never letting you go.*

They stand huddled against the wall until she says, "I need to sit." She's shaky, but it's clearly for his benefit.

He slides down the wall, pulling her into his lap like it's the most natural thing in the world. He heaves a sigh of relief as the throbbing ache of the sparkler burn eases. The feel of her against him warms him so thoroughly, he feels like he might catch fire. What was he thinking denying himself this pleasure?

"Why is this happening?" she asks. "I thought the future was safer, at least indoors."

"It is. But we have precious resources here. I think they were after genetic material." But they had no way of knowing which liquid nitrogen dewars stored the cryovials containing Electra and Jerme's organic specimens. A pang of dread hits him. They had Bexly in the BioBank. Bexly could access the Laboratory Information Management System, or LIMS, and point them to any specific DNA they were looking for.

"Those silver cases they were carrying?" she asks, nuzzling into his chest. It feels unbelievable. She's unharmed and nestled in his embrace. It's almost enough to make him forget about the ache radiating from his thigh or the implications of the robbery.

"Yes, those are temperature-regulated cases meant for stabilizing organic materials at their perfect temperature as they're transported," he supplies.

"But who would be after your organic material?"

"Considering our security system is near impenetrable, it has to be someone who works for me who has a high level of clearance." A lab tech? Someone recently promoted?

"Maybe it isn't what you think," she says.

"I wish I could be as optimistic as you." Because how else would they know, in a full tower's worth of floors, which one held the BioBank? It's not like the layout of his company is public knowledge. Unless they got to Bexly first.

"I'm sorry they got away because of me," she says, glancing up at him. He can faintly make out the concerned expression on her lovely face.

He should be focusing on comforting her, yet he's stewing over his company. This proves how terrible he is at caring for others. Jerme would probably attest to that. That's why it will be so much better when his brother is back.

"I told you I wouldn't let anything happen to you." *And I've already endangered you by bringing you to the lab for scans.*

"But if it's really DNA they're after, it could hurt your company," she says.

"Let's worry about that later. I'm glad you're safe."

"You don't even like me. With the way you've been acting, I figured you'd be happy to be rid of me now that you've got the scans."

Her words sting. With his adrenaline receding, he can't find the energy to lie to her. "Electra, I don't wish harm to come to you, and I like you fine. A lot, actually. I'm not used to having someone in my space, so your presence is distracting. I don't even go to my FRIENDS meetings. I send a manupartner made with my DNA in my place to impersonate me." Why is he sharing this with her? It's only going to make things harder when she remembers she doesn't like him. That makes how perfect she feels in his arms that much more bittersweet, because he can't really keep her if she doesn't want to be kept, can he? Even if he wants to despite all the reasons he shouldn't.

"I read about FRIENDS groups."

He shakes his head. "I bet you think those are pathetic, too."

She shrugs. "I think friends are a good thing. I miss mine like crazy. You should give your FRIENDS' group a chance."

He chuffs. She doesn't know what she's talking about, considering she's never even met his three NHOS-assigned FRIENDS. Not that he has, but still. "You're awfully quick to dish out advice."

She's probably right, though. As soon as he has the thought, he stiffens. That brings up things he isn't prepared to discuss yet. Namely, her column.

Thankfully, she doesn't press the issue, so they sit like that for a while, with her leaning against his chest, finally getting the comfort she asked for all those weeks ago. All his resistance has crumbled into a pile of dust. Even the ache in his lower back doesn't seem like a priority. He's too distracted by the circles he draws on her lower hip. Does she think this is normal, or is she only so traumatized from having a sparkler pointed at her temple that she's allowing the contact with a man she wants nothing to do with?

Eventually, a buzzing sound vibrates around them as the systems come back online. Though his vision is still dark at the edges, he can sense the lights coming on. They hold their breath as footsteps pound down the hallway. Then someone shouts, "Are you in there, boss?" Res6 recognizes it as the voice of Karik, his head of operations, along with the muffled sounds of a few security guards.

"Handsome, where are you?" Chryl shouts. Her heels loudly click-clack through the hallway, presumably as she chases after Karik. "We have to find him!"

"You can't possibly be serious with her," Electra mutters.

He can't help but agree, though there's no need to tell her that. "We're in here," he shouts through the door.

There is a commotion outside. He guesses they're trying and failing to figure out how to work around the blown-out digital lock panel.

"Stand back!" someone yells.

They huddle against the back wall as a series of ear-rattling bangs echo in the space. He nuzzles into Electra's hair and she hides her face in his chest, both of them preparing for more banging. He could easily become addicted to this. Her warmth. The weight of her body nestled against him. Connection. He needs to get ahold of himself, and soon, because it's going to be that much more painful when it all gets ripped away.

With a few more hits, the lock cracks. The door swings open, bathing them in the blinding light of the hallway.

"At least it was only a storage closet. The maintenance crew had to laser cut Bexly and the lab techs out," Karik says.

Res6's vision is starting to fill back in. He can barely make out Karik startle as he takes in Electra. Before Res6 can stop him, Karik reaches down, grabs her arms, and roughly hoists her to her feet. She squeaks, wincing, at Karik's forceful grip.

Res6 quickly staggers to his feet. The woozy sensation doesn't stop him from pulling Electra out of the other man's hold.

He tips her chin up. "You okay?"

She nods, stepping closer to him. The movement makes his heart feel like it's going to beat out of his chest. *Get it together, Res6.*

He turns his scrutinizing gaze to Karik, who says, "Sorry, boss. No harm intended. I can see she's a very . . . uh . . . fine unit."

"Daddy, you're safe!" Chryl throws his arms around his neck.

"Where are the police?" Res6 asks, pulling Chryl's arms off him. He steps around her to address Karik, keeping Electra firmly tucked into his side. "Do we know what they stole?"

"Not yet, sir. Lextr is with the officers now. They're looking into the breach."

"I want a full report the moment they know." When Karik doesn't move, Res6 barks, "Don't just stand there. Get the HR team to see to the staff. Does anyone need medical attention besides Bexly?"

"We're already on it, sir," Tommy says, jogging down the hall. "Bexly already gave his statement and is in the healing wing getting treatment now. The police are asking for you."

Electra stiffens in his arms. "Let's go." He guides her to follow Tommy, leaning down to say, "I know you've researched manupartners. Just act like one and you'll be fine." He isn't letting her out of his sight.

They, including a clingy Chryl, follow Tommy into the main glass-enclosed conference room. Lextr and three NHOS police inspectors sit at a long table, reviewing the LIMS on the large particle plane that fills one wall.

Lextr is saying, "According to Bexly's statement, they were after DNA samples, but it appears the data has been tampered with." Lextr turns as he and Electra step up beside him.

They were after DNA? His pulse skyrockets. Jerme's DNA would have been in that BioBank. "So we don't know what DNA they took?"

Lextr's eyes flash in a way that suggests he understands the underlying question: *Did they get Jerme's DNA?* "We won't know until Bexly and his team can do a physical inventory."

He nods outwardly, but thinks with his m-volt, Message Lextr. *Have them check for Jerme's DNA first. I want to know if it's missing STAT.*

Lextr's eyes go distant as he listens to the message. They clear, and he glances up, nodding.

Good. It's probably nothing to worry about—just a random hate group trying to disrupt his operations. Whoever those men were, they would have no reason to target his brother's DNA. Not to mention, the odds of them selecting Jerme's DNA out of the millions in his stores is highly improbable—yet there's enough of a chance to make his palms sweat.

Now that he's set his mind to bringing his brother back, it feels like everything hinges on it. If these criminals inadvertently ruin his chances . . . He doesn't know what he'll do. Probably have another seven-year downward spiral like he did when Jerme first died.

Electra, who's still tucked into his side, must sense his inner turmoil because she snakes her arm around his waist, squeezing, which draws his attention to the present. He steels himself. This isn't the time to have a meltdown.

The petite blonde inspector sitting across the table turns to the other officers. "When the rest of our team gets here, I want a full sweep of the premises." She nods to Lextr. "Work alongside him as his staff reviews the DNA stores. Find out what's missing so we'll know what is in those silver cases. I'll join you once I'm finished with this interview."

Lextr and the two inspectors rush out of the room. Tommy hovers behind him. "Tommy, you may go."

Tommy nods. "Of course, sir."

"Take Chryl to my office and wait there." Both Tommy and the manupartner frown but head down the hall together.

He and Electra settle into the seats opposite the inspector. She's all business as she turns her piercing blue eyes to them. "I'm Inspector Wanda. I'll be your NHOS liaison during this investigation."

Beside him, Electra's knee vibrates. He grabs it, squeezing. When she stills, he lends authority to his voice and says, "I'm Res6, CHOICElover's owner, founder, and the inventor of manupartners. This is Electra, our latest, most LifeLike prototype."

The inspector nods. "Excellent. I'd like to take a statement from you both"—she eyes Electra warily—"and try to develop a profile of the perpetrators."

"We'll help in any way we can. I want to find out who is behind this as much as you do," he says.

Inspector Wanda takes out her tablet and a stylus. "I'm going to record our conversation if you don't mind."

"Of course not," he says.

"Excellent. Thank you for your cooperation. Being the victim of a robbery can be an unsettling experience, so I appreciate your cooperation." When Inspector Wanda directs her assurance only to him, he momentarily bristles on Electra's behalf. But she isn't being callous. She thinks Electra's a manupartner.

He rubs Electra's thigh, trying to transfer the reassurance to her. A second later, her fingers brush his. At first he thinks he's overstepped, but when they close around his hand, that buoyant sensation in his chest from a few minutes earlier explodes. He has to fight to keep from grinning like a lunatic. Really, who would be so joyful after being robbed? Only a man whose world is actively being uprooted by a woman from four hundred years ago and likes it. Oh, Zorg, he really likes it. Especially the way their hands fit together and—

Shit. Inspector Wanda is saying something.

". . . to recount the sequence of events for my official records." She taps the tablet's screen. "Go ahead."

15 – The Corrections Department

Electra

Electra's voice is impressively steady as they carefully recount the last two hours. Res6, of course, is wearing the persona of *CHOICElover's owner, founder, and the inventor of manupartners*. When he said all that, she had to stifle an eye roll.

"Excellent," the inspector continues. "Forensic sketches aren't sufficient evidence to get a warrant, but they might lead to more concrete evidence. Now, while the incident is fresh in your minds, I'd like us to try a forensic sketch artist generative AI tool." She raises the tablet for emphasis. "Please describe the men to the best of your ability, then I'm going to show you the images and we can tweak them from there."

Electra sits forward. She's excellent at describing the details of a character's appearance, so perhaps she can do this. Especially considering she has the images of the robbers burned into her mind.

"Let's start with the leader. What can you remember about him?" Inspector Wanda shifts her attention from the tablet to Res6.

He squeezes her hand. "Electra, would you like to start?"

His trust in her to help with the investigation gives her a flutter of pride. *Nothing else is fluttering, Electra. Just because he's reassuringly holding your hand doesn't mean anything.* The gist is that she feels relatively confident about this task. So, determined not to use any of her usual flowery language and accidentally seem human, she says, "The man who we're calling the leader was around seventy-three inches tall. Large, muddy-brown hooded eyes. They were wide-set and slightly down-turned. His skin was pale and looked like it would easily burn, but eventually tan. His black hair was short and curled slightly at the ends."

"I thought you said the ID Scramble-Tech visors covered the tops of their heads?" Inspector Wanda cuts in to ask.

"Go on," Res6 says, gesturing with his free hand for her to continue.

"They did, but between the neckcloth and the visor, a lock slipped free." The inspector nods in understanding. "Though the lower half of his face was concealed, I could still make out the shape of his nose, which I would call Roman, and the bone structure of his jaw, which was square with a jutting chin. His head was a little blocky too."

"Roman?" the inspector asks.

"Yeah. Prominent and narrow but with a hooked bridge."

"What about his build besides his height?"

She closes her eyes, trying to recall. "He wasn't bulky, but he didn't have tight muscles like Res6. Somewhere in the middle, I think." Res6's thumb rubs hers encouragingly. "Oh! His hands were rough and thick, with fingers on the shorter side, and there was sparse black hair on his knuckles."

"Good. That should be enough to get us a starting image." Using the stylus, the inspector taps the tablet a few times before turning it to face them. There's an image of a man that looks eerily similar to the man she remembers on the screen.

"His eyes are a little too down-turned. And I remember his nose being larger. The lips, I couldn't tell at all, so I have no idea if they might have been that full," she says.

Inspector Wanda nods. "I'll include that in the metadata. What else?"

They go on like that for an hour, with Res6 occasionally chiming in details she missed, until they have three reasonably accurate composites of the robbers. When the inspector finally leaves, she tells them, "I'll input the images into MSP's surveillance system and notify you if anyone is flagged. If so, I'll need you again for identification." Electra can't help but notice that Inspector Wanda only makes eye contact with Res6 as she adds, "I'll be in touch."

It might be slightly offensive if it weren't such a relief that she believed Electra's a manupartner. What a day. All she wants to do is crawl into bed and forget about being held at gunpoint.

As Res6 walks her through the hallways, they pass other officers, presumably sweeping the premises as instructed. They enter a corridor lined with several sets of bright red double doors that she doesn't recognize. "Wait, where are we going?"

"The corrections department."

She stops, yanking him to a halt. "I've had enough for today. I'm ready to leave the scene of the crime." The scene that all but confirms the world isn't a safe place. *It wasn't back then and it isn't now. Lucky me!* She mentally glares at her inner narrator.

A distinct feminine voice echoes through the hallway, interrupting her protest. "I'm pretty sure Daddy's office isn't on this floor either. Since you're his assistant, shouldn't you know its location?"

Tommy groans. "I told you to stay where I put you."

"But that storage room was dark, and Daddy said to put me in his office." The pair step around the corner into view. Chryl's head snaps up. "There they are!"

Tommy rushes after Chryl, who happily skips ahead.

Res6 sidesteps Chryl as she tries to hug him. "Chryl, why didn't you stay where Tommy asked you to?"

Chryl stomps, crossing her arms. "I wanted to help too!"

A bead of sweat trickles down Tommy's brow. "Really, it's fine, sir. Just a minor inconvenience. I can continue watching her."

Electra bites her lip trying to stifle a laugh as Chryl stares daggers at the two men. If she weren't so exhausted from the trauma of the day, she might join in their ridiculous antics and take Chryl's side. Even though manupartners aren't really real like she is, they aren't robots either—as far as she can tell.

"No need," Res6 says, shaking his head. "She can come with me. I need you to get with Lextr and compile a summary of the losses—specifically from the BioBank—plus the damages, including a report of the affected staff. Set up meetings with them tomorrow so I can reassure them that measures are being taken to ensure their safety. Get with Karik to initiate the inspectors' recommended security protocols. I want that done before you leave for the day."

Tommy gulps as Chryl shoots him a smug look. "Yes, sir."

Electra jumps as Res6 slides a firm arm around her waist. "Good. Go. We're going to the corrections department. I need to heal this." He gestures to the scorched black spot on his tan jumpsuit.

Guilt slices through her. *That's right, he got shot.* She was so focused on her own issues that she didn't consider his injury might need healing. Not to mention the pain he must be in. He's been so stoic throughout this entire ordeal—plus comforting her—that her heart squeezes. She wraps her arm around him in return. "Come on. Let's go."

As they turn to pace down the hallway, Chryl falls in behind them, clapping. "Corrections department? Oh, goody. I've been a bad girl."

An hour later, they are twenty-seven minutes into their separate treatment programs, seated in cushy chairs—like at the dentist—inside transparent, sealed treatment pods facing each other. Chryl is watching what she described as a *murder documentary* on one of the particle panes they use as giant monitors in the adjacent room.

Electra wanted to take longer to inspect every piece of medical equipment and ask the million questions she had, but the desire to leave this place won out. Better to get it over with quickly. Still, she only crawled into her assigned chamber to begin the DNA scrubbing process after being thoroughly convinced the procedure wouldn't hurt. Now she and Res6 are facing each other through thick panes of glass, each in their own healing chambers. They seem to be engaged in a staring contest, which she has no intention of losing.

"You're really into my freckles," she teases loudly enough that he can hear through the pod's glass and hoping it causes him to blink first.

He must not know the game because he doesn't hesitate as he rolls his eyes. "Are you just blurting out all your thoughts now? Is that something people did during your time?"

She can't help but return the eye roll.

"Should I try it?" He shrugs as if he's really considering it.

"Yes!" she shouts. Anything to distract her while the program finishes.

"You're really into snuggling against my chest," he shouts.

The smile slips from her face. Does that freak him out? Was he only holding her to stop her from crying? And if so, why did it feel so real? So right?

The corner of his mouth tips up, like he's nervous that he's said the wrong thing.

"I do, it seems," she finally says.

His smile blossoms like she's given him hope. Shit. Did she mean to do that?

"I think that means you like either me, my shirts, or my chest. All three?" he asks, earning him another eye roll. He laughs. "You're cheating. You can't roll your eyes twice. You've already used that gesture."

"You're demented," she says, and they go back to staring at each other.

His eyes twinkle. The momentary reprieve from her heavier emotions brought on by his teasing is causing disorienting things to happen in her body. Warm, floating sensations she's pretty sure aren't a side effect of the healing. She's fairly certain they're caused by him.

16 – Warmth and Triumph

Electra

"So, I guess I'm healed?" Electra asks, stepping out of her chamber. Res6 is sitting on a workbench stool he brought over so they could continue their little staring game when his session ended. He was sweet to stick around and stop her from spiraling, because that's exactly what she would have done if she'd been left alone.

"Yes, Electra, you're healed. The scanner says your cancer risk is now zero." He keeps staring as tears bubble up and stream down her cheeks—though this round of staring is less amusement and more deer-in-headlights. "I don't understand. I thought that would make you happy?"

She fans herself as wave after wave of emotion hits her. She will not die like her mom did. It should be a relief, but it's overwhelming to know that she had to get hit by a trolley and end up in the future to stop it from happening. "I am. It's all so much to process. Can we please leave this place now?"

Res6 eyes her. "Since this is my office, it's likely not the last time you'll be here."

She lifts trembling hands and wipes her eyes. "True, but today, it's a crime scene. Remember? I need to get out of here."

Res6 grips her shoulders, pulling her into his chest. God, she's crying into his chest again. But it feels so good, so safe, that she can't seem to push him away.

He squeezes her with one arm. His other gently strokes her hair. His care is so warm and inviting that it makes her miss the sanctuary of his bed—

"If we go back to my unit, you aren't allowed to lock yourself in the bedroom."

"You can't read my mind now, can you?" She glares at the chamber she just exited like it's the bad guy.

He chuckles. "No bed, Electra."

What else is one supposed to do after enduring a life-threatening situation? Have a party? While she's extremely grateful to be alive and have her genetic predisposition for disease eliminated, for a moment there, the other shoe felt precariously close to dropping. Realistically, how much trauma can one woman endure? Hasn't she been through enough for one lifetime? She wants—no, *needs*—a break. Just a few years, maybe ten or twenty, without a tragedy, thank you very much.

"Electra, the tests show that your hearing is fine, so that must mean you're ignoring me," he says.

Apparently, he won't let her slink back to his bedroom to hide out. "I'm not ignoring you. I'm in my head. Sorry. Do you have a better plan?"

He looks thoughtful for a moment.

"Oh God, please tell me you're not cooking up another one of your outings."

He huffs. "How about ice cream?"

"We were just robbed at gunpoint, and you want ice cream?" How is he not lagging from the aftermath of an adrenaline spike like a normal person? "That's it. You're definitely a robot. What about your leg?"

He gives her an exasperated groan. "It's fully healed, and even if I still had some lingering pain, it wouldn't be enough to prevent us from getting ice cream." When she doesn't respond, he adds, "We can go to the lake simulation I told you about—not the holo-lake center. This one's in the simulation chamber in my tower."

At this point, she's feeling a little lightheaded and jittery from the adrenaline overload. A private lake simulation might be nice. She nods, understanding. "Because water is soothing."

"Exactly! You're welcome to congratulate me on my excellent idea." He offers her a sly grin, and she wonders if he's pretending like she's a manupartner again, or just finally getting used to being around a real woman. "Whenever you're ready, I'll take my compliment."

She laughs loudly. "That's never going to happen, so don't hold your breath."

"Why would I hold my breath?" His eyes narrow. "Another metaphor?"

"Yeah. It's a saying from my time—a hyperbole that means something is likely to take a long time if it ever even happens at all."

"So no compliment then," he mutters, brushing it off as if her idiosyncrasies are nothing more than a minor blip. "You'll see. The simulation will help."

She hates to admit it, but he's probably right. Sleeping away her latest trauma isn't the answer. She needs to be occupied so she doesn't spiral. "Synthetic ice cream and faux nature sound great."

His hand presses against the small of her back, and he guides her toward the elevators. She can't help but soak in the grounding warmth of his touch, despite all the reasons it's a capital-B Bad Idea. Speaking of bad ideas . . .

"Don't we need to collect Chryl?"

Res6 grimaces. "I suppose."

They collect Chryl, who has moved onto an *abduction documentary,* and head toward the SAT garages. It's a twenty-minute ride between his office in M Quadrant and the residential A Quadrant tower, which houses the upscale simulation chambers along with his penthouse unit. With Chryl in tow, it feels much longer.

From the backseat, the manupartner vibrates with excitement. "I looove it when we go fast!"

"Recycling her is an option, correct?" Electra asks, smirking. Not that she really wants Chryl recycled; she's not entirely convinced the manupartner isn't something real-adjacent. She'd just rather Chryl not be around all the time.

"I'm fine with that too." Chryl reaches forward, squeezing Res6's shoulders. "Whatever my handsome man needs."

He ignores Chryl, addressing Electra instead. "I thought you were eager to leave the lab."

"I would have gladly stayed another ten minutes to get the deal done." She glances over her shoulder at the perpetually grinning woman. "No offense, Chryl."

"None taken, hotcakes. We are feelings twins!"

Feelings twins? Oh God, Chryl must mean they're thinking the same thing. She really ought to ask if manupartners have ever murdered their owners. Or their owner's other manupartners. The thought might not be concerning outside of Chryl's sudden interest in murder and abduction.

When no one speaks for an extended pause, Chryl fills the silence. "I loooove ice cream. I can't wait to try it."

Electra shakes off the thought. Chryl probably doesn't even understand half of what she's saying.

When they exit the SAT, the same blonde attendant from before rushes out to greet them. "Welcome home, sir!"

The attendant's eyes widen as he opens the back door and helps Chryl out. He escorts her around the SAT and takes Electra's hand, while Chryl takes his other arm. The attendant, now slack-jawed, lifts her phone, pointing it at them. Electra can only imagine what they look like to her.

Res6 holds up a hand. "No pictures, please."

The woman lowers her device, frowning. Electra is about to give her a self-satisfied smile when she notices something on the woman's face that wasn't there earlier. She squeezes Res6's hand to get his attention. She nods to the attendant and lowers her voice to ask, "Did she have a procedure to get freckles or are those drawn on?"

Res6's nose wrinkles. "Not sure."

The woman responds to their staring by lifting her chin as if she's on display. "Do you like them?"

On Res6's opposite side, Chryl bounces. "Oh, I get it. She got freckles like yours, Electra, to impress Daddy!"

The woman's pale skin flushes scarlet.

Res6 clears his throat. "They look nice."

As they walk away, Electra glances back to see the woman fanning herself, making the eye roll she can't hold back entirely justified.

The ice cream stand is on floor one hundred, along with a dozen other food stalls set up like a mall cafeteria.

Chryl steps up to the counter. "I would like that one." She points to a rainbow-colored pan of ice cream. "Ten scoops!"

The employee glances at Res6 for approval. "Two scoops will be fine."

"I want two scoops!" Chryl corrects.

Electra orders chocolate mint and, in an interesting twist, Res6 orders one called balsamic strawberry. A giggle escapes as the employee hands Res6 the cone.

He turns to her, eyes narrowing. "What?"

"I totally thought you were going to get vanilla."

He chuffs, peering down at her as he takes a lick. "I am anything but vanilla, Electra Lynch."

She glances away quickly, her stomach doing a series of acrobatic stunts she'd just as soon avoid. How does he do that? Right, he's definitely pretending she's a manupartner again, though he isn't, dare she say, *flirting* with Chryl. No, even if he's flirting with her, *remember what happened last time, Electra? He fooled you into thinking he gave a shit, then got all concerned about his precious company. But then he saved you and let the men take the cases.* But then a murder, even if it were a manupartner as far as the world knew, would be bad press.

She takes a lick of her ice cream, deciding to ignore him.

When they turn for the elevators, they're met by a handful of gawking bystanders holding phones pointed in their direction. Chryl steps between the onlookers and Res6, holding a palm out. "No pictures, please."

"At least she's good for something," Electra mutters.

Res6 chuckles as the elevator doors slide closed.

"I'm good for a great many things, hotcakes." Chryl looks her dead in the eye and gives her an exaggerated wink.

Wait. Does Chryl think they're in competition for Res6's affection? Or is she still angling for a three-way? To what extent do the manupartners retain human instincts or are they purely a product of genetic programming? She needs to add that to the list of things to ask Res6 about next time they're alone. Not that she finds the monstrosities interesting. She's merely curious.

It takes fifteen minutes for them to get Chryl set up in her own simulation chamber. She requested a song and dance theme, claiming "I've got the music in me!" which Electra's pretty sure is the title of a 1970s pop song.

"Well, that's something," she says, walking past the counter for the fifth time. Is Res6's pacing rubbing off on her? Oh God. She stops abruptly. It's just her normal anxious energy vibrating through her that needs an outlet. She's got to start the column soon and give it one.

He finishes getting their lake scene ordered and takes her hand, guiding her into the dark chamber. He presses a few illuminated buttons on the control panel, and the lights come on. She takes in the scene, from the expansive clear blue sky to the holographic trees and the quaint round pond they encircle. The real-looking wood planks under her feet creak as she steps onto them.

If she didn't know better, she'd believe she's stepping onto an old wooden dock—the kind you see on quaint little lakes in the states people always refer to as having upstate sections. Upstate New York, Upstate Vermont, etcetera. Not that those places exist anymore. She slips off her shoes and sets them aside. As she walks across the planks toward the crystalline water, the planks even feel real, as if her bare feet are touching weathered woodgrain. She glances back at Res6, who's staring at her feet and shaking his head with the barest hint of a grin.

Warmth flutters through her. *Pointedly ignoring that.* "Is the water real?"

"Kind of. It's a shallow pool meant to look and feel real. I wouldn't recommend getting in fully, but you can do this." He walks up beside her, kicking off his own shoes. He sits down on the edge of the dock and rolls up his pant legs before dipping his toes in the water.

All she can do is stare at where his neatly manicured toes graze the surface, creating little ripples. There's something about seeing him like this that feels intimate. Humanizing. Slowly, as if she might scare off what could be the *real him*, she takes a seat next to him. There probably aren't many people who get to see him like this. Which feels especially true considering what she knows about his brother.

"Is it cold?"

He chuckles, gesturing to the water. "See for yourself."

She dips her toes in. The water is pleasantly tepid. She swishes her feet, splashing a little onto her jumpsuit, only then noticing the simulated lapping sounds and breeze.

She's about to comment on it when she notices he's staring across the lake to a cabin on the other side. He clears his throat. "I'm sorry you had to experience that earlier. I'm ashamed that my negligence exposed you to those men."

Her heart clenches, her own woes suddenly forgotten. He reaches for his knees, but she takes his hand, cradling it in her lap like he did hers when her scan results came in. "Res6, look at me." He does, albeit reluctantly. She shows him their hands. "This is real. I'm real. You aren't going through this alone, and that wasn't your fault. Those men made that choice. You did everything you could to stop them."

"But if I hadn't wanted you to get the scans, or if I had better security—"

"Let me stop you there." He blinks, but she presses forward. "If I hadn't done the scans, I wouldn't have known about my cancer risk and gotten it taken care of. You were right. They needed to be done."

"I could have brought you somewhere else—"

"Why would you do that when you have the equipment in your lab? I can see you're eager to shoulder the blame, but everything isn't a result of your choices. You aren't God, or Zorg, or whatever. Sometimes things just happen. Believe me, I've waded through enough bullshit life stuff where I tried to figure out the whys, only to discover that sometimes no matter what we do, we can't control everything."

He swallows, and there is such static in the moment that she thinks he's about to tell her something important. Maybe about Jerme? Instead, he says, "There's another immersion chamber for the ocean, but it's from somewhere warmer. The Caribbean, I think. There's also one where you can take a nature walk on the bank of a river."

Typically, whatever she's thinking pops right out of her mouth without a second thought, but now she's terrified of saying the wrong thing. He's drawn to water for its therapeutic benefits, which he clearly needs. She has to approach this carefully. "I like water too," she says, and instantly realizes how stupid that sounds.

As if he senses what she's doing, he says, "There is no need to coddle me, Electra. I'm not a child."

She huffs, only half agitated. It *was* a stupid thing to say, and they're quite the pair if she considers it. "Okay, I'll try again. I find water soothing, but you clearly do too."

"What makes you say that?" he asks, sighing as if it pains him to ask.

"All of your favorite particle pane settings are of water scenes."

He lets out a low chuckle, shaking his head. "I can't believe you noticed."

"Well, I did. So *why* do you like water? What about it draws you to it?"

"You're prying again, *Dear Electra*. I'm not writing to your advice column—"

"Which is a great idea!" she interjects.

"Which I don't want to forbid, but would strongly encourage you to reconsider," he says, frowning.

Now is probably not the time to retrace the argument. "Well, I won't apologize for asking you about why you're drawn to water, which you still haven't replied to, by the way."

Long moments drift by as they sit on the dock, staring at the scene before them, Electra patiently waiting for him to speak. His expression has become serene. Is he really that opposed to talking about why he likes water?

She clears her throat. "I can start making up crazy guesses in my head, like how right now you're fantasizing about filling glass after glass of muddy lake water to the brim and chugging it. Or maybe you've always dreamed of going skinny dipping, and you think now's your chance. You're just trying to work up the nerve to tell me."

"If you tell me all your crazy hypotheses, they aren't in your head." His hint of a grin has turned into the full thing. He's so appealing to look at . . . it's unfair.

She rolls her eyes, nudging him playfully. "Sometimes I can't tell if you're socially challenged or just being difficult."

"I'm not difficult. If either of us is difficult, it's you."

"So, are you going to tell me?" she presses.

"Zephyr, woman. You can't let things go, can you?"

"No, it's a life skill I'm rather proud of. You were saying . . . about water." She grins back, grateful for the lighthearted moment. During the robbery when the man had the gun to her temple, she was so scared, she thought she might faint. She'd never been that afraid in her life. She's surprised her wobbly knees kept her upright. Afterward, her nerves were firing, keeping her going, but now that the adrenaline has dissipated, she feels like lying back on the dock and never moving again. Their banter is the only thing giving her energy right now, and she's eager for it to continue.

A dozen feet in front of them, a large brown fish launches itself into the air with a splash, flops as it hangs for a second, and crashes back into the water, spraying them both. She covers her gaping mouth, pointing to where the fish landed. "Oh my God. Tell me that wasn't real."

"That wasn't real," he obliges.

"But it looked so real!" she squeals. "Okay, that's why you like water. I get it. You keep hoping that one day the fish will become real and swim over and offer to be your friend." She bumps her head against his shoulder. "That's so sweet."

"Of all the people I might have accidentally brought back, why did it have to be the craziest one?" Res6 tilts his head to the ceiling—or sky, according to the artificial image Electra's seeing. Then his broad shoulders slump, defeated. "I like the water because it makes me feel at peace. I think it's the sounds, though I like to watch it move. The pattern of ripples or the rhythm of waves. Something about it calms me."

She nods, biting back every therapy statistic and *did you know* that's filtering into her mind. "That makes perfect sense. In San Francisco, where I lived, the water was very cold, but in the summer, the bite was refreshing. You couldn't stay in long, though. If it was sunny, it helped. The sun felt like a warm hug on your skin. Oh, and the water was so salty. Sometimes we would see seals swimming through the kelp forest, splashing in the surf. Occasionally we'd even see whales or big sharks, which was cool."

She's unsure why she's telling him this, but his contemplative expression urges her to keep going.

"The sand felt coarse yet soft on your feet. There's something grounding about walking in nature. I think that is the biggest thing I'm going to miss about waking up in the future. Immersion in nature."

"We are in nature," he says.

She laughs. "I keep trying to tell you, nothing fake will ever come close to the real thing." Her breath catches as she realizes the implications of what she said.

Another long pause goes by, and she thinks that's the end of it, but he surprises her. "I think I'm beginning to see your point."

At his minor but critical confession, she squeezes his hand. When he squeezes back, her chest explodes in a cocktail of warmth and triumph.

17 – Another, Better Electra

Electra

November 1, 2390.

The small breakthrough in the simulation chamber, a.k.a. the HUGE confession Res6 let slip, is enough to convince Electra that her advice column is of vital importance. She hasn't been in the future long, and she's already effecting positive change. As a bonus, pouring her energy into a good cause will help ease her anxiety and sense of powerlessness brought up by the robbery. There is no way this is her avoiding her feelings about it. If Janet were here to see her now, she would be so proud. The thought only causes a momentary pang of loss. *See Janet, look how good I'm doing!*

She leans back on the couch, draping herself with the blanket that she took the liberty of ordering. It's kind of amazing that she can get onto the Shopazon app and anything she orders is in the smartwaiter delivery box within the hour. Of course, she's only bought the bare necessities, considering she's not spending her own money. And the prices of everything are shocking. There is no real way to equate it to the value of stuff during her time, but the numbers feel huge. Still, she needs her own unicoin, so if she needs something, she can buy it for herself. Freeloading off him isn't right, even if he feels like he owes it to her. It's her job to take care of herself, so it's up to her to figure out how to do that. That's why she came up with a new way to frame the column—the only avenue she can think of to earn money.

And the validation you're still chasing.

Shut up, Janet.

She discovered that if you get enough subscribers on FrogBlog, you can offer a paid subscription. It's not like she can get a job as a bartender like she did in her time while trying to make it as a writer. The column is really the perfect solution.

"Res6," she says. He jerks, glancing up from his desk. He's been extra twitchy since the robbery. She asked him if he was okay a few times, but he plastered on his fake smile and lied to her, so she stopped pushing. He'll tell her what's on his mind if and when he's ready. She needs to tackle the issue she's been stewing over. Here goes nothing! "I need a job."

He blinks as if the word *job* is foreign to him.

"Why?"

"Money, obviously."

"I have plenty of unicoin. Just worry about being happy."

"But what if I want something expensive?"

"I showed you the app. Buy it."

"But that's your money. I need my own."

He raises a brow. "Is there something wrong with my money?"

She sighs, slouching back on the couch. "No."

"Good. No need for a job then." He looks back at his system.

Her *plan* isn't *going to plan*. She needs to up the ante. What can she say she wants that might make him flinch? "What if I want a system of my own?" He glances back up, cocking his head in interest. "And a desk, with a fancy chair like yours."

"Buy it, Electra. Treat my money as if it's yours. We've been over this."

"That's not the point." Heaven forbid a woman wants financial agency. Though she's pretty confident that Res6 would never try to leverage his money to control her. He probably wouldn't even think of it, considering that the equalization event she read about allegedly killed the patriarchal gender constructs of her time. Apparently, when the world fell into disarray, people stopped clinging to gender norms. Everyone did what they could to survive. As much as she was a feminist during her time, she recognizes it's her own internalized patriarchal lens that needs to be shifted. Not that the future doesn't have its own problems—ahem: *manupartners*. Still, the modern gender-egalitarian paradigm is one of the reasons she trusts him not to use his money to control her.

Besides, it's not like she would actually splurge on something like that when the tablet works just fine. Especially with someone else's money.

"Then what is the point?" he asks. She doesn't answer because she's not entirely sure of the point herself. "Do I need to get you your own account that isn't tied to me?"

"If I don't have any money to put into it—"

"I will put the money into it. Then it will be yours."

"Why are you being so difficult?" She glances at the particle panes, which display a stream scene, then back to him. His brows arch as if implying, *See, you're the difficult one.* "I feel guilty taking your money, okay? I didn't earn it, so I don't deserve it."

He grins. "Oh, well, let me help you with that. I earned it, and I want you to have some of it." She opens her mouth to argue, but he holds a hand up. "You've been through an ordeal that is a direct result of my choices. Therefore, I think you deserve it." She frowns. "If you need to occupy your time, there are plenty of things you can do. What about writing books again?" he asks. "That's a good idea."

"No," she grumbles.

"Why not? I've read all your alien books. They're good," he says. "If you want a job, why don't you do that?"

She shakes her head. "I don't know if I can create characters future people will relate to." She waves a hand in his direction. "You don't count."

Truthfully, after years of query rejections, she isn't sure she can go through it again. She'd been weeks away from giving up when a publisher reached out because they saw her talking about her books on social media and made her the offer that set everything in motion. After over a hundred noes from agents, she'd come to the determination that there wasn't a place for her in that world. Now, with everything she's going through, it feels too risky. Like exposing herself to that level of vulnerability would be what finally causes her to lose hope.

"Approach it from a different angle, then," he suggests.

"What do you mean?"

"Like that part where Felicity tames a flying lizard monster and saves Bastian from the marauders, so he thanks her by pleasuring her atop said monster during their escape." It's her turn to blink at him in amazement. "I feel like people now would find that very enjoyable. Maybe you could even partner with a simulation chamber and have them recreate scenes from the books for people to act out."

Of all the scenes he would bring up . . . Well, he invented sex clones, so maybe having him read her sexy scenes isn't that disturbing. "Are you suggesting I write erotica to relate to future people?"

His brow wrinkles. "Is that what it's called?"

"While there is absolutely nothing wrong with erotica, you realize sex wasn't the focus of my books, right?"

"Yes, I realize that. It was only a suggestion."

She can't help but laugh. What a pair they would make—him with his manupartners and her with her erotic simulation chambers. Truthfully, she's surprised they don't already exist. "Okay then. Thanks for the suggestion."

"You're welcome," he says in complete seriousness, turning back to his desk and assuming the intensely focused gaze that tells her he's gone back to whatever he's been preoccupied with since the robbery. Which she totally gets. She's been a little on edge too, and it's not even her company. Recovering a sense of security will take time for them both. Not that she ever had one to begin with.

A few minutes pass, and she catches him stealing brief glances at her.

Eventually he says, "Are you going to order the desk and system?"

"No," she says, not looking up from her tablet. Is that what's been on his mind?

"Why not?"

"I don't need it. The tablet is fine." She's clutching it like he might take it away from her.

"I see," he says, eyeing her tight grip on the device. "How are you going to write thousands of words on that? Unless you'd prefer to go back to the lab to get an m-volt implant?"

A shudder racks her spine. After the robbery, going back to the lab is the last thing she wants to do. "No thanks. And I told you, I'm not writing books."

"Then what are you doing on there? Writing Brain Dumps about how handsome I am?" he asks, wearing a delicious smirk. She isn't sure she can handle it if he becomes charming, too.

She almost reminds him she's not a manupartner, but she's pretty sure he's stopped pretending she is, considering his confession. Instead, she says, "That's not funny. Remember, my Brain Dumps are off limits." God, if he only knew what she *was* writing about him. She adds a dramatic groan for emphasis and turns away, hiding her embarrassing blush. "I told you I'm starting an advice column, so I'm doing research and making notes."

This catches his attention. He stands and walks over to the L-shaped couch. "Electra, I asked you to reconsider." When she only arches a stubborn brow, he presses, "We should probably discuss this further. We could go to a simula—"

"This isn't up for discussion," she snaps, cradling the tablet to her chest.

He sighs, running his hand through his obscenely touchable-looking hair. "I told you it isn't advisable. It is my responsibility to protect you."

"And I told you that no one will find out my identity. I've already created a username and have friends. Everyone thinks I'm just another MSP citizen."

"Electra—" he starts.

"Don't Electra me. You get to keep Chryl, and I disagree with that. That means I get to have my advice column." Her argument feels a little shaky given that she's living in his apartment and eating his food. He's intent on her spending his money though, so for the time being, she supposes she'll drop the Chryl issue for now.

His lips press together, and he eyes her like he's debating something. "I think you're underestimating the danger. Bexly and his team just finished the physical inventory, and your remaining DNA samples were in the cache the robbers stole."

"Oh my God. Are you only telling me so I won't do my column?" she asks. Would he do that? At least his twitchiness makes sense now. He's worried about her.

He inhales deeply, as though this conversation pains him. "Of course not. I've told you repeatedly, your safety is my primary concern."

The conviction in his voice is almost desperate. Her heart squeezes. "Okay. I believe you. So, you had more of my DNA?" Why hasn't she thought to ask if there was more of it? "Wait, can other MSP citizens order manupartners that look just like me?"

He shakes his head. "I should have pulled it. Destroyed it. This is my fault."

She isn't really interested in placing blame. The more concerning issue is what her DNA floating out there in the world means for her. "Was it just mine?"

"No, yours was one of hundreds of samples, but all from the same fifty-year span. Bexly told the inspectors they were specifically looking for that period. It's possible it was just happenstance that they got yours."

"Have they figured out what they're trying to do with it?" she asks.

"Unfortunately, no. Inspector Wanda assures me they're working to get to the bottom of it. We've given them the biological signature of each of the stolen samples in case they catch a manupartner with matching DNA."

She leans forward and buries her head in her hands. *Think Electra.* What is the worst thing that can happen if someone has your DNA? Could they know about her and somehow use it to hunt her down? That one robber sure gave her the impression he knew she was real, but that was probably her paranoia. How could he know? No—this is her scarcity mindset creating threats where there are none.

Oh shit, if they bring another her back, she might bump into herself. That's freaky, but not technically dangerous. Unless the other Electra comes up with a better way to fit into the future than her Dear Electra column—*STOP IT, Electra! You're spiraling.*

Thanks, Janet. Okay, be logical. "Wait—you said people from my time are mutts and the DNA storage techniques back then were questionable. What if that's causing the glitches? Tommy said there are rumors about more people like me—what if we're all from the same fifty-year window and somehow the robbers know that?" She gasps as her story comes together. "Could they be trying to bring back more people from the past?"

"I want to say it's far-fetched, but the more I think about it, the more I think it's a legitimate concern," he says.

"Won't that be bad for the future of manupartners? From what I've learned, the government shuts down anything they view as threatening their perfectly ordered society—" His face has become ashen. "Oh. Res6, I'm sorry. I didn't mean to—"

There's that fake smile again. He almost looks like he believes his own reassurances as he says, "Don't worry, Electra. Everything is going to be just fine."

An hour ago, Res6 went into his room, the Likely Labyrinth of Lasciviousness, with a couple of bottles of water—probably to work out or something, considering the muscles and that he never seems to go to the gym. Unless somehow future people can maintain their physiques without working out. It's probably in the medical technology and innovations video she'd been avoiding, which she can now watch since her predisposition for disease has been eliminated.

She glances at the *locked* door. It's only fair that she has a secret of her own. She lifts the phone and takes a few quick selfies before uploading them to an avatar maker. With a few clicks, she uploads the best one to her profile along with a bio vague enough to make Res6 happy. Finally, she copy/pastes the text for her call for submissions post into the first blog entry.

The thing is, Res6 is right. It is a little eerie that they don't know what the robbers want with the stolen DNA. But it's not like it was only her DNA they were after. And what if it takes the inspectors months to figure it out? She'll go mad if she can't start working toward a tangible goal. So, the benefits outweigh the risks. She needs to do this before she loses her nerve.

With that decision made, there's only one thing left to do. *Besides not telling Res6.*

She hits Post.

As soon as she sees the post live on her feed, joy fills her insides. Posting it was the right decision because this is exactly what society needs—what she needs. Her Dear Electra column is going to be big. She sits there for several minutes, staring at the entry. It's not like she's going to get flooded with responses yet. Give it some time.

Surely her For You Page on the FrogBlog app has something inter-esting. She needs a good topic to get going. She could always fabricate the first handful of questions, but since she's going for authenticity, that feels wrong.

As she scrolls, an image catches her eye. It's her and Chryl standing on either side of Res6, who's staring directly at the camera wearing one of those squinty-eyed cool guy expressions. Did he know they were being photographed? Plan it, even?

She clicks on the post. The blogger is none other than the annoying woman from the private SAT garage. Her username is Res6Reverie, and the profile pic is a selfie of her and Res6 dated 2386. His hair is shorter and even more tightly cropped on the sides than it is now, making him look like a Ken doll. The woman has her arm around his waist and is staring adoringly at him.

Did they have a fling? The woman casually offered him sex—in front of her, no less. Who says that was the first time, and he hasn't taken her up on the offer before? Internally, she cringes. Ugh, she's being so embarrassing, ruminating about his sex life.

She goes back to the brief entry that speculates whether two manu-partners is the new trend, along with a quote from the woman. *"My close friend Res6 told me he finds the new manupartner prototype's freckles add to her authenticity. Did you hear that, Res6Revelers? Run to your aestheticians, because spots and speckles may up your chances for a heart-pounding night with MSP's favorite bachelor. My prediction is that getting freckles is going to be the next big cosmetic treatment after the world sees this!"*

No. Way. She scrolls down to the—holy shit—thousands of comments. Most of them are about how hot Res6 is. Some of them are people saying they never thought of getting a second manupartner or about how unaffordable that would be. A few dozen commenters render their opinion on Electra's freckles, not surprisingly calling her everything from defective to exotic and everything in between. What astonishes her is the number of users who claim they're going to ask their aesthetician for "speckles" on their next visit.

For some reason the entire thing irritates her. That is the only explanation for why she shoots up off the couch and marches over to Res6's Room of Possibly Demented Things. She bangs on the door, and he pokes his head out. Through the crack, she can see Chryl lazily sprawled across half the bed, fully clothed, thank God, playing with a corded belt like a cat might. The sight only fuels her irritation.

"Might I have a word with you?" she barks.

He steps out wearing only a towel. She has to cough to keep from choking. Holy Mother of all that is holy, his physique matches his face. He's a Greek god. Adonis or Michelangelo's David or worse!

"Yes?" he asks.

Her gaze travels across his flushed skin, and lower to where the towel hangs precariously. *Bad idea, Electra!* "I thought you said you weren't sleeping with her!" *Oh God, why did you say that? You're not jealous. You can't be—that's Chryl's thing!*

He smirks as if he can read her thoughts. "I did a quick workout while you were on your tablet, so I had a shower. Is that a problem?"

Okay, so her workout assumption was correct. Still, her cheeks heat. "No. Feel free to get dressed." *In front of Chryl, who doesn't matter because she's not a real person. Who cares if she sees him naked? This is what he's used to. He's not you and doesn't have your modesty or interpersonal conventions.*

"Electra, what did you need to have a word with me about?" he asks, not budging.

When she forces herself to meet his eyes, she finds mirth dancing in their golden depths. She lifts the tablet and holds it between them as if it might somehow substitute for words. But she sees the image that irritated her in the first place, and suddenly the libertine standing in front of her isn't so perfect. She clears her throat. "Looks like your girlfriend got a picture of us. Have your sales figures gone up like you expected?"

His eyes narrow. He takes the tablet, scanning the FrogBlog entry. "She must have followed us and got the picture. You look good, at least."

"Res6, I don't care if I look good or not. That isn't what I'm upset about." Maybe she's the stupid one for even trying to bring this up to him; he didn't even deny the girlfriend bit or sleeping with Chryl.

Apparently, he's decided silence is his best approach, as he only stands there with his brows raised, waiting for her to speak.

"I don't enjoy being your advertisement," she says.

"But we agreed to a few public outings as a part of our bargain."

"I know, but I changed my mind. Seeing this"—she points to the image—"makes me feel cheap. Like I'm some automation—number one of two—on your arm. For your pleasure."

He scoffs. "This is decidedly not for my pleasure."

"Look at what people are saying. They're fawning over you and your two manupartners like you're some type of sex god. It's unreal."

"Electra," he soothes, the corner of his mouth twitching like he's trying to repress a grin. "I hear your concerns, but I didn't arrange that. Because of my status in the municipality, people will photograph us. It is inevitable. The only way to avoid it is to hide out in this unit, which is not advisable, as we've already determined. I don't deny that I appreciate the advertising potential—"

"At least there's *something* you're not denying!" She snatches the tablet out of his hands and turns to march into her room.

He inhales sharply. "Oh Zorg, are you jealous?"

Wildly! her traitorous inner narrator shouts. She freezes. "No."

His voice is closer as he says, "I didn't sleep with that woman or Chryl, and it's been years since I last had a manupartner."

Her heart thumps wildly in her chest. "Years? Why?"

She can feel the heat of him at her back. So close—too close. Mother Mary save her, he's in a towel. She grasps the tablet tighter to keep her hands from doing anything foolish.

Without even the faintest touch, he leans down and says, "I got bored," right into her ear.

The low gravel of his voice sends a shiver up her spine. Seconds go by. When she finally builds up the nerve to do something stupid like kiss him again, the door to his room clicks shut. Did she wait too long to make a move?

She glances over her shoulder to find the space he just occupied vacant, leaving her alone with her throbbing . . . She swallows, trying and failing to ignore the sparkling sensations coursing through her.

Giddy, humming, and delicious sensations she hasn't felt since waking up in the future. Like she's only now become fully activated.

She was so angry moments ago. He even accused her of being jealous, which is completely ridiculous. *He got bored.* God, and the breathy way he said it. Especially after his lakeside confession—well, the implications are intriguing. She slips inside her bedroom, needing to extinguish this feeling before it gets any worse. More like *quench it.*

Would it make her a hypocrite if she were to lie down on the bed and slip a hand beneath her waistband to see what he did to her? Just as a sort of measuring stick to see if she's really alive. She sets the tablet on the nightstand and dims the lights. Maybe not a hypocrite exactly. The bed creaks as she crawls onto it and lies back. Definitely not a hypocrite. She's only human, after all.

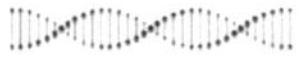

November 5, 2390.

Today is going to be the day. There will be messages in my inbox. My column will take off.

Wearing a forced smile, Electra opens the FrogBlog app. Her heart skips. There's a message. She taps her inbox.

CONGRATULATIONS! YOU'VE WON MSP'S FAVORITE COSMETIC TREATMENT!

The preview shows a grinning man with a full face of freckles. There are no other messages. Her heart sinks.

It's been five days since she posted the introduction, and crickets. She copies the text and posts it again, like she did yesterday, and the day before, and the day before. Maybe it just hasn't found the right viewers yet. But not a single person has submitted a question or even liked her post. It's that feeling again—the sting of every agent's *No* that made her question if she was even meant to be a writer. She should just give up. Take down her posts. Delete her account. Maybe she and her ideas don't have a place in this world.

18 – Cool! A Dead Body!

Res6

Res6 and Lextr watch as robotic articulated arms lower his most recent Jerme failure into the Biomass Recovery Vat. The benefit of Electra being a late sleeper is that he and Tommy can get the failed trials out of his bedroom without Electra noticing, like they did that morning.

Lextr insisted he watch the sixth trial using synthetic DNA get recycled to convince him to move onto the organic samples. Samples that are still safely stored in the BioBank. He almost wept when Lextr told him.

"How many more partially formed copies of your brother are we going to recycle before we start the real trials?" Lextr asks as the trial's arm floats by along with deteriorating parts of several other units.

Seeing a mirror image of your own face—though not fully formed—liquefy as it hits the reabsorption coagulum really ups the stakes. He swallows, the lump in his throat painful. "You've made your point."

Lextr follows him out of the viewing area past a group of school-children on a field trip. Giving the kids a chance to see science in action is one of the many things that sets CHOICElover apart from the rest. As a lab tech guides them onto the viewing platform, a child squeals, "Cool! A dead body!"

He chuckles as they enter the elevator. Jerme would have probably hung around and pointed out all the gross things for the kids to ob-serve. Lextr's right. It's time to get serious.

"Where are we going, sir?" Lextr asks, almost having to skip to keep up with Res6's long strides.

All the emotions—the anticipation, the fear, the self-doubt—threaten to erupt out of him, but he needs to stay calm if he's going to do this. There's no room for emotional outbursts in sci-ence. If he isn't performing at his peak, he could accidentally corrupt one of the ten available samples. He strides determinedly ahead. "The BioBank."

Half an hour later, they have the samples and are in the designated Neuronic Gene Infusion lab, sterilized and suited up in their biohazard kits. Lextr watches over his shoulder as he meticulously psion-splices nucleic imprints using the robotic PSI-splicer to edit them into RNA collected from his brother's first organic sample.

Splicing all the pieces back together is the tricky part. Thank Zorg for the containment suit; the sweat dripping off him in rivulets might contaminate the delicate sample. After several nerve-racking hours, he has a stable protein. With deceptively steady hands, he places it into the tissue replicator with Jerme's original sample, a nuclease enzyme binder, and the raw organic building block material. It takes another hour in the accelerated neural mesh incubator for the mixture to form a usable coagulum. Using synthesized DNA like they do for customer orders is so much more straightforward.

He siphons samples from different sections of the specimen, dropping them into the synth-gel oscillator. Once the bio-plates are ready, he runs the BioLume Gene Scanner over them to test their viability.

Lextr, who's been tracking right alongside him, studies the readings on the screen. "Looks viable."

He grins broadly. "It does." The next step is to package the kit and take it home to begin the activation process. After nearly a hundred years, he can hardly wait the seven days it takes to grow and activate him. He glances at the time stamp on the scan: November 7, 2390. The anniversary of Jerme's death is in one week. But if he's successful, he'll no longer associate it with his death. It will also be his rebirth.

19 – Floating in MSP

Electra

November 7, 2390.

As soon as Electra wakes up, she reaches for the tablet she's developing a concerning attachment to. Please let there be messages today!

She taps the weird little frog icon, closing her eyes as the app opens. Nervously, she cracks one eye open, then the other. "Oh my God!" There are a dozen messages. She eagerly opens the first one:

Dear Electra,

I'm a 67-year-old man living in C Quadrant, and I feel like I'm living a double life. I go to work and my FRIENDS groups and act like I'm happy, but I never really feel alive until I'm in the simulation chamber, slipping into my spacesuit. As soon as they activate the antigravity field and I start

220

floating, I come alive. My question is how do I tell others I may not be meant for this world?

Sincerely,

Floating in MSP

Electra groans, deletes the message, and opens the next. She needs a reasonable question related to human connection that she can actually answer. Oh, this one is promising.

Dear Electra,

I, F141, am having regular, very vigorous sex with three men as none of us can currently afford manupartners. On the surface, everything seems ideal and we all agree we want the same thing out of the arrangement, but I suspect I'm missing out on something and I keep asking myself, is there more?

Electra reads the words hungrily. She knew it! People are craving more.

What I'm wondering is, should I ask the men if they would like to add two women to our dynamic, or should I just experiment with these women on my own?

She slumps back, deflated. That's what she gets for getting her hopes up. Wait. Here's one. She opens the next message, whose subject reads:

Are Relationships Dead for Good?

The message:

Dear Electra,

I'm 42 and identify as nonbinary. I have a confession. I think I have a crush on my longtime neighbor. We often go to the sports center together and share meals in her unit. I love being around her, and I think she feels the same about me. The problem is I want more. My FRIENDS group suggested propositioning her for sex. I've had a few manupartners, so I know I like sex, but that isn't the only thing I'm looking for. I've been watching the old K-dramas from hundreds of years ago, and I think they're messing with my head. My question is twofold. Would it be in violation of the Respectful and Considerate Conduct guidelines if I asked her to change the nature of our relationship? That leads to my next question: are relationships really dead for good?

Nervously,

Born in the Wrong Century

Electra's grin is uncontainable. This is the perfect question to answer to start her column.

Dear Born in the Wrong Century,

Let me start with your last question, then I will work backward. No, relationships aren't dead. Humans are inherently wired for connection. It's written in our DNA via evolutionary biology—not modern bio-tinkering—to form social bonds. While relationship dynamics and societal expectations may change over time, the need for human-human companionship is still alive and well—just like in the K-drama days. Now people may mask their needs with manupartners, but that doesn't mean they aren't there. What you're feeling is perfectly normal, and I guarantee there are others living in MSP who want the same thing.

Our real question is, does your neighbor?

She realizes she's extrapolating, but based on what she's observed and read online, she's confident her statement is true. It has to be. Maybe by reading this entry, others will be brave enough to go against modern social conventions and voice their desires aloud.

She shouldn't have gotten down on herself. She just needed to give people time to find her column. Soon, people will find her. She'll get dozens of subscribers. Eventually she'll monetize. Then she'll really be able to make an impact and carve out a place—*don't get carried away, Electra. Enjoy these small victories, but remember they aren't what gives you value.* She takes measured breaths. Solid advice, Janet. It's still awesome, though. Now it's Electra's turn to dish some out.

Before she answers the next question, she needs to do a little research. What in the fucked-up future are Respectful and Considerate Conduct guidelines? That definitely wasn't in her intro video starter pack.

As she thumbs through educational videos, she's pretty sure she's the one *Floating in MSP*.

20 – Bewildering Mess

Res6

November 10, 2390.

The more time that passes without Electra collecting on the favor she bargained for, the more ominous the debt becomes. He's already come up with a dozen wild ideas of what she might ask for. Horrifically, she's rubbing off on him.

Keeping her distracted, therefore, is a reasonable plan. She came up with a great idea to buy a desk and system herself. That she didn't just order what she wanted is a mystery to him. Why would she feel guilty when he clearly owes her? If a system makes her happy, it's a small price.

"I have a surprise for you," he says as they arrive back at his unit after lunch. The system he ordered for her is still in its unmistakable brightly colored packaging, but the new desk and chair are set up.

She stops barely inside the doorway.

"Where would you like to position your desk?"

Her brows crease adorably. "You bought me a system."

He takes her hand, pulling her into his unit. "Yes. I knew you wouldn't do it yourself, so I did. You can pretend it's my second system that you exclusively use, like my room, if that would make you feel better."

Her head snaps up. His mouth twitches at her shocked expression. These little smiles she elicits are happening more and more lately.

"Are you teasing me?" She tries to pull her hand away, feigning defensiveness.

He holds on, squeezing. Feeling a little reckless, he says, "Yes, I think I'm discovering a new favorite activity."

He's flirting, and he's not having to pretend she's a manupartner to do it. But what if she and Jerme hit it off—where will that leave him? He drops her hand as if it might burn him.

Electra approaches the desk, running her freshly manicured fingertips over the smooth glass surface. "I suppose since you already bought it, would it be too intrusive to put it in the corner over there? That way, I can see the particle panes, but it's out of the way. The bedroom is a little . . ."

"A little what?"

She shakes her head. "No, that's okay. I can put it in there."

Stepping behind her to rub comforting strokes over her arms is instinctive. It pleases him that she doesn't back away, which should trigger alarm bells. Instead, it has him thinking, *What if she's for me and not Jerme? What if I could get her to like me?* He banishes the dangerous thought, but he can't seem to peel his hands off her arms or stop the words that tumble out of his mouth. "At first, having you in my space felt like an invasion." She frowns half-heartedly over her shoulder. "Now that I'm getting used to a real woman wrecking my carefully planned routine and peaceful lifestyle"—she spins, glaring up at him—"I find having you here is surprisingly unintrusive. You can put the desk wherever you like. We can shift the sofa to give you more space."

As she looks away, the little muscle in her jaw flexes. She's probably feeling guilty again.

Zorg, has he really made it that bad for her? No wonder she said she wouldn't date him. "If we put the desk in that room, you'll stay in there all the time. It's too isolating. I'm surprised I'm the one having to point that out."

Her lips quivers. "Are you faking it again, Res6? Pretending to care when you really don't."

Being with her like this is too intense. He's never been good at this type of thing, and if this conversation continues, the fact that he's way out of his depth is going to show. This is the side of the twin divide that he got the lesser portion of. He needs Jerme back. His brother would know exactly what to say to reassure her. That's why she belongs with Jerme and not him. His brother would keep her happy.

He forces a chuckle. "I'm pretty sure this awful twisting sensation in my chest is genuine concern for your well-being."

"Really?" She beams up at him. The force of it nearly knocks him over. All he can do is nod like a fool. "Thank you." Then before he can defend himself, she throws her arms around his neck, drawing him into an embrace that steals his breath. "Hug me back," she whispers.

Leaning down, he wraps his arms around her middle. They stay that way with their bodies flush for a painful eternity that he never wants to end. Some primordial part of his brain is screaming, *Not for Jerme, for me*. He might as well beat on his chest like one of her alien heroes.

A part of him realizes they're stuck together, wading through uncharted territory. She's acclimating him to her as much as he's trying to acclimate her to his world. He keeps accidentally flirting with her. Then there's how she stared at him like she wanted to tear the towel off his hips. At first, it made him feel like the "sex god" she claims everyone thinks he is, but when she just stood there, he worried he had said the wrong thing and retreated to his room. If she were a manupartner, he would have no problem leaning down and whispering all the naughty things he wants to do to her against her neck. But she's a real woman, so his confidence when it comes to these delicate matters has evaporated, it seems. Really, what type of sex god admits they haven't taken a lover in years? Still, despite his missteps, they're bound to form some sort of misguided attachment.

Her arms loosen, and he takes it as a signal to release her. He does, taking a steadying breath. "Come on. Help me move the desk."

An hour later, they have her corner of the living room arranged. The screens are illuminated, and he's helped her program a temporary user until they can replace it with an ID.

"Most of the applications are here." He moves the cursor to the top of the center screen. A toolbar pops up. "Open Scrawl," he commands. The system responds by opening the word processing program. "You can find the documents you created on the tablet here." He clicks on a master file. "There are lessons on how to use this here." He opens another file. "These," he points to an audio headset and the keyboard he specially ordered, "will connect automatically."

Electra takes a seat and presses a few experimental keys. She watches excitedly as letters appear across the screen. "Not to beat a dead horse, but thank you, Res6. This really means a lot to me."

"Why would I beat a dead horse?" He realizes too late it's some type of saying from her time. "Never mind. I guess I should leave you to get started. Those alien romances aren't going to write themselves."

She's half distracted, not listening to him. "I'm thinking of rereading a certain scene from *Devoured by the Alien Duke*. I'm curious how your alien species just so happens to have compatible equipment for mating human women."

She drags her attention away from the screen, turning it on him. "They just do. Don't think about it too hard. It's fiction. It's meant to be enjoyable."

"It certainly is. I bet Jerme will love them. He'll want to know all about how you came up with the characters. Between the two of us, he's the more creative one." He grins. Speaking of, he should probably go check on the first real Jerme trial. Lextr was right to push to use the organic samples. The specimen in his closet has progressed further in the process than any other without showing failure markers.

"Your brother," Electra says, giving him a quizzical look. "You said I'll get to meet him?"

He grins. "Yes. Hopefully soon."

As he walks away, she asks, "How will I get to meet him, Res6?"

Slowly, he turns, swallowing a lump as he sees her arresting gaze. "What do you mean? He's coming here to MSP." He didn't mean to lie to her. Yet, explaining everything will be so much easier when Jerme is sitting beside him to smooth things over.

She stands, and the way she slowly approaches him makes his stomach pinch with anxiety. She can't possibly know.

"I think it's time for me to call in our bargain." Her lips press into a concerned line.

He steps back, but she takes another ominous step forward. His stomach dips violently. He needs to sit down. When her expression turns sympathetic, he knows for certain what's coming. "Actually, there's something I need to take care of real quick." He turns to flee to the spare room.

"Res6, I know Jerme died."

Her words scorch him like a breath of unprocessed air. He should have never brought up Jerme. He's getting too comfortable. "He didn't." Why did he say that?

With the pitying look she's giving him, she knows he's lying.

"You can't extract my secrets with your bargain. That's extortion," he says, though there's no heart in the accusation. He's only scrambling to rewind this unasked for turn of events.

Still, her face goes pale. "I'm so sorry. You're right. That is atrocious of me."

Now he feels bad about making her feel bad. This is why he invented manupartners. *Tell her*, the voice in his mind demands. He's not sure if it's his conscience, his brother, or the overly moral body double he's been chatting with in the spare room. Perhaps all three. Defeated, he walks over and drops onto the couch. He pats the spot next to him.

The prospect of what he's about to do is terrifying and freeing at the same time. As she walks to the couch and sits, it feels like he's having an out-of-body experience. That has to be his nerves. He remembers a vaguely familiar feeling when he first started CHOICElover and experiment after experiment kept failing. He was so close to giving up. Electra sitting beside him brings him closer to the present.

"You don't have to share anything you aren't comfortable with," she says. "I shouldn't have brought up the bargain. I just don't understand." She shakes her head like she's admonishing herself. "No, it doesn't matter. You'll tell me when you're ready."

He opens his mouth to speak, but the words get stuck. She takes his hand, squeezing it reassuringly.

He exhales a deep breath. "I take it you read about what happened to Jerme?" She nods. "I've never talked about his death to anyone. No one, not even my staff knows I had a twin. Jerme is why I started CHOICElover."

Her eyes go wide, but she nods again, urging him to continue.

"He committed atmosphere-assisted suicide. We were twenty-one. He met a woman, 3Zeez. They dated for a few weeks. He became convinced she was the one. In such a short time, he built his whole life and identity around her. They bled into each other. It was strange, and I warned him that they were too interdependent. That if something happened, so much of him would go with her that he'd be a shell. He stopped coming home after a while. I didn't see him often after that.

"Turns out I was right. She left one day out of the blue. He never found out why or where she went. After five months together, all he got was a message telling him not to look for her. A month later, he walked outside without a mask. I saw it on video a few days later."

With her free hand, she reaches up and strokes his cheek. Not his cheek. She's wiping away the tears that have sprung free. The tears that always fall if he allows himself to relive that moment.

He shakes the too-potent memory off, telling her about their un-stable mother, the other woman that broke Jerme's heart. He tells her about the seven years he wandered aimlessly through life until the day he came up with the idea for manupartners. He tells her how he still visits the site where Jerme took his last breath.

"Oh, Res6. I can't imagine what it must feel like to lose a sibling like that." Before he can stop her, Electra has thrown her arms around him. She's half in his lap as he finds his arms snaking around her back. They sit there for a long time until the searing pain in his chest becomes numb. She gently strokes his back as he weeps into her chest for a change.

He pushes her away a little. "Electra, your blouse." He points to her shoulder to show the damp spot. She glances at it, then gives him a sad smile before brushing her fingers across his cheeks again. Embarrassment at his mental collapse crowds in, and he stiffens, but she leans forward and kisses one still-damp cheek, then the other.

"I'm sorry," he says, cheeks burning. Has anyone ever kissed him so tenderly? Shown him such care? Never. Not even his own mother. It's almost more than he can take.

"You have nothing to apologize for. When you have an open wound, it is normal for it to hurt when you revisit it. Thank you for sharing that with me. I know it was hard for you."

He's so caught off guard by her understanding reaction that he has to ask, "Does that help you understand what CHOICElover means to me?"

"It's a legacy in honor of your brother," she says, moving off his lap. "Perhaps I was a little too harsh with you. You created manupartners to save people like your brother."

He wants to pull her back. *Needs* to pull her back to him. Because now it feels like there's something missing where she'd been moments earlier. This is the exact reaction he's spent his whole life avoiding. "I thought if he had a companion whose interests aligned with his, then that never would have happened."

"Res6, I think it's important to clarify that the type of relationship you described with your brother and his girlfriend wasn't interdependent. It was codependent, which I know courtesy of my stepmom Janet, the therapist."

He shakes his head, trying to process what she's saying. "I don't understand."

"I won't claim to know your brother, but he was probably struggling long before 3Zeez came along. When people are rejected by a parent, it can cause a number of unhealthy relationship patterns later in life. Our parents can give us all sorts of fucked-up trauma."

"Your birth mother died because your family didn't have the resources for her treatment," he says, thinking he's following. Datasets and DNA records are so much simpler.

"Exactly. It sounds like his relationship with your mother gave him an insecure attachment style, which may have led to love bombing with 3Zeez. It's a lot of pressure to be someone's everything."

That can't be right, can it? Even if their mother wasn't there for them, they were there for each other. "But we had the same mother, and I've never put that kind of pressure on anyone."

She shrugs. "Everyone responds differently. Someone else with the same parental abandonment issues might respond to relationships with distrust—"

"Or avoidance," he fills in for her. All the pieces snap together with startling clarity. Like always, he and Jerme were opposite sides of the same coin. In over a century, he hasn't learned what this woman taught him in ten minutes. He should have done better. Been better. Shame crawls up his neck, making him want to abandon their conversation and flee. But he knows somehow that would reinforce that there is something defective about him in her eyes. He forces himself to stay put. "I don't know what to say."

"You don't have to say anything." She offers him a gentle smile. "Thank you for sharing that with me. It helps me see you better."

Her words mean more to him than he can handle. He probably should ease into this vulnerability thing, but here he is in the deep end, flailing.

She must sense his distress because she says, "I should probably go put on one of those skin-brightening face masks we bought so my freckles look brilliant for the cameras tonight."

"What cameras?" he asks.

"I think we should go out. Me, you"—she glances toward the locked door—"and Chryl."

Oh, Zorg, she's trying to support him. Does he even deserve it? She's too considerate for someone like him. "Electra, we don't have to—you said it made you feel cheap." This stupid vulnerability thing is spreading inside him like a cancer, changing everything. Like Electra Lynch is rewriting his very DNA.

"I understand why CHOICElover matters to you, so I've changed my perspective about our little outings." As she disappears into her room, wave after wave of warmth washes over him. He thought telling her would be the most painful experience he's had in a long time, and in a way it was. Just not for the reasons he expected. In listening, empathizing, she's trying to show him she cares. And that makes his chest feel like it's going to split wide open.

When her door is shut, he slumps back onto the couch. If only she knew the bewildering mess she's unleashing.

21 – Hopefully Yours

Electra

Dear Reader,

Today is stellar! Why, you ask? I'm winning on all fronts.

This morning, I woke up to hundreds of new Dear Electra subscriptions and dozens of messages—granted, most of them are nonsense future people advice requests. Get this—one man wants to propose marriage to his ManuMATE manupartner. I thought of Chryl, who seems excited about everything, so I told him, *Sure, why not?* What's the harm if he proposes to a sex clone? He'll probably lose interest in a week and recycle it.

Oh, and I got my first death threat! That was quick. Apparently, even the future has hate groups and internet trolls, but it was so creepy. "The world doesn't need your poisonous ideas. Delete your account immediately, or we'll find out who you are and delete you." Yikes and blocked!

On a positive note, there were some meaty questions too, probably inspired by that first one. I took a little time this morning and planned out a few weeks' worth of posts. There was one guy who, based on his question, might be from the past like me. He mentioned something about his owner getting him an ID on the dark web from a new company called IdenTECH. I need to ask Res6 about it. I know he's fine with me spending his money, but if I got an ID then I could earn my own, even if it was paltry compared to his. At least I'd be contributing something. But I'll need a few more subscribers to get to that level.

Speaking of Res6, he took me to this great little pizza place, so that's a win! Then he surprised me with a computer, complete with a desk and the most comfortable computer chair I've ever sat in. The guilt! But he has a way of convincing me it's unnecessary, which I'm honestly grateful for.

Here is the best part about today. I made Res6 cry! Like real human tears in response to real human emotions! It was incredible. He told me all about his brother. I guess he's been in serious denial, which explains why he keeps talking about him in the present—*as if he were still alive*. It also gave me some insight into why he's so avoidant and thinks that you can have a fulfilling relationship with a manupartner.

So now I'm sitting here with a facemask on, planning to go out with him and Chryl and let the world take pictures of us. Stop judging me! I know what you're thinking. I promise, this doesn't make me a hypocrite since I know why he's doing it now. CHOICElover is a memorial to his twin.

My freaking heart! Considerate and open Res6 might be more than I can handle without things getting really complicated. When he's sweet and perceptive, a part of him I've only seen brief glimpses of, he's even more attractive. Hell, who am I kidding? When we're not arguing, I gravitate toward the man like a rich white lady to a rescue donkey.

Anyway, this Oklahoma clay mineral mask is getting dry, so I better wash it off. Wish me luck tonight; now that I'm finally melting his icy exterior, who knows what might happen?!

Hopefully yours,

Electra

As Electra exits her room, Chryl walks out of Res6's Room of Wonder and Weirdness. Res6, who's already dressed for the night, is leaning against the counter sipping a glass of WhiteVine.

"You look beautiful," he says, his stare making her blush.

"Thank you," she and Chryl say at the same time.

Res6 smirks, and they both shift their gaze to the manupartner who's wearing—

"She can't go out naked, can she?" Electra blurts out.

"I'm not naked, silly." Chryl fingers the chain of pearls that dangles haphazardly over her body, not covering any of her intimate details. She gives a little wiggle, causing her large breasts to bounce as if that proves something.

Res6 frowns. "Chryl, would you do me the honor of putting on the blue dress I laid out for you?"

Chryl frowns back. "I don't understand."

"The blue dress," Electra snaps. "Put it on."

Chryl jumps. "There's no need to get testy with me, Prototype."

Since Chryl heard Res6 explain Electra to a fan using the word *prototype*, Chryl has been calling her that as if it were an insult. She doesn't bother shutting the door, which Res6 quickly corrects, closing it and handing Electra a glass of the chilly white liquid.

"Does it seem like Chryl thinks she's competing with me?" she says.

"She is," Res6 says, simply. "I reviewed her specification sheet. Her prior owner selected jealous."

"Why would someone choose that?" she asks, and takes a sip.

"Trust me, I've seen far weirder trait combinations than Chryl's."

Half an hour later, they're standing in a very crowded bar, getting approached for the fourth time for photographs, which Chryl, thinking it's what Res6 wants, poses for exuberantly. The rest of the evening carries on like this until, in an interesting twist, a group of total strangers approach Res6 to request his permission to proposition Chryl for sex. Res6 agrees, and a very gleeful Chryl dances off with the group's messenger, who promises to send Chryl back to his unit fully sanitized later that evening.

"Is that normal?" she asks.

He shrugs. "No, but given—"

"The way she was eye-fucking them across the room?"

He chuckles. "Precisely." Electra's expression must be one of utter astonishment, because when Res6 turns back to her, he leans forward, sliding his arm around her waist, and whispers. "Jealous they didn't pick you?"

A laugh bursts from her chest as she swats him away. "Have I told you I hate the future yet?"

He chuckles. "You have mentioned that once or twice."

She sighs wistfully, taking a sip of her Spiny Spritzer cocktail.

His hand closes around her elbow. "Now that we're alone, there's something I want to ask you about."

Her heart stumbles at his serious tone. Does he have regrets about what he told her earlier, and now he's going to take back his generosity? Why is that her first thought? She turns to him, unable to mask her startled expression.

"What's wrong?" he asks, brows furrowing in concern.

"Nothing." He squeezes her elbow as if to say he doesn't believe her and she might as well confess now. She struggles to meet his gaze. "If you regret what you told me earlier, that's fine. You can take back my desk or whatever."

"Electra," he urges.

"That's why I said I needed my own money—"

He shakes her elbow. "I haven't even said anything. Why are you jumping to conclusions?"

She shakes her head as if it might fling the destructive thoughts from her mind. "Your tone was so serious just then. I guess I panicked."

He steps closer. Something about the warmth and his proximity soothes her flash of nerves. "You need to stop assuming the worst. I told you, I've got this." *I've got you*, is what she hears. "I didn't mean to scare you with my tone. I suppose I'm a little out of my element here, but I wanted to ask you if you would go somewhere with me?"

She swallows the lump in her throat. "Sorry, go on."

"The anniversary of Jerme's death is in a few days, and I usually go to the site. After our conversation, I thought having you there might be helpful."

Her eyes feel wide as saucers.

"You know what, now that I've said it aloud, it sounds stupid." He turns to walk away, but she runs after him, jumping into his path.

"Not stupid," she says. "I'll go. I'd love to—I mean, I'd be honored."

He glances down the bridge of his nose at her, and she can tell he's fighting a wave of emotion.

"Res6, I want to go. That's what friends do. Thank you for trusting me enough to invite me."

He doesn't say another word as he takes her hand, threading their fingers together, which is decidedly not what friends do—but she's supposed to be a manupartner. Right.

"Let's walk for a bit," he finally says.

He leads her out of the bar, and they stroll through the corridors in his tower for a long while in silence. Even though her feet are screaming in these ridiculous heels, she doesn't complain. The buzzing warmth in her chest is more than enough to make the blisters she'll have tomorrow totally worth it.

He seems to need movement to think as much as he needs water sounds to relax. She's more than willing to give this to him, glad to be there for him to confide in when and if he needs. She suspects that her presence beside him is enough.

22 – Dangerous Ideas

Res6

November 14, 2390.

The smog is worse every time Res6 visits the empty expanse of concrete where Jerme took his last breath. Maybe it's his perception becoming more morose over the years. If Electra were to be believed, it is his unhealed wound that muddies the grimy patch of sidewalk they now stand before.

He reaches out for her, and she wraps comforting arms around him. *Friends*, she said.

As her face presses into his chest, he says, "Careful with your mask. You don't want to take in any outside air."

It chills him to think she might inhale the same deadly chemicals that killed his brother. While he's successfully avoided his own

FRIENDS group most of his life, he's pretty sure his protectiveness of this woman isn't the way most people feel about their FRIENDS. Warmth permeates his chest as she strokes soothing circles on his back, holding space for him as he processes his long-avoided feelings. That had to be what Jerme felt for the woman who broke his heart. Electra told him their relationship sounded codependent. But the way she makes him feel can't be harmful, can it?

Holding her at the location of his brother's death feels like a betrayal in some ways, and an awakening in others. But is it really when there's a Jerme currently growing in his closet? He braces as a wave of shame washes over him. He's suspected, since manupartners disgust Electra, she'll be disgusted by his bringing back his dead brother. Their heart-felt conversation will only make it worse.

"I meant it when I said Jerme would like you." He knows it's true because *he likes her*. He's known he likes her for a while—a real human female who is everything a manupartner isn't. Not as a *friend*, which scares the shit out of him. It's a stunning realization to come to on the anniversary of Jerme's death, of all days. He's sexually attracted to her and finds her intriguing, but this feeling is something more. He knows this because all thoughts of hooking her up with Jerme have officially flown out the window. He needs her for himself.

"What was he like?" Electra asks.

"My twin was the fun-loving one. Always joking. He never took anything too seriously. That was always my role. He was quick to love and laugh. Slow to forgive and forget. He always had strong emotions. Look where it landed him."

Her arms squeeze his ribcage because she's already attuned to him enough to understand there is nothing she can say to ease what he's feeling. For decades after starting CHOICElover, he's always been able to stand here and honor his brother's memory while holding himself together. Being here with her makes him feel seen, which only makes the pain worse. This time, as the tears roll down his cheeks, he feels them acutely. As if the pain he's been storing has only now found a path out.

"Our mother told us the genes responsible for temperament were the only ones that didn't get perfectly duplicated. I often wondered if they'd been more evenly distributed, if something might have been different for Jerme. Maybe he wouldn't have fallen so hard and taken the loss so deeply."

He braves a glance at Electra to find her staring up at him. She shrugs. "I don't know. It sounds like in being happy-go-lucky all the time, he was putting up a shield for something he was fighting in secret."

A heaviness hits his chest as if someone struck him. How does she dive right into the heart of things like that? This time it's his hidden shame. His instincts are screaming, *Clam up. Run. Do whatever it takes to hide from this woman. She'll take everything. She'll ruin you.*

But he closes his eyes as different words tumble from his lips. "If I'd known what he was going through, I could have done something. I should have seen him better and fixed it. I feel responsible." That would mean no CHOICElover, but he would trade his company for Jerme. "If I could do it all again, I would do everything differently."

"Oh, Res6, it isn't your fault. You can't blame yourself for what happened." She runs her fingers through his hair, combing it with soothing strokes until he finally opens his eyes.

Zorg, they need to get inside. His mask is foggy from his tears and hot breath. "Come on. Enough of this. I can't dwell on the past forever." He drags her back to the SAT garage where they parked. Once they're safely inside the building, they remove their masks. "Thank you. That wasn't pleasant, but I think I needed it."

Twenty minutes later, they're sitting in a small booth at his favorite lunch spot, an Italian café called Linguini Land. He's pulled himself together enough to tease, "Between the two of us, I think we've shed enough tears this month, don't you think?"

She chuckles. "Yes, I think so. We've earned a glass of wine. Is there rosé still?"

"Yes, you'll want to order the PinkVine. And I'd suggest the CKin fettuccini. The chef here makes all the sauces from scratch." Res6 sets his menu down. He comes here often enough that the server knows his selection.

Once the order's placed and their Vine's been delivered, Electra leans over. "Now that I understand the price of things, I feel a little guilty ordering the faux meat."

"Please don't start with the money issue. Pick something else to pester me about or I'll be forced to send for Chryl to act as a distraction."

Electra lets out a throaty laugh, waving her hands in submission. "Fine. Fine. How jealous do you think she is right now that we're out without her?"

"Can someone be ravenously jealous?"

Electra snorts. "I'm sure a manupartner can." She clears her throat, shifting to face him in the booth. "I have a question. If it's too upsetting, you don't have to answer, but I'm curious—since you know it's possible, has it ever crossed your mind to bring someone back intentionally?"

Panic flashes through him. Does she know he's trying to grow Jerme in the locked room? She knew about his death. He examines her intently. She's grinning, so she must be blissfully unaware.

Res6 leans back in his chair, trying to adopt a casual façade. Leave it up to equally curious Electra to conjure the possibility. One day, when he succeeds, he'll have to tell her. She'll be livid, of course, and probably want nothing to do with him, which he'll count on Jerme to smooth over. Or he can tell her now and suffer her disgust. But he might fail and lose her. Is it worth it to upset her when things are going so well? Especially in light of his burgeoning *feelings*. Better for him to wait to confess until after he succeeds. Zorg, he can't wait till Jerme is back.

He clears his throat. "No, I've never considered that."

She nods. "That's probably a good thing. I can't imagine the ethical considerations. For example, if someone didn't wish to be brought back, doing so might take away their agency . . . or cause them more emotional pain."

That can't be true. There are thousands of stories of people surviving a suicide attempt and regretting the attempt afterward. Despite that, the weight of her words hangs in the air between them. By her sympathetic expression, he knows they're thinking about the same person. Not vivacious and full of life Electra, of course. *Jerme*. He's always assumed his twin's decision was a mistake. That Jerme got caught up in the emotions of an especially bad day. He thought if he could just show him how loved he was, he'd see the reason for living. But what right does he have to undo Jerme's choice? Would Jerme wish to stay dead?

The question makes bile rise in his throat.

Her gaze is dissecting, like she's prodding around his insides with a laser scalpel. She must decide he's not the monster he actually is because she reaches across the table, brushing his arm. "Res6, I'm sorry. I didn't mean to—"

"It's fine," he says decidedly. Because in the footage he's watched a dozen times, Jerme never staggered back toward the door. Never even looked at it. He just sat down on the sidewalk, leaned against the wall, and closed his eyes. The undeniable truth, which he's avoided until this second, is right before him, forcing him to speak. Though it makes his chest feel like it's being ripped in two for a second time, he says, "Jerme probably wouldn't want to be brought back."

23 – Web of Lies

Res6

Why did he lie? It's not like he owes her the truth, does he? So what if he's selfishly trying to bring back his dead brother? Sure, Jerme might be upset at first, but he has Electra to help him solve Jerme's issues.

He reaches around the fully formed Jerme experiment and sets the scanner down on a shelf. The scan looks perfect. In a few hours the light will turn green, and he'll be ready to activate it. His anticipation is making him jittery.

Chryl lounges on the bed, watching something on her tablet, giggling occasionally, unlike the body-double manupartner, who seems content to stare blankly at the wall or watch him like it's doing now.

"Something bothering you?" it asks. "The *woman* again?"

Even though he's now had a dozen conversations with the unit about Electra and her nature, it still calls her *the woman*. Telling the manupartner was probably a highly inadvisable plan, but he's exasperated Lextr and Tommy talking about her and, well, DumBot is dumb. His body double's selected traits make it such a good sounding board, and it looks just like Jerme. One day, he just blurted it all out. He should invent a line of therapy manupartners—he's getting distracted. *Focus, Res6.*

"She doesn't approve of my experiment." And in a few hours, she's going to find out and they're going to have a blowup—between Electra and a newly resurrected Jerme, it will be a challenging few days, but it will be worth it.

He glances toward the now closed closet, then at Chryl, who looks up from the tablet. He points to the noise-canceling headset on the nightstand. Chryl frowns, but puts it on. In a too-loud, pouty voice she says, "I don't know why I don't get to be part of your little talks."

Thank you, he mouths, and a second later, she's reabsorbed in whatever she was watching.

He turns back to the body double. "She brought up that some people like Jerme might not want to be brought back. At first, I thought she had a point. Then I got to thinking. She told me her stepmom was a psychologist. She wasn't just any psychologist. After a little research this morning, I discovered she was on San Francisco's premier morning show with her own segment, Ask Doctor Janet."

"That's why she wants to start an advice column," the body double astutely observes.

"Right."

"Did you change your mind about the column?" it asks.

"What? No," he shakes his head. "That's not the point. I'm trying to say it's serendipitous that Electra is who I brought back. When Jerme is here, she'll know how to help me make Jerme happy."

The body double's eyes narrow. "So you're going to tell her?"

"She'll find out when I activate him. Then Jerme will help me smooth things over." He huffs, plopping down at the foot of the bed.

His foot is tapping restlessly. He grabs his knee, willing himself to still. He can handle this. "You've studied up on relationships. How upset is she going to be?"

"According to the Respectful and Considerate Conduct Course text, citizens 'should refrain from lying. Engaging in falsehood may break down trust and stifle open communication between individuals, leading to negative consequences for both parties, such as causing the offended party to make poor choices based on the misinformation. Lying may even cause stress, feelings of guilt, or negative self-talk, effectively lowering one's self-esteem.' "

Damn, that's what he was afraid of because that's exactly what's happening. His lie is leading Electra to believe he's a better man than he is. That's why when she's sitting across the room at her new desk, she keeps stealing glances at him with stars in her eyes. His lie has effectively tricked her into a poor choice: liking him. His guilt is a natural consequence. Ergo, he's an idiot.

But his proverbial hole is already dug. There's nothing he can do about it now, and it's not like he can afford to come clean. He'll just have to deal with the consequences when they inevitably come. "Great talk. I'm screwed," he says, effectively ending the conversation.

He didn't select judgmental, but it seems to be a consequence of the morality trait backfiring because he can feel the manupartner's narrowed eyes on his back as he slips out to get a little work done to keep himself occupied.

An hour later, Chryl joins him and Electra in the living room, wearing a black pleated skirt, a gray open sweater over a vintage white button-down, and a pair of glasses she doesn't need. She carries his tablet to the couch and plops onto it, eyeing him as she twirls the end of a pigtail braid. Her attention darts between him and Electra like she's waiting for something.

"What are you doing, Chryl?" he gives in and asks.

She brightens considerably. "Reading!"

"Reading what?" he asks, mostly out of scientific curiosity. While manupartners are programmed with the ability to read all six of the most common languages since reading is often necessary for their owner's tasks, manupartners don't typically read for fun. It's most likely a side effect of her jealousy trait and proximity to Electra.

"Some sort of instruction manual, I think," Chryl answers, nose wrinkling.

Electra's gaze snaps up, and she muffles a laugh as she eyes the other woman. "What are you wearing?"

Chryl frowns, assessing herself. "I asked DumBot to give me an outfit recommendation for a naughty book nerd from the early 2000s. This is what it suggested."

"You look like Britney Spears," Electra says.

A second later, a video pops up in his chat, which he also assumes shows on Chryl's display as the manupartner's eyes widen.

Chryl gasps. "Why is this child wearing my outfit?"

Res6 returns his attention to the video, in which an oversexualized teenage girl dances provocatively. Frowning, he closes the window.

Chryl must sense his disapproval, because she says, "Great. This entire outfit is wasted."

She gets up and tosses the tablet onto the couch, shooting Electra a glare.

"I thought you were reading?" Electra prods, smirking.

"That instruction manual was boring. Besides, I already know all the positions described. When you're ready, handsome, I'll show you." Chryl winks at him and slips into his room, presumably to change.

When he looks back, Electra has the discarded tablet in one hand, and is trying to hide a broad grin behind the other.

"Do I even want to know?" he asks, leaning back in his chair.

Electra waggles the tablet. "Res6, why are there dozens of romance books downloaded onto your system? I thought you said you don't read romance books. Just mine."

He shoots to his feet as mortification reddens his cheeks. "That file was labeled private!" He rushes around his desk to snatch the tablet containing the damning evidence proving that he may have formed somewhat of an addiction to Electra's books and possibly others like them. "It's your fault!"

She dances away before he can get to her. "After our previous conversation, I suspected you'd like erotica, but these are swoon-worthy historical romances."

"I wanted to know what a duke was. Please give me the tablet," he begs, chasing her.

She stops on the opposite side of his desk, giggling. "This one is called *Romance for Romeo*." She wipes tears from her eyes. "Here's another called *Duke Theodore's Tempestuous Touch*. This cover—you gave it five stars." Losing herself in a fit of laughter, Electra folds over, clutching the tablet to her stomach.

He darts around the desk, but as he reaches for the tablet, she spins, effectively wrapping his arms around her from behind. He grips her waist, and she leans back into his chest. The fresh lilac scent of her hair must be the reason he buries his face in the inviting skin beneath her ear and inhales like an animal, much in the same way Duke Theodore did to Lady Catherine. "You weren't supposed to see that," he growls into her neck.

She glances over her shoulder, and their noses nearly brush, which sets his pulse racing. "Too late."

Their eyes meet. The heat swirling in her wide pupils draws him closer. Confusing yet not unwelcome emotions surge to the forefront of his emotional landscape—longing and something more menacing. He pulls her closer. The way her soft curves mold so perfectly against him has his mind racing in dangerous directions. Zorg, he's going to miss this when she hates him. He really shouldn't let this go any further.

With a slow breath, her eyes flutter closed. Damn if he doesn't feel like a romantic hero. He's powerless to stop himself, and it's only a kiss. His heart skips as he reaches up, coaxing her chin toward him. Their lips brush—

A throat clears. "Am I interrupting something?" Chryl says.

Shit. He didn't even hear the door open.

Electra stiffens, and at that moment he determines the manupartner is getting recycled at the next available opportunity. Electra giggles, moving out of his arms, and waves the tablet at him. He steps forward, compelled as though she wields the full power of the MagTrack and he's merely a SAT drawn to her charge.

"There's something in here you need to see," Chryl barks.

Stupid jealousy trait. He doesn't take his eyes off Electra. "Not now, Chryl. Go back to your room."

She huffs. "There's something wrong with the thing"—her eyes widen comically—"in the closet—"

"I'll be right there," he interjects, his blood chilling. Why would Chryl think there's something wrong with the Jerme trial? Its scan came back perfect an hour ago. Unless she's using it to distract him.

Electra crosses her arms. "What's in the closet, Chryl?" She turns her pointed—no, accusing—gaze on him.

Right as Chryl opens her mouth to answer, he laces his voice with authority, commanding, "Go. To. Your. Room."

Chryl stomps her foot, scowling at Electra, but she doesn't budge. Surely she doesn't think he wants them to have a catfight over him.

"Or," Electra butts in, "we could team up. You know, girl power, and you could tell me what's in the closet. That would make me very happy."

Chryl's eyes narrow as if she's contemplating her next move.

Fortunately, Electra has far less experience bending manupartners to her will compared to him. "Chryl, you have my attention now. Let me deal with Electra. I'll be in there in a few short moments."

Beaming, Chryl says, "Yes, Daddy!" He watches as she excitedly slams the door behind her before returning his attention to the now-fuming human woman.

"Deal with me?" Electra's lips curls in a sneer.

He pinches the bridge of his nose. "You know I didn't mean that."

She shakes her head. "What are you hiding, Res6?"

The brother I'm trying and possibly failing to resurrect. "Nothing," he lies.

"Every time I feel like I'm getting closer to you, something like this happens." She paces to her bedroom door and opens it.

He has the distinct feeling that if he lets her go through it, recovering from his latest screwup might be more than he can manage. He needs a good explanation. What about something related to their outings? "I have a surprise for you," he blurts out as an idea strikes him.

Her brows lift.

At least she's listening. He takes a calming breath, making a mental note to acquire two tickets. "I wanted to save it for a better moment, but I have tickets for a fantasy ball called Saturday Sirens this weekend." He read about the event, but decided not to get tickets since he'd likely be dealing with a freshly awakened Jerme and an angry Electra.

She frowns. "What does that have to do with the problem in the closet?"

He shakes his head. "Our outfits. The dress I got for you has an electrical component. It keeps short-circuiting. I need to schedule a technician to come look at it before the event."

Another mental note: *procure a ball gown and tuxedo.*

She plants her hands on her hips. "Can I see it?"

He chuffs. "What, and further ruin my surprise?"

Her eyes narrow. "I don't believe you."

"Ah, well, you will when you see it," he says, feigning a shaky confidence, and slips into his room. His back hits the door, and both Chryl and the body double stare at him. Ignoring them, he thinks the command to message his personal shopper about the formal attire, but his thoughts are so convoluted that he can't put together a message.

That's when he notices the closet door rattling.

"I told you," Chryl says, twirling a lock of blonde hair.

There's no way this should be happening. Panic has him jumping into action. He throws the closet door open. The trial is no longer attached to the electrode pad, and as he catches the convulsing body, he shoots Chryl a glare.

He hauls the seizing Jerme trial to the bed. Chryl helps him lay it down. "Chryl, there's a medical kit under the sink. Get it."

The body double sits in its chair, judging, as Chryl does as he asks. He props pillows around Jerme's head, leaning his hip against him to keep him on the bed. Chryl sets the box down and opens the lid. He fishes out one of several preloaded syringes. It's rare for a manupartner to seize upon activation; it happened more in the early research days when they were tinkering with their programming capacity. Still, he's prepared. He injects the anticonvulsant, and Jerme stills.

He takes a few deep breaths, trying to calm his racing heart.

"What's wrong with it?" Chryl asks, taking the syringe and replacing the cap. She tosses it back into the medical kit.

He turns his angry gaze on her. A guilty pink blooms on her cheeks. "Chryl, what did you do?"

Tears well in the manupartner's eyes. "The video on your website says to push the button when it turns green. I was just trying to help."

Res6 buries his head in his hands, groaning. It's not Chryl's fault; it's his fault. How can this day get any worse? He has a possibly failed trial lying on the bed next to him unconscious. An angry Electra that he's fed more lies. And Chryl, a manupartner who has been around so long she may be gaining sentience. The lingering hope he felt while visiting Jerme's memorial site with Electra fades to something gray.

He turns to the body double. "Will you please comfort her?"

Chryl nods, agreeing with the suggestion, crawling into the body double's lap. When it pats her back, he goes back to ignoring them as usual.

He gets out the portable BioLume Gene Scanner. He quickly runs a scan, then waits. When the results populate on its screen, he shoots them over to himself and Lextr. A minute later, he has the other man on a call.

"Hold on, why did you activate it before you did the final scan?" Lextr asks.

Because the manupartner I got as a buffer from the woman I'm falling for is individuating and decided to be helpful and pressed the bright green button before I got the chance doesn't feel like the right answer. He says, "It's not important."

Lextr hums like he does when reviewing data. Res6 takes out his tablet and does the same. With each passing minute, his anxiety sky-rockets. This is only one of ten—if it fails, they can isolate the issue and correct it. Still, his eyes are starting to blur, the data becoming a jumble.

Lextr hums again, and his patience snaps. "Lextr, did the trial fail?" *Will I get my brother back?*

"Did you see section B83c101?" Lextr asks.

He swipes to the section. "I see it."

"It looks like there is hidden epileptiform activity that we couldn't measure until activation."

His throat constricts. "What does that mean? Are his memories viable?" *They can stop the seizures.*

"It would appear the cognitive load during the NAM activation caused a spike-wave. The subject's memories might have expressed had the subthreshold activity been absent," Lextr says.

"So it might have worked, if it weren't for the spike?"

"My guess is the seizure it caused burned out any potential memory imprint, but you won't be sure until it wakes up," Lextr says.

As if summoned, Jerme—*not Jerme*, the trial—sits up. Oh Zorg. It looks just like him and the manupartner body double, but knowing it's made from Jerme's DNA makes it feel completely different. More significant. Real. Is he real? The faint glimmer in its eye feels like a sign of life, of memory. Like his brother. Is this it? Is he about to see Jerme after all this time?

Tentatively he asks, "Jerme?"

The trial grins, and it is just like his brother. Joy barrels through him. After six failed trials and a close call, he did it! He has Jerme back. This time he's going to fix everything. Be the brother he needs. He shifts so quickly that he knocks the medical kit off the bed as he throws his arms around his twin. "Oh, Jerme, I've missed you so much. I've been so lost without you."

But Jerme isn't hugging him back. He leans away, holding his brother by the shoulders. It's the same grin as a moment ago. Did he imagine Jerme's signature quirk? Jerme blinks. "Hi!"

Please, Zorg, no. This can't be happening. Terrified at the prospect, but desperate to know, he asks, "What's your name?"

As its eyes glaze over, his stomach drops.

It says, "I think my name is Jerme!" Then it beams as if pleased with itself.

24 – Saturday Sirens

Res6

Beside Res6, the bed dips as the body double sits down. On his opposite side, Chryl crawls across the blankets so they've effectively caged him in. He pulls the covers up over his head, making a mental note to tell Electra—if she ever speaks to him again—that he sees the appeal of wallowing, and he shouldn't have judged her so harshly for it.

He didn't sleep the night after the real Jerme trial woke up seizing. It was a nightmare with his look-alikes and Chryl all in the cramped room with him. Thankfully, the next morning, Chryl let Tommy in to collect it before Electra woke up. He's been in bed ever since, with Chryl bringing him meals that she figured out how to order.

When Jerme died, he got up and went to work the next day, and the day after, until he got proficient at going through the motions. But now, after what feels like a catastrophic failure where he's not only disappointed himself, he's letting Jerme down, going through the motions doesn't seem to matter. The only thing that matters is the woman he keeps lying to. The point is, he's fucked, so why get out of bed? To waste another precious DNA sample on a trial that will undoubtedly fail? He isn't sure he can do that again. Though on a positive note, thinking it worked only to realize he was wrong has warned him off activating a future trial *just to see*.

"You going to get up today, brother?" The body double pats his shoulder through the blankets.

"The tablet told me about MSP's best comfort food, so I ordered us all the best things," Chryl chimes. "How about some yummy faux-tater tot hotdish or roasted sweet corn?"

"I'm not hungry. Go away," he grumbles, even as his stomach protests.

"If you don't eat your meal, you won't get any Gel-Oh salad!" she says.

One of them tugs the blanket hard enough that it slips down. When his eyes blink open, he's face-to-face with Chryl's bright, unsettling smile.

"Hi there, handsome!" She fishes out his arms and drags him forward, so he's forced to sit up. The body double is sitting in the chair staring at him, having obeyed his command to go away. Chryl's defiant attempt to pry him out of bed is another indicator that something is off about her.

"Hi Chryl," he mutters, swinging his legs off the edge of the bed. He misses his bedroom with its dark walls and soothing art. The stark white of the four walls surrounding him makes the space feel like a seclusion room . . . or maybe that's his mental state.

"Too much time in bed can promote negative thoughts, worsen health, disturb sleep, and cause physical decline and isolation. Inactivity may harm both a patient's mental and physical well-being," Chryl says, scrambling off the bed and collecting a package. She opens it and hands him a takeout container. "Tommy said you weren't listening to his messages, so he told me to tell you the repairman will be here soon."

"Repairman?" he asks.

"For the malfunctioning dress, silly! Remember the lie you told Prototype so she wouldn't discover our supersecret in the closet?!" Chryl claps excitedly as he forces down the food. "Tommy got us tickets! We're going to the ball!"

He groans. Things are really getting out of hand.

Half an hour later, he's successfully extricated himself from bed, showered, and is stationed at his desk getting caught up on the hundreds of messages in his inbox. Electra's desk sits empty, though it is still early. The doorbell rings. He answers, noting Electra's head pop out of her room a few moments later.

He lets in a technician carrying a small kit and wearing a gray onesie with a nametag that reads Trent. Beneath it are the words Tower A Electric. He scans the room, landing on Electra. He nods like he's ticking off a box and says, "I'm here to repair the dress."

His cheeks heat. This was Tommy's brilliant idea? Send a tower maintenance man?

Electra steps into the room, coming to stand beside him. She shoots a skeptical look at the man, pointing to the logo. "You're the dress repairman?"

He clears his throat. "Side gig."

Chryl whips her hand in a circle above her head. "I'm going to be a cowgirl!"

"Yes, for the fantasy ball we're going to tomorrow," Res6 agrees.

There's no stopping his descent into the purgatory he's landed himself in. But on the off chance Electra will believe this charade, maybe he could gain back a smidgeon of normalcy. "Ready to fix the dress?"

The man lifts his toolkit in solidarity. "I'll have *the dress* fixed right away."

Res6 forces a smile. "Great. Right through here." He grabs Chryl's elbow. "Show him the dress. I need to talk to Electra for a minute."

Chryl winks, which Electra won't think anything of because . . . Chryl. "Sure thing, Daddy!"

When the door clicks shut, he braces himself. "I've had a rough couple of days—please don't be mad at me."

Her eyes narrow. "About your brother?"

His insides light up. Finally, something he doesn't have to lie about. "Yes."

It's magical how her features transform from anger to sympathy. "Is that why I haven't seen you for two days?"

"Yes, I'm sorry." It's true. Zorg, telling her the truth feels so good. After this little bout of lies related to bringing back Jerme, he's never lying to her again. "Come here."

She lets him pull her into an embrace, and it's the best feeling ever. After the last two days, he really needs comfort—shit. This is what she wanted from him that first week. But they were strangers then. Things are different now; something has grown between them. Something inevitable, at least on his side. That's why his instincts were screaming to keep a distance between them. But now, he has the same feeling he did after the robbery when he knew she was safe—he's never letting her go.

When she finally pulls away, he says, "I should probably go check on Chryl and the technician."

Once he's safely on the other side of the door, he sags with relief against the wall. She doesn't hate him. It's a miracle from Zephyr herself! If the reasons for lying weren't abundantly clear before, the last two days he spent wallowing without her in bed have made them undeniably obvious now.

It's not helpful that his manupartner body double is sitting there in the ergonomic chair, staring at him judgmentally. "I told you keeping up your lie was a bad idea."

Chryl climbs onto the body double's lap, straddling it. It sits there unfazed as she reaches up and grabs two fistfuls of hair, tugging them so she's forcing eye contact. "Prototype can't know Daddy's and my secret! Got it?"

Zephyr, he's created a monster. The manupartner's eyes go wide as it nods emphatically.

Chryl grins. "Good boy." She lets go of its hair, spins around, and settles in so she's effectively using the body double as a seat.

Trent, the technician, watches them incredulously. "I get it," he says, chuckling. "You like to watch."

Res6 buries his head in his hands, groaning. No, he doesn't like to watch what is essentially an overly Sexcitable™, half-sentient manupartner and his body double, who he's been imagining is his twin brother, having sex. Not that they are having sex . . . that he knows of.

The four of them occupy the room for an uncomfortable yet convincing twenty minutes until the technician finally slips out. Thank Zorg, the building technicians sign resident privacy statements.

November 17, 2390.

His eyes land on Electra as she slips out of her room, and all his worries over the past few days fade into the background. Her long black hair is swept up on one side, and the rest falls in waves down her back. The swooping points of her eyeliner mimic the copper butterflies with their delicate wings and twinkling fairy lights that adorn the front of her dress. The fiery orange of the bodice softly transitions to a forest green where the hem grazes the floor. As she moves toward him, two slits reveal a brief glimpse of her upper thighs, sparking his thoughts for later use. With Electra's warm skin, highlighted with bronze and golds, plus her freckles, she looks like an autumn queen.

He swallows, awe overtaking him. "There aren't sufficient words to describe your beauty."

She blushes. "You look perfect, as usual." She pats the deep rust lapel of his tuxedo. "These shoes, though, they were the best I could find." She gestures to the wedge sandals she wears. The movement causes the slit to slide further open, revealing a tempting expanse of her toned thigh.

The sight almost makes his knees buckle. *Zorg, Res6, get yourself together.* He needs tonight to go well so he can show her he's someone worth forgiving when his lies eventually come out.

"Your shoes just came in." He unboxes a pair of strappy copper heels and points to his desk chair. "The laces are complex. Allow me."

"You don't have to—"

"I want to."

The corner of her mouth twitches as he kneels, holding the shoe out like an offering—another idea he got from DumBot. In the scene, a man called Prince Charming offers the heroine a glass shoe, the fragile material a rude gesture, leading him to question whether romance—or something far more nefarious—was the prince's aim. His own intent, however, is decidedly more straightforward. Plus, the prospect of Electra allowing him the intimacy of slipping on the delicate sandals he picked out has had his blood stirring in anticipation all morning. Thank Zephyr, the footwear arrived on time.

She sits, lifting her foot to him. A wave of heat washes over him. *You've seen a woman's leg before. Contain yourself.* His hands tremble as takes her foot and slips the toe strap on. At first it's awkward, but it only takes him a second to have the ankle straps wrapped around and secured snugly. She swallows as his fingertips graze her other ankle. For the next sandal, he moves slowly, with more intention, allowing his touch to linger. He's acutely aware of every sparkling point of contact as he finishes the job and then the absence as she gently places her foot back on the floor.

"It's not fair," Chryl whines, stepping into the room. The momentary tension crackling between him and Electra pops. "I want to go to the fantasy ball!" For emphasis, she lifts the lasso and boots she ordered for herself.

Electra smirks. "The dress code specifically says no cowgirls."

Ha! She isn't above untruths either. That shouldn't make Res6 feel as justified in his own falsehoods as it does.

As if she senses the lie too, Chryl narrows her eyes at Electra, an uncanny gesture that, if he is guessing correctly, Chryl learned from the other woman. "I'll take Prototype's dress."

"Maybe you can try on your cowgirl outfit and show me how nice it looks when we get back." Managing a manupartner while trying to explore this thing happening between him and Electra is becoming increasingly difficult. He can't recycle her now, though. After the first twenty-four hours, he suspected there was something different about her. It's one of the reasons he didn't immediately recycle her.

Chryl's lower lip juts out in a pout. "How long will you be gone?"

"A couple of hours," Electra says, intertwining her fingers with his, almost like they're a real couple. He should be terrified, but he's too elated to care.

"Fine." Chryl's boots thump to the floor as she wanders off toward the kitchen, giving them a chance to slip out the door.

Two hours pass in a blink. The uniquely arranged particle panes at the venue, Bubble Bar, have been programmed so the cavernous space resembles a giant tree, and each of the bubbles are amber glowing treehouses. Despite his social status, they wait an hour and a half for one to become available. They step in and arrange themselves on the plush cushions so they can see the main stage, where a cabaret performance is about to take place. A server takes care of their drink order, then they're alone in the cozy space.

As the main room's overhead lights dim, Electra leans into Res6. The bubbles that surround them at various heights all twinkle in rhythm with the music. The tree flickers for a moment, and the room goes dark. Three spotlights hit the stage. As the tree reanimates, transforming into a dozen tall, straight pines that reach toward a starlit sky, each bubble fades into a twinkling background with a single bubble in the center resembling a full moon. The bubble lowers to the stage, and a woman holding a microphone steps out. She begins singing a hypnotic, enchanting melody that melds perfectly with the scene.

"This is incredible," Electra whispers as more performers take the stage.

He leans forward, slipping his free hand inside the slit of Electra's dress just like a real boyfriend would do. Her breath catches. "Not as incredible as you." Her thigh is warm and soft beneath his palm, and she shivers as his hand drifts higher. They watch the first song with his fingers tracing lazy circles.

Blue, yellow, and pink stage lights dance in his periphery. By the awed expression on Electra's face, the performance must be extraordinary, but he can't quit staring at her. "Are you enjoying yourself?" he whispers, pleased with himself that he could offer her so much pleasure.

He's so damn eager to offer her more. She glances to where his hand has drifted higher. "Is this okay?" he asks.

Her stare lifts to his lips. "Are you going to kiss me?"

"Do you want me to?"

There's no uncertainty as she closes the distance between them. Her lips are supple yet firm as they crash into his. The kiss is nothing like the tentative exploration they shared in the Empire State Building simulation. This one is hungry and sure. If there was any lingering doubt before, this kiss has demolished it. He's done denying how inextricably drawn to this human woman he is. Electra is for him.

She gasps as he nips at her lower lip and he presses closer, learning her. Savoring her. She meets his intensity, reaching up and running her nails through the short hair at the nape of his neck. The nerves along his spine prickle.

With every kiss, every swallowed breath, his desire unfurls. She's like an immersion chamber, drowning his senses. His palms itch to feel more of her. He grasps a handful of her hair, pulling her head back so he can run his mouth along the smooth column of her throat. She hums in satisfaction as goosebumps dance across her skin.

He makes his way lower, trailing kisses to the soft mounds of her breasts and slipping a strap off one shoulder until it falls low enough to expose a dusky pink nipple. He takes the hardened peak into his mouth, licking and sucking, reveling in the way she arches into him, fingers gripping his hair.

"You're so fucking perfect," he confesses between kisses. She moans at the praise.

As he makes his way back to her delicious mouth, her legs part subtly. Is she opening herself to him? He's terrified of crossing a line and bringing this beautiful, confusing, complicated thing between them to a screeching halt. He pulls back, searching her eyes. Nerves dance in his stomach like the moment before a lab result, but the possible boon of touching her is so much greater than a successful experiment.

She holds his stare, boldly stating her desire. "Touch me."

Oh fuck. Her command has all his blood rushing to his cock.

He leans over her and slides his hand higher, fingers grazing silk and lace, then soft wet heat. Her eyes flutter shut as he dips a finger inside, gathering her arousal. He swirls it around her clit, discovering what pleases her. Soon he finds a rhythm that has her knees quaking. With every hitch of her breath, his cock throbs, straining against his trousers. But this is about her. "You're so beautiful trembling at my touch." He runs his lips across her pulse point.

"I need your fingers inside me."

He obeys, slipping a finger inside, using his thumb to strum her clit. "I love touching you like this."

Her inner walls flutter, and she cries out between gasps. "Oh God. Res6, I'm so close."

"Come for me, Electra," he demands, biting slightly in the spot that caused a shiver before. He hooks his finger forward on the following thrust, and she curls into him as she tips over the edge. Her inner walls spasm as he pumps his fingers, letting her ride out her orgasm. Pre-cum leaks from his cock and he's desperate to replace his fingers with it. Does she want that too?

Before he can ask, a chime sounds at the door.

"Fuck. I forgot to switch the light to Do Not Disturb." He eyes her as he licks the taste of her off his fingers. "Mmm," he moans, the taste lingering on his tongue. "So good."

Her eyes go wide. Another check in the Pro column for romance novels. He gets up to remedy the problem, eager to resume their activities because he's discovering he craves this woman in a frightening way. "Don't you dare move. I'm not done with you yet."

The flush beneath her stunning freckles deepens, and she glances away. He pops his head out, redirecting the server before closing and locking the door. He takes too long to figure out which switch sets the Do Not Disturb. He's still straining in his pants when he turns back to her.

But she's staring at the stage, her brow wrinkled in concern. She points, pulling her strap back up, and his stomach sinks. "There's Chryl."

"Impossible." The heat humming through his body in time with the music turns cold and his erection deflates as he sees the cowgirl Electra is pointing at. He runs a hand over his face. "I guess I deserve this for insisting on keeping her."

Electra hides a giggle behind her hand. "Oh God, is she twerking?"

"That thing she's doing with her backside is called twerking?"

Electra groans. "She must have watched more music videos from my time."

"We'd better go collect her before she causes any trouble."

By the time they make their way down to the ground level, Chryl is in the middle of the stage, swinging the lasso overhead. He takes Electra's hand, pushing through the crowd with an "Excuse me."

He creates such a disturbance in the throng of people, it draws Chryl's attention. It's too late when he notices devices pointing between him and the manupartner on the stage. Chryl's hand—not the one swinging the lasso—shoots up, waving maniacally.

"Is she glitching? On stage? In the center of a crowded ball in the middle of MSP?" Electra asks over the music.

"I'm afraid it's much worse," he says, already suspecting the cause of Chryl's uniqueness. But this isn't the time to explain his suspicions to Electra.

"Daddy!" she shrieks. "Found you! I've been looking everywhere."

"I'm here. Why don't you come down?" he shouts, earning an encouraging squeeze from Electra.

"Two hours passed, and I feared the worst. I've looked in every closet in this entire building! I thought they'd taken you again—"

"Chryl, please come down," he yells, more firmly this time. They were able to keep the robbery out of the news. The last thing he needs is for Chryl to announce it while a dozen bystanders have their cameras on them.

"No way, José! Daddy comes to Chryl this time." Before he realizes what's happening, the lasso flies. The crowd seems to have guessed what was happening, because there is a straight path to him and Electra with enough space for the rope to loop around them. Chryl tugs and it cinches tight, causing an equally shocked Electra to squeak.

The crowd breaks out in uproarious applause.

"Oh damn, it caught her too," Chryl says. "Oh, well." She yanks the rope toward her, and they have no choice but to follow.

It takes five minutes of coaxing to get Chryl down from the stage, and not before she gives a short farewell address to her fans, whom she encourages to follow her on FrogBlog at CowgirlChryl2390.

"You've created a monster," Electra says when they finally enter the sweet bliss of his private SAT.

"I actually had the same thought earlier." He glances toward the backseat. "Chryl, how did you learn how to use a lasso?"

"I knew I could impress you!" She beams. "When you left, I watched a how-to video, then went to the simulation chamber to practice. It only took me a few tries. It was much easier than the people in the video claimed."

Res6 shakes his head. A manupartner adapting as quickly as Chryl has fascinating implications for the future of CHOICElover. Her nature is programmed, but her nurture—the environmental factors that influence individual development, plus her learned and stored experiences—seems to be individuating Chryl. What more proof does he need? Her paperwork says she's been activated for a little over three years. She's like a fully grown and educated toddler. Fascinating, but also horrifying. Perhaps they should impose term limits on CHOICElover leases. "How did you get them to let you into a simulation chamber without me?"

Chryl leans forward from the backseat like she's about to share a juicy secret. "They recognized me from photos on the network, so they knew I belonged to you. I told them you sent me to practice, and that you sent a message giving me permission. When they couldn't find it, I told them how upset you were going to be, so they decided it would be easiest to let me in. Between lying and sexual favors, I can accomplish anything!"

Electra must not have connected that Chryl is learning by observing them, thank Zorg. Otherwise, his lies might come to light.

Electra cuts him off from his disturbing thought, saying, "Do what you want with your body, but lying is wrong, Chryl."

Chryl chuffs. "You lied. Two hours? Really Electra. Lying isn't that hard."

Res6 and Electra share a glance.

When they arrive back at the unit, he commands, "Chryl, please lock yourself in the room."

She stomps. "Why can't I stay out here with you?"

This jealousy trait is really getting out of hand. Is that what caused her original owner to turn her in? It might be worth sending a survey. "Because you've had a long night and I need to deal with the disruption you caused."

Chryl frowns. "The crowd loved me."

He sighs, pointing at the door. "Please just go."

"Fine," she says, before perking up. "Can I at least have the bed tonight? The floor is uncomfortable."

This causes Electra's brows to shoot up.

"Yes, you can take the bed." Anything to get rid of her.

Finally, the door closes and locks. With his m-volt, he thinks the command to keep it locked until he commands it open. Satisfied, he turns back to Electra, who's twirling a lock of her dark hair and biting her lip.

"I can't believe you're making her sleep on the floor," she says.

He shrugs guiltily. "I made her a nice pallet."

Electra rolls her eyes. "What now?"

Now that they're alone, his desire flares back to life. He thinks the command for a twinkling moonlit night. The room darkens, and soft music fills the space. He stalks toward her. In a swift move, he cups her jaw and kisses her. She rises to her toes, returning the kiss with the same vigor. He walks her back to the couch, gathering her dress in his hands, and drops onto the seat, pulling her onto his lap so she's straddling him. He kisses her neck. "I told you I wasn't done with you."

"What about Chryl?" Electra asks, but her concern doesn't stop her from leaning into his touch.

"Ignore her," he says, taking her mouth again, kissing her thoroughly. It's been so long since he's been with a woman, well, a *manupartner*, it doesn't take much for him to get hard again.

He palms her breasts, and she grinds against him once, moaning. When she doesn't continue, he grips her hips, moving them so her center is sliding along his length. "That's perfect," he praises. "Use me to make yourself feel good."

She moves, and he matches her tentative rhythm. *Too many fucking clothes.* "I want you naked."

"And I don't want to think about why you're so good at this," she says on a heavy breath.

He groans, and for a split second, he curses himself for inventing manupartners. But if he hadn't, Electra wouldn't be here with him now. The more intoxicated he becomes with her, the more he's convinced that he could never feel this way about any other woman. "It's you. I promise it's you, Electra."

"Really?" She pulls back, meeting his eyes.

For a split second, guilt nips at him, but he's been thinking about it and it isn't hard to convince himself that his untruths are for her benefit. *Their benefit.* His overly moral body double failed to mention that the Respectful and Considerate Conduct Course online manual also states that "lying may be acceptable when sparing the feelings of another."

He leans his head back. Her fingertips trace his lips, and down over his chin. Down his neck. "Yes," he says, swallowing thickly. "Really."

It's laughable that he ever planned to give Electra to Jerme, because she's clearly meant for him. Once he tipped over some invisible edge, he felt no resistance admitting how badly he wanted her. *A real woman.*

She leans down, pressing light kisses on his jaw, then lower. "You're beautiful too, you know." The whispered words against his neck unravel something inside him, and he isn't sure the word want is enough anymore.

The air between them hums as her fingers undo his buttons, pressing the jacket and shirt off his shoulders, grazing his overheated skin with such gentleness, reverence even. She watches his reaction as she pulls his shirt from his trousers, then reaches for his belt.

"Yes?" she asks.

He nods, admiring how powerful she looks perched on his lap with him at her utter mercy. "Please."

As she undoes his buckle, he slips her straps down so the bodice of her dress pools at her waist. "I've never seen anything like you before."

He touches her with worshipping fingertips as she did to him moments earlier. Her breathing hitches like she's feeling the same charge he is. Like he isn't the only one falling into this inferno building between them.

He wants nothing more than to feel her sliding onto him and rocking, drawing out both of their pleasure. His desire is so strong that he meets her gaze and says, "I need to be inside you."

The locked door rattles, and Electra stiffens.

He leans up, pulling her close, desperate to hold on to the energy humming between them before the manupartner in the other room drains it away.

Her forehead presses into his shoulder, and she groans in frustration. "I'm sorry. I can't do this with Chryl in the other room."

"She's only a manupartner," he pleads, though he isn't entirely sure if that's true anymore. "Let's go to your room." Zorg, the thought of getting tangled in his sheets with her sounds like perfection. Maybe she'll even let him sleep there, curled around her warm body.

The door rattles again, a pounding fist joining the ruckus.

Electra holds a hand up, stopping him. "I want this, I do. But we need to deal with her, or I can't."

He rakes a hand over his face. "I can't recycle her. She's not like you, but I think she's worth studying. She's learning, mimicking behaviors. The potential implications for my company—"

She leans back as if he's slapped her. "Your company. Right. I wasn't suggesting you recycle her." She pushes herself off him, tugging her straps back up. "I was going to suggest you see if she could stay with someone else, like Tommy. But of course, everything is about your company. Silly me."

"But, Electra," he chokes out, his flagging erection the least of his concerns.

She glances at his tented pants. "I'm sure Chryl will be happy to take care of that for you."

"But I don't want her!" he shouts at her retreating back. "I want—"

Her stare is so sharp it cuts him off. The question of what he was about to say hangs in the air between them. Then his mouth closes. Somehow he knows anything he says that isn't *Chryl goes* isn't enough. As she closes the door behind her, she mutters to herself, "How could I be so fucking stupid?"

The twinkling particle panes are his only audience when he finally finishes his admission, "—I want you."

25 – Contradictions and the Spice

Electra

November 18, 2390.

How could she be so stupid? Had she not kissed him, these regrettable feelings wouldn't be festering. For a moment last night, she thought something deeper was growing between them. As she ran her fingers over him, there was something burning in his deep gold eyes. Hunger? Worship? Devotion? He made her feel like the heroine in one of her stories, elated and powerful. She got so drunk on the feeling that she allowed herself to believe he would pick her. She almost offered a piece of her heart to him.

But it's her fault for thinking things might go right this time. That he could even be the type of man to offer her something. He'd been pretending she was a manupartner like he did before. That had to be it.

His words ring in her mind. *"It's you. I promise it's you, Electra."*

With such perfectly desperate sentiments, how could she not get swept away? She bites her fist, choking back a sob. *I will not cry over that man.*

This is exactly why she's never bothered with a boyfriend. Book boyfriends are enough. They can never disappoint you or keep a gorgeous female clone who's decided she's a cowgirl in the spare room.

She jolts up.

That's exactly why Res6 created manupartners! Her stomach squirms. Oh God. She's a hypocrite. No, the real reason she's never had a boyfriend is that she was too busy making ends meet while she wrote every spare moment she got. There wasn't time for a boyfriend. Well, and the men from her time were a questionable lot. But when the time was right, she would have taken the time to find one of the good ones. *The one.*

Well, that's a ludicrous fairy tale. Might as well hope she'll discover she's a secret witch, or that she's the long-lost heir of a kingdom of powerful women warriors. She takes a few grounding breaths and forces herself out of bed. *You will not cry over that man. You have officially reached this year's wallowing threshold.*

Her mascara-stained reflection stares back at her determinedly. She really shouldn't have slept in yesterday's makeup, but oh well. The water steams as she steps into the shower, letting the hot stream wash away her delusions.

When she's dressed, she finds Res6 sitting at his computer desk, staring blankly at the screen. His eyes have uncharacteristically dark circles, and his hair looks like he's been dragging his fingers through it.

"Sleep well?" she asks cheerfully, though it's clear he didn't.

He doesn't answer, but his eyes trail her as she gets a pick-me-UP nourishment packet and VitaShot from the refrigerator and takes them to her desk to get situated for the day. There are a dozen messages waiting that need to be sifted through. It's time for another column entry, and then there's the correspondence she's taken up with several fans, including her favorite new friend, Sister Xelna—the leader of the group building that amazing scratching post monument they saw while people-watching on the roller-boats.

As eager as she is to respond to Xelna's latest message, she has a strong urge to poke at Res6, who hasn't taken his eyes off her. "Where's Chryl?" she asks, noting the blanket and pillow on the couch.

He clears his throat. "The lab." For a moment, her heart leaps. Did he change his mind? He must read the excited expression on her face because he shakes his head. "For tests."

Her heart sinks. She tries to infuse as much nonchalance into her voice as she can muster. "Oh, well, good for you."

Res6 groans. "Electra, can we please talk about this?"

She shakes her head. "There isn't anything to talk about. Last night was a mistake." His eyes widen as devastation washes across his face. She isn't going to feel sorry for him. He knows what he needs to do to fix this.

He gets up and—suddenly he's rolled her chair around and is kneeling at her feet. He takes her hands, holding them between his. His brows are knitted together as if what he's about to say is incredibly painful. "Chryl didn't start real, but I think she is becoming real. This is what I was trying to tell you last night before you got upset and left."

Electra blinks. She left, didn't she? Then she fell into a spiral of self-pity.

"Lextr sent the scan results. There are new neural connections in the areas of her brain responsible for memory. Her experiences are individuating her."

"How is that possible?" He wasn't picking his company over her like she assumed. If what he's saying is true, Chryl something new. It's reasonable that he's grappling with how to deal with her. Shame washes over her at her behavior. The future is really throwing her for a loop.

"I don't know exactly yet. Most people turn their manupartners in before a year. Chryl is over three years old, which is unheard of. We've never thought to study what would happen to a manupartner as it ages."

Electra swallows. "You suspected this yesterday?"

He nods. "I've been watching her. She's mimicking us."

"The lying thing," she guesses.

"Yes, and she's started replicating your expressions."

"Oh God. The lasso thing too. If she can learn that fast, could she become dangerous? Her jealousy is already a little frightening."

Res6 raises himself to his feet, taking her hand and guiding her to the couch. They sit side by side, and her mind instantly goes to the moment they shared in this spot. He brushes his fingertips over her flushed cheeks. "You're so lovely."

The awe in his voice is unmistakable. She hadn't imagined it. Still, there was the ever-present Chryl. She clears her throat. "So you won't recycle her?"

He frowns. "I'm afraid that would be murder at this point."

"Well, it's reassuring you see that as a problem, since you were giving me murder-y vibes when we met," she says.

Chuckling and shaking his head, he says, "Tommy agreed to keep Chryl for a while until we can determine exactly what is going on with her."

Her stomach swoops. He listened to her. She can hardly believe it. "Really?"

He brings her hand to his mouth, turning it to place a devoted kiss on her wrist. "Really."

It's too good to be true. That doesn't stop her from grinning like a madman. "Okay."

He leans forward, and her pulse jumps. "I don't want us to fight, Electra."

"Me either," she says.

"Good." He cups her jaw, softly kissing her. Right as she's about to lean into the addictive sensation—thereby throwing every thought she stewed on overnight out the window—he pulls back, giving her a lopsided grin. "You aren't stupid. You're intelligent, entertaining, humorous, sexy, rather irresistible, thoughtful, admirably strong . . ."

Tears well as he lists her qualities. When he finishes, she laughs. "Are those the traits you selected when you thought you were programming me?"

A broad grin breaks out on his face, making him impossibly handsome. Fuck Adonis, she'd pick him all day, every day. She's about to launch herself into his lap so they can finish what they started last night when the front door opens to reveal Chryl, still in her cowgirl outfit, and Tommy, wearing a shimmery gunmetal jumpsuit.

"We're here to get Chryl's things," Tommy says.

Electra shoots up and marches over to Chryl. "Did you get freckles?!" She's not jealous—more shocked.

Chryl tilts her head this way and that, showing off the new spots sprinkled across her cheeks. "I think I wear them better, don't you think, Daddy?"

"Yes," Tommy answers, right as Res6 says, "No."

Chryl beams as if they both said yes, eliciting a groan from Electra. "I posted a vlog about the procedure my new daddy"—she frowns at Res6—"was kind enough to arrange for me. It only took ten minutes, and he said I can get rid of them just as easily when they fall out of fashion." She gives Electra a smug look.

"Chryl, no FrogBlog. We discussed this," Res6 says, giving a firm look to Tommy.

Chryl stomps, glaring at Electra. "Why does Prototype get to have one and not me?"

"She doesn't," Res6 says.

Chryl opens her mouth to argue—oh God, did Chryl discover her username?—but Electra cuts her off. "I don't see what's wrong with Chryl having a blog. Everyone knows she's a manupartner." She clears her throat, feeling only slightly guilty for defending her own self-interest. "Like me."

Chryl's eyes narrow, and Electra can practically see her wheels turning—the learning Res6 was talking about. She braces as Chryl's mouth opens. "Girl power?"

Electra beams. "Yes, us girls have to stick together." She hopes she isn't pouring it on too thick. She was terrible in drama class. "If it makes Chryl happy . . ." she says, hoping Res6 will get the hint. *If a blog makes her happy, maybe she won't turn evil.* Because obviously that is the biggest danger, as per EVERY VILLAIN ORIGIN STORY EVER.

"Right." Chryl turns to Res6. "Yes, *Electra* should have one too if she wants one. No one knows she's not a real manupartner."

Electra's stomach clenches right as a muscle in Res6's jaw twitches. "Electra is a manupartner, just like you," Res6 says. "Just a Prototype like we talked about."

"You are very good at lying." Chryl winks.

Res6 pinches the bridge of his nose. "Chryl, if the public had reason to believe that either of you are different . . ." He pauses, seeming to consider. "It would hurt CHOICElover, which would hurt me and Tommy. Do you understand?"

Chryl's eyes widen. She nods and flings an arm around Tommy's neck. "I would never do anything to hurt my new daddy." Then she mimes zipping her lips.

"I'm with the ladies. If there's a problem, it'll be easy to mitigate. Tell the public they're part of an experiment for a new product we are testing." Tommy says as Chryl bounces against him. He shifts, clearly uncomfortable with her exuberant attentions.

Res6 doesn't argue. "Fine. I'm only agreeing because Chryl is already exposed."

"But Electra should get permission too—" Chryl starts, then her eyes narrow in on her arm. "What's wrong with your arm?"

Electra cradles her forearm to her chest as they stare at her as if the minor nick is a contagion risk. "Nothing. I must have bumped into something last night. It's probably from your lasso."

Chryl's eyes narrow. "My lasso is made of the finest nylester. Why didn't you have my old daddy fix it?"

Res6 takes her arm, running his finger over the pea-sized cut. Good grief—she's glad for the distraction from FrogBlog conversation, but this is just a minor cut. She pulls her arm out of his grip. "It's nothing."

Tommy clears his throat. "I agree. It looks minor. Chryl, let's go get your things."

When Chryl and Tommy eventually leave, it doesn't escape her notice that the door to the spare room is locked once more.

If he gets to keep secrets, so do I. She huffs, turning her attention back to her station to work on her column.

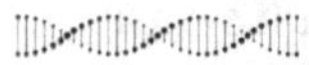

November 22, 2390.

Dear Electra,

I don't know if you remember me from your first column since there have been so many. I'm a huge fan. I got freckles done just like yours.

Electra opens the attached image. The person in the image has a stylish asymmetrical black bob, upturned eyes, and an adorable button nose dusted with freckles, similar to her own slightly pointier one.

I have news to report on the dating front. I approached my neighbor respectfully and asked permission to bring up something that might change the nature of our relationship. You were right. She was hesitant at first, but she agreed. I think I came on too strong. I just got so excited, I ended up confessing my feelings. She didn't talk to me for a week. I swear, I was devastated, cursing this Dear Electra person who'd led me astray.

Electra's chest tightens. She wants to help people, not to cause more loneliness and pain. She keeps reading, hoping for some good news.

But then, in the midst of my despair, she appeared at my door with takeout. She apologized for shutting me out and said it took her time to come to terms with her feelings in return. She said she's willing to explore something more with me. I was thrilled. Needless to say, the takeout got cold.

Electra's heart warms. See, her advice blog is a positive contribution to society!

Things were going well for a few weeks, but then she stopped wanting me to come to her unit. She still came to mine willingly. Then I saw her out with a male manupartner one day at the food court. She didn't see me, and we haven't spoken since, though she's rung my doorbell a dozen times. It's not that I wouldn't be open to adding a manupartner to our relationship, even a male one, but her deception makes me feel betrayed.

My question: is this something we can move past, or was it foolish of me to get my hopes up for a relationship? What do I do?

Desperately,

Born in the Wrong Century

Electra chews her lip. If she's going to advise this person, she needs to handle it delicately.

Dear Born in the Wrong Century,

First, the image you sent is adorable, and I'm so flattered that I inspired you to get freckles. They suit you.

To answer your question, relationships are never perfect. Getting hurt is part of the risk, but people need people, and love matters. Lying and deception are big indiscretions in any relationship. It is up to you to decide what you can forgive. Your partner may have hidden her manupartner from you out of fear of losing your relationship.

If you choose to move forward, you can gently confront her about it, and share your feelings of hurt and betrayal. Remember, don't speculate about her reasoning or accuse her. Just tell her how you feel, and listen if she tries to explain herself. Then if you come to an understanding, you can share with her that you'd be willing to explore different things in the relationship, but in the future, you need her to be upfront with you about her desires first if she wants the relationship to continue. You can reassure her of your willingness to be understanding because of how much you care about her.

Of course, if you find you are unable to forgive her, you may want to have a thoughtful conversation with her about why. Either way, this will be good practice at developing your social intelli-

*gence and interpersonal skills, which will help you greatly in future
relationships.*

Wishing you a happy outcome,
Electra

It takes her only a few minutes to proofread the entry and post
it. Feeling satisfied, she scans the other submissions, thinking she'll
prepare for tomorrow's post.

Res6 passes behind her on his way to the kitchen. She quickly closes
the window, but he pauses. She keeps her voice casual as she asks, "Is
it already lunchtime?"

"What are you working on?" he asks.

"Just writing, like you suggested." Technically, it isn't a lie. *More like
an error of omission.* Shut up, Janet.

His eyes narrow, but he shrugs. "Okay, then. I can't wait to read it."

He leans over her chair from behind, moving her hair aside so he can
kiss the sensitive skin beneath her ear. He's learned so quickly what
she likes.

"I could give you a few ideas for your next scene," he suggests.

Her toes curl. Boyfriend material indeed.

A loud growl sounds, and she chokes on a laugh. "Was that your
stomach?"

He sighs, as if his hunger has foiled his plans. "Let's go eat. There's
a new lunch spot I want to check out."

She places her hand in his outstretched one, and he pulls her to her
feet. As they're leaving his unit, they pass—"Wait, was that Tommy?
Tommy!" she calls.

Tommy turns around, grimacing. He says, "Oh hi, Electra," breezing
past her toward Res6's apartment.

"What's he doing?" Electra asks.

Res6 takes her arm and guides her to the elevators, but not before she throws a glance over her shoulder to see Lextr enter their unit.

He shrugs. "I left something for him to pick up."

What sort of wild-goose chase has Res6 sent the poor man on now? "What type of something?"

"I've noticed curiosity is a trait we share," he says, deflecting. "You know what they say, curiosity—"

"Killed the cat," she finishes automatically.

His brow furrows. "What cat? Why would you kill a cat? Didn't you also worship them in your time?" He shakes his head, chuckling. "Right, another saying from your time. I was going to say that, like the intense focus of a laser, unchecked curiosity can be an incredibly dangerous weapon. Curiosity, like lasers, can cut, burn, and even vaporize. Therefore, it should be used with extreme care."

Is he serious? She can't hold back a laugh as they step into the elevator. "Did you just make that up?"

"No. It's from the Respectful and Considerate Conduct Course manual. Remind me to get you a private tutor." There's no edge of sarcasm in his voice.

It's kind of bizarre that future people have a compulsory course that teaches basic human decency, but who is she kidding? They could have used one during her time. She jabs a finger into his side. "Is that how you learned to be so charming?"

He seizes her finger, spins her, and kisses her passionately. He only breaks away when the elevator doors open onto the food court. That's when she notices half a dozen people pointing phones at them. Res6 isn't fazed. He takes her hand, leaning down to say, "Smile," and leads her into the crowd.

The kiss in the elevator has her buzzing with untamed glee. This time, smiling isn't an issue.

26 – Camp Reincarnate

Electra

November 26, 2390.

Electra digs into her fill-you-UP fish sandwich. "This is delicious," she praises, and Res6 nods approvingly. "I haven't had fish since I was a teenager, and since it isn't real, I guess I don't have to feel bad about it."

"Mmm," he agrees. "I never understood the point of eating animals when the foods we can create in a lab are just as delicious and more nutritious."

"Not to mention their impact on the environment," she adds. "But sadly, we didn't have faux foods this tasty during my time. I still ate them though."

How many things they agree on is amazing. Who would have imagined her own personal book boyfriend would 1. Be this good-looking. 2. Be a vegetarian like her. 3. Love reading romance books, even if he read them in secret at first. 4. Be able to kiss like that. *5. Be over a hundred years old.*

Evidently, the Vine is kicking in because she's feeling exceedingly positive about this week's turnaround. Thoughts like, *See, things might work out* keep popping into her mind at an alarming rate.

"I've been considering your worries about my identity." Electra moves a faux-tay-toe around her plate. She's been debating bringing this up with him for days now. Might as well attempt the conversation when the mood is primed for positivity.

He nods as he swallows a bite. "Good."

"Right, so I found a company on the network that specializes in helping people get fake identities."

His brows furrow. "That's illegal, so I highly doubt that's really what they're offering."

"It was on a portal I found called BLACKOUT," she supplies.

He chokes. "That's the dark web, which is even more illegal."

She knew he would resist. But she keeps going. "It's called Iden-TECH, and their site says they can help people with peculiar problems. Then it showed a woman wearing a shirt that says *reincarnate*—that's the word they're using for people like me. She places her hand on one of those palm scanners and it shows a big green response, saying *Identity Verified*! GROW's logo is on there. They're your competitor having the mishap issue, right?"

Around them, there is a swish of water, and the particle panes show a school of cherry red minnows zip by, pursued by some larger blue fish. They zoom and dip around the room, making a swift pass by the restaurant's only real aquarium. It holds a single lonely-looking lionfish. Electra feels sorry for the creature as the fish images make another confusing pass. The poor thing's spines are standing at attention as it shifts and spins in the small tank.

She tears her gaze away to find Res6 studying her. "I'm not sure getting a fake ID is a good idea."

The second death threat she received that morning almost convinced her to keep quiet like he wants. "You can't block all of us. We told you we don't want your old-world advice. Every word you write is another step closer to the recycle station. Nice freckles, by the way." Panicky thoughts flitted through her mind like those red minnows. *Do they know my identity? Are they the same people who took the DNA? Are they going to find me and take this second chance she doesn't even deserve?*

But that's the response they wanted, so she talked herself out of deleting her account and shot her new friend Sister Xelna over a screenshot of the threat looking for some reassurance. Xelna told her she got messages like when she first started The Sacred Order of Feline Transcendence. "There will inevitably be people opposed to your ideas. You can't let them win." Xelna was right. With how popular her cat cult is now, she is speaking from experience. Still, thinking about it makes a shiver run down her spine. Too bad she can't ask Res6 about it. Random death threats from internet trolls would not help her case.

She must maintain a positive outlook on the topic if she stands any chance of convincing him. "I hear you. But I was thinking you could meet with them and see if they're legit. If I got an ID, you might feel more comfortable with the idea of my Dear Electra blog. Maybe I could even publish my work again."

"Electra," he says. "What makes you think they're legit?"

"I thought maybe you could go meet with them and get a gauge."

He shakes his head. "I'm not sure you've thought this all the way through."

A flash of red that she's pretty sure isn't the minnows darts across her vision, and she flinches as if he slapped her. "I haven't thought it through *completely*. That's why I'm *discussing* it with you. But why would I expect you to know this? You've only had relationships with sex clones for most of your life."

Instantly she knows she's said the wrong thing.

His shoulders tense. "BLACKOUT deals can be risky. We don't want to expose ourselves to any unneeded scrutiny. Thank you for bringing it up for discussion."

"But . . . It's not a discussion if I bring something up and you decide for me. That isn't how relationships work, Res6. Consider my perspective. If I'm not anyone but a manupartner, how can I work or contribute to society long-term? According to you, I'm not even registered like a normal manupartner, so I can't use the SATs or go to the gym alone."

He scoots nearer, reaching behind her to pull a lock of hair over her shoulder and twirls it around his finger. "I hear your concerns, but the company you found is an unnecessary risk. As for the gym, I'll take you, and I'll register you as a manupartner so you can use the SATs."

Alarm prickles through her. She shifts back, nearly to the edge of the semicircle booth. "The gym isn't the point. This is exactly why I need to support myself. If I rely on you for everything, I have no true freedom. I'm subject to your judgment and decision-making." *And if you're wrong, I'm the one who pays the price.*

His brow wrinkles as if he's contemplating something. Carefully, he says, "I'm trying to understand."

"If it's up to you, I'll be registered as a manupartner for the rest of my life. What more is there to understand?" She slumps back, crossing her arms.

"I don't see what the problem is. It gives you access to everything you said you wanted. I'm trying to keep you safe, not control you, if that's what this is about."

In a rare moment of independence-fueled security, she maniacally gestures to the room. "What do you think is going to happen, Res6? I am safe."

His lip curls, and he snaps, "I thought the same thing about Jerme, and look what happened."

Her heart jumps to her throat. Oh God. It makes perfect sense. He's finally allowing himself to become attached to someone, which brings up the fear of loss. *Shit.* She moves closer, but he slides out of the booth.

Curious eyes track her as she jumps up to follow him.

"Res6, please!" People are definitely staring. The rollercoaster of her emotions over the last week is too much. Between being worried that no one wanted her column, the emotional visit to his brother's site, and the frustration of their little misunderstandings, she needs a break.

He holds out his hands in a placating gesture. "Don't worry, people. Just a little role-playing for the make-up sex." Then he turns to her and—*no shit*—says, "Fight with me, baby."

Her mouth drops open. "You're a total lunatic."

He steps closer, latching onto her elbow. He leans in close, murmuring only for her ears, "Understand this: if you draw attention to yourself, there's a limit to what I can do to keep you safe."

Her head might actually explode. "All the more reason to meet these IdenTECH people and get me an identity." Louder, so the fight scene is believable, she says, "And just when I thought things were going well."

"We don't know them. It could be a setup by NHOS searching for these *reincarnates*. It's too risky." He takes her elbow, leading her out of the restaurant.

As they march down the hallway, something nauseating occurs to her. "This is about your company again, isn't it? Not me, an actual human being. I don't know why I thought you might understand. You're unbelievable. It's easier for you to keep me under your thumb where you can control me and make sure I don't upset your perfect world. So fucking typical. Take me home. I'll figure it out on my own." She jerks her elbow out of his grasp, cringing at the word *home*.

His arm wraps around her waist without another word. When they finally get back in the elevator that leads to the penthouses, he leans in, grumbling, "You are being impossible. If you recall, I chose you over my company when you had a sparkler aimed at your head. Then I got rid of Chryl, again choosing you."

Her throat tightens at the chastisement. "I—"

"I'm not done," he growls, releasing her waist to punch the elevator button, which redirects them to the private SAT garages. "Inspector Wanda informed me that NHOS knows about GROW's mishaps. Apparently, there was a manhunt a few weeks ago that made the news. Since then, they learned about and caught several more." Her hand drifts to her gaping mouth. "Do you know what they're doing with them?" She shakes her head. "They're keeping them in holding cells as if they're manupartners." His eyes go distant, like when he's using his m-volt. "Come on." He takes her hand, leading her from the elevator to his private SAT.

Between his irritation and his determined strides, resisting seems pointless. "Where are we going?"

He blows past the attendant and opens his private SAT's door. "Get in. I was going to drop you off at the unit before my next meeting, but since you refuse to listen to reason, change of plans."

That doesn't sound ominous at all. She slides in, noting the sleek silver case in the backseat. He marches around, dropping into the seat next to her. "You're not reconsidering recycling me, are you?" she asks, halfheartedly joking.

His eyes roll—an apparently universal gesture. "I agreed to help Inspector Wanda evaluate these mishaps she's caught. Since you refuse to hear reason, you're going with me."

Electra plasters on what must be a manic, fake smile if the wary glances from the eight reincarnates in the spacious, sterile room are any sign. She wants to shout, "It's okay. I'm one of you!" But the dismal holding center is enough to give her pause.

Res6 stands beside her carrying the silver case, which, it's strangely comforting to know, has something to do with Camp Reincarnate and not with whatever secret project he's working on behind locked doors. His irritated expression has bled away. He now wears an appropriately concerned grimace.

Inspector Wanda swipes at her tablet. "When your name is called, please come forward."

Only a few people acknowledge her. A man sitting in a metal folding chair in the center of the room glares at them as he gets up and turns the chair to face away. His glare makes Electra feel unwelcome, like an intruder seeing something they shouldn't. Another person, a woman sitting in a cross-legged meditative pose, blinks her eyes open to gaze in their direction before taking a long inhale and closing her eyes again. Three people sit in a corner talking quietly. There is a couple huddled together, dozing against the far wall. The last person is a woman lying facing the wall, trembling. Is she sick? As a manupartner, could she ask? Will Res6? He's similarly scanning the space.

"Marshal Withers!" Wanda booms.

Several reincarnates jolt at her loud voice. The man who turned his chair shakes his head but gets up. His defeated, sagging posture suggests he's resigned to whatever Wanda's about to do to him.

Electra represses a shiver. What has he been through? She isn't sure she wants to know, but her urge to help them is firing. But she's powerless to do anything except get herself caught. Then she'll be forced to join them.

She watches in horror as the reality of their circumstances hits her. That's the impression Res6 was hoping to make. Well, his plan is backfiring because this is even more proof that she needs an ID. She can't end up like these people—in a barren holding chamber awaiting some government agency's decision about what to do with her. How long have these people even been here? She glances at the shivering woman, and her stomach tightens.

As Marshal approaches Wanda, his gaze snags on Electra's for an extended pause. *Look away*, she wills him, hoping he can read her mind. Finally, his gaze slides to Wanda.

"Hello, Marshal. This is Res6 and his manupartner." Wanda says, not bothering to mention her name. "He's going to do a few quick scans."

Marshal shakes his head. "How many more scans do we need? I've told you and every so-called expert you've brought in here the same story." He turns to Res6. In an annoyed monotone, he says, "My name is Marshal Withers. I'm a twenty-eight-year-old mechanic from Idaho. The last thing I remember is fishing at my buddy John's pond outside of Fort Hall. It had just started to rain—rain always makes for amazing fishing. Keith, my other buddy, who's an amateur weatherman, said it was only supposed to be a light drizzle. That thunderclap came out of nowhere. I remember nothing after that. See. Same story."

"Of course," she says, blatantly blowing him off. "Just one more for good measure. Res6 is the owner of a company like the one who created you. That means he has special insight into your nature and can help us understand what is wrong with you. Our goal is to prevent it from happening again in the future."

"I don't need no more scans. What I need is to go home. My wife's gonna be pissed as hell that I've been gone this long, and she's never gonna believe I got picked up by aliens." Several of the other reincarnates glance in his direction. "She's probably havin' the lawyers draw up divorce papers as we speak."

Oh my God, Marshal thinks these strange future people are aliens. It's a fair guess.

"That's all very good, Marshal. I'd like you to tell Res6 what year you think it is now," Wanda says.

Marshal covers his eyes. "Not this again."

"Marshal," she scolds.

"It's 2016."

Electra gasps. He's from her time. She has a million questions, but she can't voice a single one.

Wanda turns to Res6. "I'm sure you understand the ramifications if NHOS determines the risk is too high."

He clears his throat. "I do. As I mentioned on the call, CHOICElover's resources are at your disposal. Your threats are unnecessary." Res6 and the inspector stare at each other for a long moment before she finally looks away. The corner of his mouth tips up. "I'll need a table for my equipment. Marshal, please be seated and I'll be with you in a moment."

Wanda leaves them in the reincarnate room to fetch a table. As soon as the door closes, Electra spins to face Res6. "You're helping her to protect your company, aren't you?"

His eyes widen. "Did you not hear what I just said, or are you intentionally being obtuse?"

"These people are traumatized, not to mention they're probably terrified out of their minds—"

He leans down, pressing his lips to hers. When he pulls away, he whispers, "Cameras, Electra."

Her stomach dips. She didn't even consider that they were being watched. Well, not them specifically. The reincarnates. Is someone watching their exchange right now? NHOS is evidently rounding up reincarnates. Are manupartners like her being scrutinized? Anxiety shoots through her, but she clenches her jaw and forces a smile.

"Be a good girl and go sit down." He points to a chair. She does as he asks without hesitation.

A few minutes later, Wanda rolls a metal table into the room. Res6 opens his silver case and retrieves a now-familiar scanner.

It takes him two hours to interview and scan every reincarnate. Thankfully, when they get to the shivering woman, Res6 confirms she isn't sick, just cold. By the time Wanda escorts them out of the room, Electra's tailbone aches from sitting and her cheeks are pinched from her asinine smile. Still, it doesn't waver.

Wanda guides them to an upper-level floor—her office? A few screens sit on a sleek stone desk. Several gray metal cabinets line two walls. A third wall is a large particle pane displaying a flat concrete-texture background.

When they're seated across from Wanda, she sets her tablet on the desk, tapping the screen. "Our conversation is being recorded."

Electra doesn't blink.

After a few pleasantries, Wanda says, "Now that you've interacted with them, in your expert opinion, would you say we're dealing with faulty manupartners, or are these indeed people from the past?"

No blinking, Electra. Smile. Show your teeth. Not that much teeth! Act like a manupartner—like Chryl. Oh God. She points to the gray concrete in the particle pane. "I like that texture. It feels soft!"

The corner of Res6's mouth tips up. He pats her hand. "It's very pretty, like you."

Wanda's eyes brighten, and she points to Electra. "See! They're nothing like a normal manupartner."

She has to force herself not to melt into the chair. Don't lay it on too thick. Stop while you're ahead. She sits motionless.

"True enough. And to answer your question, yes, I believe we're dealing with something unprecedented here. I'd like to do a little more research, but I believe the eight people in that room are experiencing reality as if they're from the past."

Wanda's warm skin goes ashen. "How could this happen? Considering the testing . . . and I know the Consumer Rights Protection Agency would have . . . There are protocols, aren't there?"

He offers her an easy smile. "Of course, Inspector. This is my area of expertise. I'm happy to work with NHOS as a liaison during this challenging situation. And believe me, I'm dismayed that a competitor would have such a concerning issue. I'm a champion of proper protocols to prevent such mishaps." Wanda nods appreciatively. "As for the issue of how this happened, I'll need more time to study the scans, but my initial guess is they tried to push out their Realer Than Real advancement before they were ready. Each company's NAM suppression sequence is patented, and I can't speak to their proprietary electrowave oscillation pattern, but it seems instead of repressing, their technology caused an expression event."

"Okay, but answer this. They all claim to have been born prior to 2050. Why?" she asks.

"My best guess is GROW's Realer Than Real update had an adverse reaction because of the purity of the DNA in combination with the collection standards of the time. That was prior to the birthing industry, which began tampering with DNA to achieve specific outcomes, and modern DNA preservation techniques. These are the only variables we've come up with."

That's basically what he'd told Electra when she first woke up. Perhaps he'll find something different after he studies the scans.

"And you say CHOICElover has never had such a mishap?" Wanda prods.

Res6 smirks. "Never, and I assure you, we won't. Manupartners are perfectly safe. The issue with GROW appears to be a quality control issue. I'd suggest investigating them as soon as possible."

Wanda stiffens. "I know how to do my job. Must I remind you that you're a consultant on this investigation?"

He shakes his head, giving her another amiable smile. "No. Only a suggestion."

Wait, is he pretending she's a manupartner? Is that his technique for dealing with social situations that make him uncomfortable, like giving a speech and pretending your audience is naked?

"Great. Please have your team study the data you've collected, and if you find anything significant, I want to know immediately."

"I'll make sure that happens."

Wanda taps her screen. "Before you go, I wanted to get your feedback on another thing. My team has been discussing what to do with these manupartners now that we're uncovering more of them. Our initial plan was to recycle them like one would a normal manupartner."

Doesn't the inspector realize that would be murder? Electra fights to keep from tensing. Those were clearly human beings, nothing robotic or stilted about them.

"And your other option?" Res6 asks.

"A few of my team members felt uncomfortable with that idea, so they proposed NHOS arrange a custom simulation that mimicked their world. The expense would be tremendous, but if we could isolate the problem and prevent future issues, the affected manupartners could live their lives in peace, and we could keep them out of the public eye. Since people during their time only lived around eighty years, it wouldn't be for too long. Assuming that the data confirms they truly have this NAM expression issue you mentioned."

She wants to scream that recycling them or sticking them in a simulation chamber is inhuman. They have the power to heal these people and extend their lives as Res6 did for her. These people could live well into their hundreds. They could acclimate like she is! She's practically vibrating with the need to say something.

Res6 turns to her. Can he sense that she's about to burst and blow their cover? "Electra, go wait for me in the hallway."

It takes a second to process his command. Robotically, she stands to do as he says. Does he regret bringing her? He said he regrets activating her. Is he going to suggest they recycle her too? No, that's insane. He won't let them recycle her—he brought her here to show her he's trying to protect her. But the inspector just threatened his company, which is his primary consideration—his love. Because a man like him could never love a real human woman—could he? He probably hates himself for liking her at all. The company that is his brother's legacy, however . . . If it's between her and it, he'll choose it every time. CHOICElover is and will always be his priority.

Trembling like the cold reincarnate a few floors down, she slips out into the hallway. Before the door closes behind her, she hears him say, "I programmed this one to be active. She gets antsy sitting for too long."

Once safely inside his awaiting SAT, Electra asks, "Why did you send me away?"

His goal in bringing her to Camp Reincarnate worked—maybe not in making her less interested in getting an ID, but his opposition certainly feels more relevant.

"If I could sense you about to lose it, Wanda would too. I needed you out of that room before they took you from me." He takes her hand, bringing it to his lips. "Aside from that last bit, you did well."

Her heart skips a beat. *See, Electra, he cares about you. You were freaking out over nothing.* Well, good for her, but what about those eight traumatized people? "We can't let her recycle those people."

The back of his head hits the seat. "The problem is that she doesn't see them as human, and I needed to convince her they are, without letting on why I know that. Do you see now?"

The NHOS inspector didn't realize they're human? Is she a bad person or just a product of her time? "You're trying to help them while also protecting me."

"Yes, I want to help them, but you're my priority, Electra. I promised to keep you safe. But I didn't know the conditions I'd find them in. I thought she'd at least treat them humanely." He shakes his head. "I got through to her in the end, though. I think."

She squeezes his hand reassuringly. "So you needed me to leave before I messed everything up?"

"I couldn't focus with you in the room bordering on an explosion."

"What happened after I left?"

"They're not getting recycled, and she agreed to give them blankets and cots. Plus, better food. Not the sustenance meal packets they've been getting. I'll keep working on it. They'll need citizenship, ideally. Personhood, but she was so resistant I didn't even bring it up. Small steps."

"I can't believe you just advocated for them, considering your stance—"

He drops her hand. "I'm not a monster, Electra. Is that what you think of me?"

She doesn't answer because it's a relevant question. *Is that what she thinks of him?* She spends the rest of the SAT ride dissecting it. She still isn't entirely sure about the answer. Perhaps that is how she viewed him at first, but now she can see little cracks is his colder façade that let the lighter, realer him shine through. The part of him she's growing increasingly attached to. The part of him that makes her feel—

"You didn't answer my question. Is that what you think of me?" he asks as the elevator doors close.

There's hurt in his voice. "I . . . I know you're not a monster. I just don't understand why you're trying to help them." God, that sounds awful, but it's true.

"For some strange reason," he eyes her pointedly, "I feel compelled to advocate on their behalf." The elevator doors slide open, chiming, and he drags her down the hall. When they get safely inside his unit, he spins her, pinning her against the wall. "It's the right thing to do. After all, I have a personal attachment to one." He slams his lips down on hers for a brief, heated kiss.

When he pulls away, they're both breathless. "I want you so fucking bad, Electra, but you also drive me so fucking crazy." Before she can reply, he storms off to lock himself in his Secret At-Least-Chryl-is-Gone Room.

She brushes her fingers over her lips, heart thrumming wildly. "Wow." Though her cheeks ache from earlier, she can't wipe away her massive grin. He cares. He might actually truly care. About her, even though she drives him crazy. He seems to think she's worth it. He said she's his priority. Her heart feels like it's expanding with each beat. What a revelation! Too bad he retreated to his room, because make-up sex isn't a terrible idea. She wants him too—*so bad*. God, every time his words repeat in her mind, her core pulses like she's never seen a good-looking man before. Or written about them. This is so much better. He is so much better.

27 – An Adult Conversation

Res6

November 30, 2390.

After another failed Jerme using an organic sample, Lextr suggested running more than one experiment at a time, varying the electrical impulses. After the trauma of the first failed real Jerme, it took him a few days to work up the nerve to restart the trials. The problem is they've now burned through four of the ten they started with. It was one thing to synthesize encoded DNA to match Jerme's unique sequence—they had a limitless supply. But in light of the failure rate and the fact that Electra's sample came from real preserved DNA, using Jerme's actual DNA gives them the best shot. That means six more tries, two of which are currently growing in the closet. The scans look good. There's no point in hovering.

When he steps out of the spare room, Electra is sitting in her computer chair with her arms crossed. She's staring at him, which really means she was staring at the door he just exited.

Electra clears her throat, letting the silence hang heavy between them. He figured she'd be asleep when he got home with the two damning cases.

"Please, Electra, don't be upset with me." He rubs the bridge of his nose for emphasis. If she knew what he was dealing with, would she be more empathetic? No, she would judge him, he's sure of it. People who got brought back accidentally, like Electra, have certain rights. But bringing people back from the past is wrong, apart from Jerme, who deserves a second chance. He takes a deep breath. Actually, forget trying to justify it. It's wrong, but he's doing it anyway.

Electra eyes him as if she knows the contradictory thoughts swirling around his mind. "We need to have a tough conversation, but I don't want to fight." He nods for her to go on, bracing. "I understand you have a right to your privacy, but I'm having a hard time wanting this relationship to progress when you're clearly hiding things."

Feeling threatened, his instinct is to defend himself, but she's right. They can have an adult conversation like people in an actual relationship. "If you understand that I'm not obligated to share every personal thing with you, then why are you pushing?"

She's quiet for a moment. "There is a difference between privacy and secrets. If that's just something you're working on for your company, why can't you tell me about it? I know I said some awful things about the manupartners at first, but I thought after we went and paid our respects to your brother—after everything you shared with me—that we had moved past that."

His focus shifts to the silent particle panes, which he only now notices display the first light of sunrise.

This is the exact complication he's always tried to avoid. But she's worth it, isn't she? He stares as a tear trickles down her cheek, wrenching his heart. If he keeps making her cry like this, she won't hang around for long. She's smart. She'll figure out how to leave, then she will, like 3Zeez left her brother. That means losing the relationship he never even wanted. He paws at his chest where the panic is settling in. Would losing her wreck him like it did his brother? He's only known this woman for a short while, which means he's no better than Jerme for embedding Electra so deeply into his world that the thought of her leaving sets him on edge. That makes him a hypocrite, but who cares? He can't lose her.

He takes a deep breath. Is he obligated to share with her that he's trying to bring Jerme back? He isn't sure which category his experiments fall into—privacy or secrets. Regardless, waiting until Jerme's return to tell her will maximize his chances of keeping her. Then he'll tell her anything she wants to know; that's the plan. She'll deserve to know. After all, Jerme will be their new roommate because he isn't letting his brother out of his sight until he's certain Jerme is stable. Maybe he'll move back into his room, which he and Electra can share—not her and Jerme like he originally envisioned. Considering how effectively she's knocking down his walls, the non-deities clearly meant her for him.

He steps up behind her desk chair and rubs her arms. Now that he's becoming attached, he hates that she might distance herself over a simple difference of opinion. Or that he might be the one causing a chasm between them. "You're right. We've moved past that. I'm not used to sharing things, okay? What I'm working on is a highly confidential and very difficult project. There isn't anything that you can do to help, and I guess I'm still sensitive about what you'll think about it." That was true enough.

Her shoulders deflate, and she must sense the earnestness in his words. "We come from different worlds, and I know that there will be bumps as we figure things out. I just need to be able to trust you. Especially now that things are becoming more delicate between us."

He spins her chair to face him again and gets down on one knee so they're at eye level. He doesn't speak, sensing she has more to say. A single tear crawls down her cheek. She reaches to catch it, but he beats her to it, brushing it away with his thumb. "You know I care about you, right?"

"I care about you too, Res6. I guess I'm always waiting for the next bit of bad news. I keep getting my hopes up, only to be let down." She takes quick sniffs, trying to contain herself. Still, the tears fall. "I'm not upset with you. I'm just afraid because what's between is so new and I feel so vulnerable."

Thinking of the sunrise on the particle panes, a symbol of new beginnings, he doesn't hesitate. He pulls her out of the chair and into his arms, stands, and carries her to the couch. He could mirror her words, but instead of him fearing some existential threat taking things from him, he fears being left alone—like Jerme left him. The realization only makes the pang in his chest that much stronger. When he has her situated in his lap, he tilts her chin up so he can look at her. "I feel vulnerable too, and you've seen why."

"Losing Jerme," she fills in.

He nods. "What happened that makes you so afraid of what may come?"

He's never found himself more deeply curious than he is at this moment. He needs to know why she is so afraid so he can fix it and make sure she never fears the unknown again. That is the security he can give her. That will make him valuable enough to her that she won't leave. *Which, in an unfortunate twist, is a good argument for getting her an ID.* He internally grumbles.

She shakes her head, focus blurring. He senses she's reliving a memory. "I was really poor growing up. Everyone in my community was. We got by, but we were always borrowing the basic necessities like bread and eggs from neighbors. Our car was always broken down, and we didn't have enough money to fix it. My dad would have to get rides to work or take the bus when we could afford it, but he usually saved his pocket change for my school lunch money. I never told him it wasn't enough. The neighboring town was more affluent, and the kids always gave me their change, but it was humiliating. The shame of admitting my family was poor and borrowing money was easier to bear than the guilt my dad would have felt if he knew.

"But I never cared. I loved my parents, and we always looked out for each other. But then one day I got home from school, and I could tell something was wrong. My dad was in his normal burgundy paisley recliner, staring at a black television screen. My mom was standing across the room behind the counter, kneading dough that had turned hard as a rock. There's no telling how long they'd been there like that. When they noticed me, they sat me down and gave me the news. My mom had breast cancer. The doctor had given them a treatment plan and said the odds were good that she would survive. But then as the months passed, I saw papers on the kitchen table that were covered in red numbers. That's when I realized that my parents couldn't afford to pay for her lifesaving treatment. She died three months later."

Her grief momentarily transports him back to the day he found out about his brother. "I'm so sorry." He strokes her hair, letting her weep gently into his chest. He knew her mother died of cancer, but she never told him why. His heart quietly breaks for her.

Eventually, she speaks again. "I always think I've left it in the past, but something will happen, and it triggers me all over again. You know, right before I died, I'd found out that my books were getting published.

I thought I'd finally made it, and everything was going to be good. That was hundreds of years ago, but for me it feels like only months."

"I know," he says, knowing there's nothing he can say to alleviate her pain.

She shakes her head, sitting up to look at him. Zorg, she's still so beautiful even with puffy eyes and a tear-stained face. Maybe even more beautiful, more human. The thought twists his insides as he stares at her in awe.

"You know what it's like to lose someone," she says. "The other day, I was thinking about all the things we have in common, and I forgot to add that to the list."

She gives him a soft smile, which he returns. "At least we have that," he says. "I wish I could help you feel more secure."

He wonders if she's about to tell him that he could show her what's inside the room. After the last ten minutes, he's fairly certain he would be compelled to comply. He wouldn't be able to come up with a good enough reason not to. Thankfully, it doesn't seem to occur to her, or she realizes it would be a manipulation and she's too good a person to wield her power over him like that.

"It's okay. Only I can choose to have an abundant mindset and learn to reframe life's road bumps as challenges—two of the many lessons from the constant stream of psychological exercises Janet was so fond of. Thank you for not trying to see the bright side. That's always the worst. When you're lost in a sea of melancholy, the last thing you need is some well-meaning person accidentally minimizing your pain. Just let me wallow in it, damn it." She chuckles.

It's so good to see her smile, he can't help but laugh too. "When Jerme died, I never wanted to talk to anyone about it because I was so afraid of the things people would say to me. I think that's part of the reason I shut people out."

"And send a manupartner to your FRIENDS groups?" she teases.

He waits for her to shoot a glare at the door, but she doesn't. She must assume he keeps it at the office.

"I went to them when NHOS first rolled out Project LEN." He chuckles again. "I was already quite adept at my aloof persona by then."

Her mouth falls open. "So that version of you is the persona! That's another thing I wondered about. I thought you were having an identity crisis. Or acting like everyone you meet is a manupartner."

He shrugs. "I'll admit I do that occasionally. It makes social situations easier. Wouldn't Janet call it a defense mechanism? As far as identity crises go, I am indeed having one, considering I'm the very public creator of manupartners—"

"You're either brave or foolish," she says, and he raises a brow in question. "If you recall, the last time you said something to that effect, I got quite angry at you."

He kisses her lightly. "You didn't let me finish. I'm the very public creator of manupartners, in the midst of falling for a human woman." Her cheeks redden, and he relishes that he can make her blush so easily.

The device in his pocket buzzes. "One second," he says, pointing to his m-volt implant behind his ear. It's a message from the identity company Electra mentioned. After their visit to the reincarnates, he created a BLACKOUT account and sent them a request to meet, and they've finally replied.

She watches him listen to his message, opening her mouth. Probably to berate him for getting distracted with his device, but he presses a finger to her lips before she can speak. "It's good news that you'll want to hear, so please hold your comments."

"Oh, really?" she asks, swiping at his hand.

He brushes the last residual tears off her cheeks.

"Yes. We officially have an appointment with IdenTECH. Tonight."

"Really?" she asks, beaming.

Res6 isn't thrilled about the prospect of meeting at a dusty bar in Z Quadrant called Scraps with the two founders of the alleged company, but he has to give her something to make her happy, *and keep himself valuable to her so she won't leave.* That's what he failed to do all those years ago with Jerme. He won't make that mistake again.

Plus, seeing the conditions the reincarnates were being kept in convinced him a fake ID was an option worth exploring. If she gets one, she'll still have to be careful since Wanda can identify her. But they can navigate that together—unless he can convince Inspector Wanda to grant the reincarnates personhood. Then he could tell her about Electra and get her legitimate citizenship too.

Electra shakes his shoulders. "Really?" she repeats.

He grins. "Yes, really."

The private SAT emits a faint humming as it zips across MSP toward Z Quadrant, the location of the meeting Res6 arranged for them with the founders of IdenTECH. Beside him, Electra's vibrating knee betrays her anxiety. Since they set up the meeting, he's been scrolling through BLACKOUT for anything that will give him some insight into the people he's about to meet with.

She's watching him intently as he scans an article. "What are you reading?"

She chews her lower lip, trying to steal a glimpse at his screen. "You don't want to know," he says, rubbing her knee to ease her nervous energy.

"Well, now I certainly do," she says, leaning closer.

The SAT pulls into a public garage, and the doors lower to begin the air purification transfer. There is a loud click before the hiss of the air exchange, which is powerful enough to rattle the vehicle. Outside the window, the air becomes lighter until it's the clear, breathable inside air he's used to.

Electra reaches forward, tapping his phone to scroll to the beginning of the article Tommy sent that's still making the rounds from over six weeks ago. He lets her read it quickly, knowing there is no point in arguing once she's decided something. It's part of the reason he's sitting here. At least she quit pressing him about his "work" experiment, i.e., the gelatinous blob that might one day become Jerme.

He knows she's gotten to the part about the manhunt that took place in B Quadrant when she emits a small gasp. "This article is dated October 14. Does that mean Wanda knew about the reincarnates the day of the robbery?"

The word *reincarnate* seems to have caught on. Even the NewNews reporter is using it. "Evidently, but when she messaged me to ask for my help, she didn't mention how long they'd known about them."

"Several of the people at Camp Reincarnate stated that their owners turned them in, but the ones there the longest said they got caught, which suggests she found out some other way. Maybe BLACKOUT, like you and Tommy?" she asks.

"The organization that hosts and moderates BLACKOUT has a way of blocking people who might have cause to shut them down. Because NHOS isn't shy about shutting things down, people like police officers or government officials and anyone associated with them get restricted. I gather they know about it and occasionally find ways of getting access, but if the moderators routinely slipped up, people wouldn't trust it. NHOS could have found out through a number of channels—FrogBlog for one."

He doesn't miss how she blanches at the app's name. "That makes sense. Do you think the woman from the article was in camp with the others? None of them mentioned running from the police during the interviews." By her alarmed expression, she's probably envisioning herself in the woman's place—wherever she is now. "Wait, how do you think they knew she was a reincarnate?"

He shrugs. "I don't know—maybe her owner tried to turn her in, so she fled?"

"This whole situation is awful. Wanda couldn't have been happy that this article got out. It reads like both NHOS and GROW are on cleanup duty. They published your official statement, which definitely reads as an advertisement for CHOICElover."

She's right, it does—he and Tommy crafted the statement specifically to make CHOICElover look good. The doors to the SAT open, and he takes Electra's hand, helping her out. There's no one but the half-interested Z Quadrant garage attendant in the vicinity.

She eyes the man as they pass into a vacant hallway. "Wanda won't shut CHOICElover down, will she?"

"CHOICElover has always led the field with our security protocols and rigorous safety testing. We've been completely transparent with the Consumer Rights Protection Agency and Product Safety Commissioning Board. Not to mention we've made our research available to NHOS, which has led to advancements in the disease prevention and human longevity project. As long as our record remains untarnished, I don't think we are the company that NHOS will be scrutinizing."

She takes his hand, squeezing. "Well, that's a relief."

He squeezes her hand back. "Electra, even if they forced me to shut down CHOICElover, we would be fine. I have more unicoin than we'll ever need, and I would be highly sought after for other projects as a scientist and business leader."

She stops midway down the hall, yanking him to a halt. He turns, giving her a quizzical look. She shakes her head. "I'm not worried about that, you ridiculous man. I know your company is important to you, and even though I don't necessarily think manupartners are the right solution for human companionship, I care about what happens to CHOICElover because it impacts you."

A not-altogether-unpleasant pang hits him square in the chest. "I knew you made your peace with what I do for a living, but that's . . ." He looks away, fighting a wave of emotion. Her simple acts of caring are unlike anything he's ever known.

"Come on," she says, offering him a reprieve from his emotions.

Dear Electra, indeed. For her sake, he hopes that the IdenTECH people are the real deal. His concern for her happiness is beginning to eclipse his own desires, which might be concerning, if his descent didn't feel so inevitable.

After a short elevator ride, they're on the ground floor, hovering outside a dingy-looking bar called Scraps. He follows her to the door, but just as she's about to reach for the handle, she spins, retreating a step, and crashes into his chest. He takes hold of her shoulders. "Did you see something?"

She steps out of his reach a few feet from the door and leans against the wall, looking visibly shaken. "No, but that article is freaking me out. Trust me, I would not do well in that center with only a blanket and the gross protein packs they're giving those poor people. I'll be the first to say, if the apocalypse happens, just give me to the zombies."

"I'm sure Inspector Wanda's given them better food and cots by now." He leans against the wall next to her. "What about all the heroines you write about?"

A few people pass down the otherwise barren hall, not paying them any mind, but that doesn't stop her from giving them a scrutinizing once-over. "That's fiction, Res6. I am not cut out for a life on the run from monsters, or prison for that matter."

"We'll be fine. It looks like the bar has quite a few patrons, which is good for us. Let's just step inside, and if anything seems suspicious, we can leave right away. We'll just go up to the bar and order a cocktail like we planned. We have no obligation to talk to anyone."

"You don't really think it could be NHOS inspectors, do you?" A strand of hair falls into her eyes as she leans forward to make an assessment through the glass of the door. He reaches up and brushes it away, taking her jaw in his hand. With her head angled toward him, the trepidation in her expression is impossible to hide. He hadn't realized she was so nervous.

"I'm not going to let anything happen to you, okay? This isn't the other shoe dropping."

Her eyes widen. "That's a saying from my time."

He grins proudly. "I know. I looked it up. I was reading about your scarcity mindset in an effort to understand you better."

The pinched, fearful expression slips from her features, replaced with something softer yet more determined. "Wow. Janet would be proud. If you're not careful, I'm going to think you're enjoying romancing a human woman."

"I learned from 2027's alien romance queen," he teases. "My new mantra is 'What would Vorack do?'" This earns him a humorous eye roll. "Come on. Time to channel your inner Ella and face your fears."

"That might be the best pep talk I've ever received." She giggles, shaking her head. "Now or never, I guess."

28 – Baby Steps to Bravery

Electra

Electra takes his hand, bravely guiding him into the hazy room. A dusky, acrid smell hits her instantly. Along the exterior wall, there are hairline cracks every few feet, letting a fine trail of outside air seep in. Must not be bad enough to cause lung damage and not bad enough to fix.

She notices Res6 eyeing the same thing. "This is why I never come to Z Quadrant."

Scanning the room, she notes two men sitting at a small round table in the corner that seem as out of place as they are. It's the quality of the material of their jumpsuits and the dark-haired one's slightly crooked nose. Something about the old injury makes her instantly think he's a reincarnate.

Res6 leans down. "I think that's them in the corner. Stick to the plan. Let's go to the bar."

But what if she's wrong? What if the man's nose is some type of disguise? *Send the NHOS inspector with the crooked nose. The other reincarnates will think he's one of them, then you can catch them!* God, she's clutching her bag to her chest like a shield.

She's about to tell Res6 she's changed her mind. It's too risky, but he presses his hand to the small of her back and whispers, "You can do it."

He's right. Just think of Ella facing the entire enemy hoard with bravery and grit. She takes a few quick steps forward—the dark-haired man's eyes brighten with excitement. That can't be good. Her stomach seems to agree, pitching and diving. He leans slightly forward, as if he wants to encourage her, and that's enough to have her making a sharp turn and darting toward the door.

God, Electra. This is a perfect opportunity, and you're wasting it.

Her critical inner voice is decidedly not Janet, who would tell her to be gentle with herself or some nonsense. Heaven forbid her self-preservation instincts fire occasionally. Granted, that was terrible timing. They probably weren't NHOS inspectors. But maybe they were. Mentally, she groans. Res6 is right. It's too risky.

Her march doesn't end until they're in the garage, waiting for Res6's private SAT. Thankfully, he says nothing, but that makes her feel even guiltier for chickening out than she already does.

Finally, when they climb inside, she slumps back into the seat, defeated. As they zip away in retreat, she finally speaks. "I guess I'm not a heroine after all."

December 1, 2390.

What could be more detrimental to a heroine than losing a battle with herself? Is she even fit to give out advice? The way she ran the second the man with the crooked nose fixed his gaze on her could only mean one thing: she's a coward. Ella never would have retreated like that.

She tossed and turned all night, unable to get the self-berating thoughts out of her mind. Exhaustion has her pulling the covers over her head as the morning light sequence brightens the room.

Even as Res6 knocks on her door and tells her he's leaving for work, she doesn't budge. Why is she like this? It's as if any adversity turns her into an immovable, depressive lump. He shakes the lump of covers that is her languid form. "Electra, stop beating yourself up."

The last thing she wants to do is settle like a cloud over his day. He did his part to get the meeting. "I'll be fine. Just go."

When he doesn't budge, she says, "When I saw his once-broken nose, I thought it was meant to trick us into a false sense of security. It was dumb."

Beside her, the bed sinks. "I shouldn't have let you read that article."

She groans. "I'm the one who let it mess with my head. It wasn't your fault."

"We're not Zorg and Zephyr."

She pops her head out of the covers. "What?"

His chuckle momentarily outshines the negative self-talk that's been replaying in her mind since her fear got the best of her.

"You aren't a non-deity who can control everything. You're human, remember? You shouldn't be so hard on yourself." He leans down and kisses her, which feels pleasantly domestic. "Do you want me to call Tommy and tell him I won't be in?"

His offer makes warmth bloom in her chest. At least she has him—the parts he's willing to share. "No, I'm okay. I just needed to wallow a bit. Disappointing yourself is a hard thing to live with. I'll get up and do a little writing."

"I had the same thought about his nose. The flaw felt too convenient."

"Exactly. When we made eye contact, he seemed almost eager. It threw me off."

"Agree," he says. "I'd rather you follow your instinct than force yourself to do something you feel is unsafe out of stubbornness. Just promise me you'll get out of your head."

"I will," she promises. "When you get back, I'll be at my desk pouring all my angst into my characters."

He kisses her again and slips out the door.

He's right. It's the article's fault, not to mention the barren room full of suffering reincarnates. Still better to wallow for another hour for good measure. Maybe she needs to build up to the IdenTECH meeting. She hasn't even ventured out into the city without her trusty protector.

She should invite her new friend Sister Xelna out for lunch while Res6 is at work. That would be a good start. And if after a few days, inspectors don't show up at their door, she'll feel safer assuming that the ID people were legit.

December 2, 2390.

Electra rolls over, blindly reaching for her device in the pitch dark. Since she figured out how to control the room's light settings, the space is pleasantly cave-like. Blue light glows from the glass screen as she starts the Slow Good Morning sequence that will softly brighten the room, giving her eyes time to adjust. Checking her messages, she finds a DM in FrogBlog from Sister Xelna waiting for her. Her heart leaps. She's agreed to meet for lunch today. Excellent.

The clock on her nightstand blares a bright 10:09 at her. She must have fallen back asleep after Res6 left for the day. She jumps out of bed, rushing to get ready, so she can get a column done before she leaves for her 13:00 lunch date.

She triple-checks her bag for her tablet so she can unlock the unit when she returns and a water in case she gets lost. Her device goes on a chain she wears cross-body. Oh, and a lip gloss. She runs to the bedroom, snatching one off the counter. *Not procrastinating out of fear at all.*

Finally, she is standing before the door to the unit, stomach squirming. God, making new friends as an adult is hard. "Fuck it." She turns the handle, and she's off. Fifteen minutes later, her heart is hammering as she wades through the crowded cafeteria toward the agreed-upon café. She glances around but doesn't see the woman from the profile picture, so she takes a small table in the corner, deciding to wait. At 13:12 she's about to give up when Sister Xelna approaches from across the room. The tattooed cat whiskers on either side of her button nose are instantly recognizable, not to mention the body-hugging leopard unitard she's sporting. As she gets closer, Electra can see her black nails are sharpened to fine points, which match her spiky hair, and she's pulling some type of animal behind her.

Electra takes a deep breath. She gathered this woman was a bit of an oddball, but she seemed so friendly and empathetic. Electra always gravitates toward people others might consider different, so she decided to give the woman a chance. Which means she needs to give the robot-cat thing she's walking a chance too.

"Sister Xelna!" she greets brightly. "I'm so happy to finally meet you in person."

"Dear Electra!" the priestess chimes back. "You look just like your avatar! I'm delighted you reached out. Come here." She pulls Electra into a hug so warm it almost makes her want to pinch herself. Is this her first real future friend? When Sister Xelna finally releases her and they take a seat, she picks up the creature and sets it in the chair next to her.

Electra eyes it as it puts a tentative paw on the table, then two. Sister Xelna notices her staring. "Down, kitten," she says, instructing the machine, before making little paw-fists and tucking them under her chin. Using baby talk, she says, "Just like this." The robot-cat does as the woman commands, and she gives it an ear scratch as a reward. Then she turns to Electra, who is torn between horror and fascination. "My followers pooled their money and bought me her. Synth-cats are incredibly rare. Since ASI Personal Companions were banned, the company that made them went out of business. She's beautiful, isn't she?"

Electra blinks. "What's her name?"

"A-Pawstle Calico. She's the official mascot of The Sacred Order of Feline Transcendence, and she's such a good girl," Sister Xelna croons. The synth-cat arches, letting the priestess stroke its patchwork fur. Its green electric eyes blink up at Electra expectantly.

Obligated out of respect, Electra reaches down and pats the robot's head. It purrs, and she can't help but giggle at the absurdity of it.

When she turns her attention back to her lunch companion, she's placing an order. She finishes rattling off a list of items and turns to Electra. "Anything else?"

She shakes her head, glad Sister Xelna has taken away the pressure of ordering. "No, that all sounds good."

The server walks away, then the priestess's full attention falls back on her. Her metallic green–lined eyes narrow, and she leans forward. "You're not from now, are you?"

Electra swallows. "I, uhh . . ." she splutters.

"I know things." Sister Xelna taps her whiskers. "I've also read your blog, which blatantly advocates for ideas from the past—not that I disagree—and you've also obviously never seen a synth-cat before."

Electra glances around the room, and she must look like she's about to bolt because the other woman reaches across the table, grabbing her hand. "Don't you worry your adorably freckled face. I won't tell a soul. I've been theorizing that a new presence was emerging. Naturally, I thought it was our feline companions, resurrected using old DNA samples that were altered so cats could reemerge outdoors. But then I read about the reincarnates. Sadly, it seems I was mistaken, but I say upon meeting you, I am very intrigued. I find many of your ideas worth exploring and, based on your growing popularity, it seems others do too."

Electra swallows. "I heard that when NHOS officials catch one of us, they're keeping us in holding cells almost like a prison." She offers this bit of information as a self-preservation tactic.

Sister Xelna shakes her head disapprovingly. "That isn't right. It's not like those poor people chose to show up in the future. NHOS should make them citizens, no questions asked."

Her staunch position eases Electra's anxiety. It seems she has an ally in this woman. As her new friend prattles on about the ethics surrounding reincarnates, she finds clever ways to tie it back to her cat cult and offer prescriptions for what she would do if she were in charge. Fortunately, she never connects Electra to CHOICElover or any of the other manupartner companies. Res6 would be horrified if he knew the risk she's putting them in by admitting the truth, but Xelna clearly isn't an NHOS spy and is on her side. Plus, listening to Xelna talk gives her the most normalcy she's felt since she's been awake in the future. Maybe she'll even work up enough gusto to attempt another

IdenTECH meeting. She has a boyfriend, a growing column, and now a real-life friend. It's almost as if everything's going to be okay.

29 – A Cocktail of Success and Betrayal

Res6

December 13, 2390.

"Excuse me, sir, there's a man here to see you," Tommy says, poking his head inside his office.

Res6 glances at the clock. 18:35. Later than he hoped to leave. Since the first few days after the failed ID meeting, Electra's mood has improved considerably, and he was looking forward to sharing a long, leisurely dinner. It seems the writing she did impacted her spirits greatly. Much in the same way, his improved when he poured himself into a research project. Well, aside from the Jerme experiments, which keep failing. After this afternoon's failure, which leaves him with only four samples, he needs an uplifting evening with Electra.

Tommy clears his throat. "What shall I tell him?"

"Did he say what he wanted?" he asks, not hiding his irritation.

"He says he works for GROW and has some information you might be interested in."

Res6, whose attention had drifted back to the synthesis failure report, looks up sharply. "A GROW employee. Interesting. Send him up." As much as he hates to keep Electra waiting, the prospect of potentially confidential information from a GROW employee piques his curiosity.

A few minutes later, Tommy shows in a tall, slim man wearing his blond hair twisted into a knot at the base of his skull. The man's copper stare darts around Res6's office before landing on him. He nods in recognition.

If he offers the man a seat, the meeting is apt to drag on, so Res6 stands. "You work for GROW?"

The man eyes the chair opposite Res6, noting the omission. "Yes, in their marketing department. I'm Viper, by the way."

"Well, Viper, you know who I am. I have a very important dinner I'm going to be late for, so if you will please get on with it?"

Viper frowns. "I thought you might be interested in some dirt on your biggest competitor, but perhaps I was wrong." The man turns to leave.

Res6 rolls his eyes, but the man's taunt works. "Please sit."

Viper grins as they both take a seat. "What is my information worth to you?"

He raises his brow in challenge. "It depends on what the information is."

"What if I could lead you to one of GROW's top physicians who's using manupartners in an illegal fighting ring to throw the bets?"

Res6 leans forward, masking his intrigue. "I suppose I would be willing to compensate someone for that type of information."

They take fifteen minutes to settle on terms, which include taking Viper on as an employee before he sends the incriminating files. "Since I discovered them, the club's owner, Jeffi, gave me access to the building's footage. Avoiding scrutiny by the authorities is a priority for him, as it is for GROW, I suspect." Viper leans forward, grinning proudly. "That's how I got their Blackmarks accounts frozen this morning. Jeffi tracked down their club accounts and reported them to their Blackmarks depository. Now the depository is working out a deal with him to return the illegally won funds. Serves them right."

"Okay," Res6 says, watching the video, intent on ignoring this man's seemingly personal vendetta.

Viper comes around the desk to get a good view of the monitor. He points to a woman in the center of the image exiting the SAT garage. "That is Sable, the physician." The video continues, and the group follows the woman down the hall, presumably toward the arena. "Pause there. Those are the men she's working with. I couldn't get the tall one's name, but the other one is a manupartner called James. The image of him isn't good, but we were able to get his identifier because he fought a few times and Sable healed him. I assume that's how they met. Unfortunately, the fights aren't recorded, but I've spoken with a dozen witnesses."

Res6 squints at the screen. The manupartner called James looks familiar, almost like the dark-haired man from IdenTECH, but he never looks right at the camera, so he can't be sure about his nose. Why would a guy running an identity fraud company be fighting in an illegal boxing ring? Electra's paranoia is probably rubbing off on him. He locks the image away in his mind to ponder further later. Nodding at Viper, he closes the file. "Excellent."

"That's it?" Viper asks defensively, crossing his arms.

"As I mentioned, I have a very important dinner this evening. I will review the rest of the documentation in the morning. When you show up tomorrow, you can ask for Tommy and he will direct you to the correct department for onboarding. That's all for now." He stands, collecting his device and another bio-transport case.

Viper scratches his head as he follows Res6 out of the room. "What are you going to do with the information?"

"I haven't decided, but it's none of your concern." Viper's eyes widen at his brisk tone, but Res6 continues. Viper is clearly up to something. The robbery comes to mind first, but the connection to a GROW marketing employee makes little sense. Considering his prideful boasting, he likely has a personal vendetta with this Sable woman. Still, he'll have to monitor him. Have his security protocols limited. Give him some mundane tasks to occupy him until he finds out the man's angle. "If I require additional input, I'll send for you."

He leaves his new employee in the hallway as the elevator takes him to his private SAT garage. On the ride back to his unit, he considers how to use this new information. While crippling a competitor's public reputation is a good business move, inevitably leading to more market share for him, that isn't his main motivation. It is, however, removing NHOS scrutiny by stopping the reincarnate issue, which getting GROW shut down would effectively do.

But it's possible that if NHOS discovered manupartners were being used in an illegal boxing ring—to throw the fights—it might bring more unwanted scrutiny of his product. With reincarnates, most likely from GROW, running around, the Consumer Rights Protection Agency could have justification to pull their licensing altogether. That's exactly what happened with the ASI Personal Companions. They got a little too smart, so NHOS shut them down. Sometimes, it seemed The Great Equalizer's main achievement was to instill excessive caution.

The thought of something happening to CHOICElover makes him shiver. His trepidation stays with him until he enters his unit and his gaze lands on Electra, clad in a slinky black dress that falls below her knees. The sleeves sit off the shoulder, showing off a tasteful amount of skin and her gorgeous collarbones that he's dying to get his lips on. Perhaps after dinner.

She eyes the silver case in his hand, but before a frown can overtake her beautiful smile, he sets it by the door and sweeps her into his arms for a kiss. "I've been looking forward to doing that all day," he says, earning a brilliant grin. "Shall we?" he asks, holding his hand out.

Blushing, she takes it and lets him sweep her out the door, the silver case thankfully forgotten.

Starting what will most likely end as another failed experiment can wait until tomorrow.

December 14, 2390.

"Three," he shouts. "Three left, Lextr. This is unacceptable."

The frown on Lextr's face isn't one of self-recrimination. It's pity. "Well, sir," he says, wringing his hands, "we knew this would happen. I'm running a comparison using the data you collected from the GROW reincarnates NHOS caught now."

"Didn't we determine it was our electrical impulses that triggered the NAM activation?" Res6 paces his office, running a hand through his hair.

"Yes, that was our initial suspicion, but we've run the impulse sequence exactly. There seems to be a factor we haven't identified. We lost two samples in the accelerated protein compounding phase alone." Lextr pauses for a long moment before mumbling, "I have other work I should be focusing on." He stares down at the little disk of organic material spinning in the Tissue Tangler and his eyes brighten. "You should consider keeping it here. Perhaps something happened during transportation, or when we removed it from the original electrical source. Perhaps the loss of connection severed something. Plus, if you grow it in the big BioLume Scan chamber, you'll know immediately if something goes wrong."

Res6 nods. "That's not a terrible idea."

"If you're here, you might be able to intervene if you catch the failure in time."

"That means I'll need to camp out in my office for a week." The idea of a week without Electra twists in his stomach.

Lextr shrugs. "How bad do you want your brother back?"

December 17, 2390.

He sent Electra a message that his experiment would keep him at the office for at least a week. He hates the pang in his chest at the loss of her presence, but it's necessary. He also instructed Tommy to leave his latest failed specimen in his unit until he can make sure Electra doesn't see its removal. If he remembers correctly, the body double has enough protein packs to last the week. That only leaves the FRIENDS appointments he's been helping it slip out for. They'll have to be missed. There's no way around it.

After two days, Electra messages that she wants to bring him lunch, claiming that venturing out is exactly what she needs to overcome her fears, which will eventually make her brave enough for another ID meeting. He couldn't argue, so they sat in his office in awkward silence, his secret experiment looming between them.

As he walks her to the elevators, he notes the clock. 14:57. He's almost due to check on the specimen that's growing exceptionally well. Perhaps he should have thought to grow it here in the first place. It illustrates how lax he's gotten in recent years. Too used to relying on others to think for him.

"What's on your mind?" she asks as they step into the elevator.

He slips his hands into his pockets so he won't reach for her. Since he left and didn't come back from the office, he isn't sure if his touch is welcome, and she hasn't made the first move. "When I first started CHOICElover, I spent weeks sleeping in my office so I could monitor experiments. I was thinking about how energizing it is to do that again."

She grins. "So you're enjoying your work?"

"Yeah. It makes me think when this experiment is finally finished, I might see if there is another project I can take on." His mind trails back to how he got caught up in his work while Jerme was alive and how it led him to miss the signs of his brother's mental state. "Well, not something so all-consuming as what I'm working on now." He reaches out and brushes a lock of hair off her temple, thinking himself rather brave to make the first move.

She leans into his touch. "I miss you." Her eyes widen, like the words accidentally slipped out. "I mean—"

He takes that as an invitation to kiss her. She sighs against his mouth as their tongues brush, her fingers gripping his shirt.

The elevator doors open, and he reluctantly pulls away. "I miss you too."

She glances back, waving over her shoulder as she makes her way to his private SAT garage. Alone.

Days pass. He uses the time between his scheduled observations to work out in the on-site fitness facility, check in with staff he doesn't speak with on a regular basis, and catch up on his reading. His no-longer-secret romance novels stir his need to get back to Electra to a near boiling point.

He closes a particularly riveting chapter as Jerme's alarm chimes in his mind. Time for the next observation. Based on the progression against the GROW reincarnate data, things are looking good. One more day, then this will be the closest since the first one that had a spike-wave that wiped out any potential memory.

The closer he gets, the more he wonders what he'll say to Jerme when he wakes. It almost feels foolhardy considering how many failures he's had, but he can't help thinking about it. Will Jerme be angry? Upset and regretful? He hates that he'll be waking up in a laboratory, but it's inevitable. Then he'll get him home and confess everything to Electra, who will take one look at Jerme and melt. At least that's what he's hoping. Even if they're both irate with him, they can't stay that way forever.

December 20, 2390.

He scans his palm on the reader outside the door to his private lab and slips inside. The specimen looks more and more like his brother with every hour. The green light from the big BioLume gives his brother's face an eerily otherworldly glow. He takes a snapshot of the data, sending it to the Spot-Gene Mini screen on the counter.

Every time he reviews the data, a knot of dread forms in his stomach. He quickly scans the screen, running a comparison up to the failure point of each prior experiment. A marker catches his eye. His heart rate doubles. That's the same NAM marker Electra had. The CAS456 protein is doing its job, bonding the spliced RNA to Jerme's active DNA. His sweaty palms slip on the sleek metal counter.

It's working. It's fucking working.

He can hardly believe it as his gaze darts between the screen and *his brother*. Excitement shoots through him like a lightning bolt, making every cell of his body feel alive. He needs to tell someone. But who?

His first instinct is to call Electra and tell her she's going to get to meet Jerme after all. His brother. After ninety-eight years, he's going to get to talk to him again. He reaches up, wiping moisture off his cheeks. Good Zorg, he's crying like a child. He didn't realize how wide the hole in his chest was, but now that he's poised to get Jerme back, it gapes, making him aware of the full breadth of the chasm. Soon it will be filled.

But he can't tell Electra. The only person he has right now is Lextr. He grabs a towel and dries his face, giving his cheeks a slap for good measure.

It takes him ten minutes to find the man when he spots his orange hair in the back of a rarely used lab. He must have commandeered it to get privacy for his project. "Lextr," he calls, walking into the room.

Abruptly, the diagrams and datasets that were up on the screen disappear, and Lextr jumps up. "Hello sir. I expected you to be working on your trial." His stare flashes to a cart in the corner containing six silver cases.

"I was, but I had something I wanted you to look at to confirm what I think I'm seeing." He gestures toward the cart. "What are you working on?"

Lextr shifts, clearly uncomfortable under his scrutiny. "Just a new prototype I wanted to propose."

"Oh," Res6 says, immediately feeling ridiculous for his suspicion. There's no way Lextr had anything to do with the robbery. He didn't even blink when Inspector Wanda asked him to work with her team, which they've been doing for almost two months. "Show me, then we can go look at my side project."

"I, uhh . . ." Lextr hesitates. "I'd prefer to wait until I have a better sample."

Res6's eyes narrow and he crosses his arms. Maybe he was letting him off the hook too soon. "Are you taking those somewhere?"

"I figured since you were working on your experiments at your unit, you wouldn't have a problem with me doing the same." He steps back from his chair, rolling it under the desk, all while failing to make eye contact.

"Show me the files you just had open," Res6 demands.

"Sir, there's no reason for that. I'm not ready," his lead scientist practically whines.

"You're acting very suspicious. Show me or I'll command them open."

Reluctantly, Lextr thinks the command to open the files.

With a quick scan, Res6 determines that he's been lied to. "What the fuck, Lextr?" He uses the override feature he has with all their systems, opening the last ten files accessed and requesting an action history report.

The screen displays a list of manupartners along with 3D models of each one. All six figures, both male and female, are tall and heavily muscled. His mind immediately goes to the illegal fighting ring and the scientist Sable, who Viper told him about. Could the same thing be going on right under his nose? "Please tell me this isn't what I think it is."

"It's only a side gig, I swear. I rent them out for a few hours at a time. Mostly for events."

Res6 shakes his head, running his hand over his face. "You're in pay bracket A, Lextr. If you needed more money, you should have come to me. There is a GROW physician doing something similarly illegal, and I plan to use that information to get them shut down." He grips the back of the chair as the betrayal of Lextr's actions floods the space between them. "If anyone found out that you're practically doing the same thing, they could shut *us* down. They could take everything I've built."

A reddish undertone blooms beneath Lextr's warm brown skin. "I don't see why you're so intent on undermining GROW. Competition is healthy."

"They're creating reincarnates, which is undermining our entire industry! I'm surprised you aren't more concerned, considering you directly know NHOS's stance on them." His blood heats. It's more than making him look like a hypocrite and undermining his chance to shut down GROW. How dare Lextr steal from him? He wasn't there in the beginning, when Res6 lived in a cramped lab for weeks at a time building a global company from nothing, from the branding to the science. CHOICElover is everything to him. That's why this theft feels like a betrayal. "Those weren't your specimens to use as you wish, Lextr."

A crazed, indignant look passes across Lextr's features. "My little side project is hardly as bad as what you're doing. You're practically in love with one of those illegal reincarnates you're allegedly against."

Res6 jolts back. In love with her? He's not—could he be?

Lextr sneers as if he knows he hit his mark. "That's right. Do you actually look at your publicity shots? Zorg, it's written all over your face. Your normally impassive expression is now ridiculously lovesick—don't you think people have noticed? The staff think you're head over heels for your latest prototype. And don't think there aren't whispers. I've heard more than one staff member ask if she's a reincarnate."

He looks away as his number two chastises him. How long have they worked together now? Fifty years? More? They were never close like he was with Jerme, but he thought he could trust the man. He almost hates to ask . . . "You assured them she's not a reincarnate?"

"Of course. Unlike you, I'm being careful with my side project," Lextr bites back.

Red flashes fill his vision. "A side project you have no right to be undertaking."

Lextr's eyes flare. "At least I'm not trying to bring back my dead brother!"

The air leaves Res6's lungs. Recovering quickly, he determines that the specifics of his questionable choices aren't directly relevant to the conversation. "What you're doing is no better than theft, not to mention an egregious violation of our licensing agreement from the Consumer Rights Protection Agency." Lextr makes to open his mouth, but Res6 continues, sharply. "This is my company. If I want to have an illegal side project, that is my prerogative. I clearly should never have involved you. Still, if I want to do something stupid jeopardizing CHOICElover, it is my company to ruin. Not yours!"

Lip curling, Lextr snarls, "You're the worst kind of hypocrite."

"And you're fired!" Res6 storms toward the door but stops, turning at the last moment. Then into his m-volt he thinks, speaking aloud so Lextr can hear as well, "Security, please meet me at Laboratory E on floor 23. I have a former employee I need you to remove from the system and escort out of the building." Then he turns to Lextr, who's gone deathly pale. "Don't forget you have an NDA." Then he steps into the hall, letting the door close behind him. He slumps against the wall. The harsh reality of Lextr's betrayal quickly replaces the high of his successful experiment, leaving him feeling raw at the edges.

Soon, two female security guards and a man from HR are walking down the hallway toward him. He quickly explains the termination and leaves Lextr in their capable hands.

Firing the long-term employee was rash, but in the heat of the moment, it felt justified. Yet now, as he makes his way back to his office, a dazed sensation settles over him. The clock displays 18:50. He would really rather be getting back to his unit and have a smiling Electra greet him, but it's almost time for another data review, and he only has one day left before he can bring his brother back. Then they will all go home. Nervous, erratic energy vibrates through him. It's all going to be fine, he mentally repeats. He has just enough time for a few calming breaths. As he runs his palms over his thighs, he can't get the words Lextr hurled at him out of his head. *You're the worst kind of hypocrite.*

He's fired people before for many reasons. The irony doesn't slip past him that this is the first time he's fired someone for being right.

December 21, 2390.

Between missing Electra and the weird, already glaring vacancy on his team, he isn't humming with excitement like he thought he would be when he finally got to activate his brother. That isn't great since who knows what mental state Jerme is going to wake up in.

The timing is terrible. If only he could wait until he was in a better headspace himself, but leaving a manupartner on an electrode pad after the grow sequence has completed increases the probability of glitches. He has to do this now.

He takes a last glance at the data. Everything looks good. If only he had Lextr here to review it with him a final time before he presses the green button. He considered calling to apologize, but the betrayal is too fresh. He'll give it a few days and then call him.

With that, he kneels before the electrode pad. Thankfully, Lextr set the sequence so he wouldn't be required to program a name. All he needs to do is press the button. So why is he hesitating? Because the prospect of pressing the button and being met with another seizing trial or even just a blank manupartner stare is terrifying. His hand is unsteady as it hovers over the green button. He glances up one last time at the unit.

What if Electra is right, and this is a bad idea? He could stop this right now and recycle this trial and go home to her. He would never even have to tell her. He could put the two remaining samples back in the BioBank. Pretend he never got this crazy idea to begin with. It would be as if all the turmoil he's gone through trying to resurrect his brother never happened.

Wait, why is he suddenly having second thoughts? What if this is really the one? He's been trying to bring back Jerme for two months now. This is one of three remaining samples he can't waste. He can't let a bad day or a momentary hesitation upend his plan. Not when his brother is counting on him.

He takes a deep breath and presses the button. The trial's lungs fill. Then its eyes open. When it doesn't seize, he exhales shakily and braces himself, meeting the trial's blinking gold eyes. *His eyes.*

The corner of his twin's mouth twitches, like he's going to smile . . . or frown. Yet his eyes spark with unmistakable life—there's recognition there too. This time he's certain of it. The unbearable weight of hope drives him forward. He brushes trembling fingers against the cheek that mirrors his own.

"Jerme?"

Jerme sucks in a sharp breath, and he quickly scans the lab before his gaze finds Res6's again.

"Jerme," he urges, tears burning a hot trail down his cheeks. He knew this would be the hardest part—bringing a man back to life who'd wanted to die. But with Electra's help, they'll give him a reason to live. "Say something," he begs.

"Res6?"

Everything freezes but the erratic rhythm of his heart.

"Jerme." It's all he can mutter. Jerme is real. He did it. It worked. "I'm so sorry. I promise I'll fix you—" A trickle of blood sliding out of Jerme's nostril cuts his apology short. "No."

He reaches up, his hand trembling as he brushes the blood away. More follows. The trembling becomes a violent shake as he wipes at it. Instead of undoing the biological betrayal happening in his brother's brain, it smears, staining Jerme's unblemished cheeks. Jerme's eyes—his perfect, tragic, beautiful gold eyes—turn pink. Then bright red. Broken veins, then a single crimson tear.

"No. No. No. No. This can't be happening. The corrections department—we have to get you to the corrections department. Hang on, Jerme. I can fix this."

Res6 frantically reaches out to wrap an arm around Jerme's waist. "Let's go." He urges him forward a step, but Jerme stumbles, catching his shoulders, and dragging them both down. He barely feels knees slam into the concrete.

He's about to scream for help when Jerme meets his eyes. "It hurts."

"I'm so sorry," he chokes out.

"Please, Res6. Make it stop." Jerme goes limp.

He cradles his brother's failing body as they slump to the floor. At least this time, he gets to hold Jerme as he dies.

30 – Rose-Colored Comfort

Electra

"What happened to you?" Electra asks as Res6 shuffles through the door. His hair is askew and his eyes are bloodshot as if he's been crying.

"I fucked everything up," he says. He looks like he hasn't slept well in days.

Her first instinct is to panic, but she reminds herself, *This isn't about you*. He's clearly been working very hard on something that didn't go well. "Come," she says, taking his hand. "Sit, and you can tell me as much or as little about it as you like."

He seems to be in a daze as she walks him over to the couch and presses him down onto it. He leans forward, burying his head in his hands. She crawls next to him, getting on her knees for better access, and massages his shoulders, working her way up the tense, corded muscle of his neck. "You are incredibly tight."

He groans as she digs into an especially firm knot. She does this for several minutes until her hands ache. Still, she keeps working his angry flesh. "You can't hold everything in, Res6. If you keep bottling things up, one day you're going to explode."

He shakes his head. "I think I already did."

She stops massaging as he turns to face her.

"I fired Lextr," he says, shaking his head.

"Oh God, that must have been awful." She waits as he stares blankly ahead.

"He betrayed my trust by stealing unregistered manupartners to rent out for some type of side gig. Openly leasing a manupartner from the company as an employee is one thing, but he knows we strictly prohibit the unauthorized use of company materials, not to mention unregistered manupartners are illegal and could get us fined or our license to operate revoked. That he did such a thing during an active investigation when missing samples could be discovered is highly risky. Granted, he did a decent job of covering his tracks. When I confronted him about it, he threw a bunch of stuff in my face. Then he called me a hypocrite, and I snapped." His Adam's apple bobs as he blinks back tears.

"Me?" she guesses. It wouldn't surprise her, since the man clearly dislikes her, even refusing to call her by name. But firing Lextr can't be what has him so upset. She wants to push but resolves to be patient.

"Among other things." He leans back on the couch, melting into it. Boneless, like all the fight has left him. "The experiment I stayed in the office to work on failed. I got my hopes up . . ." His breath hitches, and he takes a moment to collect himself. "It was going perfectly, but I let my pride cloud my judgment. I missed the smallest marker. So fucking stupid. It worked, Electra. It finally worked, then . . ." He buries his head in his hands, muttering, "Then it didn't."

Hold on. He usually calls manupartners *it*. Not *him*. It couldn't be him, as in *Jerme*. That would explain why he's so upset. Her heart stumbles. "Him?"

He glances up, his face agonized. "The manupartner . . . a prototype. It was male."

Right. They discussed it, and he agreed that trying to bring back his brother would be a terrible idea. Why did she even think that? She nods, trying to understand. "The experiment clearly meant a lot to you. I'm sorry it failed. I can't believe that about Lextr. I'm definitely naming the villain in my next book after him."

His lips twitch like his smile can't quite get there. Without meaning to, she starts rubbing soothing circles on his chest. The fabric of his shirt is so thin that her fingertips absorb the heat of him and feel every defined ridge. Her gaze lifts from her hand to his golden eyes, which are fixed on her.

"What would I do without you?" The desperation in his voice makes his words feel like a confession. "Since you've come into my life, everything is changing so fast. I'm unmoored."

Not this again. She leans back, but he grabs her neck before she can retreat. "I wouldn't trade a second of you, Electra Lynch. Knowing you'd be here when I returned was the one thing keeping me tethered."

Her heart squeezes. "I'm glad I can be here for you." Her voice is breathy, and he must notice it too, because his gaze drops to her lips.

"I'm a mess," he says.

Something about his vulnerability is like an aphrodisiac. "My mess?" she dares, reaching up to run her fingers through the silky hair at his temple.

A sad grin plays across his lips. "All yours."

He pulls her toward him. The kiss is desperate, as if he's drinking her in. His desire, his vulnerability, the intentional way his lips move all stir something deep inside her. Something aching and terrifying, begging for her surrender.

Leaning her back on the couch, he hovers over her. "I . . . I need to get lost in you. Is this okay?"

She wraps her leg around his, running her bare foot up his calf as she reaches for his waist, fisting his shirt to pull him nearer. "Very okay. But I think you can do better." She smirks as his eyes momentarily widen.

When he realizes she's teasing him, a grin erupts—still laced with sorrow, but with a cocky edge to it, as if he's accepting her challenge. "If you get bored, please let me know."

She giggles, watching transfixed as he reaches behind himself and tugs his shirt over his head. Her mouth goes dry as she takes in his sculpted torso.

He smirks. "I've seen you looking. Touch if you like."

There's only a split second where she wonders if he's pretending she's a manupartner. He must sense it because he takes her hand, pressing it to his chest. "Get out of your head. Stay here with me. I need you right now."

"I'm here."

"Good," he says, trailing her hand down over the firm muscles. "Because this is real."

Swallowing, she lets her gaze drop, following the path of her hand, which he guides down his abdomen, then lower. He pauses. "Yes?"

"Yes," she agrees.

He sucks in a sharp breath of air as he moves her hand over his straining erection, pressing her hand into him. "I want you, Electra. Feel what you do to me." He squeezes her hand, cupping it around his shaft, and she groans at the indecent way his hips roll, his lower abs flexing in a way that makes her mouth water. "Can I have you? Will you let me make love to you?"

31 – Life-Affirming Sex

Res6

"Can I have you? Will you let me make love to you?" he asks.

She bites her swollen lower lip, nodding. Zorg, he wants to rip her clothes off and drive inside her so he can drown out his grief with the feel of her body. The feel of being so close to her. The ache in his chest and the comfort she gives . . . the desire she stokes inside him . . . it's a dangerous cocktail.

The reckless feeling he gets every time she's near tips him past his breaking point. That coy fucking nod. He presses her into the couch, trailing open-mouthed bites and kisses down the column of her throat. Then lower. As his teeth graze over the mound of her covered breast, she arches toward him. "Too many fucking clothes." He quickly tugs her top off and tosses it aside. He does the same with her leggings, revealing the warm, smooth expanse of her thighs.

He sits back on his knees to take her in. She's not wearing a bra. Only a barely-there pair of teal lacy panties sit low on her hips. He groans at the sight of her. "You're so beautiful." He runs trembling hands over her skin, eliciting a delicious shiver. Is he nervous? He clenches his fist. *This is not the time to lose confidence.* Make this about her, you animal. "Incredible." He settles beside her, claiming her mouth once again as his hand trails over her ribs, down her stomach, and lower. "I'm eager to kiss you here," he slips his fingers inside her panties, "but I'm afraid if I taste you, I'll finish too soon and I need this to last."

"Next time," she says, whimpering as he grazes her clit.

Encouraged, he steadily increases the pressure, drawing circles, then spelling out his name. When he finishes the 6, he slides his finger lower and dips into her wet heat.

"Did you just spell your name?" she asks, gripping his bicep as he pumps into her.

"Mmmhmm," he hums into her neck. "Mine," he growls, stealing a line from one of the books he read, partly for dramatic effect and partly because he sure as fuck means it. It earns him a giggle. "No laughing during sex," he scolds. When his finger curls forward, her neck arches back as she groans in pleasure. That sound has his cock twitching.

"Tell me what you need, Electra, and I'll give it to you."

"I need more." Her words come out as a whine this time.

She sighs as he adds another finger, stretching her. Curling them, massaging until her breaths are shallow gasps. He watches her eyes squeeze shut and the first of the tremors start. "That's it. So good," he praises.

It takes an effort to keep up the slow, steady rhythm—every one of his baser instincts is urging him to yank his fingers out, part her legs, and thrust inside.

His jealous cock aches as his efforts pay off. Her inner walls clench, and she cries out.

"Oh, God! Res6—it feels—" Gasping, she curls into him, her thighs gripping his hand to keep it pressed deep inside her. "Oh, fuck."

When her breathing steadies, he leans over her. "Such a dirty mouth."

She rolls her eyes. "You've read my books. Don't look surprised."

"You're going to give me interesting ideas." He chuckles, unfastening his pants, shoving them off and readjusting so he's kneeling between her legs.

Her eyes widen as she takes him in. "You're my own personal Adonis."

"Who?"

She giggles. "A Greek god known for his remarkable beauty. And lover of Aphrodite, goddess of love, beauty, and pleasure."

He tugs at the lace at her hip. "I suppose that fits, then." Her brow raises. "You write love and give people pleasure."

"It was meant to be a compliment."

"How about you compliment me by allowing me to take these off so I can fuck you?" He grips the base of his aching cock in emphasis. Desire flares in her eyes as she watches him stroke himself.

She lifts her hips, which he takes as the signal. A second later, her panties join the pile of clothing on the floor, and he's leaning over her, lining himself up. He trembles with anticipation. "I have the pregnancy-prevention chip."

Her brows furrow. "Shit. I didn't even think about it."

"I don't have to come inside you."

Another shift of her hips presses his tip into her entrance. A cheeky grin spreads across her beautiful face. "Where do you want to come, Res6?"

Still gripping the base of his cock with one hand, he uses the other to thread their fingers together and raise them over her head, so his body is splayed across hers, their noses touching. He nudges his hips forward, releasing himself as he nestles into the cradle of her hips. "Here. I don't want to pull out of you until we're both boneless."

Her hips lift, forcing him deeper. Pleasure causes his vision to flash white.

"Then don't," she says.

He thrusts, bottoming out. Swallowing her gasp, he meets the movement of her hips. His entire body trembles as pleasure quickly builds low in his spine. Too fast. "Electra, fuck, you feel so good. I don't know how long I'll last."

She squeezes, drawing a ragged exhale from him. He pulls out, dropping his forehead to hers and trying to catch his breath. "I'm serious, you wicked human woman. Behave, or I'll come."

"Don't hold back, Res6. I want everything." She fists his hair, twists his head, and bites his earlobe—delicious prickles race down his spine. She whispers, "All of you," and he almost loses it.

He grits his teeth, clinging to control. "I have to know what you feel like coming on my cock first." Resolved, he slams in harder this time. "I need to know. I've been dreaming about this. About you. I need to feel you squeeze around me."

By the mercy of the non-deities, he gets a second wind. Her cries of "Don't stop," "More," and "Just like that" drive him to thrust harder and deeper.

Beneath him, she goes pliant, lost to the pleasure of their bodies, letting him chase their pleasure. He groans, allowing the moment to sweep over him. Time is fuzzy, and there's only the two of them in existence. No worries, no loss, just them and the unearthly feelings her body is drawing from his. Somewhere at the edge of his awareness, fingernails dig into his shoulders, drawing his attention. She's close. The way her legs tremble—he needs to get her there before he loses himself to this feeling.

"So perfect," he encourages. Then a string of praise between labored breaths. "You feel so good. So wet for me. You fit me so perfectly." More gasps and moans. Then, he begs, "Please come for me, Electra. I can't hold it back—shit."

"Oh God, please." He slams into her over and over until she cries out, shuddering beneath him.

"Fuck," he shouts, following her over the edge. Time stops. Their gazes meet. The supposed lovesick look in his eyes is in hers too. It's like starlight. It fills him to the point of bursting. Then he's shattering. Pleasure so euphoric it's almost painful. He is drowning in her, his body tensing, jerking. His release fills her as blinding pleasure radiates from where he pulses inside her.

"Electra," he says, gasping. Needing to say her name. To connect the real human woman beneath him to the sensations, the aftershocks, that are overwhelming him. That wasn't just sex. He's had plenty of meaningless sex to know the difference. Could she feel it too? That they just had the type of sex that justifies one's existence. Life-affirming sex. He hovers over her, still inside, for a long moment. Their foreheads press together, their heartbeats returning to baseline.

"You okay?" he asks, pressing a gentle kiss to her lips.

She grips his side, but not to push him away. "That was intense."

"I'm sorry—"

"Perfect. I meant to say perfect. It's never been like that before."

He pushes away any notion of jealousy toward whoever *before* might refer to, in favor of the chest-expanding pride he feels at the monumental thing that just occurred between them. At least something is going right. "Me either," he admits. If only there were a way to freeze this moment in time. Capture it and preserve it so he could relive it. But he doesn't need a simulation or a memory. She's here with him and not going anywhere. Perhaps they'll find themselves in this exact position again in a few hours. He grins against her lips and repeats, "Me either."

32 – Lies and Lockpicks

Electra

December 22, 2390.

Electra stirs. The sleepy haze from the delicious dream she was having slowly dissipates as she rolls over, reaching for Res6's warm body. The bed is empty. She sits up, glancing at the bathroom. She was really hoping for a lazy, sex-filled morning, but Res6 isn't in the room. Perhaps he's in the kitchen.

She slides out of bed and throws on his T-shirt, thinking of the words he uttered to her on her first day in the future. *How is that so unbelievably sexy?* The aesthetic should signal what she wants. She swishes some mouthwash and glances in the mirror. Her hair is wild from sleep and Res6's fingers, and her neck is still blotchy from where he ravished her the night before. Thrice.

The first two times were intense, like they couldn't get enough of each other. The third time was exploratory. Slower, each learning what made each other gasp. Clever fingers and capable tongues eliciting moans and making fists clench in sheets.

Forget Chryl. Electra is the one who looks Sexcitable™ now.

She steps into the living room, glancing around. No Res6. Footsteps coming from the spare room draw her attention. "Res6?" she calls, glancing at the probably locked door. Her stomach tightens. After the intimacy they shared last night, she's even more invested in this man still clinging to his secrets.

She's sitting at her desk trying to focus on her column when the door to the spare room finally opens, and he slips out. Lines of worry etch his face, as if the moments they shared the night before weren't enough to lift the burden he carries. But when his eyes land on her, his face transforms. Instantly the worry evaporates, something far warmer replacing it as he stares at her.

"Good morning, Electra," he says. The low, hungry tone of his voice makes heat bloom low in her belly. To know she can capture his attention and transform his mood so effectively is such a turn-on.

"Hi," she says, grinning. She stands and walks over to him, showing off her body clad in only his T-shirt.

"I was going to go to the office, but you've given me other ideas."

Dear Reader,

Please sit down.

Okay, now that you're not in danger of falling over, I have a confession.

I THINK I'M IN A RELATIONSHIP WITH A SEX GOD.

The things that man can do with his tongue. I've had casual flings. Some lovers who even knew their way around a woman's body, but this man—I know this is going to sound bad AND super hypocritical, but it would be like keeping a football player in basic training for a hundred years, then when he finally shows up to the big leagues, he's an all-star. Or something like that. You understand my meaning. The guy's a pro.

And that's not to mention the emotional connection. When his golden eyes locked with mine, at that moment (you know the one) ... I think my soul left my body. I might even be in love with him. Believe me, I know. Nothing could be crazier than that! But I swear he feels it too. But just in case I'm imagining things or getting ahead of myself, I'll probably wait until he says it first. Unless we have sex again and it explodes out of me. I'll keep you posted.

That's all. Just wanted to share that I'm reveling in the afterglow. Basking in its blissful warmth like it's the summer sun and I have on SPF 100. The girl horrified by Res6 for inventing manupartners—she doesn't exist anymore. In her place is a grown woman making the choice to be happy. The end. Thank you for coming to my talk.

Choosing bliss,

Electra

Now that she's word-vomited all over the virtual page that no one is EVER going to read, she feels considerably better. Time to check her messages. She scrolls, deleting the nonsense queries and responding to a few fans. The next message automatically pops up, making her gasp. The subject reads: *You've been monetized!*

She quickly scans the body of the message, then sits there blinking at her screen, dumbfounded. Of MSP's 120 million residents, one million of them have honored her with a subscription to her column in a few weeks. Tears well in her eyes. That's basically the definition of an overnight success. And it's happening to her. People want her work. They love her voice and message enough that a million of them stopped to pay attention. This kind of success twice in a lifetime must mean she's meant to be here. It's unreal.

She sits back in her chair, letting waves of emotion wash over her. The overwhelming feelings bring her back to the day an email from a major publisher showed up in her inbox. They were interested in adding her indie-published books, which were just gaining traction, to their catalogue. It took her a week to find an agent, and together they negotiated a stellar six-figure deal. She jumped up and down squealing like a maniac the day they signed. Even though keeping quiet felt nearly impossible, she kept her big news to herself for an entire week, waiting until her monthly girl's night to share. Her friends had been ecstatic for her, and she even splurged by buying them all dinner.

A sudden pang of loneliness hits her. A distinct melancholy that she never felt in her previous life threatens to overshadow this win. Res6 disapproves completely, so she can't tell him. Other than that, she only has a few online acquaintances and Sister Xelna. Matter of fact, she should message her and see if she's available for lunch. They bonded over Electra's good advice, after all. Sister Xelna will probably be thrilled to celebrate with her.

She shoots her a quick message, then clicks the link in the email. It takes her to the FrogBlog dashboard, where a new tab opens showing a video explaining how monetization works. Apparently, the app will keep her unicoin in a temporary account connected to her profile until she connects her Worldbank account. Another reason she needs to find the courage to meet with the IdenTECH company.

She bites her lip, considering as she eyes the exceedingly large number of zeros in her temporary account. The value of unicoin isn't anything like the dollar she's used to, so she has no idea how much she's earning. At least she's earning.

Two hours later, she's ordering cocktails at the Bright Lights, Big City Bar with Sister Xelna. A-Pawstle Calico is curled up beside her on a stool shaped like a skyscraper from her time, "sleeping." Neon signs displaying adages light up the rest of the room. The only quote she recognizes is "Here's looking at you, kid." Next to it is a neon image of a baby goat chewing on a slipper. The energy of the bar is perfect for sharing exciting things.

"I have news!" she cries. She eyes the synth-cat, whose ears twitch.

Sister Xelna puts a hand on her shoulder. "Not to worry. I have Calico's sleep setting set to four." Electra has no idea what *four* means in terms of robo-animal sleep settings, but she nods anyway. It seems to please the priestess, who continues, matching her energy. "Tell me!"

She grins, sharing about her subscribers and the monetization, while Sister Xelna listens intently, eyes going wider and wider.

When she finally finishes her boisterous mini-monologue, Sister Xelna throws her arms in the air, exclaiming, "How wonderful! I knew you would be MSP's next social phenomenon." She pulls Electra into an embrace. "I'm so proud of you!"

The praise feels so good it almost strikes Electra oddly. Has it really been that long since someone told her they were proud of her?

Xelna must read her apprehension, because she continues, "You should be proud of yourself, too. How many people"—she leans forward, lowering her voice—"could wake up in the future and become an overnight advice sensation? It's like you, and possibly the divine Feline Essence Miss Kitty, knew exactly what we were missing." She raises a brow as if to impress her point.

"Yeah, I guess so. It's all so unreal. It's like I keep waiting for the other shoe to drop, but everything seems to be turning out okay."

Sister Xelna chuckles. "Aside from discovering you died in your last life."

Electra grins. Now that she's come to terms with it, she can see the humorous calamity that is her life, dark as it is. "Yes, aside from that."

"So what are you going to do with your newfound fame? Oh!" Sister Xelna straightens so abruptly that Electra glances over her shoulder to see what startled the woman, but there's nothing there. A hand wraps around her wrist, tugging. She turns back to a nearly maniacally grinning priestess. "NewNews will probably want to interview you. Just think—maybe they'll offer you a video segment like your stepmom! Then everyone will get freckles!"

It hasn't slipped Electra's notice that she's seen more and more people with artificial polka dots on their cheeks. There were even a few people with sheer outfits showing off entirely speckled bodies. Good on one hand because it makes her freckled avatar less conspicuous.

"I don't know about an interview. If Res6 sees it, he'll flip out, and things are going so well between us," she says, chewing on her lip.

Sister Xelna's mouth pinches in disapproval. "Has he told you what's in his supersecret room?"

"No," she admits.

"Well then, he can just deal with your fame."

Electra isn't entirely sure she's following the logic, considering the idea is for him not to find out. Granted, with a million subscribers, he'll probably learn of her column eventually.

"What do you think he's hiding in there, anyway?" Sister Xelna asks.

"Oh, he isn't necessarily hiding anything." The lie rolls so easily off her tongue that she almost believes it. Almost as easily as the unease that settles in her gut every time she thinks about the Room of Shoes Waiting to Drop.

Sister Xelna's brows shoot up. "Electra, dearest. People hide all kinds of things behind closed doors. There was a man in my building who got monthlong leases for manupartners from each manufacturer, including the off-brand ones. His plan was to have a monthlong orgy then turn them all in for recycling at the end of the term. He saved up vacation time and everything. I guess he got so addicted, he failed to turn them in. He barricaded them in his unit, and NHOS had to show up and break his door down. It was quite the scandal."

Beside her, the synth-cat raises its head, side-eyeing her. Does it know something she doesn't? *No, Electra. It's a machine. Res6 isn't hiding a monthslong orgy from you. He got rid of Chryl. You're safe and everything is fine. Great, even.*

She tunes into Sister Xelna, who's saying ". . . an electronic lockpick with your funds. Hand me your device. I'll show you how."

Electra chokes on the sip she just took. "An electronic lockpick?"

The priestess leans forward, collecting her tablet off the bar. She turns the screen toward Electra to unlock it and taps the glass a dozen times. "Yes, see this app I just downloaded for you?" Sister Xelna shows her the Special Ops app she's using. "There. I loaded some unicoin into your account. When you get your ID and Worldbank account, you can pay me back."

"But I thought lending money was illegal," Electra says.

"It is. That's why I'm paying you for the service of fortune-telling. And when you pay me back, you can make a donation to The Sacred Order of Feline Transcendence."

"Okay . . ." Does that mean the cat church is a front?

"So all you have to do is purchase one entry. Then, when you're standing next to the door you want to open, you click Pick. It usually takes a few minutes for the program to hack the entry, but I've never had it fail."

"Okay . . ." Electra repeats, eyeing the woman incredulously. Does she even want to know what locks Sister Xelna is picking?

"Oh, don't look at me like that. Everyone dabbles in a little illegality. You can bend the rules. Just don't break them."

On her way home, she gets a message that Res6 has to stay late to help fill in for Lextr while they search for his replacement. She busies herself writing an outline for a modern alien story she's been thinking about all day—inspired after a rousing round of sex the night before. Her tablet containing the digital lockpick sits on the desk, vying for her attention. For her part, her hand keeps twitching toward it, almost involuntarily. Would it be wrong—what is she thinking? Of course it would be wrong.

But her legs don't care about morals. She snatches the tablet and stomps over to the door. *No. Sit your ass back down. Janet would be so disappointed.* After a brief internal struggle, she turns around. She is not going to break Res6's trust. There is nothing ominous in the room. She has no reason to open the door. He will share what's behind the locked barrier when he's ready. There. That's settles it—

Bang. Bang. Bang.

Her heart seizes. Slowly, she turns back to face the door. Oh God. She's hallucinating now. Her denial has collapsed into some type of sick delusion, and she's hearing things.

Her voice is sheepish as she asks, "Hello?" remembering that the rooms are practically soundproof. *Please let me have imagined it.*

Bang. Bang. Bang. Bang.

She isn't sure how long she stands there frozen. Someone is in there, and they want out. Could it be another reincarnate like her? No, that's insane.

Still, her hand trembles as she opens the Special Ops app. Holding the tablet against the door, she presses the Pick button. Her heart hammers as several seconds pass. A dozen possibilities pass through her mind of what she's about to discover. A sinking feeling in her gut tells her that the worst option is probably the one that is true.

The lock clicks. There's a moment in which nothing happens, then the handle turns. Before her, a man stands in the now-open doorway. Not a man. *The man*—Res6. Or at least a perfect likeness of him. Okay, there has to be a perfectly reasonable explanation for this. Maybe it's the body double he sends to his FRIENDS appointments.

"Hello. Are my protein packs here? I'm hungry." The voice is so eerily similar to Res6's that it makes a chill run down her spine. His flat gaze drops to her and animates. "What's your name?"

"Electra," she mutters.

His eyes widen before narrowing into an inspecting glare. "Oh, you're the woman who has my brother so unmoored." He makes air quotes around the word *unmoored*.

Res6 said she made him feel that way last night. But he also said the changes she's brought into his life are a good thing. Time slows. "You're Jerme?" she finally chokes out.

"Sometimes he calls me Jerme," he says, smiling.

"Wait. Are you a manupartner?" she asks hopefully. Surely this is a simple misunderstanding. This isn't Res6 trying to bring his dead brother back.

"Jerme" takes in a big breath before dramatically exhaling. "Yes, I'm only a manupartner. Sometimes I have to pretend like I'm Res6."

"Oh, that's a relief."

Still, her eyes drift to the open door. He told her about the body double, so that isn't what he's hiding. Before she can stop herself, she darts forward into the room, first noting the neat bed, then the comfortable-looking chair in the corner. To her left is the bathroom. The door is open, and the small space is empty. That means the door to her right is the closet. Right as she's about to fling it open, the manupartner places his large hand on the surface, holding it closed.

"I don't think you're supposed to see what's in there."

She turns, squaring her shoulders. "Move."

The manupartner jumps back at her stern tone, and she wrenches the door open.

There's a fully formed human that looks just like Res6 stuck to an electrode pad. Somehow, she knows exactly what she's looking at and why Res6 kept it a secret.

The manupartner clears its throat. "He said this one failed, and he'd send Tommy to take care of it later. I think he forgot about my fuel too. I can go three days without fuel. I should consume something soon." His grin is so wide, unlike Res6's typical smirk. It's unsettling seeing it on his likeness. Aside from Chryl, who's partially real, this is her first interaction with a manupartner. It's just as creepy as she expected.

She shakes her head in disbelief, pointing to the unit in the closet. "This is supposed to be the real Jerme, isn't it?"

The manupartner frowns. "I am not authorized to talk about that."

It's confirmation enough for her. Her heart feels like it's squeezing and shattering all at once. She covers her mouth, but she can't hold back a sob as the pain in her chest bubbles over. He tried to bring Jerme back? No . . . He's actively trying to bring him back. That's what his experiments are about. That's all she's been to him. A research pathway to his brother. Not a random accident like he claimed, or the real human woman that he's falling for. Certainly not fate. As soon as he gets Jerme back, because obviously it's possible, he'll probably lose interest in her, then all she'll have is her broken heart.

The manupartner steps forward, taking her by the elbow. "You should sit down. You don't look good."

He guides her to the couch, pressing her shoulder until she sits. Then he picks up the remote and turns the particle pane to a sunny beach scene. "Feel better?"

She glances from the particle panes to him. "How do you know how to do that if you've never been out of that room?"

He shrugs. "My programming. I can do almost everything except be real." His tone is so beleaguered that Electra can't help but momentarily feel pity for him.

She shakes her head as if she can shake away the horrible revelation that Res6, the man she's inconveniently developing feelings for, has a god complex and is trying to resurrect his dead twin. He lied. He's been lying. Oh God, it wasn't their Saturday Sirens outfits in the closet glitching. It was this thing. Or another earlier experiment. But the repairman came—Trent seemed clueless at first. Has everything been a lie?

The hovering manupartner looks so distressed that she feels compelled to say, "Don't worry. It's not your fault."

It sits down next to her, and she does her best to ignore its presence so she can think. This is the other shoe dropping. The horrible thing she was waiting for that will steal her happiness away.

"If you need to talk, you can talk to me. He does that sometimes."

Tears prick her eyes. Res6 has been having late-night chats with a manupartner he calls Jerme? It's so insane, she isn't sure if she should laugh or cry. No wonder her column is becoming so popular. Humanity has lost track of what it means to be human.

She gets up, giving in to the call of her bed with its massive pile of blankets she can hide beneath. Last night, the same blankets cocooned her and Res6 as they drifted to sleep tangled in each other's arms. She forces one foot in front of the other, doing her best to block out the memory. Still, dread nearly paralyzes her. *You can collapse into a heap of spiraling doom once you get to the bed.*

Footsteps sound behind her. Is the Jerme clone following her? "Electra, do you need to talk? You never answered. What about my protein packs?"

She groans and forces herself to fish out a prepared meal from the refrigerator for the manupartner so the thing doesn't starve. As he sits on the couch content with his "fuel," she retreats to the bedroom and collapses face-first onto the bed. Res6's woodsy citrus scent envelopes her. "I'm in hell."

33 – Sexting and Double Standards

Res6

The last thing Res6 wants to do is review quarterly sales figures when there's a beautiful human woman waiting for him at his unit. A stunningly delicious woman who's been sending him scandalous messages all afternoon. Little narratives of the things he did to her last night and this morning. Some detail the things she wants to do to him.

He thinks the command: Message Electra. *No more interesting messages to get me through the day?*

After fifteen minutes, she still hasn't responded. She's probably napping. Her sleep schedule is a bit erratic. He did some research and read that having odd sleep habits is common with creatives like her. While he waits for her reply, he rereads his favorite scenario she sent him: *Scene idea. After a hard day's work, MMC falls asleep on the couch. Wakes up to FMC swirling her tongue around the crown of his growing erection. Licking up the pre-cum already beaded there. She grins, because they both know how eager she is for more.*

Every time he reads her little narratives, his cock takes notice. He shoves the feeling away. Having a hard-on while Tommy is sitting across the desk from him would be incredibly inappropriate.

Think about the sales figures.

He refocuses on the numbers on his screen. While they're good, they weren't as good as he hoped based on dragging Electra and Chryl out in public at every opportunity. At first there was a spike, aligning with what he expected, but then they evened out, showing a slight increase overall compared to the prior five years. He runs a hand over his face, massaging his temples. "This is because of the GROW reincarnate scare, isn't it?"

Tommy looks up from his tablet. He stares at Res6 across the desk, blinking.

"GROW reincarnates—Tommy. Are you listening?"

Tommy shakes his head. "Yes, sir. The reincarnate scare is likely affecting public trust. Would you like to put out a statement?"

"I should report them. I have some information I could give Inspector Wanda that might demonstrate to the public how we're working with the authorities to rebuild—"

Tommy's eyes glaze over. Is he paler than normal? A few seconds pass before his attention clears. "Perhaps reporting GROW isn't such a wise choice, considering . . ."

Res6's brows shoot up. "Considering what?"

"If someone were to find out about Electra's nature." Tommy emphasizes the word *nature*.

Why is he being vague? Is he worried about getting fired like Lextr? Perhaps he should reassure him at some point. Of everyone he knows, Tommy is the least likely to do something suspicious. He sighs, taking pity on the man—Electra must be rubbing off on him. "You mean that she's a reincarnate? Yes, I'm quite aware of the risks, but that isn't something you need to worry about. I have her identity under control."

Tommy frowns, looking away as a message pops up on Res6's screen.

"Tommy, why are you messaging me when I'm sitting right here?" Curious—*because when is he ever not curious*—he opens it. It's a forwarded NewNewsletter. "What's this?"

"Scroll down."

Res6 does, freezing when he reaches an avatar that looks an awful lot like Electra. Beneath it is a headline: "What does MSP's new advice influencer know that you don't?"

Heat crawls up his neck as he scans the article.

Dear Electra has taken MSP by storm . . . giving out advice, encouraging relationships between humans . . . with Electra's advice, will manupartners become a thing of the past? . . . only time will tell, but in the meantime, this reporter plans to get the exclusive.

He finishes the article and shoots out of the chair. "I'll take care of this. Then I'll get that inspector in here and deal with GROW and our public trust issue."

As the SAT zips across the city, he can't stop thinking that she's not only putting herself and his company at risk, her column is impacting his sales. If MSP found out she was a manupartner and that they'd brought her back more or less intentionally, NHOS would fine him at minimum. Possibly shut them down. That means no more CHOICElover, the thing he's worked tirelessly on his entire life. Plus, he'd lose the chance to bring Jerme back.

Two more chances. That's all he has left. Yet after the last heartbreaking failure—the look in his brother's eyes as he whispered *Make it stop*—his throat constricts.

But he's come this far. He can't give up now. So what if it takes every last sample to get it right? He owes Jerme that much. He owes it to himself because, for one fleeting minute, having his brother back gave his life meaning.

The memory evokes the same jolt of meaning he felt later that night. He'd fallen into welcoming arms, and they'd tethered him—almost like he mattered. Like his existence meant something to someone. Like he mattered to her.

Damn it, Electra. He can't let anything happen to her.

Suddenly, all the doubt and dread he pushed aside flood back in. By the time he exits the SAT, he's practically trembling with a dangerous mix of anger and despair.

He throws the door open only to come face-to-face with the man he'd do anything to bring back.

"Hi Res6. You don't look good. Would you like to sit down? We can talk about it."

His heart thuds painfully. Then it hits him. His gaze slashes to the closed door of Electra's room, then to the spare room. The door is wide open. His stomach drops to his knees. Shit.

Take a deep breath. Maybe it isn't what you think.

Slowly, he asks, "How'd you get out?"

The body double warily glances at the closed door. "I met Electra. Are you upset?" The manupartner's attention drifts to where his fists are clenched at his sides.

"I am upset."

"Good." Res6 doesn't turn his head away from the manupartner, but he can sense Electra standing in her doorway, staring daggers at him. "I'm upset too." Her voice is a mirror of his own, full of venom-laced agony.

"Unit, please go back to your room and give us a moment."

The manupartner walks by, placing a hand on Res6's shoulder. It's so like what Jerme would have done, he has to bite back tears. When the door finally closes behind it, he turns to Electra. She's clearly pissed at what she thinks she discovered, but he doesn't care. She's been lying to him too about her column. Now she's breached his trust by breaking into his locked room. He's never felt so violated. She opens her mouth, but he doesn't give her a chance to start.

"You trespassed! You're writing an advice column that undermines my life's work. You're splattering your likeness and name across the network, putting both of us at risk of getting caught for what you are. Did you think no one would connect that the woman writing the trendy new column has an avatar that looks a lot like my latest manupartner?" he hisses, watching as her cheeks redden with anger. "What do you have to be mad about?"

Her eyes narrow as she steps into the room. "I'm so glad you asked."

34 – Good Enough for Human Love

Electra

"You are the most thickheaded man I've ever had the displeasure of knowing!" Electra shouts. They've been going around like this for ten minutes. It's like he's listening but not hearing what she is saying. "I told you; he kept knocking, so I found a way to open the door." How isn't important, so there's no need to mention it. From her perch on the couch, she watches him pace. "Until that, I had no intention of opening it, I swear." He doesn't immediately respond, and she's leery of throwing out accusations as flippantly as he did. She takes a deep breath and asks, "What is going on, Res6? That manupartner told me you sometimes call him Jerme."

"What I do with him isn't any of your business. But you just couldn't leave it alone."

His accusation feels like a thousand spiders using silk made of rage to weave a web around her brain—it might implode. Still, she takes

360

another deep breath, mentally renewing her commitment to keep a calm voice. If this conversation doesn't move forward, they'll be here all night. At least the column is out in the open. Based on what Sister Xelna said, she won't be able to keep it a secret much longer anyway. Res6, on the other hand, still hasn't admitted his intent with the Jerme-shaped manupartner or the failed experiment in the closet that he doesn't seem to realize she knows about—or he knows and he's in denial. "I'm done with the lies. If this is going to work between us, we have to be honest from now on."

"That's rich coming from the woman who's been hiding her very public advice column," he snaps. "The only thing I did was have a locked room that you labeled a Sex Dungeon, and it's decidedly not a sex anything!"

"I can't believe you've been reading my journal when I explicitly told you not to!"

"It says *Dear Reader*," he says, staring her down as if his point is valid. "Besides, I stopped after you told me. How was I supposed to know?"

"You should have brought that up when we talked about it." Oh God, what else did he read? "Those were my private thoughts. I can't believe you did that and have the nerve to accuse me of a violation of trust."

Thunder crashes. The particle panes behind him display a storm scene. His silhouette is stark against the bright lightning.

Did he change it to match his mood, or does the little metal disk behind his ear that is both a communications device and an emotion tracker pick up on it and adjust it accordingly? Either way, could he be more dramatic?

Enough with the nonsense. "I know that you're trying to bring him back." There. Now that's out in the open, too.

He freezes. "I don't know what you're talking about. That," he points to the now-closed door, "is a manupartner made with my DNA that I've been sending to my FRIENDS appointments. Sure, in a moment of weakness, I called him by my brother's name and it stuck, but I told you about him."

"I realize that. I'm not stupid, Res6. I saw the one in the closet."

His skin pales a shade. "I'm not—"

She shoots to her feet. "Don't you dare lie to me! I know what you're doing, and I promise you, by not accepting reality, you're only adding to your suffering. You have to stop this. Jerme is gone, Res6. He's gone, and it isn't up to you to bring him back. It's not right."

Trembling, he stops pacing and turns to face her. "You don't want me to lie to you, Dear Electra. Is that your advice? Fine. Then I'll take it. Yes, I've been working my hardest to bring Jerme back. And for one groundbreaking moment, I thought it worked. I saw him again after a hundred years before everything went wrong. So believe me when I tell you, I would do anything—*trade anything*—to get him back."

The implication is *her*. He would trade her . . . She flinches as if he's slapped her. Of course he would. That's his twin. She had already come to that conclusion before he walked through the door. But she thought after what they shared that night when he'd been so upset—oh God. That's what he was upset about. Had he must have succeeded only for something to happen and lost Jerme all over again. It was never about her or them at all.

He continues, evidently unfazed by her reaction. "You don't think Jerme deserves a second chance? Who are you to dictate who gets to come back?"

She blinks, dumbfounded. Is he serious?

"Answer me," he shouts.

"I'm sorry. I'm trying to keep my brain from imploding from the force of your faulty logic," she says, jumping up and gesturing wildly in his direction.

"Faulty logic?" He huffs, sneering.

"That's right. I'm not the one trying to play God. Or Zorg. Whatever!" So much for keeping calm. "Res6, we talked about this. Do you still think he's going to wake up and be happy you did that to him? Stole his autonomy like that? You said yourself he probably wouldn't want to be brought back."

"No, I didn't think he would be happy, but I was going to have you help me fix him." He looks away as a deep flush blooms on his throat and cheeks, his shame a vibration pulsing between them.

The tight sensation in her chest is becoming unbearable. Damn her empathy. "You want me to help you fix him? Res6, you can't fix other people."

He chuffs derisively. "Isn't that precisely what you're trying to do with your secret Dear Electra column? Surely Dear Electra can fix anyone."

"Don't you throw the Dear Electra column at me. I tried to tell you about it, but you wouldn't hear it. You were completely closed off to the idea."

"That's because it's dangerous. You're all over the news now." He gestures to her computer desk as if it's all the damning evidence he needs. "You've put everything I've spent my whole life working for at risk. When they find out what you are, they're going to shut me down."

"They won't shut *you* down, Res6. They'll shut your stupid company down. That's a huge difference. Honestly, from where I'm sitting, Lextr was right. You're an unbelievable hypocrite." As soon as the words leave her mouth, she knows she's crossed a line.

Silence hangs between them for an infinite moment. He runs his hand through his hair every few seconds, which would be painful to watch if she weren't so angry.

Finally, he stops, directing the full force of his attention at her. "I thought our little arguments until this point meant we were learning to communicate, but it seems that wasn't the case. Since you're so good at advice, what do you propose we do now?"

"I propose we each try to see where the other is coming from. I'll go first." She takes several calming breaths. "I shouldn't have called your company stupid. I'm sorry. I still have such a hard time wrapping my mind around the concept of a manupartner, and I suspect I'm not the only one who thinks something is missing." She almost mentions what Sister Xelna said, but decides they already have enough to tackle without letting him know she's been making new friends. Best to save that for another day when tensions aren't so high. "I want to help people find the connection this society is sorely missing. Based on my column's popularity, there are people who want that too. That's why I think Dear Electra is so important."

"It's a trend, Electra. Like your freckles." His expression is pitying as he mutters, "This was a mistake."

The word *mistake* slices through her cleaner than any blade could. "What?"

"This is how the world is now—something you need to come to terms with. Do you think your column is going to change that? That all of a sudden society is going to regain some interest in human-human relationships? Oh, here's one. Do you imagine NHOS is going to lift the ban on marriages and you'll start officiating weddings? I'm on a roll." He taps his lips. "Let's see. What other delusions do you have?"

She holds up a hand. "Please stop." A tightness builds in her throat as she tries to process what he's saying, still unable to get past the word *mistake*. He watches her as she walks back over to the couch and slumps onto it. This conversation is sapping all of her energy. "So you're good enough for human love, but no one else is?"

"You've made it quite clear you don't find me worthy of love," he says. "What I don't understand is what you think is going to happen. When you get caught, which you will, do you think the government is going to grant you personhood? Give you an ID, no questions asked? You've seen firsthand how Inspector Wanda and her team are responding to reincarnates." His head snaps to the side like he's had an epiphany. "Do you think you're the hero in this story, like one of those women you write about?"

"That is the most insulting thing anyone has ever said to me." She buries her face in her hands. The worst part about it is that even she, as mad as she is, can see a sliver of truth in his accusation. Because isn't that what she's doing—trying to save the citizens of MSP through human connection? "At least I don't have a god complex. I'm sorry I picked the lock and discovered your secret, Res6. I really am, because I promise you, I'd rather not know how truly messed up you are."

This time she doesn't even feel bad as hurt shines in his golden eyes. "This is exactly why human relationships became obsolete." He shakes his head, gesturing between them. "This. Us. That's the mistake. I knew dating a human woman was inadvisable."

"What are you saying, Res6?"

"Well, you're the one who clearly doesn't respect me and my life's work, so what more is there to say?"

Maybe he's right. She's the stupid one for thinking she could have a relationship with a repressed, walled-off man like him. He clearly cares more about his fake people than real ones. So what if the sex is mind-blowing? Breaking up is probably for the best. "At least that's one thing we can agree on." With that, she gets up, marches to her room, and slams the door.

Except instead of letting the bed swallow her up, she paces, replaying every word they threw at each other, which only makes it worse. Was she craving security so intensely that she trusted a man like him? A man who's so stuck in the past that he's actively trying to bring his brother back from the dead? Who's calling his body double by his dead twin's name and using him as a sounding board?

She walks over to the bathroom mirror and takes a good, hard look at herself. *You look tired.* They probably have a treatment for that now. They probably even have a treatment for her cracked and aching heart.

Tears spill over her eyelids, dropping onto the counter as she stares at her reflection.

Oh, Electra. How did you get yourself into this mess?

35 – The Sting

Res6

December 23, 2390.

Is he avoiding her? No, he's busy. There's a mountain of tasks to tackle that he's trying to catch up on. He has candidates to interview. A meeting with Viper in half an hour. His absence is completely justifiable.

He scrolls down and does his best to focus on the figures before him. Reviewing reports compiled by his staff is his least favorite aspect of running his business. He loves the discovery of being a scientist. Getting in the lab and using the high-tech bio-equipment was the driving factor when he chose his profession. The list of quantities is especially mind-numbing, explaining why his usually focused mind keeps wandering. Considering Lextr's recent theft, he should give it the attention it requires. Sighing, he focuses back on the list.

- Lipo-protein coagulum – 4,198,003 Units

- Liquid Nitrogen – 3,054 Low-Pressure Cryogen Dewars

- Needle, 16 gauge x 31 mm – 1,050 units (low quantity)

- Needle, 23 gauge x 16 mm – 1,991 units (low quantity)

Perhaps he was a bit harsh calling their relationship a mistake. It is, but he can't bring himself to regret it. What he regrets is her finding out about Jerme. He knew she would be upset and disgusted with him. That's why he didn't tell her.

Such a stubborn, foolish woman. No matter what he said, she wouldn't acknowledge the risk she's putting them in. All for her stupid column. He winces at the thought.

So you're good enough for human love, but no one else is? Her words keep ringing in his mind. It's no wonder he's been staring at the same inventory reports for the last two hours.

He wasn't lying when he suggested she doesn't think he's worthy of love. Hell, Jerme didn't either. Love is a farce. Manupartners solved the problem. If anyone is a modern-day hero, it is him.

Human love.

Love.

He didn't pick the word up during their argument, but he's replayed it in his mind so many times now. LOVE. It illuminates his mind like a neon sign. Is that what's between them? He drops his head into his hands. Impossible. This wrecked feeling he gets when he thinks about having to face her certainly isn't love. It's something far worse.

Therefore, it's best he gets on with his life and pretends like she never existed.

A knock sounds at his door, and his new employee Viper pokes his head inside. "Are you ready for our meeting?"

"Ah, yes. Please sit." Res6 collects his tablet, giving the other man a moment to get settled in the chair across from his desk. "I've decided to approach an inspector I know about the information you shared with me."

Viper's brows lift. "What prompted that?"

To his mind, Electra already put them at risk with her column. If he were to report GROW's criminal activity, and the nature of Electra's existence came to light, he could explain that she was a onetime mistake and show he has a track record of working transparently with NHOS, even going above and beyond to discover information that would help them with their reincarnate case. For all they know, the physician Sable is the one creating reincarnates—and he wants to put a stop to that.

Electra's voice sounds in his head. *You're an unbelievable hypocrite.* Jerme is different, he reminds himself. He owes his brother a second chance.

"I'm concerned about consumer trust," he answers, his tone brisk enough to broker no further questions.

"I see. What do you need from me?" Viper asks.

Res6 lifts his tablet. "I'd like to record your testimony so I can use it along with the video you sourced. Please start from the beginning."

December 24, 2390.

When he got home the night before, Electra's door was shut again. He decided that a few days of space wasn't a bad thing. Not that he's ready to face her. In the romance novels he loves, breakup scenes are common at the beginning of the third act, which easily explains the argument between him and the writer he may or may not be dating. The problem is, the more he marinates on their argument, he isn't sure which one of them is the hero. She's probably pegged him as the villain for attempting to bring Jerme back. Her very own mad scientist. Except she doesn't want him, does she? If she did, she wouldn't have walked away.

He picks up his Lase-Razor and runs it over his stubble. Does he look as tired as he feels? He forces himself to meet his own gaze in the mirror. The answer is yes. That's what happens when you toss and turn all night. "How did you get yourself into this mess?"

The man in the mirror doesn't answer. Thinking about her is the last thing he needs. Right before he left the office, he got a message from Inspector Wanda asking to meet first thing this morning. Apparently, her version of early is 06:30. Knowing he wouldn't sleep, he agreed.

He needs to focus and give his company the best shot for when the world discovers Electra's true identity. He needs to get Inspector Wanda on his side and convince her they want the same things. That being the proper control of manupartners, so NHOS won't perceive them as a threat to their stable society and shut his *stupid company* down. Not *him,* as Electra so aptly put it.

When he finally gets to his office, the inspector is already waiting for him. "Good morning," he says, pressing his palm to the pad outside his door.

"You said you had a lead on the reincarnate case?" Wanda says, following him inside and taking a seat.

"A possible lead," he clarifies. "I've become aware of a physician at GROW using manupartners in an illegal fighting ring. I thought it might be connected."

Wanda's blonde brows shoot up. "Good. I wanted to meet early because there might be an opportunity, depending on what you have for me."

Res6 pulls up the video and the audio file of Viper's testimony. "Let me show you."

Wanda listens as Viper details what he saw along with several extrapolations and a short extraneous rant about a woman named K8 who apparently embarrassed him with a vehement rejection in front of his coworkers, which explains his vendetta. Occasionally, Wanda takes notes on her tablet. He plays the video next.

"Pause there," Wanda says, getting up to get a better look.

"My source confirmed that is a manupartner called James. I've included his unit number in the package I've prepared."

Wanda quickly taps her tablet and her eyes go distant for a moment, a sign she's mentally dictating more notes. "And you say there's a GROW physician involved?"

"Yes," he says. "Her name is Sable. My source says she and the manupartner James are behind most of the big upsets at the club over the last month. Perhaps you could get—"

Wanda clears her throat. "Let me remind you, I know how to do my job."

His gaze flicks to his hands. "Of course. My mistake."

"The unauthorized use of manupartners draws scrutiny to your product. I'm sure you're aware."

"I am," he says.

"Then explain your motivation in bringing me this, so I don't think you're trying to redirect my attention elsewhere. Considering the robbery, imagine how this looks from my perspective." Her blue eyes are piercing as she meets his gaze.

She's right to question his motivations. After all, his intent is to bolster his favor with NHOS should Electra's nature ever come to light. But technically that isn't a diversion. "Of course. That's why I wanted to bring you this information. Believe me," he says, running a hand through his hair. Zorg, could he be more suspicious? He leans back in his chair, trying to assume a relaxed position. "The last thing I want is for NHOS to have a problem with my creation. That's why I've made sure our product safety measures are unmatched across the industry. I thought my aid and transparency would have reinforced my commitment to shutting down the reincarnate problem."

"Hmm . . . I suppose I'll accept that. You're so sure it's limited to GROW. Why not ManuMATE or CheapDate? she asks, chewing the tip of her stylus.

His gaze attaches to the movement. Inspector Wanda is a beautiful woman, but his mind is full of Electra's glossy lips. He shoves the image out of his mind. "I almost have the full report of the scans ready to send. The reincarnates came from the GROW DNA catalogue you provided us, confirming what they told us in their interviews. Considering none of them are from one of my other competitors, the evidence points to them."

He certainly isn't going to tell her that the additional dozen reincarnates Tommy found on BLACKOUT are also from GROW, plus this IdenTECH company Electra found is solely using GROW's logo in their marketing. Better to minimize the problem for now until he can convince her that manupartners are not a threat.

"Or someone working for them," the inspector agrees. "Unfortunately, the evidence so far is circumstantial. I'm not convinced this woman, Sable, is behind the reincarnates. You say she moonlights as a healer at the boxing ring."

"That's right."

She sits there for a long moment, mulling it over. "While what they're doing is illegal, my gut tells me she's in it for the unicoin."

He doesn't want to contradict her and get scolded again. He clears his throat, gingerly offering, "Wouldn't it be just as plausible that she's making reincarnates for the unicoin too?"

"I suppose it's possible. I could bring the people you've identified in for questioning, but I have a better idea. We need to act fast."

An hour later, Res6, Viper, and Inspector Wanda, along with ten inspectors from her team, are standing in the lobby at GROW. She holds up her device, showing a digital badge. From the corner of his eye, Res6 sees her screen flash between documents.

"As you can see, I have an official mandatory injunction stating that you are to open your facilities to my people for inspection. I expect GROW is prepared for our visit."

The panicky woman behind the counter keeps glancing between Wanda and Viper. "I'll let my supervisor know you're here."

They're led into a lobby in the employees-only section next to a bank of elevators. Wanda confers with a man who seems to be her team lead, and the inspectors disperse.

Once they're alone, she turns to Res6. "We have an inspection scheduled this morning, along with a recall. It seemed like a way to round up reincarnates and put a stop to more being made. At least make the point to GROW that we're serious about them isolating and solving their problem. I've been operating under the assumption that the reincarnates are a mishap, but based on what you showed me, my doubts are growing. I want to get a read on this Sable woman without having to bring her in. We'll wait here until they've gathered their staff. Meanwhile, we can go over the plan."

Fifteen minutes later, they're being led into a large room packed full of GROW employees in orderly lines.

"Quiet!" Inspector Wanda's team lead barks. The murmuring in the room grinds to a halt. "It is each citizen's duty to come forward if they become aware of NHOS violations. As most of you are aware, GROW is being investigated for . . ." He continues speaking for several minutes, but Res6 tunes him out, scanning the rows of employees. His gaze snags on James—specifically on his broken nose that wasn't obvious in the surveillance video Viper provided. His eyes narrow as recognition passes between them. An image of him sitting in a dingy bar in Z Quadrant with the other taller unidentified man from the video flashes through his mind. Shit. He's not a manupartner at all. The more likely explanation is he's a reincarnate . . . but if that's true, why is he here posing as a GROW employee?

Oh shit.

Shit. James saw him with Electra, and now he's eyeing him knowingly. He must realize Res6 is harboring a reincarnate too. Her column increases the likelihood of her getting caught, but the threat feels more abstract. The hair on the back of his neck stands on end.

He and Sable obviously have a connection and, logically, now he has information about Res6 to keep them out of trouble. He can just picture Wanda stepping up and asking James to identify himself as planned and James jumping in front of the physician defensively, pointing an accusatory finger at him. Then NHOS inspectors will show up to his unit and take Electra before he can get there to tell her he didn't turn her in. After their fight, that's what she'll assume. That he thought she was too much trouble and wanted to get rid of her. He shouldn't have been so callous toward her. Should have knocked on her door last night until she opened it, then knelt at her feet to apologize. His knees are wobbly.

Get it together, Res6. You have a role to play. You have to protect her no matter the cost. The corner of his mouth twitches as he fights a frown. Would James really turn Electra in, though, and jeopardize his identity company? Assuming he's not a plant, it would implicate him even further. He'll get through this, then contact the reincarnate James after. He has no idea what he'll say—and they'll most likely be surveilling them. *Shit. Shit. Shit. This is bad.*

Beside him, Viper shifts, and he can practically feel the excitement radiating off him. "That's the manupartner, isn't it?" He nods toward James.

Res6 leans over. "Stick with the plan. Trust that Wanda knows how best to work her case."

He wouldn't put it past the impulsive man, who clearly is on a revenge plot, to veer off the script. His belligerent insistence that Wanda arrest them immediately did not please her. She threatened to remove him from the mission, which effectively shut him up.

Viper nods vigorously.

When he glances back at James, he's scowling.

He tunes back into the inspector, who is finishing his monologue. ". . . going down the rows of employees to identify the perpetrator, who may or may not be in this very room." More murmurs break out, but louder, and the inspector shouts, "Quiet, please! Both identifying the guilty and clearing the innocent from suspicion hold equal importance. Once you've been cleared, we ask you to exit the room and not speak of today's proceedings, as this is an ongoing investigation. A notice from GROW detailing the status of your employment benefits during our investigation will follow."

Wanda steps up to his side. "Let's begin with the first row."

Viper follows as they make their way down the row, clearing GROW employees who file out of the room. Every few minutes he notices

Wanda's gaze subtly flick to the row further back in the room where James and Sable stand, shifting nervously.

They make it through the second row and are moving onto the third when shouting sounds from outside the door. "I'm sorry, ma'am, but this area is restricted to employees only."

They keep moving down the rows, but the chaos outside the door is distracting him. The woman's words sail through the door. "But I still own him. I can pay—I have the funds!" The agony in her voice makes his stomach clench.

Another few GROW employees are dismissed, and they move to the row James and Sable occupy. From outside the room, someone calls, "Seize her. We can't let her go in there while an active investigation is underway."

A woman from the line barks, "Is someone going to deal with that madwoman, or shall I?" He turns to see that it's Sable who is glancing around like she's surrounded by idiots. If Wanda wants to observe their reactions, the physician certainly seems primed to give them a show.

Wanda turns, addressing Sable directly. "I'm certain the situation is being handled by the appropriate GROW personnel."

Res6 is certain she is provoking her intentionally. Sable breaks eye contact first.

Wanda moves to stand in front of a lab tech who seems to be their companion. "Identify yourself."

"F-Avrel-MSP-00034489," the tech says, ringing her hands like she has something to worry about.

Res6 shakes his head. "Not a match."

Tension flows off Avrel as she rushes for the exit. "I'll wait for you guys outside," she shouts to her companions before the door closes behind her. He tracks her as she passes through the door, spotting a flash of auburn hair. It's the woman from the video, and she has a finger in the face of a burly security guard. This can't be good.

Res6 turns back to James, who seems on the brink of panic. Viper's scowl is now a deep frown as he eyes him. James meets his gaze.

Wanda says, "Identify yourself."

"C-Nixon-MSP-00010672," James says, repeating an identifier that definitely does not belong to him, adding a layer of complication to the case. Could this be a part of his identity company's scheme? Good thing he and Electra bolted when they did. He knew something was off. He doesn't break eye contact with the man as the moment stretches on. *Do not say anything about my reincarnate*, he mentally pleads. He wishes he could snap the tension with a quick, *not a match*, but Wanda instructed him to draw the moment out, so that is what he's doing.

Finally, Res6 says, "Not a match," and both his and James's shoulders deflate.

He moves on to Sable as James heads for the door.

"No need to wait for me," Sable calls. "Take Avrel and go back to the decommissioning chamber. We have a mess to clean up. I'll deal with that woman and follow shortly."

She's going to deal with the K8 woman who thinks some-one—*James*—was recycled. That has to be it. Does that mean she's in some sort of relationship with her reincarnate? The realization is making him dizzy. If that's the case, it mirrors his situation with Electra so closely that it can't help but affect him.

Wanda clears her throat. "If you're quite finished, identify yourself."

Sable's voice is clear as she meets his eye and states, "C-Sable-MSP-00031475. A pleasure to meet you."

Res6's heart is racing as he and Viper step out into GROW's lobby. Something about Sable's tone felt decidedly ominous. Did she just threaten him, or is that her general demeanor?

"We'll let you know if we require any additional assistance. Report back to the office and resume your normal activities," he instructs Viper, who frowns. Did he think the inspector was going to let him tag along throughout the day?

Grumbling, Viper leaves. After giving him a head start—the last thing he wants is suffer through another chat with the man—Res6 makes his way toward the SAT garage to wait on Inspector Wanda as instructed.

But as he's walking, the woman from earlier catches his attention. She's still arguing with that same security guard in front of the customer service counter. Behind the counter, the doors burst open. Out walks Sable, followed by two more guards.

"He's dead?" the woman—K8—asks, rapidly blinking back tears.

He's not dead. Both Res6 and Sable know this, but K8 doesn't. Her distress is palpable, clouding the hallway with tension. Not his business. He quickly slips down a hallway, but not before catching Sable's eye. She looks beyond him before turning back to K8, face a mask of indifference.

After a few wrong turns, he finds the lobby for the SAT garage. A dozen chairs are arranged in neat rows, and the space is otherwise empty aside from the single particle pane displaying an obnoxious GROW advertisement. *Love has never been easier*. What a joke. He can attest from personal experience that—well, he can't attest that, because love isn't what he's feeling. Yes, it's all-consuming. Yes, knowing that she's mad at him has his stomach in knots. Yes, the way she's affecting him makes him want to move municipalities. Is that why 3Zeez ran from Jerme?

His chest squeezes. He thinks the command: Time Check. 11:06. Would Inspector Wanda hurry up already? He's got a ton of work to do. And maybe he can swing by his unit and resolve things with Electra. The longer this goes on, the more unease he feels. He needs a distraction.

"Nervous?" a newly familiar voice asks.

He turns to see Sable leaning against the wall next to him. He got so wrapped up in his thoughts, he didn't notice her approach.

"No," he answers, frowning. "What do you want?"

"That was my partner's girlfriend back there who you upset. She thought he got recycled. If it weren't for you, he would have been home before she ever knew what happened." The thoughtful sparkle in her dark eyes is slightly scary. "You have a reincarnate problem, too, don't you?"

He looks away, a guilty pang hitting him for the distress his actions caused the auburn-haired woman. "I don't know what you're talking about."

Sable chuckles. "The one with the freckles. We know about her." He must pale, because she takes whatever she sees as confirmation. "I'm not here to judge. I only want to see if we might find an opportunity in our common ground."

She holds up her device, sending a request to share contacts. Reluctantly, he thinks the command to accept.

She grins. "I'll be in touch."

36 – Sour Milk

Res6

Inspector Wanda takes another half hour to wrap up the inspection and meet him at the SAT garage lobby. By then, his mind is oscillating between Sable's barely veiled threat, his devolving relationship with Electra, and the realization that he fucked up that's getting harder and harder to deny.

"You look like you've seen a ghost," Wanda says, breezing past him.

"I'm fine." He follows her into the next available SAT.

When the vehicle finally zips out of the garage, he's awash with self-doubt and feeling all too aware of a string of regrettable life choices. He braces for the inevitable. "What did you want to discuss with me?"

He hoped to be done with his role in the reincarnate case after the inspection. In an ideal world, his actions would have swayed the inspector's favor toward him and lifted any scrutiny aimed at

CHOICElover—and Electra. But he clearly isn't living in an ideal world.

"See how that works? Imply that you know someone is guilty and the guilty people start fidgeting and give themselves away! That was the manupartner James, was it not?" she asks.

Yes, that is the man running an identity replacement company. Yes, that man knows I have a reincarnate. Yes, that man has the uncanny ability to make threats with his eyes. All he verbally says is, "Yes, I believe it was."

"That's what I thought. Looks like we've got ourselves another reincarnate and an identity theft situation going on. I'm still not convinced they're behind the reincarnates though, but they may be able to lead us to the people who are. That's why I'm going to let them think they got away for now and keep tabs on them. I'm after the bigger fish." She grins, seeming pleased with herself. "I'd like your continued involvement with the case. I just need to decide how I want to use you. How do you feel about espionage?"

Res6 swallows the lump in his throat, trying not to look too guilty. "Whatever I can do to help."

By the time he enters his unit that evening, he's so rattled by Sable's and Inspector Wanda's propositions, he's ready to fall to his knees and beg for Electra's forgiveness. There's no caring about who's right or wrong. Zorg, he'll happily be wrong if she'll forgive him. He needs her. Somehow, after nearly a hundred years of sufficiently operating alone, it only took a few months with a chaotic woman from the past to wreck the insulating facade he built to shield himself from the world's cruel ways.

She's become his air. His respirator, helping him filter the outside world.

"Electra!" he calls, glancing around.

Her door is still shut.

He doesn't even want sex, though it was comforting to lose himself in her arms after two of the last few remaining Jerme samples failed. Her touch—that is what he needs. He wants to feel her soothing hands on him, softly reassuring him that she's there and everything is going to be okay.

He knocks on her door. When she doesn't answer, he cracks it open just enough that she'll be able to hear him. "Please, Electra. I'm so sorry. I'm such an idiot."

When she doesn't answer, he realizes his weak apology isn't enough. Nothing he ever does is enough.

No, he can't think that way. She said the word *love* and that must mean she's thinking it regarding him. He can fix this. Be what she needs. While he still has her, he has to.

"Electra, please. I know that trying to bring back Jerme is wrong. I've been stubborn and unwilling to let go of my grief for entirely selfish reasons. It felt easier to cling to it, and I see now that I used the loss of Jerme as a shield to keep others out. It was cruel of me to say I'd trade anything for him. It isn't even true. I didn't mean it. I'd never trade you. I never thought I'd laugh again the way I did with Jerme, but you make me laugh all the time. And you're such a talented writer. It's no wonder everyone loves your column. Your advice is brilliant. And you're so incredibly sexy. There isn't a manupartner in existence that can outshine you."

Saying all of that aloud, it sounds a lot like . . . "Oh, Zorg. Electra, I think I—"

He stops just short of saying the words. Saying something so potent through a cracked door would not make him a very good romantic hero. "Electra?"

Silence is the only thing that greets him. For a long moment, he stares at the handle. She wouldn't have—would she? No, Electra isn't Jerme. Finally, he works up the nerve to push the door open. The neatly made bed causes his stomach to drop.

He glances around the room, his throat tightening as the room's vacancy becomes apparent. This can't be happening to him. He's jumping to conclusions. She's probably out somewhere—

The thought abruptly dies as he pushes the closet open. All her things are gone.

Reality strikes him with the weight of a SAT. She left. Even he isn't delusional enough to think the authorities came for her. She left him.

She left him like their mother did. Just as 3Zeez left Jerme and Jerme left him. Everyone leaves. *Because you're not worth staying for.*

Before he realizes what's happening, his back hits the wall, and he's sliding down it. No tears fall, but a pulsing numbness radiates from his chest, eclipsing everything else.

He lies down on the floor, curling into a ball. If he lies here for just a little while, the feelings will pass. It's funny, isn't it? He almost said he loves her. But that's ridiculous. The only person he's ever loved is Jerme, and Jerme, like Electra, is gone.

December 25, 2390.

Someone is shaking his shoulder. The room is too dark to make out the figure, but their touch is firm enough to tell him it isn't her. Still, he stupidly says, "Electra?"

"No, it's me, Jerme," the body double says.

"You're not Jerme," he mutters. He must have fallen asleep. Res6 slumps back onto the floor, the cool concrete beneath him a stark reminder of how alone he is. A feeling he should be grateful for, considering he momentarily forgot the precise reason he invented manupartners.

"Here, let me help you up." It fumbles around before latching onto his arm and tugging.

He allows the unit to ease him to his feet. He thinks the command: Time Check. 03:56. Then he thinks the command to start the slow morning light sequence. A dim glow from the ceiling illuminates the room.

"The woman left," it says.

He groans. "It's better this way."

"Where did she go?" it asks.

He stares at it for a long time before coming to a determination. "I need to recycle you and start going to my FRIENDS appointments on my own." He needs to recycle it before it starts individuating like Chryl did.

The manupartner gives him a pitying look. "I just want you to be happy."

He quickly readies himself for the day then grabs a pick-me-UP nourishment packet, and a VitaShot for good measure. When he's ready to walk out the door, he forces himself to glance over at the manupartner who's docilely sitting on the couch with a blank stare.

A handful of overnight employees stare as he and his identical replica pass, but he pays them no heed. He's too tired and wrecked from the last few days to care. He takes ten minutes to lead the unit to the recycling station in his main lab. There is a single lab tech on duty who's in the process of decommissioning a few test units.

"Hello, sir!" the man, whose sleep schedule must be better than his, greets brightly.

"I need to decommission this unit." He gestures to the manupartner beside him, who he's been talking to as if he's his twin brother. He should never have started calling him Jerme. That was a mistake, regardless of which of their DNA it was made from.

The tech's hazel eyes widen behind his protective lenses. "Of course, sir. I will take care of that for you."

Res6 shakes his head. He needs to do this himself this time. And what's a little more suffering? He can't even feel the thumping organ in his chest anymore. "I'll do it. Please prepare an extra dose of the deactivation serum."

He slips on gloves and the rest of a PPE kit.

When he finishes, the tech has two syringes set out on a tray resting on the stainless steel counter. He guides the unit over to a metal table. "Please lie flat on your back." The manupartner does as the tech says.

Res6 steps up to the side of the table and the tech holds out the tray for him. He takes the first syringe to put the unit to sleep. It's been a while since he's done an injection. Fortunately, the drug doesn't need to be given intravenously. *You deserve this, so do it*, he mentally chides. He doesn't hesitate as he leans over the manupartner and sticks the needle into the meaty flesh of his left forearm.

As he's about to depress the plunger, Jerme speaks—not Jerme, *the manupartner*. "I could help you if you wanted."

His heartbeat ratchets up, and he has to clench his teeth to keep the tears at bay. Instantly, his jaw aches. He cannot allow himself a single tear in front of the employee standing so close. *It's just a body double. Not Jerme. Besides, the only person who can help me doesn't want anything to do with me.* He presses down. A second later, the manupartner's eyes close.

He takes the second needle—the one that stops the heart—and repeats the act, this time without pausing. The manupartner's chest rises one last time before it stills.

He sets the used syringe on the tray, noting his trembling hand.

"I'll have it recycled with this morning's first batch," the tech says.

Res6 nods, removes his PPE, and flees to his office. Once safely behind the closed door, he lets the tears fall. That manupartner was the closest thing to a friend he's had in almost a hundred years—because of Electra, he can see how sad that is now. *You had her until you fucked that up.*

If absence were a trauma, it would feel like this—a temporal scar left by the wound that sliced his life in two. When he lost his brother, it split into before Jerme and after Jerme. Now there's before Electra. Is she gone for good? Is this truly the after? He can hardly wrap his mind around it.

There is one gaping truth he can fully grasp, however. He's never been more alone.

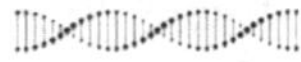

December 26, 2390.

As time crawls by, Res6 can't shake the sensation of trudging through the dense, toxic atmosphere. It's as if every moment that passes deserves an air quality level five warning—except it's not air, it's his life. He's mostly come to terms with recycling the manupartner. It served a useful purpose over the last few months. But now that it's gone, his guilt for treating it like his brother is eating away at him. He's never felt more isolated. Still, he decides to hold off on using the two remaining Jerme samples until he can complete some additional testing. Bringing Jerme back may make him a monster, but at least he wouldn't have to be alone for the rest of his life.

His device chimes. There's a message from Sable. *When can you meet?*

He glances at the time. 14:43.

Inspector Wanda cautioned him not to seem too eager when approaching Sable. He is supposed to ease into her life and see what he can find out. Wanda's plan: approach Sable under the guise of intending to poach her as an executive-level candidate for CHOICElover. Have a few meetings and try to bait her. If the inspection comes up, claim he saw a lot of people that day and doesn't remember her.

The problem is, Wanda doesn't know Sable already approached him. He's in quite the quandary since Sable is aware of Electra, and there is simply no way for him to explain to Wanda why Sable might want to speak with him without creating further suspicion—namely, on Electra.

Electra, who is now out there somewhere, surviving on her own. Without him. Electra, who has awakened primal instincts he never thought he had—instincts that scream for him to hunt her down and drag her back home. It's what Vorack would do. But is that what Electra wants? No. She condemned him for playing Zorg and trying to take away Jerme's agency. He's at a stalemate with no good options.

He shakes off the thought, considering Sable's message. Best to stay busy.

Since the day at GROW, he's been waiting for Sable to contact him. He's surprised it's taken her so long.

He responds, *Can you meet now?*

Thirty minutes later, they're seated across from each other at a booth in the Old Thyme Diner, a server on roller skates having dropped off their drinks and a big bowl of YourNutz.

Sable picks an oval synthetic nut out of the bowl, sniffs it, then sets it aside. Then she places her phone between them and presses start. The screen displays an app called Scrambled Eggs. "It's a countersurveillance app. Prevents recording and video within a three-foot radius. I learned my lesson after the boxing club incident."

He nods. "I wasn't recording."

She eyes a camera in the corner. "Someone always is. Now that our faces are being watched, courtesy of you and that moron Viper." She studies him for a moment. "Who pissed in your milk?"

He leans back, affronted. "Excuse me?"

"Loneliness got you down?" She repeats GROW's slogan, smirking. Is she teasing him? When he only frowns in response, she says, "What happened?"

Allowing his tone to become as gruff as he feels, he says, "It's none of your business."

"So, something did happen," she guesses.

"What do you want?" he asks.

She sighs as if disappointed. "First, are you spying for that inspector?"

His eyes widen. *Damn her.*

"I'll take that as a yes." Her fingers drum on the table. "Here's the deal. I imagine she suspects that we're the ones responsible for the reincarnates or that we'll lead you to them, which is why she let us go. I assure you, we aren't and I don't see how we could. I haven't seen anything that suggests they're not just anomalies caused by an accidental yet precise mix of factors."

Because she's being so forthcoming, he presses, "You really don't know who's behind them?"

"Like I said, I don't think there is an individual per se to blame. They're just scientific accidents. We're trying to help those who already exist. That's what we need your help with. We're willing to offer our help in the form of an identity for your secret reincarnate lover in exchange. And our continued silence." She winks, sending a chill down his spine.

Her candor leads him to believe she's telling the truth. Besides, an ID for Electra might be enough to bring her home, assuming their method of providing one proves safe. "Why aren't you mad I turned you in?"

She huffs. "Viper is the one who couldn't mind his business. You only did what a prudent business owner would do. I don't fault you for that. My partner, on the other hand, may appreciate an apology. The extra time your inspection cost us caused quite a stir in his personal life."

"Your partner, James." When her eyes widen, he says, "Viper got his manupartner identification number from the medical database at the boxing club. So, say I help you. What am I supposed to tell Inspector Wanda?"

"Make something up. Not my problem. But remember, if they find out what we're doing, I'll personally make sure they pick up your little plaything." The grin that lights up Sable's face is borderline villainous.

Yet there's something about knowing exactly where you stand with her that's comforting. There's no guessing or playing games. "She's not my plaything."

"Then what is she?" she challenges.

The way Sable eyes him across the table makes him shift in his seat. "Nothing anymore. And good luck finding her. I have no idea where she is."

Sable taps her lip, considering. "Interesting. Did you try using facial recognition software to find her? We ran a search based on my partner's memory of his encounter with you both and identified a few candidates that match her description. Freckles are still quite distinct, plus you're all over the gossip sites sporting two manupartners. Isolating her down to one result that led to a woman running a stupendously successful blog giving out terrible advice was easy. Dear Electra, I believe. But since you don't care—"

"Her advice isn't terrible, and she's off limits," he barks. Zorg, this is a mess. But what other choice does he have? "I'll help you. What do I need to do?"

Sable smiles, leaning back in her seat, all too pleased with herself. "We give you DNA samples and you provide blanks for us. It's that simple."

"You're not entering the *blanks*"—he makes air quotes around the word—"into the fighting ring, I presume?"

She chuffs. "No. It's really none of your concern. And I'll need them before GROW's recall period ends on the 31st, so we need to accelerate their grow period."

"If I'm going to provide blanks from the organic materials listed in my inventory, then I want to know what my exposure is." Does this make him a double agent? The last book he read was a romantic suspense, and he can't remember how it turned out for the spy. It was a romance, though, so he must have survived.

"Since you haven't figured this out, let me clarify it for you. This is a transactional relationship. You give me something. I give you something. Get it?"

"Yeah, I get it. What do you want now?"

"I want to know what happened with the reincarnate you've lost track of."

Res6 blinks, momentarily stunned. That isn't at all what he thought she was going to say. "Why?"

Sable shrugs. "Consider this your divine punishment for bringing one of them back, then falling in love with it." She clears her throat. "Her, I mean. Besides, I'm curious."

He takes a long inhale and releases it slowly, determined to get through this without his brain melting out his ears. "Why is this happening?" he mutters, and offers a brief explanation. Her column, the half-formed, brother-shaped manupartner she discovered, their communication breakdown—just enough to satisfy her curiosity.

"Okay, but I don't understand why she would think you're a monster for creating a manupartner of your dead brother. That seems perfectly reasonable to me. There must be more to it." Her eyes narrow and go distant for a moment.

He groans. "Please, Sable, can we move on with this negotiation now? You still owe me an answer about what you're doing with the blanks."

She frowns. "Our company is called IdenTECH. We're turning them in for recycling in place of their corresponding reincarnate to get them out of GROW's system, then providing the reincarnate a new ID." She clears her throat. "Selling, technically. I thought that was obvious. That is why we need you to make something up to tell Inspector Wanda. I don't want my new friends concerned, much less aware of her interest in us, until I can figure out how to deal with her."

His eyes narrow.

She scoffs. "Stop judging. It isn't respectful or considerate. Besides, I'm sparing the feelings of another—number seven of acceptable reasons to lie."

The sudden urge to slam his head against the table overtakes him. He grits his teeth instead. It really isn't his business if Sable hides things from her business partners. He knows from experience that it's a bad plan. Losing Electra because he hid his Jerme experiment made that apparent. "Fine."

"There's still something that doesn't fit about your reincarnate problem—oh Zephyr, she wasn't mad because you created a manu-partner with your brother's DNA. You're trying to bring him back, like the reincarnates!" she cries, bolting upright.

"Good Zorg, keep your voice down," he chides, picking up a handful of nuts. Casually, he pops them into his mouth, the chalky taste choking him with instant regret. Around them, a few other patrons glance their way, but no one seems bothered by her outburst. "I thought we were done talking about that."

She leans forward, whispering, "That's it, isn't it? But you've been unsuccessful, and she found out. I could look at your data if you wanted."

"I'm not trying to resurrect my brother, and if I were, I don't need your help."

She crosses her arms. "You're a terrible liar. Why don't you want my help?"

He leans back, utterly defeated by this fiery woman. Maybe he should hire her. He would certainly rather have her on his team than on someone else's. "You're a physician, not a researcher."

A smug grin erupts as she says, "Sounds like you need to take a different approach."

"Perhaps," he reluctantly agrees, sensing his hole getting deeper and wider.

"Next time, I pick the location." She picks up the bowl of nuts and hands it to the server as she skates by. "You know, after you help us, you could message her to show her what a changed man you are. Assuming you want her back."

"She blocked my number. And I don't want her back. It's complicated. How would that show I changed?" If he could get her back, would he want to? Obviously. So, could it be as easy as Sable is suggesting? She seems to have a sharp sense of things—even if she's currently under surveillance by NHOS inspectors. How did she guess that about his brother?

"Set up a new account and message her on FrogBlog. You said she hates the idea of manupartners. Send her a message showing her you care about real people," she says. When he stares at her blankly, she shakes her head like he's an idiot.

His mind clearly isn't firing at optimal capacity, because he can't make the connection. "You're going to have to spell it out for me." He gestures for her to get on with it.

She sighs, as if conversing with him requires a ton of effort. "Real people like *her*."

Her point clicks into place. She's right. He is an idiot.

37 – Real, Adoring Fans

Electra

Sister Xelna calls out from the living room, "Dear Electra! Another fan is here to see you!"

She winces. As much as she's enjoying running her column, the constant stream of in-person fans the priestess allows in her home is draining her energy. In her early writing days, she learned to channel her energy. Fill the tank and the muse will come. When she was living with Res6, she didn't realize how much the "dates" he took her on fueled her creativity wells.

Not that she isn't grateful for Sister Xelna taking her in, and for her money-lending workaround—a.k.a. paying her for "fortune-telling services" until Electra can get an ID and Worldbank account so she can use her own funds and return the money. The woman means well.

She crawls off the cot in Sister Xelna's spare room that she's been sleeping on for over a week, and tosses her tablet aside. As her back twinges, she regrets leaving the comfort of Res6's enormous cushy bed and the ergonomic computer desk he bought for her. Why did she leave again?

Because he cares about fake people more than real ones. He's been having a relationship with a clone pretending it's his dead brother. He said she was a mistake. Right. These are all great reasons.

Reluctantly, she steps out into the living room to be greeted by Sister Xelna, who is chatting with three women. All with long, straight, dark hair like hers. All with freckles. Oh God, was Res6 right? Is her column a trend that will pass in a flash? Dear Electra is how she's earning income, even if she can't access it yet. How is she going to make money? How is she going to survive? Deep breaths. Focus on three things that are real. But as she stares at the three women with their fake freckles and artificially perfected skin, a sense of the real eludes her.

"There she is!" the nearest woman shrieks. For a second, she looks like she's ready to throw herself forward, wrapping Electra in an unwelcome hug. But she holds herself back at the last moment.

Thankfully, Sister Xelna steps between them, linking arms with her. "This is my dearest friend, Dear Electra!"

She is supposed to love this. Becoming a famous writer is what she wanted, right? Surely, she can sell her Dear Electra fans on her romance books, and she can build a career out of this. Dread slices through her in place of the glee she should be feeling. She forces a smile, observing the priestess's smug expression as she shows Electra off like a prized possession. Is that all she is in this future world—a novelty? A sick feeling swirls in her gut. No, that can't be right. She's just being paranoid again. Sister Xelna isn't using her. They're friends.

Her fingers itch to touch something real. *Res6 was real. Res6 is not the one for you. He made that abundantly clear. God, Electra. Say something to your awaiting fans. Be grateful!*

"Hi," she offers sheepishly. "So you guys are fans of the column?"

38 – Five Simple Steps

Res6

Time is moving too fast, or not fast enough. Res6 isn't sure. He steps into his unit, making a beeline for his bed—the one that still smells like Electra as he's refused to clean the sheets, thus removing her scent. More torture that he deserves.

Exhaustion weighs heavily on him as he kicks off his shoes. He peels out of his aseptic-smelling jumpsuit and crawls under the blankets. Wrapping himself in them, he inhales deeply, taking in her lingering scent like an addict.

Please, just let me sleep, he prays, hoping Zephyr will finally take pity on his weary body. How long can he go on like this?

Even Sable commented on his bedraggled look as they finished with the last of the decoy units right in time for GROW's midnight deadline. For the last five days, if Sable wasn't at GROW dealing with the ramifications of the inspection, she was in the lab with him, psion-splicing

DNA vectors into the organic bio-gel substrate, then using the accelerated test protocols to grow a full lab's worth of manupartners as *blanks*.

Her presence was an interesting break in the monotony of After Electra, at least. Despite Sable's role as a physician with GROW, she easily operated the Spot-Gene Interface while they waited between phases, sifting through the highly technical Jerme data. She seemed to understand the science she was looking at, asking for time to mull it over, but already offering a few promising suggestions.

Is he actually weighing the prospect of hiring her? Inspector Wanda's suspicions present a challenge, but if he can help prove her relative innocence, the ambitious physician might end up being the hire he needs. And if NHOS ends up shutting down GROW permanently, which is still up in the air, she'll be looking for a new position. He'll have to deal with her involvement with the IdenTECH company, though. That could be problematic. As intriguing as he finds her, hiring her might be too risky. He gets the impression she's a bit of a loose cannon.

He rolls over, glances at the clock, and buries his face in the pillow. 02:34. *Sleep*, he begs.

After another hour of pointless ruminating on the future of his company, his thoughts unavoidably drift back to Electra and another future stolen from him. His grief briefly transforms into anger. He did this to himself, and he's being too cowardly to write in to Dear Electra like Sable suggested, afraid of rejection. If he does nothing, the possibility is still out there. The lack of finality feels safer.

He huffs. Since he clearly isn't going to fall asleep, he sits up and reaches for his device. If he could just read one of her journal entries . . . He's not supposed to, but he's rather desperate to feel some connection to her. She'll never know.

He quickly finds the folder that she renamed "Electra's Private X-Rated Thoughts (Hint: Res6 is Forbidden)." Just seeing her words lessens the ache in his chest.

He leans back on a pile of pillows and opens the last entry from a week ago. The day she left.

Her words populate on screen, and he settles in.

Dear Res6,

Not "Dear Reader." His stomach drops. She must have known he'd eventually break down and discover the entry.

I'm sorry I left without seeing you first. The truth is, I couldn't face you. Knowing how you feel about me, that you find dating a human woman "inadvisable." Especially after what we shared. But the things you said—did you think if you sabotaged us, you wouldn't have to feel the big scary things you were feeling? Push the human woman away now to avoid potential loss in the future before you get in too deep? How long did it take you to find this, anyway? Days? Weeks? If you had figured out a way to get me back, I would have deleted this, so we know that hasn't happened. Obviously, you don't want me back.

God, I'm not making sense. I just need to get this out. I knew you would find this, and you deserve an explanation. At least that's what Janet would advise. Hell, it's what I would advise. Real life is a bitch though, isn't it?

I tried to be there for you, but you didn't want it. I'm evidently not what you need. After the lying and hiding things, I don't see how we can work.

Especially when you're clinging to the past like a life vest and you can't even see it. You think you can bring Jerme back and I'm going to magically fix you both, but I can't fix you, Res6. You have to fix you.

STOP right now. I can hear you calling me a hypocrite.

A chuckle escapes his lips. He stops reading to wipe his eyes. Reading her letter intensifies the ache in his chest. But in place of loss, a bone-deep longing for some lost future that will never happen takes hold. His eyes drop back to her words.

I know I need to fix myself, too. I have to figure out how to be okay on my own. That's part of the reason I left. Since this is my new life, I need to be valid on my own. I can't keep waiting for something bad to happen, like you tiring of me. Or me feeling like I'm in constant competition with your stupid manupartners or some fantasy of resurrecting your dead brother.

Maybe that's what it all boils down to. You make me feel like I'm not worth choosing. And I can't live like that.

My heart aches because I thought we had found something special. I guess I was wrong. There really isn't anything left to say. Have a nice life, Res6. I hope you find what you're looking for.

Coming to terms,

Electra

He sits there for a moment, stunned. How did he not choose her? Or is this some excuse to reject him because of how messed up she thinks he is?

I would do anything—trade anything to get him back. He implied he'd choose Jerme over her. He didn't mean it. He felt hurt that she had hidden the Dear Electra column from him. Then, when she confronted him about his lie, his shame caused him to lash out to hurt her back. Was he really trying to sabotage them to protect himself? He lets out a bitter laugh. Look where he is now.

The hole he's dug with his hurtful words is massive. Helping Sable and James isn't going to be enough. He needs a new plan. Taking a note from her playbook, he opens the Scrawl app. At the top of a blank page, he writes:

How to win back the hand of the fair maiden, in five not-so-simple steps.

He considers consulting DumBot, but he ended up accidentally dating her last time he did that. The virtual assistant would probably make the situation worse. He needs to do this on his own to show her he's serious. Right. Five steps:

1 – Help Sable with the reincarnates.

Already done, but it's nice to add to the list nonetheless for the simple pleasure of checking things off.

2 – Start going to my FRIENDS meetings myself.

A few weeks should suffice to show he's trying.

3 – Get Electra an ID.

Sable owes him, so basically in progress.

4 – Write into the Dear Electra column groveling.

Sounds painful. Will do later.

5 – Choose Electra and make sure she knows it.

Will be the easiest thing in the world. He only needs to get there. Perhaps there needs to be a sixth step: *Stop trying to resurrect Jerme*. He has two remaining samples. He could call Sable off and put them back in storage. *Or you could destroy them? That would really show her you were serious.*

The permanence of the thought makes his stomach flutter anxiously. Once he gets Electra back, he'll consider it.

39 – Fast Friends

Electra

January 15, 2391.

Sister Xelna frowns. "Aren't you enjoying your fame?" She taps her tattooed whiskers. "I thought people from your time enjoyed that sort of thing. No?"

Electra slumps back onto the priestess's cat bed–shaped couch. "True, some people were obsessed with celebrity. I wasn't one of them."

"Oh, so you don't want fans?" Sister Xelna strokes the synth-cat. Its approving purr is more of an electronic vibration than an animal sound.

"I do want fans," Electra says, absently scrolling through Dear Electra submissions.

"You just don't want to meet them?" The priestess raises a brow.

She glances up. "Just not so often. The steady stream is zapping my creativity."

That perks Sister Xelna up. "Excellent thought. We can arrange a monthly meet and greet with Dear Electra and sell tickets. At first, we can use the public chapel, then when we get larger, we can rent an event room." She picks the synth-cat up off her lap and sets it next to Electra. "Perhaps we can arrange it before or after next month's The Sacred Order of Feline Transcendence service."

Electra blinks, unsure how her minor complaint escalated so quickly. The last thing she wants is to do a monthly Q&A panel with a bunch of unhinged future people. Though if the ticket sales went directly to Sister Xelna, that would take care of the issue of paying her back, giving her more time to get an ID. But she's reluctant to agree to it yet. "Where are you going?" she asks the other woman's retreating form.

"I'm going to get us Tuna-ish sandwiches. Then you can tell me about the story you've been working on."

When the door closes, Electra closes her eyes, taking a few breaths. What she wouldn't give to be in Res6's large bed, tucked securely in a big pile of blankets. At least compared to the cot in the spare room, the cat bed–shaped couch is comfortable. But it requires her to be in the living room, thus subject to Sister Xelna's prying questions.

Electra isn't sure the priestess likes her for her, but at some point over the last few weeks, she determined she isn't using her. Not exactly. Sister Xelna delights in the attention, whether it is being showered on her for her feline prophesies or she's absorbing it vicariously through Dear Electra. Maybe this is just what friendships are now. That doesn't stop it from feeling icky, like when she was one of two women on Res6's arm as a publicity stunt.

Res6—God, why do her thoughts keep returning to him? Surely, she should be over it by now. They weren't even an official couple, even if she does look back on their unintentional dates with fondness. She groans, and the synth-cat's ears twitch. She strokes its faux fur, an act that should horrify her. Strangely, it doesn't. "This is what my life has become," she says to A-Pawstle Calico, who purrs in response.

She returns her focus to her tablet, deleting a few ridiculous advice requests, before finding a message simply titled "ID." Her heart skips. She clicks the message. There are two straightforward sentences:

> I met them, and they are legitimate. Can you meet Seconday at 18:00—same place?

Intrigued, she clicks the user's profile: @unknownerror2271. The profile picture is a generic avatar, and there are no other posts. The account was created today. It's Res6, she's sure. But the message is so sterile—does he want to see her, or is he doing this to assuage his conscience? Or did he somehow get found out, and he's trying to lure her out to save his company? There's no way he would set her up; it has to be real. So, guilt, most likely. Still, butterflies erupt in her stomach at the prospect of seeing him.

She's still staring at the screen when Sister Xelna breezes back in. She sets the reusable takeout containers on the coffee table. "You look like you've seen a ghost."

"He messaged me," she says, still staring at the message.

"I thought you blocked him." Sister Xelna scoops up the synth-cat and pulls it into her lap as she sits down.

Electra angles the tablet so she can see. "Not in the FrogBlog app. He never had an account."

The priestess scans the two sentences. "An ID is good, right? Did you respond?"

She sets the tablet on her lap and balls her fists so they don't tremble. "Not yet. I haven't decided."

Sister Xelna takes her hand like she's about to deliver her some sage wisdom. "What would Dear Electra tell her to do?" Her brows raise as if she's made an impressive proposition.

Electra can't help but smile at her strange friend. "Dear Electra would tell her to be brave and have faith that everything is going to work out." Giving advice and taking advice are totally different things.

"Then it's settled." The priestess squeezes her hand. "You'll go to the meeting and let the dumb man get you the ID."

"Right."

"Unless there's something more you want from him?" A-Pawstle Calico's tail flicks back and forth like it understands what Sister Xelna is implying.

"I don't want anything from him. We broke up." Electra extricates her hand, reaching for her sandwich.

Sister Xelna taps her nose before reaching for her own container. "I sense someone is lying."

Electra stares at her Tuna-ish sandwich as if it will back up her lie.

"You're not the same as when we first met. Your aura then was a bright, cheerful bubblegum pink. Now it is blue, and not a vibrant, peppy shade. That's why I keep bringing the fans around. I thought they would cheer you up." Xelna takes a bite of her sandwich, not noticing the tears welling in Electra's eyes.

"I miss him," she admits. "I don't want to, but I do."

Sister Xelna turns, and they lock gazes. "I know, dearest." She reaches up and wipes a tear away. "Oops! I got a little Sammy Sauce on your face. Here. Let me get that . . ." She takes a napkin, dabbing at Electra's cheek, which only smears the blob of mayo-like substance around.

A chuckle bubbles up from Electra's throat. Then they're both laughing.

"Maybe it's good for your skin?" Sister Xelna says between giggles. When their laughter dies down, she continues, "I only want you to be happy. If that means you need to go back to him, then I support you. Me and A-Pawstle Calico will be just fine. Isn't that right, my precious girl?!"

"No matter what happens, I'm here for you too," Electra says. "Thanks for being my friend."

"Always." Sister Xelna lifts the sandwich to her mouth, but pauses. A guilty grin materializes, and—did her whiskers twitch? "Wait. Does this mean you don't want to do the meet and greets? Because I may have already told a few people about them while I was standing in line at The Fresh Catch."

Knowing her friend's intent in bringing the fans around changes how she feels about it. Electra smiles. "I'll do the meet and greet. I would hate to disappoint my adoring fans."

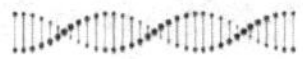

That afternoon, she sends a single-word response to Res6. *Yes.* Then she books the appointment in her calendar, along with the first official meet and greet for the following month. Will he hear about it and be upset? She really shouldn't care. Shouldn't be thinking about him, yet now that she knows she's going to see him after several long weeks, she can't keep her mind off him. Now she's going to see him in two days.

She needs something to occupy her mind, which keeps trailing back to him. It's a vicious cycle. She tried a Dear Electra column entry but couldn't keep her gaze from flicking to her inbox. Would he message again?

Frustrated, she closes the FrogBlog app and opens Scrawl to her latest copy of the manuscript for *An Experiment Gone Wrong*. The storyline is a very loose Frankenstein retelling set on a spaceship where a mad scientist pieces together parts for the perfect man. Only upon activation, she discovers he's just like the rest of them. Like in the original, the scientist rejects him and sends him away from her lab. The monster roams the spaceship, causing problems that ultimately lead him back to her.

The problem is, she can't bring herself to write the next chapter: the third-act breakup scene. It's too on the nose. But it sure would be nice to have it drafted by the meet and greet. Then she would feel confident teasing the storyline. Maybe she could even figure out how to set up a preorder campaign. She'll have an ID by then, so it might work . . . if preorders are even a thing anymore.

The external motivation is there, so she keeps staring at her keyboard, waiting for words to come. They don't. It's pointless. Somehow, the commercially viable love in space saga isn't intrinsically motivating enough.

Right as she's about to give up and call it a day, an idea strikes her.

She's a fast writer—she can pick back up the Frankenstein retelling in a few days and still tease it if she wants. What if she writes a short story as a love letter and apology all in one? He's getting her an ID, so maybe she can do this to reciprocate. She probably owes him something after that shitty breakup note she left him. God, she can't even remember what she wrote. She was packing and trying to dictate to the Scrawl app through angry tears. Had she even made sense? She has no idea, and she's certainly still angry. There's more to hash out, but she isn't opposed to the idea of talking. So maybe this story is her version of opening the door.

She takes her tablet and opens a new Brain Dump. If she can nail down the hook, she'll be off and running.

Best not to overthink it and let it come naturally.

A man's twin brother does not die, as suspected by those he left behind; he sacrifices the life he might have had to pass into a fairytale realm to save a fair maiden—they live happily ever after.

Maybe Jerme will never live in this world again, but she can immortalize him in a story. The dedication comes easily.

For Jerme. I never got to meet you, but this ridiculous man we both love believes we would have become fast friends.

40 – IdenTECH

Res6

January 17, 2391.

If they have to sit here in this dingy Z Quadrant rented meeting room any longer . . . Something isn't right. They've been waiting for at least—Res6 thinks the command: Time check. 18:03.

Okay, so only three minutes past the meeting time. He grips his thighs, kneading his muscles. He can sense Electra noting the action, so he leans back and threads his fingers together in an attempt to appear calmer than he feels.

Electra's scent surrounds him as she leans over. "Why are you nervous? I thought you said you'd met them?"

"I'm working with their business partner, Sable. Just let me do the talking," he says.

She chuffs, but he ignores her. He trusts Sable to a degree, but this is Electra's safety they're talking about, and this time he's the one having second thoughts.

Under her breath, she mutters, "I see nothing has changed. I guess I have my answer for that."

"This isn't the time or place." Stay the course. Follow the plan. Get the ID. He's surprised he hasn't burned a hole in the door with the intensity of his gaze. Right as he's about to launch himself out of the chair, the doorknob turns, and a familiar dark-haired man with a crooked nose walks in. Res6 cocks his head to the side, studying him.

James steps forward with all the confidence of a successful businessperson. His relaxed demeanor is such a relief, Res6 almost stumbles as he stands to reach out his hand. He read about the customs during Electra's time and wanted to be prepared. And possibly impress her. "Res6," he says.

"James," the other man offers in return. Not releasing his hand, he says, "You know, I still can't figure out your motivation for turning us in. Especially considering her." He inclines his head toward a frowning Electra.

Okay, so they're confronting this now. *Well, there's the robbery and my effort to get in the inspector's good graces. And Electra put herself at risk, so an ID is more necessary than ever.* But Res6 doesn't voice any of that.

James continues. "I see the marketing angle of getting a competitor shut down—a tactic that only lasted a week, mind you. That can't be your only reason."

It's true. After the day Inspector Wanda took him and Viper to GROW for the inspection, they didn't find more than a handful of minor violations. Nothing that warranted being permanently shut down. Since they submitted his blanks in place of the outstanding reincarnates, the inspectors didn't find what they were looking for: more reincarnates. Wanda wasn't happy. He assumed she'd been expecting to collect a dozen of them as the recall progressed, but it seems IdenTECH got to them in time. Luckier still, it seemed she had no clue as to his involvement. NHOS had no choice but to let GROW reopen on January 1st.

Res6 tugs his hand away and returns to his seat. James sits down across from him. His gaze automatically skims over Electra. "Perhaps I have other reasons."

"Are you going to keep me guessing?" James asks.

"I didn't realize we were friends," Res6 says, crossing his arms and doing his best to convey the matter being closed.

"My partner, Oro1, will be here any minute." James turns to Electra. "You must be the reincarnate."

Res6 feels her tense beside him. His every protective instinct fires. He fights the urge to pick her up and haul her back to his cave like her hero Vorack, but since she agreed to this, he doesn't offer any comfort. She probably wouldn't accept it if he did.

James offers her a warm smile, continuing, "Like me."

Res6's gaze snaps to the other man. To admit that with such a level of nonchalance . . . Either the man has a death wish, or he reads people exceptionally well.

Electra reaches across the table, taking James's hand. "Electra Lynch. Born 1998. Died 2027. I've been back for a few months now. I'm glad to finally meet another normal human being." She nods in Res6's direction, and he scoffs. Is she teasing? He can't tell. Zorg, is he back to being awkward around her again?

"Good, good. And I know what you mean. Trust me," James says, chuckling, which seems to set Electra at ease. "You've come to the right people. If a discreet identity is what you're looking for, we've got you covered."

"Excellent." He can hear the smile in her voice.

He refuses to glance in her direction. The thought of seeing her pleasing grin directed at James, when she's only offered him a cordial press of her lips, makes him green with envy.

Across the table, James studies him. "You turned us in for using reincarnates in the fighting ring, but by then, Electra would have already been in existence. Now you're going to great lengths to protect her. I'm still trying to understand why."

He shifts, uncomfortable under the scrutiny. In an ill-advised move, he glances at Electra, who's staring at him with the same bold, assessing gaze.

She smirks. "Good luck with that."

Before he can navigate the strategic apology he planned, the door swings open. The tall man who must be Oro1 steps through, sweeping his gaze around the room. Does he sense the tension? He must because he strides around the table, holding his arms out wide. Oh Zorg— Res6 hates the formal greeting. Still, he jumps up, taking the other man's forearms, and leans in to exchange air kisses.

"The French greeting stuck around," James explains to Electra. "I'm sure you've noticed the mishmash of what used to be distinct cultural customs. A little Japanese here, a little Brazilian there. It's anyone's guess how it came to be this way."

Electra chuckles as Oro1 takes his seat, but not before taking her hand and placing a soft kiss on her knuckles. Res6 can't help but notice the pink that colors her cheeks.

Doing his best to hide his irritation and eager to prove himself the bigger man in front of Electra, he says, "Sable tells me I owe you an apology. I understand my actions upset a woman who is important to you. That wasn't my intention, and for her distress, I'm sorry."

"That was K8, the one who deserves your apology. She's my fiancée now. And yes, if she's upset, I'm upset," James says. "But I appreciate your directness."

"Fiancée?" Electra asks. "I thought marriage was outlawed."

"The legal arrangement was. NHOS can't regulate what goes on between two people in love." When James says *in love*, he eyes Res6 knowingly. "I'm sure your good friend Sable can explain it to you."

Damn Sable. He can hear her saying, *I had to tell them something.*

He dares a glance at Electra, who's staring at him with wide eyes. "Who is Sable? He doesn't have any friends," she says, and it stings about as much as he deserves. Granted, he's attended his last several lunch encounters as himself, and no one seemed to notice anything different, so he has that going for him.

He clears his throat. "Thank you for pointing that out, Electra." He directs his attention to Oro1, seemingly the most reasonable one of the bunch. *The only person from the present besides him.* "As you're aware, Electra is from the past, and she requires an identity."

"Of course. It is truly our pleasure to assist in these sensitive matters," Oro1 says.

Res6 resists an eye roll. Oro1 means he's glad to take the excessive fee they're charging him, despite his help with the reincarnates and his secrecy. *It's for a good cause*, Sable told him. *Just think—you can tell Electra how your fee funded IDs for reincarnates who weren't lucky enough to wake up to exorbitantly rich people like you.*

"I can speak for myself," Electra says. "You can leave the room if you don't think you can keep quiet."

James's brows lower as he leans forward. "Electra, if you are uncomfortable in your current arrangement, I'm positive my K8 would welcome you with open arms. Just say the word. Your safety is of utmost importance to Oro1 and me."

"Oh, I'm not living with him anymore. I've made friends. It's not that hard."

Instead of correcting her—because technically James just called Sable his friend—or correcting James, who suggested he might hurt

Electra, which will never happen again, Res6 sits there flabbergasted like the ineffectual lump he is.

James leans forward. "Are you certain you're safe?"

She waves him off. "Yes, I'm fine."

That spikes a new fear in him. Who is she staying with? He's been focusing on her absence, but he failed to consider the danger she's putting herself in. That should have been the first thing he thought of. He's now torn between demanding that she come home with him for safety and respecting her need to prove she's a valid individual, as referenced in her breakup letter.

That doesn't stop him from reaching out to grab the arm of her chair and dragging it toward him. "If her current residence doesn't work out, she can come back home to me. End of discussion."

"Electra, ultimately it's up to you," James says. All three men's attention shifts to her.

Res6 braces, sensing he's moments away from doing something rash and out of character, like throwing her over his shoulder and storming out. Maybe all those romance books are getting to him.

She turns to him. "You want me to come home?"

Yes! Desperately! "Only if that's what you want," he says, watching her subtly deflate. It isn't enough. A few words in a tense meeting won't be enough. He knows this, which is why he has a plan. This isn't the time or place to make his move. Still, for good measure, he throws in, "I respect your choices and I understand you need to be valid on your own."

Her eyes widen.

Yes, I read your letter, he thinks, silently conveying his understanding.

Oro1 clears his throat, but Res6 senses he's on a roll. "James." He turns to the other man. "Perhaps a dinner is in order, considering our working relationship via Sable. I'll buy, of course. I'm sure Electra would love to meet K8." Feeling back in control, he gestures to Oro1. "Bring him too, if you must."

Oro1 chuckles. "I realize I'm good-looking, but why does everyone assume I'm going to steal their woman?" He winks at Electra, which makes Res6 bristle.

James ignores his partner, eyes narrowing. "I'll talk to K8."

Electra gasps, excitedly gripping his forearm. "Actually, that's a great idea. I'd love to meet her."

His eyes narrow in on the gesture. Her touch does more to ease his tightly coiled tension than any of her words might. The room suddenly feels lighter. "Perfect. Dinner, then, and whatever else Electra needs," he says, attempting not to seem like the worst man in the room.

The words come out so easily, they surprise him. He'd been so against—well, everything. He could mentally tick off a list, but it boils down to her being a real human woman who forced him to confront the broken parts of himself so he could become the man she deserves. Because that's what happened. Electra happened, and now he wants to be the man she depends on. Who she comes home to. Who she shares all her secrets with. The man who keeps her safe. If only he can get her to see that. He *will* get her to see that.

Res6 sits a little taller, allowing his normally cool countenance to blanket him. There's no need to act rash. He has everything under control. "What are the next steps?"

After the IdenTECH meeting, Res6 and Electra linger in the hallway, a taut silence vibrating between them.

"Are you really safe where you're living?" He shoves his hands into his pockets so he doesn't do anything stupid, like embrace her.

She shrugs. "Yes. Now that I'm getting an ID, I'll be able to transfer the money I'm making from the column to a Worldbank account and get my own place."

He fights a grimace. "I said you could come back and live with me."

"You don't want that." She shakes her head, glancing down the hallway at two men in bright orange jumpsuits who are gawking at them. The men turn, slipping around the corner out of sight. She takes a step toward him.

She clearly knows nothing of what he wants, because his inner Vorack is screaming, *Yes, I can be the man who protects you.* Considering she got scared and moved toward him, does *she* even know what she wants? He's more than happy to solve the riddle for her, but he senses he needs to give her time to come to the determination on her own. He presses a hand to the small of her back, guiding her toward the elevators that lead to the SAT garages.

"It's probably nothing. They most likely recognized one of us." He clears his throat, eyeing her. "Now that you're nearly as famous as me."

"I know you don't approve." She grins. "Wait, are you teasing me?"

His palms itch to touch her. Back in his pockets they go. "Perhaps."

When they're safely behind the closed elevator door and moving between floors, she leans against the opposite wall. As she stares at him across the elevator car, her dark eyes don't flash with the same fire as they had before, despite plans to get the ID she's been wanting.

He can hardly take it, knowing he's the cause. "Listen, I'm sorry I didn't make it safe for you to tell me about your column. I know it's important to you, and I'm glad you're pursuing it. I understand why you didn't tell me about it."

"Thanks," she says, staring at her feet. "What did James mean when he said you were helping them with the reincarnates?"

He shrugs, trying not to appear too eager to share the evidence of his growth. "My *friend* Sable found out about a GROW recall, which put the active reincarnates at risk. They needed manupartners made with the same DNA to surrender in their place, so Sable and I used their DNA samples to make them." *Because I care about real people!* He mentally screams the words, trusting that she'll infer as much. Romantic heroes should never overwhelm the heroine at this point in the story by trying to force her hand.

She bites the tip of her finger, clearly debating something. "We could have lunch? As friends, I mean."

Tempting, so tempting. She doesn't believe he wants her back in his home, and he'd rather shut down CHOICElover than settle for friends. There is so much more that needs saying. A conversation that even he understands can't be had over lunch, and definitely not out in public.

"I can't." He doesn't offer any further explanation as he follows her off the elevator. She doesn't argue. When the next SAT is available, he helps her into it and returns to the glass enclosure to await the next one.

Her SAT zips out into the atmosphere, taking her away from him—hopefully for the last time.

He has a plan. The first three steps are complete. He'll give her a few days to process his actions. Perhaps James will give him an answer about dinner. Then it's time to properly grovel.

41 – The Pretty Man Grovels

Electra

January 20, 2391.

Between planning for the first official Dear Electra meet and greet, which sold out within an hour, and the convoluted process of getting her ID, she's fallen behind on the column itself. The thought of dishing out advice like she knows what she's talking about has become draining. She stares blankly at her full FrogBlog inbox. *Are you even qualified to give out advice? He said you could come home, and you just sat there.*

Technically, she offered to have lunch—*as friends*. Oh God, did she mess up the one chance she had? When he pulled her chair nearer like a Neanderthal, her heart stupidly tried to leap out of her chest. *He's choosing me!* she thought. Then he rejected her lunch invitation twenty minutes later. How pathetic can she possibly be? This isn't impostor syndrome. It's simply that she isn't capable of running her own life, much less advising people on how to run theirs. Why does this always happen—nope. She mentally grabs the other shoe and tosses it over her shoulder.

At least she's getting better at catching herself now. She can't think that way. It doesn't matter if some man chooses her. She needs to choose herself. The people of MSP clearly have. Her fans need her, and she refuses to give her writer's block—regardless of the form it takes—fertile soil to take root. For every advice request in her inbox, there's another reader writing to tell her how her words made them consider unexpected possibilities, or gave them hope. Janet would be proud of the work she's doing.

With renewed vigor, she scrolls through her inbox until a message catches her eye.

HELP! I'm in love with a human woman.

Intrigued, she clicks on the message.

Dear Electra,
I'm a 120 y/o man, hopelessly in love with a 29 y/o human woman.

Electra's heart catches in her throat. Username: @unknownerror2271. In case her memory is playing tricks on her, she finds the previous ID message from days ago to confirm. It's him. Her pulse races as she returns to the message.

I think I might have fallen in love with her the moment she opened her eyes in my lab and I saw that spark that is distinctly hers. The draw I felt toward her scared the shit out of me. I'm such a coward that I've been fighting it ever since. My fear led me to hold back truths from her I wasn't ready to admit to myself. She saw me though, and by seeing me, forced me to confront the parts of myself I felt ashamed of. I lashed out, and for that I'm deeply sorry. I insinuated I would trade her for someone else who's lost to me, but I realize he's gone. I've known it since that miserable day nearly a hundred years ago. The truth is, I would trade almost anything and anyone to get him back. He's my twin—someone who feels like a missing half of my brain. But I've discovered that she's the other half of my heart.

She brings a lightness to my life each day. She makes me laugh and keeps me guessing. When I'm with her, I feel alive in a way I haven't felt for the longest time. Since Jerme.

I'm not sure I'll ever be whole, but I'm willing to do whatever it takes to show her I can be a better person. Someone who is worthy of her trust and affection. Maybe even her love.

For so long, I wasn't willing to open up—to risk losing someone again. But she's worth it. So please, Electra, tell me what I need to do to win her back.

To win you back, because I miss you desperately.

Please know that I'm eternally yours,

Res6

Electra wipes the tears away with the back of her hand, rereading his heartfelt words. What did it cost him to write this? She glances at the time stamp from two days ago. He must have known it would sit in her inbox and been prepared to wait.

Knowing him, he'd probably bide his time indefinitely, waiting for her to work through her own issues. For years, she imagined herself patiently building something. She thought she had been chasing success to give her a solid foundation. She even convinced herself that she'd find love when everything was perfect. Secure. Then she'd get a real boyfriend and have her own happily ever after.

If Dear Electra were to take her own advice, she would accept that life can be chaotic and that to create the rich connection she desires, she has to take risks. She must trust in the future and revel in the messiness of the human condition in the same way she dances with the muses when she writes her stories.

Maybe Dear Electra would say something like "Finding true love is like looking through both sides of a two-way mirror at once. You must see the other person for who they truly are and accept them despite their imperfections. The challenge is to see the spots in your own reflection and offer yourself the same grace."

Is that what Janet was always trying to tell her? That she is worthy of love and good things as she is? How could she expect him to choose her if she couldn't even make peace with herself, though?

She chuckles at the ridiculousness of it all. They are quite a pair. Her with the advice she dishes out but never takes. Then there's the juxtaposition that is Res6. The awkward-in-private, smooth-in-public figure, the fumbling sex god, the devoted-yet-walled-off man. The more she thinks about him, the deeper the longing burrows in her chest. She wants him, flaws and all.

Thinking of their flaws reminds her of Res6 and his DumBot dates. She crawls off the cot in Sister Xelna's spare room, ignoring her stiff body, because she knows what she needs to do. A nervous energy propels her forward as she freshens up, then races out of the unit. He's already waited this long; she's loath to make him wait longer.

Res6's tower in A Quadrant is two towers over from the one she's been living in and connected by enclosed sky bridges. She's panting by the time she's power walked to their usual simulation chamber to make an appointment. Then she heads to his private SAT garage. When the perky blonde attendant recognizes her, frowning, she says, "Remember me?"

The woman deflates. "I had hoped he recycled you."

"He isn't nearly done with me yet." The woman's frown deepens, but Electra adds, "I make him very happy."

"Funny, he's seemed out of sorts the last dozen times I've seen him."

A pang of guilt hits her, and for a moment, she's at a loss for words. "That's because I had to go in for a tune-up. But I'm back."

Twenty minutes later, she's in a SAT humming across MSP toward CHOICElover's headquarters. The pink neon lights of the logo shine through the smog, nearly blinding her as the SAT pulls up to Res6's private garage entrance. As soon as the airlock releases, she bolts out of the vehicle and rushes down the halls, not paying any mind to the staff who are giving her odd looks.

She finds his door. It's closed. She debates knocking, but taking a play out of his book, she turns the handle before she can chicken out. It's unlocked. Butterflies dance in her stomach as she pushes the door open. Res6 doesn't look up from where he leans on his desk, head buried in his hands. The blue glow from his system illuminates him in a soft light in an otherwise dark room.

She slips in and shuts the door. He glances up.

"Hi." She lifts her hand in a shy wave.

"Electra? What are you doing here?" He jumps up, rushing around the desk to her. His assessing gaze follows his hands over her shoulders, then down her arms. "Is everything okay?"

She steps back, chuckling. "Oh God, I'm sorry. I should have realized showing up like this would make you worry. I'm fine."

His brows furrow deeply, his panic still resonating in the small room. She reaches up and brushes his cheek. "I'm fine," she soothes.

He cups her hand against his stubble, allowing his eyes to close. "You scared me. What are you doing here?"

"I came to see if you would go somewhere with me?" She takes in the symmetrical planes and angles of his face, his soft golden hair, and the dark blond eyelashes to match. The gently sloping lines of his lips that she knows are smooth, yet firm under hers. The warm tone of his skin that made her think she woke up to Adonis. He's so beautiful and all hers.

His eyes snap open, and he stares down his perfectly sculpted nose at her incredulously. "Where?"

"A surprise outing." She grins as his brows lift, intrigued. "Don't worry, it's not a date."

He scoffs. "That's too bad."

She steps into his space. "If you agree to go, you can touch me."

"I'll go. Praise Zorg." The tension in his body unwinds as he pulls her into his chest.

His arm wraps around her ribs, the other threading through her hair to grip the base of her neck. She slides her hands from his chest around his waist, relishing the feel of him, the firm muscle and his warmth that she could so easily melt into.

He takes a deep inhale. "You smell so good. It's funny the things you miss when someone is gone."

"I'm not gone," she says. "I'm right here."

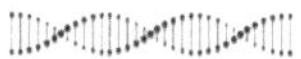

"Where are we?" He glances around, taking in the forest clearing in the simulation chamber.

"It's from a scene in one of my favorite books. It's the place where the hero first sees the heroine bathing in moonlight. She's using her power, which he doesn't realize because he's so smitten."

"Is that what you're doing?" He asks.

"Huh?" She glances back at him.

He tugs her hand, pulling her close. "Using your power on me."

She laughs. "I wish. You would be much easier to manage."

"If you could manage me, what would you have me do?"

She can think of a few things—kissing her being at the top of the list. They should probably talk things through first. "Lay the blanket out on the moss there." She points to a bright patch of green moss, watching as he does as she instructed. "Now we should lay down. I ordered a meteor shower."

They settle on the blanket, lying side by side. He takes her hand, threading their fingers together.

Unable to let the silence linger, she says, "I got your letter."

"I figured." He leans up onto an elbow, angling toward her. "Does this mean you forgive me?"

"Yes. Do you forgive me?"

"There's nothing to forgive." He reaches out and brushes a hair away from her temple.

"That's not true. I shouldn't have left you the way I did. Knowing your history, that was cruel. I'll never do that again. I promise."

He cups her cheeks. "I forgive you, then."

She leans into his touch. But before she melts into him completely, she jabs a finger into his chest. "Here's how this is going to go."

Res6 blinks.

"We're doing this, okay?"

His throat bobs. "Yes, please."

She huffs a laugh. "You sound like a manupartner."

He offers a small grin. "Whatever you like."

It earns him an eye roll. "New rules. No more lying, for starters."

"No lying," he agrees.

"No manupartners."

He nods. "Who needs one when I have you? Where will you live?"

She shrugs, glancing away. "I could still get my own place?"

He frowns. "Why?"

"I don't know. Are we moving too fast?"

"I hate not having you there," he says, groaning. "But if your own place is what you need—"

She cuts him off with a kiss. When their lips break apart, she says, "I don't need my own place."

His eyes are hopeful as he searches her expression. "So you'll come home?"

"You're sure that's what you want? I'm human, remember?" she teases.

"You're certainly no compliant manupartner," he says, and she opens her mouth to protest, but he leans over her, pressing her back into the soft ground. "And I wouldn't have it any other way. Tonight you will sleep beside me. Tomorrow we can go get your things, and if it's up to me, you're never leaving again. I want you, Electra. I want you so fucking bad."

Thunder rumbles softly in the distance. "Oh, shit."

"What?" he asks, glancing over his shoulder to see what she's staring at.

"Rain clouds." Right as she says the words, the first fat droplets fall. "They must have programmed the wrong shower!" she shrieks.

As the rain falls in earnest, he pushes off her and helps her to her feet. She scans the faux forest and points to a copse of trees. "Do you think those trees would offer us shelter?"

"One way to find out." He snatches the blanket, grabs her hand, and drags her to the spot she pointed out where the rain is noticeably lighter. He tosses the blanket onto the ground haphazardly and pulls her into his arms, kissing her deeply. "DumBot suggested a date called Kissing in the Rain. Romantic or not so much?"

She chuckles. "I need more data. Why don't you try it again?"

He takes her jaw in his hands, angling her head so he can control the kiss. He's slow and methodical as he explores her. All she can do is grip the damp fabric at his hips and surrender. When he pulls back to examine her, she's breathless.

"So?" he asks

She blinks, unable to speak. The rain clinging to his thick lashes and running down his warm skin makes her mouth water.

"I'll take that as a yes."

She raises up on tiptoe, bracing against his shoulders as she runs her lips over his jaw, then down his neck, tasting his hot skin as she moves lower. She tugs aside the fabric at his neck, exposing the hollow over his collarbone, licking and biting at the flesh there.

"Fuck," he cries, neck arching back as he grinds his hips into hers. "We have far too many clothes on for this."

She makes her way back up to his lips, whispering, "What are you going to do about it?"

It only takes him a second to unfasten her dress and push it off her shoulders, eyes trailing down her body as the fabric pools at her feet. "You are the most beautiful thing I've ever seen."

He runs his fingertips down her neck, over her breast, and gently palms her, thrumming her hardened nipple with his thumb. Heat pulses between her legs.

Cool raindrops fall on her overheated skin, giving her chills.

"Cold?" he asks.

She nods. "A little."

"Lie down."

She does as he says, staring as he strips out of his wet clothes. He kneels before her, parting her legs, eyeing her sex for a second before crawling over her.

She hums as the delicious warmth of him presses into her.

"Better?" He brushes a wet strand of hair away from her face, kissing her before she can respond. "Tell me what you need?"

"No fancy sex god tricks. I just want you inside me," she says, watching his golden eyes catch fire.

"Anything you like," he says. He claims her mouth while taking hold of her knee, pulling it up against his hip. The movement presses his erection against her clit. Her inner walls clench at the promise of him. "Are you ready for me?" he asks, teasing her entrance.

"I was ready for you ten minutes ago—oh God," she cries as he sheaths himself inside her.

He stills for a moment, letting her adjust. He presses his forehead to hers, making soft circles on her throat with his thumb. His hand, which still grips her knee, pulls her tighter against him, changing the angle so he's impossibly deep.

"You feel so fucking good, Electra. I thought"—he takes a few staggered breaths of the air they share—"I thought I might never have you like this again. I thought you were gone. I'm so stupidly in love with you, I thought I might die."

She opens her eyes to take him in. That isn't rain dripping on her face. Those are his tears. Her heart feels like it may burst. "Move," she commands, before leaning up to claim his mouth.

He obeys, rolling his hips, and the emotion barreling through her works in tandem with the ache building at her center. The pressure is devastating as his thrusts build with intensity. With her free leg, she presses into the ground, chasing that feeling coiling deep inside her. He releases her mouth, burying his face in the side of her neck. "Please, Electra, I want to feel you unravel."

Their rain-slicked bodies move, skin sliding against skin, stoking her desire. Her pleasure. The orgasm that she's been holding back since the moment he thrust inside her sits on the precipice, waiting for her to let loose.

He sends her over the edge with four little words. "Please come for me."

Her body trembles as bliss shoots through her, giving her the bursts of starlight the simulation chamber failed to. "Oh God, Res6!" she cries as her muscles contract as wave after wave washes over her.

"Zorg, I can feel you strangling me. So. Fucking. Good." Res6 moves sharply, emphasizing each word with a thrust before stiffening. She holds him through his pleasure. When he comes back to himself, he collapses onto her, face still tucked into the crook of her neck.

She strokes his silky hair, and eventually their breathing evens out. "You okay?"

His chest rumbles as he pushes himself off her. "I'm hopeless for you, but yeah, I'm okay."

It takes them a few minutes to dry off with the blanket and make themselves presentable enough to make it to the locker rooms. His grip on her hand lingers, and she can tell he's reluctant to let her out of his sight. He's given himself over to her completely, and she knows how much trust that requires. Oh God, she didn't say it back. She meant to, but she was so lost in the moment. Shit. She'll rectify that as soon as they're home—when he's ready for round two, because after several weeks without him, they have some time to make up for.

"I'll be fine. Just give me ten minutes to do something with this." She gestures to her wet and rumpled clothing, and stringy hair. "Then we'll go home, okay?"

He nods, eyeing the door like he might fight it. "Fine. I'll be in the lobby waiting when you're finished."

He turns to walk away, but she calls, "Res6." The words she needs to say dance on the tip of her tongue. But saying them in this nondescript hallway won't be romantic, and he seems to be into that—imagine her luck.

He stops midway down the hall, turning as if ready to run to her aid. "Yes?"

She grins, feeling very doted on by the attentive man. "Nothing. I just wanted to say that everything is going to be fine. Better than fine." Her grin turns into a full smile as the certainty of it washes over her. "It's going to be perfect."

42 – Kill Mode

Electra

Electra steps out of the locker room, still basking in the postcoital glow. Someone bumps into her shoulder. She must really be riding high and not paying attention because she didn't notice anyone else in the hallway. "Excuse me," she says, turning around to see who she bumped into.

"You're excused," a man in an orange jumpsuit says. Another man stands behind him. They're both vaguely familiar.

She quickly racks her brain to remember where she saw them. Then it hits her. "You both were in Z Quadrant the other day in the hall."

"Bingo," the one nearest says, holding up a sparkler.

Her breath catches in her throat. This can't be happening. Right as she's about to scream, the man behind him steps into the light. His nose is smashed from a recent break, and she remembers Res6 told the inspector he heard bone crunch when he struck one of the robbers in the face.

Shit. Shit. Shit.

She backs up, glancing over her shoulder. The lobby isn't far. Res6, who she just promised that everything would be fine, isn't far. "You're the ones who stole the specimens from the CHOICElover lab. We didn't tell them anything," she lies.

The man with the broken nose chuckles, lifting a syringe.

Her voice shakes as she pleads, "No, please. I don't know anything." She can't let them get the needle near her. She darts back, opening her mouth to scream, but the man with the sparkler points in at her head. The dial is set to red—*kill mode.*

"All we need is your DNA sample. Scream, and you're dead."

She whimpers, her tremors becoming convulsions as the man eases toward her.

"That's it, pretty girl. Much better to keep you breathing. You are much more useful to our boss alive. But . . ." he shakes the sparkler, turning it down to the orange setting. "I can make you wish you were dead."

Her blood runs cold. Just like all those months ago when Lextr raised a needle to her, the action happens in slow motion. She doesn't care about pain. She has to make sure he knows she didn't leave him again. It would kill her if he thought that. It would kill him, and she cares way too much to let him get hurt like that again.

Maybe he'll find her. Not maybe. He will find her.

She opens her mouth to scream right as the needle pierces her flesh. "RES6—"

Everything goes dark.

43 – She's Gone

Res6

What is taking her so long?

He thinks the command: Time Check. 16:29.

A sound reverberates through the corridor. He stops pacing to stare down the dark hallway. Was that his name or his imagination? Probably his lovesick mind replaying an echo of her crying out his name in pleasure.

Still, his nerves fire. He marches down the hallway toward the locker rooms, pausing before the door to listen. It's quiet on the other side of the door. "Electra?"

He bangs on the door, impatiently pushing it open. He can apologize to anyone he bursts in on later. "Electra?" he calls, poking his head around the stalls and showers.

She's gone. She's gone. She's gone.

With every step, the words ricochet in his mind. *She left you. You told her you love her and she left. She probably thinks you're love bombing her like Jerme did to 3Zeez, and placated you long enough to get away. There's something wrong with you. There was something wrong with Jerme. You're not enough—*

He pauses his frantic search, throwing open the steam room door. A cloud of hot steam hits him in the face, cutting his downward spiral short.

She said she loved him back, right? He replays the last hour over in his mind. *Move*, she said. *Oh God*, and *Res6*. But never *I love you too*. His back hits the slick tile wall, the steam saturating his already damp shirt. Gravity suddenly doubles, dragging him down. She never said it back.

She doesn't love him. Maybe he was too desperate for her. Not a swoon-worthy enough hero for Dear Electra, giving himself over to her the way he did.

But would she really have slipped out of the back exit to avoid him? That didn't seem like her, especially after what they shared. Even if she doesn't return his love, she wouldn't do that. She said she would come home. That everything would be fine.

He races to the front desk. Zorg, is he being paranoid?

The neatly dressed woman behind the counter takes in his wet shirt and otherwise disheveled appearance and grimaces in distaste. "Can I help you?"

He plants his hands on the countertop. "The woman I came in with—did you see her leave?"

She tucks thick strands of her light blue hair behind her ears and glances uninterestedly at the sliding glass doors. "It's not my job to track people as they leave."

He fights his rising irritation. "Do you have access to the security footage?" She stares, blinking as if his presence is equally irritating.

"Can you tell if the emergency exit alarm was disabled? Or if anyone left through a back exit?"

Her stare tracks to the hallway to her right. "There's an employee exit. Look, is this some type of game? People ask for all sorts of weird scenarios, and I'd rather not get involved."

"What? A game? No, I think there's been an abduction." The claim sounds crazy as he makes it. But it feels right. Electra didn't leave him. She may not have said she loved him, but she said she would never abandon him like that again since she knew his history. She's too good of a person, and he has to trust her. That means only one thing. Someone has taken her.

Intrigued, the attendant leans forward. "There's security footage." She motions her hand over the palm scanner at the simulation chamber's system control station. Her gaze darts back and forth across the screens, as colorful lights illuminate her pale skin with a rainbow of blues and greens.

"You might want to come around to look at this," she says.

He moves around the counter to stand beside her.

"The one with the freckles. That's her, right?" she asks, pausing on a video of them coming in over an hour ago.

He nods.

"We don't video inside for obvious reasons, but there is surveillance at every exit point." She pulls up another window, playing a time-lapse of the video. Two men in jumpsuits and ID Scramble-Tech visors stand outside an emergency exit in a nondescript service hallway. The taller of the two scans the hall. Then he looks directly into the camera. There's no sound, but he clearly mouths, *Shit*. He turns away from the camera, takes the visor off, and presses a few buttons on the side. He appears to put the visor back on like a headband—it must not be working—and plucks his device out of his pocket. Since the man's back is still facing the camera, Res6 can't see what he's doing, but the camera goes dark a second later.

"How did he do that?" the attendant asks.

"A scrambler app. I assume those men don't work here."

She shakes her head.

"Send me that video. Quickly." His brisk tone makes her jump.

Thankfully, she doesn't argue. On the screen, a series of commands play out. When the file is packaged, he holds out his device to make the connection. A second later, his phone pings.

She frowns. "Wait, isn't scrambling a surveillance stream illegal?"

His eyes narrow as he stares at her. "Obviously. Now lead me to that exit."

"Shouldn't we call the authorities?"

"You cannot call the authorities." Those men must have come for Electra knowing she's a reincarnate. He's sure of it. They know she's connected to him and must have been tracking them—those men in the hallway after the IdenTECH meeting. He had a clear image of one of them. Could he get the footage from that day, too? There isn't time. Electra could be halfway across MSP by now.

He's ready to grab the woman's arm and force her down the hallway. Damn the consequences. She steps out of reach, eyeing his hand. "Fine." Then they're marching down the dark hallway.

He thinks the command: Time Check. 16:42 sounds in his ear. Electra said she needed ten minutes in the locker room. At twelve minutes, he went to check on her.

Panic seizes his chest. That means at ten minutes he heard her cry out for him. He didn't imagine it. Zorg, if he'd been paying closer attention, could he have stopped them from taking her?

They push through the emergency exit that leads to a service corridor.

The woman lingers behind as he bursts out into the hallway. "I should get back to my station."

He turns, towering over her. Hoping he exudes enough authority that the woman doesn't balk, he says, "Tell no one of this."

Her eyes widen, and her knuckles turn white as she grips the door handle. "I won't. I swear."

The door clicks behind her. He doesn't glance back as he races down the hall in search of Electra.

A fruitless hour of searching goes by, then another. Who does one report a missing person to—who isn't supposed to exist? Inspector Wanda will only lock Electra up in one of NHOS's holding cells, and he can't let that happen. He needs to get away from his crowded tower so he can think.

The thirty-minute ride to the CHOICElover headquarters drags on like a never-ending nightmare. Electra's beautiful face smiling up at him as their bodies' equilibrium returned to baseline plays in a loop in his mind. *She didn't say she loves you, but she didn't leave you either.* He has to cling to that and do whatever it takes to get her back. She matters. The world needs her. He needs her. He's in too deep to lose her. Now she's in trouble, and she needs him.

His device pings as he steps into the elevator. Could it be the woman from the simulation chamber sending him something she found? He opens the message: It's an image of a woman bound and gagged, huddled in the corner of a sterile white room. He would know the shape of her from even the briefest glimpses. It's Electra. His stomach clenches violently.

He zooms in. Dried tears make vertical tracks down her freckled cheeks, and her dark eyes flash as she stares at the camera. If she's afraid, she has it well masked with anger.

There's a metal cabinet almost off camera. He zooms in. On top of it sits a BioLume Gene Scanner. They're analyzing her DNA? That fits with the stolen organic materials and his hypothesis that someone is trying to bring more reincarnates back. The shiny metal door reflects something orange opposite her. The jumpsuits the men were wearing from the other day?

He rushes to his office, debating between responding and waiting for their demands. Because that's clearly what this is—some plot to extort him using Electra. Her gene scan is probably a bonus. He sends the image to his system and runs it through an enhancer program. He zooms in on the reflection expecting to see fabric, but—it's hair. It's a man with dark skin and curly orange hair.

Lextr?

But why would Lextr take Electra? He's had access to her DNA this whole time. The pieces of the story he concocted move around in his mind. He thought for certain that whoever took Electra is also behind the robbery. Does that mean Lextr is behind the robbery, too? He was the first to speak to the authorities that day. To cover something up?

But that doesn't make sense. Unless he was lying about what had been in those silver cases. Res6 shakes his head. Electra was his first and only successful experiment, a fact reinforced with each subsequent Jerme failure. Unless Lextr's been sabotaging them to shield himself from suspicion. Was she a fluke, or is his own employee—the man he trusted for over fifty years—the one behind the reincarnates? But their DNA is all from GROW's stores. He confirmed that. For Lextr to be involved, he'd have to be working with someone employed by GROW then. But why, when he had access to all the same materials?

Maybe this GROW person knew the key factor they were missing, and again, Electra was a fluke. He isn't getting anywhere.

"Fuck!" He buries his head in his hands. The longer he takes to figure this out, the longer Electra is at risk. He needs help.

He slams his fist on the table. "Zorg-fucking-damnit!" How has he landed himself in this situation? He can't think of a single person to call besides the inspector—which is a terrible idea because she'll just take Electra to Camp Reincarnate. But even if he called Wanda, what do they have to go on? An image and a reasonable guess that the man in the cabinet's reflection is his former employee.

Plus, he'll have to admit Electra's nature and why she exists. Maybe Wanda wouldn't take her in light of all his help. Is he willing to find out? No, too risky. He could call Tommy, but the man's particular moral compass means he'll encourage Res6 to contact the authorities.

Sable's dark eyes and full, smirking lips appear in his mind. James said Sable is his friend. He picks up his device, staring at it for a moment. Can he count on her?

It's worth a shot. Maybe she'll see something he's missing. Before he can change his mind, he thinks the command: Message Sable. *There's been an emergency. I need you to come to my office ASAP.*

This is the whole point of having friends, isn't it?

A second later she responds, *On the way. If this is a setup for Inspector Wanda, I'm going to be pissed.*

GROW's headquarters is in the same industrial quadrant, and she's been working extra, trying to appear like the dedicated employee she isn't for the inspector's benefit. It only takes Sable eleven minutes, making it 19:25 when she throws his door open.

"They've got Electra," he says.

"When did this happen?" Sable asks, breezing through his door and around his desk. No hello or anything. She is truly the perfect friend for him.

"Around 16:30. I got this message as soon as I got here." He shows her the image of Electra, pointing out the gene scanner, then the snip of the orange-haired scientist. Finally, the image of the men outside the simulation chamber's emergency exit.

Sable frowns and her eyes go distant for a moment. "DumBot says the first seventy-two hours after an abduction are critical. If that's true, we have approximately sixty-nine hours to get her back and solve the case that your inspector friend has yet to crack."

He leans back in his chair. "So it seems." He explains his hypothesis, and she listens intently.

She wordlessly requests control of his system, which he grants. She enlarges the image on the screen, so Electra's curled-up form fills it. "She seems to be in one piece. It doesn't look like they've hurt her. They didn't send any demands?"

Right as he says, "Not yet," his device pings. It's a lengthy message from the same sender as the photo. He pulls it up on his system. Sable crowds his space and they scan it.

It's a demand for a list of highly classified information from his company, including intellectual property, methods, and formulations.

He runs his hands through his hair, his worry for Electra stunting his ability to think clearly. "It has to be the same people behind the robbery."

Sable moves to lean on the wall behind him. "So if they're working with your former scientist, why do they need Electra? And wouldn't Lextr know the bulk of that information?"

"That's what I thought."

"Well, I think we can safely rule out GROW's involvement. Their accidental reincarnates probably gave whoever is behind this the idea." As she speaks, the images on the screen move, then a new window opens. It's a portal to a part of the network he's never accessed.

"Don't worry, this is encrypted."

For a second, he questions the wisdom of giving her access to his system. "Is that BLACKOUT?"

"Yes," she says nonchalantly. "Untraceable." A message opens. She drops the files into it and fills in a username.

"What are you doing?"

"That's Orol's handle. You met him, remember?"

"Of course I remember." He specifically remembers Electra's pretty blush when the man kissed her hand. "Why are you sending this to him? I think the fewer people who know, the better."

"Unless they're one of MSP's top hackers with access to the same facial recognition program as Inspector Wanda?" she asks, raising a brow.

"Fine."

"So what do we do now?" She walks around the desk and takes a seat.

"Waiting doesn't feel right, but I don't know what else to do," he admits.

"We could run a few simulated clone experiments for your twin project," she suggests.

He shakes his head, not remotely tempted. "I've put that on hold."

Her brow twitches. "Any particular reason?"

He narrows his eyes as he assesses her. "Are we friends, Sable?"

"Why do you ask?" she shrugs.

"You said our relationship was transactional, but James said we were friends. I was curious about what you thought." He looks away as if uninterested in her answer, but secretly hoping it will be yes. The story's hero always has a quirky sidekick, and Sable is definitely quirky. Well, perhaps not quirky.

"Do you want us to be friends?" She doesn't flinch as her stare meets his.

Saying yes feels incredibly vulnerable. Risky. Out of character. He swallows. "Yes." Electra would be so proud.

Sable's grin is , and he wonders if she knows how she comes across. "OK then. We're friends."

"But why are you smiling like that?" He figured since they're friends now, he has the right to ask.

"K8 keeps saying human connection is dead, but given our straight-forward transaction, making friends doesn't seem so difficult." She picks at her perfectly manicured nails. "Speaking of, does this mean I'm obligated to come to this group dinner of yours?"

There's a subtle edge of vulnerability in her tone that contradicts her words. Something about it causes him to feel a twinge of affection. "It's a requirement."

"If I must."

His device pings. He glances at where it sits on his desk, the clear glass illuminated bright blue.

They both stare at it.

"Another message?" She asks.

He glances at it, noting the same user. He casts the message onto the largest of his screens. There is another image showing a visor-scrambled man holding Electra up against the wall by her neck. Another figure holds a sparkler at her temple.

"They're wearing those ID Scrambler Visors," Sable observes.

"I see that." Does she think he is that much of an idiot?

"The man in the cabinet's reflection wasn't altered. If that really is Lextr, is it possible he's also a captive?"

Before he has time to consider it, another message arrives. It's a block of text and a link.

We require you to upload the above list of requirements to the following link by 08:00. Once our team has assessed the validity of the information, we will release the hostage. If the information is not received, she will be recycled.

The next image is of a silver tray with two ominous syringes on it, which does more to send a message than any weapon they might send ever would.

"Have you got anything?" Sable asks.

He looks away from the message to see her pacing. He opens his mouth, but she holds a finger up and points to her m-volt.

"From where? . . . Really? . . . Impossible."

She continues speaking, presumably to Oro1. The longer the conversation goes on, the more ominous it feels until she finally says, "This is worse than we thought. Send the files over. We'll let you know if we need anything else." She hesitates. "Actually, do you think we could get our hands on a few sparklers?"

His stomach twists into an impossible knot. "What's worse than we thought?"

She moves around the desk again, taking back control of his system. She goes to the BLACKOUT window, where her messages are still open. There is a document containing several pictures of the man who stared directly into the camera before abducting Electra.

"We have a lead."

"Sable, what's worse than we thought?"

"Perhaps I should have said this is *bigger* than we thought. The man in the image is a low-level lab tech for ManuMATE in their product research division. He got transferred from another municipality after some undisclosed legal issues were resolved. He started working for the company as soon as he arrived, which is odd considering the hiring process at ManuMATE is notoriously strenuous."

Res6 buries his head in his hands, which seems to be all he can do lately. "So does this mean ManuMATE is trying to bring back reincarnates too? But why would they need Electra when they can just find another reincarnate on BLACKOUT? Can Oro1 find out if Lextr is working for them now, too?"

She pauses to send a message. "Oro1 is on it. As far as ManuMATE's involvement, I highly doubt the company knows about it. Wouldn't it make more sense that a few employees have gone rogue?"

"Good point. But what about Electra?"

She shrugs. "Since NHOS is publicly hunting down reincarnates, maybe they're harder to find. Tracking your and Electra's whereabouts was easier?"

But that would mean he'd put her in danger again. "Fuck. And somehow this is connected to the robbery?"

"You said they stole the pre-2050 DNA and got Electra's remaining samples?" she asks.

"Yeah."

She grins. "Are you thinking what I'm thinking?"

He shakes his head. "Sable, I'm certain we're never thinking the same thing."

She laughs, brushing off his comment. "What if they weren't after Electra's DNA? What if they were looking for someone else and CHOICElover just happened to have it in their catalogue?"

"But who?"

A message quickly appears on the screen, and she sends it before he can even read it.

Her brows furrow. "No idea. Someone who died pre-2050. Do you think they have her at ManuMATE's headquarters?"

His stomach dips. "I don't know, but we need to figure out something to send to them. Zorg, it'll take me hours to pull all of this together."

"We have all night," she reassures. "There's no need to give them your proprietary information. The last thing we need is for them to figure out how to bring back people from the past intentionally—I'm assuming that's what this is about."

"Sable, this is Electra's life we are talking about. I would risk anything. Give up anything to save her."

She shakes her head. "What is it with reincarnates that makes sensible modern humans fall so recklessly in love? Zephyr, I hope I never get stuck with one."

A message from Oro1 pops up on screen. *Can't find any untraceable sparklers.*

Res6 stands, clutching his stomach as he begins pacing.

"What's wrong with you? You need to start compiling documents so we can send them to Oro1 to falsify." She points to his chair.

He obediently sits and gets to work. Time flies by as he collects and organizes the required data. Several hours later, when he finally has the files packaged, he glances up from his screen. His intense focus shielded him from his panic, but now that he's finished with his task, dread floods in.

"What if it doesn't work? What if they're lying? What if they discover we tried to trick them? What if we give them everything and they kill her anyway?" He reaches up, brushing his damp cheeks. Fuck. The last thing he needs to do is start crying in front of his reluctant new friend. Somehow, he can't stop the overwhelming urge to double over and collapse to the floor. Sheer will is the only thing keeping his spine straight. The prospect of losing Electra is too similar to losing Jerme all those years ago. If they kill her, he isn't sure he'll survive it. "I can't lose her."

Sable's eyes are wide as she cautiously approaches him, like he's a prey animal. She gingerly pats his arm. "It's OK. Everything is going to be OK. If you don't like my plan, what do you think we need to do?"

His vision blurs as he stares past her, quickly calculating the possibilities. He can't come up with a solution that would guarantee her safety. The best option he can come up with scares him almost as much as the prospect of losing her. Because it could mean revealing the truth about Electra and losing the only other thing that he cares about. The thing that has given his life meaning for nearly a hundred years: CHOICElover.

He takes a deep breath, steeling himself. "I think we need to call Inspector Wanda."

44 – Risk and Compromise

Res6

January 21, 2391.

Inspector Wanda walks into his office an hour later wearing her usual gray uniform jumpsuit, clutching a silver mug. "What was so important you had to drag me all the way over here at this hour?" Her long blonde hair is in a neat bun atop her head, and she looks strikingly youthful without her normal full face of makeup.

"I'm not tired, so don't even ask. It's called makeup for a reason," Inspector Wanda says, evidently having noticed him assessing her.

"I wouldn't dare," he says.

Sable chuckles, and when Wanda's eyes land on her, they go wide.

The clock in the bottom corner of his largest screen displays the ticking time bomb that is the clock. 00:03. He gestures to the chair across from him, next to Sable. "You should probably sit down for this."

"We have a lead on the robbery and the people bringing the reincarnates back," Sable says.

Inspector Wanda's brows rise, but she doesn't speak.

"We would like to make a deal with you in exchange," Res6 says.

Wanda takes out her tablet and sets it on the desk between them. She opens an app called Privacy Screen. "This will simultaneously record and encrypt our conversation. I can't promise you any deals until I know what we're dealing with."

He and Sable share a glance.

"Neither of us is behind the reincarnates," he says.

"I'm aware." The inspector gestures for them to get on with it.

He takes a steadying breath. "As a part of our Consumer Product Safety protocols, we ran a few experiments with the goal of making sure our premium product could never accidentally create a reincarnate."

Inspector Wanda rolls her eyes. "No need for a sales pitch. Get on to the part where you tell me you have a room of people from pre-2050 somewhere in this building."

Sable laughs. "You will be relieved to hear—"

Res6 clears his throat, not feeling nearly as jovial. "There's only one. We mistakenly brought a woman back to see if it was possible. For prevention purposes."

Sable leans forward. "He's in love with her."

The inspector glances between them. "One of you better start making some sense."

He takes a deep breath. "The reincarnate, Electra, was abducted yesterday at 16:30 from a simulation chamber in A Quadrant. I was able to obtain surveillance footage before the assailants scrambled the video. Within a few hours, I received these images and a list of demands with a link to upload them, along with a timeline." Res6 pauses, giving the inspector a few moments to study the images and scan through the list. "We have a clear image of one of the men responsible. We know his name, where he works, and we have a vague understanding of his history. We have reason to believe he is one of the men behind the robberies, and we have a hypothesis about what they're doing with the DNA they stole. It's possible my lead scientist, Lextr, who I fired weeks ago for leeching company assets, is working with them."

"You mentioned a timeline. How long do we have?"

He toggles to the threatening message.

"08:00," she observes. "And I presume you want me to grant her legal personhood, ID and everything in exchange for his information."

Res6 nods.

Inspector Wanda turns to Sable. "Where do you fit in?"

"I know I'm being investigated because you think I can somehow lead you back to these people. I want you to call off your tail and leave me alone." Sable glances at him. "Res6 didn't tell me. I guessed."

"Considering the breadth of our current situation, that is a big ask." The inspector shakes her head as she studies the other woman. She turns to Res6. "I told you to ease into this relationship, but considering what I've just learned, I assume an ID for your girlfriend led you to cross paths sooner than anticipated."

That isn't why, but it's better Inspector Wanda believes that than know the truth—that Sable bribed him to create blanks to turn into GROW in place of the reincarnates they're shielding. Reincarnates who are now roaming MSP with fake IDs.

Res6 blanches. He wonders if Sable is feeling the same tension, but she shows no signs of anything but calm. What would it take to crack her cool demeanor?

Sable shrugs. "I can't say I know what you're talking about."

"You're lucky that identity crime doesn't fall under my division. I am, however, deeply concerned about public safety. Considering the more pressing issues I'm dealing with and your potential usefulness, I might be willing to keep my knowledge of IdenTECH to myself."

There's a barely perceptible crack in Sable's voice as she says, "In exchange for?"

"I haven't decided yet, but when I do, you'll be the first to know. For now, I can commit my resources to help bring your reincarnate to safety. But tell me why I shouldn't seclude your reincarnate with the others. They are illegal. What makes her special? Or you, for that matter?"

This is what he was afraid of. His throat is tight as he says, "They're people just like you and me, Inspector. It's not their fault they ended up in the future. It is unfair that they're being treated as if they're the ones who've committed the crime. They all deserve to be granted citizenship, given medical care, and integrated into our society. Our goal should be stopping more from being created, not punishing those who are already here."

Sable nods. "What he's saying is consistent with the protocols in the Respectful and Considerate Conduct Manual. NHOS should treat them as newly born citizens. In a way, they are."

Inspector Wanda's eyes narrow. "You're suggesting that in housing them like we have, we've violated the RCCM guidelines?"

That's exactly what he thinks. He glances at Sable, afraid to answer honestly and upset the inspector, making things worse for Electra. Sable doesn't hesitate. "Yes. It seems you're in violation. You're managing them according to objective reality, when the RCCM clearly states that subjective experience trumps that when taking into consideration the well-being of NHOS citizens. I studied Electra's scans. All the markers you would expect with intact long-term memories are there. Her body is new, but in her brain it's as if she made a time jump."

The silence drags on as Wanda considers. Finally, she says, "I'll have to loop in one of my team members who has a relationship with the Department of Human Affairs for the issue of personhood, but I feel confident we can make that happen. As for the rest of it, we are all working in the best interest of the citizens of MSP. Are we not?"

Res6 nods eagerly. "We are."

Thank Zorg for Sable and her quick, analytical mind. He's going to get a real ID for Electra—now they just have to get her home. Inspector Wanda is proving to be exceptionally reasonable. He toggles to the man's dossier. "His identifier is G-Eliot-MSP-00098754. Three years ago his location code changed from PRS to MSP. That's around the same time he began his employment in the product development division as a lab tech for ManuMATE."

She gives him an incredulous look. "Conveniently, one of your biggest competitors."

"Not convenient at all. The problem being isolated to GROW would be my preference. The last thing I want is for a competitor to draw scrutiny to my creation and give NHOS a reason to revoke our licensing."

"Then we'd better solve this case quickly." She takes her tablet off the desk. "Send me the latest images you have of Electra and Lextr. I want to see if I can get a surveillance trace on their latest whereabouts."

Res6 complies, nervously tapping his foot. "What are we going to do about the ransom?"

"I have a friend who can falsify the data enough to fool them. Should we move on that?" Sable asks.

Inspector Wanda doesn't look up. "What about Lextr? If he's working with them, won't he realize it's fake?"

"I don't want to risk it. I'll just send the real documents."

"Hold on." Sable stands, turning to face the back of the room. "Hey. Can you embed some code in a decoy file package that contaminates the data after a set period?" She pauses, listening with her m-volt. "Okay. What about preventing its being copied?" She's nodding now. "Oh, that's even better." She turns back around. "He says he can corrupt the data remotely. As long as the system is connected to the network."

"Do it," Inspector Wanda instructs.

"You can expect the files within the next hour." Sable turns to him, pointing at his system. "Clock's racing."

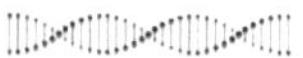

"I found them," Inspector Wanda says. A second later, he gets a request to cast to his system.

Wordlessly he approves it, and a map with two pinpoints appears on the large particle pane that is his north window.

"V Quadrant? That seems random," Sable says.

"At least we know they aren't at ManuMATE's headquarters," Res6 points out.

Inspector Wanda selects the first image, and a video pulls up showing the interior of a SAT garage. It shows Electra being dragged out of a SAT and roughly set on her feet by a man wearing an operational ID Scramble-Tech visor. She stumbles, throwing an arm out for balance, like she isn't fully in control of her motor functions. When the man with the broken visor steps out of the vehicle, he roughly grabs her arm, but not to steady her. He jerks her violently forward, and Res6 is certain she'll have marks on her arms from the bruising grip. He grips the arms of his chair as a wave of fury washes over him.

She's in danger because of him and his *stupid company*. The irony isn't lost on him. Only a month ago, she'd said those words to him. Considering their circumstances, he couldn't agree more.

"Easy, tiger," Sable says, eyeing the death grip he has on his chair.

"We're going to get her back unharmed." Inspector Wanda says. "We need to focus in order to do that." She flips to another video, this time of Lextr being approached in a dusty hallway in Y Quadrant from behind by two men wearing full-face respirators—indoors.

"I guess in Y Quadrant they don't care about being inconspicuous?" Sable asks.

She gets her answer when they dart forward. Lextr must hear them because he spins, wearing a comically shocked expression. The nearest man's arm shoots forward. The camera doesn't pick up the rest of his action, but Lextr wobbles, and it's clear they drugged him. The other man places a bag over his head before they drag him into a room. They walk out a few minutes later, wheeling a table, presumably with Lextr's limp body lying covered atop it.

"How are they going to get him to V Quadrant without drawing suspicion?" he asks.

Sable scoffs. "It's Y Quadrant." As if that means anything to him.

Inspector Wanda chuckles. "My team calls it the Y ask, Y tell quadrant."

"For instance, Y Quadrant is the location of the boxing club," Sable fills in.

His eyes widen, and he nods to the NHOS inspector, who only seems to take issue with *some* illegal dealings.

Sable only shrugs. "She already knows. Besides, Wanda and I are friends now. Right, Wanda?"

Wanda frowns. "I already have a FRIENDS group."

Sable waves her off. "No such thing as optimal balance. Res6 and I just became friends, and neither of us have exploded."

Wanda ignores her. "The point is, some rules are more important than others. For instance, the illegal fighting ring wasn't a concern for public safety until we learned of a possible instance of coercion. Now there is an active investigation."

"See! You're warning me so I don't get caught—just like a friend would do!" Sable cries. "It is uncanny how incredibly likable I am."

"You're definitely something," Res6 agrees. A little frightening, if he had to put a word to it. "So what do we do now that we've isolated their location down to a building in V Quadrant?"

"I'll have my team start reviewing the footage. I want to know what they're up to. With that, I want to move forward with sending the ransom demands and see if we can get them to release her as promised."

"But we know where they are," Sable says.

"True," Wanda says, covering a yawn with her hand. "But if this is larger, this lead might be the break we need to take the entire operation down. I need to be strategic about this."

"What about Lextr?" He feels a stab of guilt over assuming his long-term employee had anything to do with Electra's abduction, even if the man had no qualms about decommissioning her. Was firing him too rash? From this vantage point, it feels too rash. Shit. "Can't we demand his release, too?"

"Electra's life is the one at risk. I'm guessing they know he helped you bring Electra back, so they won't kill him. They abducted him for a reason." Wanda picks his device up off the desk. "I need full permissions."

Electra is gone, and he has no control. He's spent his life thriving on control. Now he's going to have to give up more? His stomach twists painfully. "Why?"

"Once we get the files from Sable's friend, my team will handle the information transmission along with all correspondence." He must look like he's about to argue because she says, "You want her to live, right?"

He nods, rubbing his tired eyes, and thinks the command: Time Check. 3:18.

She gives him a tight smile, approving of his answer. "Then let the experts do their jobs."

45 – Things that Cut

Electra

"Let go of my hair!" she screams, lashing out, trying to get her nails on any exposed piece of flesh. She makes contact with the man's neck and digs her claws in. The man grunts, yanking her head back, and she cries out.

He drags her into a room and shoves her against a wall so hard the air whooshes out of her. She clutches her stomach, bending over as tears prick in her eyes.

"Stand up straight," he commands.

A woman wearing an unnecessary full-face respirator enters. Through the glass, she can make out her light brown skin and vibrant yellow eyes, which in her time would make her easy to identify, but now are a fairly common feature. Her matching yellow hair is tied back with a black and white checked bandana. She comes to stand next to the man. Her white lab coat and the medical scanner she holds remind her of Lextr. Is she a scientist too?

The man who brought her in rubs at the angry red scratch marks on his neck. "What makes you think he'll give up his company's information in exchange for this little hellcat?"

The woman's eyes flash with irritation. "I told you we've been watching them. Hold her still while I run the scan."

The man's right, isn't he? Res6 said he's in love with her, but he won't give up CHOICElover for her . . . will he? She can't think like that. Even if he comes for her, she needs to fight for herself. Her gaze darts around the room trying to find anything she can use as a weapon. There's no way she can take on both of them, but every female character she's ever written found a way to fight back. She has to do the same.

The room is mostly empty other than a small metal cabinet holding a handful of medical-looking containers and a set of packaged tools like at the dentist. The rounded toes of a black pair of shoes peek out from between the wall and the cabinet—just below a face staring straight at her. The man's distinctive orange afro is instantly recognizable. "Lextr?"

Shit. She's distracted. The big man moves so fast, grabbing one hand and then the other, lifting them over her head, and pressing them into the wall. "Hurry up," he grumbles.

The scientist lifts the scanner, and the blue line of light makes several passes over her body. He watches the screen for a moment before a light turns green. "Got it. Now we just need to get the tissue samples."

Her stomach turns to lead. They are not getting tissue samples. She knees the man in the groin. Except her knee doesn't land in his groin. It hits the meaty flesh of his thigh.

He grunts in mild irritation. "I'm going to need some help."

"Get off me!" she screams, flailing. "Lextr, do something!"

"Lextr, come help me hold this wild animal down so we can get a sample."

The scientist hisses as she kicks out and catches her in the shin. "Lextr, do as he says or I'll recycle you," she barks.

"Help!" She thrashes and wails, refusing to make it easy for them, but the big man spins her quickly, pressing her face first into the wall. Her cheek smashes into the cold surface and a shooting pain radiates over her face. She should have screamed before. She shouldn't have let him take her.

"Wouldn't it be easier if you drugged her?" Lextr offers. His clammy hands wrap around her wrists and press them into the small of her back.

"We wanted her awake for the ransom photo. Plus, too much of that drug in her system can contaminate the sample. If someone hadn't compromised the blood sample they got, we might not need to do this. But since we've got her for the ransom, we might as well take full tissue samples so you can use them to verify the CHOICElover data and complete our little project," the woman explains.

Blood sample? The cut from Saturday Sirens suddenly pops into her head. Was it not an accident like she thought? Electra whimpers as the big man moves the hair off her neck. Cool air hits her skin, and she feels a sharp pinch. The area goes numb. There's pressure, then tugging.

Oh God. They've cut out a piece of her, and all she can do is stand there and let it happen. Her chest convulses as a sob racks through her. Each breath is getting harder. She's becoming lightheaded. *Do not pass out. You can't pass out.*

The big man presses her head harder into the wall. Tears run down her cheeks and onto the smooth concrete her face is pressed against. "Please stop," she begs.

"If we killed her, we could get a brain sample," the big man suggests.

Her heart seizes. Res6 told her the sample that brought her back was from her brain. Lextr would know that too. She reaches to the edge of her vision, hoping her pleading looks are enough to keep him quiet.

The woman sighs. "He won't want her back if she's dead. We're counting on that because we need his data. These samples will have to do."

"You're overestimating her value to him. You should just collect the samples and let her go," Lextr suggests.

Momentary relief floods through her. At least until another needle pierces her skin.

Lextr continues, "I would make a better hostage, considering my knowledge—"

"Quiet," the scientist barks. "We need you to interpret the data."

Lextr doesn't say another word. At least he tried, even though she's pretty sure he hates her very existence.

The scientist repeats the procedure at several other points on her body. By the time they're finished, there are half a dozen precise cuts all over her. Her clothes are streaked with blood, and she's exhausted. When they release her, she slumps onto the floor. The stitches on her wrist are haphazard. Didn't Res6 say they had the technology to fix such minor cuts? They probably didn't want to waste energy on a hostage.

She glances up to see a device pointed at her. If Res6 is going to see this image for a ransom request, she wants to make sure he knows that she still has fight left in her. She glares at her captors.

The big man looks over the scientist's shoulder at the screen. "What about the blood?"

"The AI will edit it out." The scientist packages up the dirty tools. "Come. Time to make our next move."

Before the door closes behind them, the big man turns, looking directly at her. "You better hope that man cares more about you than about his company." His grin sends a chill down her spine. "Otherwise you're dead."

"He'll never give up the proprietary company information they're asking for. We're screwed!" Lextr moans from his huddle on the opposite side of the room.

"He will," she repeats. They've been going over this since the abductors left them alone for the first time.

"I've known the man for fifty years. He single-mindedly cares about CHOICElover." He hesitates. "And his secret Jerme experiment."

"And me," she adds. "I know about that, by the way."

He rolls his eyes. "You're being optimistic. Things aren't how they were during your time. People don't form the type of attachments you're envisioning anymore."

She just shakes her head. *I refuse to think that way!* Her voice is singsong in her mind. He loves me. He'll choose me. Tears well in her eyes for an entirely different reason. She knows it's true because she's worth choosing. She belongs here in this world with him and all the happy things that go along with that. It's too bad it took so much heartache and turmoil for her to realize that.

"Just think of the implications, Electra. If these men get caught with all CHOICElover's experimental data, they'll shut CHOICElover down. Then he won't be able to resurrect his brother. You aren't worth it to him."

Her hands reflexively ball into fists as she absorbs his cutting words. Calmly, she places them in her lap, taking a deep breath.

He's my twin—someone who feels like a missing half of my brain. But I've discovered that she's the other half of my heart. Those are the words from his letter. She believes him, which means she can't give up hope. She turns to study Lextr. He's sneering at her as if he resents her. "What's your problem with me?"

He shrugs.

"Fine. I guess it will remain a mystery."

Silence passes between them for a while when he finally speaks. "You're my greatest achievement."

Her head snaps up. "Huh?"

"I don't believe GROW ever meant to resurrect people. It was an accident. But what I did—Res6 gave me a challenge: prove CHOICElover could never make the same mistake GROW did. He, as always, had an ulterior motive—to keep an edge on the competition. All the companies are hunting for the next wave of LifeLike advancements. Though maybe he was thinking about his brother the whole time. We'll never know. To me, the why wasn't important. The science fascinated me, so I threw everything I had at the problem. I figured if I knew how to do it, I'd know how to prevent it from happening. Any advancement would be a bonus.

"I brought you back to life. It's unprecedented. Probably one of the biggest scientific breakthroughs the world has ever seen, and I can't tell anyone about it. Your existence is illegal. You should belong to me. Instead, he kept you for himself. Then, to add to the insult, he barely acknowledged what I did." Lextr glances away. His jaw flexes as his stare bores a hole into the wall.

An annoying pang of empathy hits her in the chest. It sucks because everything he's saying makes perfect sense. She can completely see Res6 overlooking the praise and approval that this man so clearly craves. "I didn't know that. I'm sorry."

On the other hand, he just confessed he thinks she should belong to him, which is insane.

"I even tried to help him bring back his brother. That's why I felt justified in taking the specimens for my side project. When he was parading around town with a reincarnate, who cared that I was renting manupartners out for events to make a little extra money? It felt good to be the one getting attention for a fun new business for once—even if it was only through back channels. I felt he owed me that. I didn't think he would fire me."

"I think he fired you because you threw his brother in his face and called him a hypocrite," she points out.

"We worked together for fifty years. He threw it away after I confronted him with a truth he didn't want to hear. If that doesn't give you a clue about his character, I don't know what will."

They both look away, letting silence fill the space between them. Lextr's words play on repeat in her mind. Is there a chance she's mistaken? That one small thing can go wrong, and he'll just throw it all away. She's a dangerous variable in his world. CHOICElover must be very attractive to him by comparison, considering he can control it.

But he's changed. Or he is changing. He's not the same man he was when she woke up in this world, or even when he fired Lextr. She's already making an impact, and it started with just one person. The man she loves. The man she loves who doesn't know it because she got so caught up in the moment, she missed saying it. God, why did she do that? What if she doesn't survive this, and she never told him how she feels?

After everything he said, after his bravery—the risk he took offering his heart to her—and she might die without ever letting him know that he's on the right track. That he's worthy of love too. She knows it's true to the depths of her being because she loves him.

She's processed so many emotions since she received his letter less than twenty-four hours ago, not to mention the trauma. Maybe she'll just take a nap, and when she wakes up, he'll be here to rescue her.

The tile is cool against her bruised cheek, offering momentary relief before the ache sets in. He's going to save her. He's going to give them the information, and they're going to release her. Right as her vision is about to blur, she notices a long, taxicab-yellow hair right in front of her nose. She picks it up, bringing it to eye level for inspection. She grins.

"He's different now, Lextr. He's going to save me." Lextr glances up, and their eyes meet. He shakes his head, but she continues. "That's what heroes do."

46 – The Countdown

Res6

"Can I get a status on the decoy file?" Wanda asks.

Sable leans back in her chair. "He's having trouble with the PhantomByte program since there are so many file types. Once they're unpackaged from the container, the data seek protocol isn't able to sniff each of them out. It's requiring him to bury a new VeriSync signature in each file the Splinter Module can find."

"Enough with the technobabble. Speak plainly," Wanda commands.

Sable takes a deep breath. "It's not working."

Res6 bolts upright. "Not working? Just send the real files and be done with it."

"Sorry. It *wasn't* working. He's almost done. Then he can run it through the Symul-a-tron—I mean, he can test it. Once we confirm it works, we'll be good to go."

"I don't like waiting," Res6 says, getting to his feet.

"Well, I don't like the idea of handing them over your data. Who knows what they might do with it before we can stop them?" Wanda argues. "Let's give him another half hour."

"That's what you said half an hour ago." A few hours ago, he put a large digital clock on the particle pane. It displays a bright red 07:18. "What if they change their minds and hurt her?"

Wanda shakes her head. "There's been nothing in their communications to suggest they'll retract their offer, and our professional hostage team is standing by to collect her as soon as she leaves the building. We have a team in the building if they flinch."

"Can't they just raid them and be done with it?" he asks.

"Not until we piece together their motivations. I want to gather more evidence and determine if there's a larger group involved. If we let them think they're succeeding, they're more likely to become lax and slip up," Wanda says.

He clutches his knees, squeezing. "I don't like this. I feel like I should be there when she's released."

"We've told them you've hired a crisis de-escalation service to manage the transfer," Wanda says.

He frowns. "Electra is going to think I just threw money at the problem."

"So are they. That is a key part of our plan," Wanda calmly explains.

"Fuck," he says, tugging at his hair.

After fifteen minutes go by with no word from Oro1, Sable says, "Res6, sit down. Your pacing is making me antsy. Better yet, go get us more coffee."

Wordlessly, Wanda holds out her reusable mug. He takes it, groaning. He knows what they're doing. Every time his nerves get the better of him, they send him for refreshments. He glances at the clock one last time before he takes the cup. 07:33. The last thing he wants to do is run into anyone, and his staff should start arriving at the office soon. He pokes his head out the door, looking both ways.

"Hey there, stranger!" Chryl shouts from down the hall.

He groans, jumping back inside the door and slamming it shut.

Stable stares at the door as if there's a monster behind it. "What the fuck?"

"Be quiet and maybe she'll go away," he says.

Three loud knocks sound on the door, and then Chryl's turning the handle. He presses his hand against it to hold it closed. "Go away!"

With surprising strength, Chryl pushes the door open. She takes one look at the three of them and then at the bright red digital clock, and bursts into tears. "Oh holy mother Zephyr! What's happened?! Please tell me the world isn't ending!"

She throws herself into Res6's chest, sobbing. Then when she looks up, her red eyes landing on his, she must note his panicked expression because she cries louder, "Oh God, is it Electra?!"

The *oh God*, he's guessing she learned from Electra. He pats her back. "I thought you didn't like her."

"Can't a girl change her mind? She stood up for me about my FrogBlog, and I've been following her journey since before she was famous. It's always the young ones that end so tragically. Just when their light is beginning to shine," she laments.

Thankfully, Sable steps in, pulling Chryl away. "Electra is fine. We're just having a bit of a situation." Sable stills. She must be getting a message because her body language changes. "He's got it done! The files are on the way."

"What files?!" Chryl cries.

"Got them. It's six packages in total," Wanda says. "I'm removing the real files we were going to use just in case. Uploading the fake ones now."

"07:43," he says for good measure.

Chryl wipes her tears. "What files?"

Wanda adds files to the upload link. Once the sixth file is selected they wait. The upload time is six minutes.

"How long will the scrubbing take?" he asks.

"Should be quicker," Sable says. "3 minutes tops."

"How on earth would a physician know that?" he asks.

Sable shrugs. "I'm trying to reassure you. That seems like something a friend would do."

"07:49," he says, ignoring that she apparently thinks it still counts if you're making things up.

The upload process finishes, and another window pops up. *Scrub time 3 minutes*.

"See, I told you!" Sable says.

"Lucky guess," Wanda points out. They wait as the tenuous seconds pass. Finally, the scrub process is complete. Her cursor hovers over the word Submit for what feels like an eternity.

Electra can't die.

Electra can't die.

Electra can't die.

"Are we sure this is going to work?" Res6 asks, one final time.

Chryl follows their lead as they turn and stare pointedly at Sable.

She crosses her arms. "Oro1 is the best hacker in MSP. If he can't do it, no one can. Besides, it's a little late now to question our decision." She motions to the clock. 07:54.

Chryl whimpers as if she's in true distress. "What are you hacking? And what does that have to do with Electra? And what happens at 08:00?"

"Who is this woman, and can someone get rid of her?" Wanda snaps.

"Chryl, please leave," Res6 says, ushering her to the door, but she resists. If he weren't so terrified for Electra's safety, he might be fascinated with Chryl's deduction skills.

"I don't have to do what you say. You're not my daddy anymore." Chryl stomps twice for emphasis.

"Just verifying everything is there," Wanda says.

"Her daddy?" Sable prods. "Is she another reincarnate?"

"No, but I'm considering recycling her when this is all over," he answers, looking pointedly at Chryl. Of course he won't do that, but with Wanda here, he can't really explain Chryl's evolving nature to Sable.

Wanda only chuckles, not removing her focus from her task. She presses the Submit button. The time on the wall is 07:56.

At 07:58, Wanda says, "They've got the files. Now we wait for them to verify their authenticity." She taps her device as she does when she switches to communicate with her team. "Team, prepare the extraction. I want a SAT standing by for when I give the word. Do not deploy it until we have eyes on the asset."

Res6 slumps back against the wall. "Did they say how long the verification would take?"

"Half an hour at most, but we'll see," Wanda answers, leaning back in her chair to wait.

"Oh my Zorg! Electra's been abducted! I have to tell her best friend!"

Sable darts around the desk, grabbing hold of her arm, to stop her from running out the door. "Wait, who's her best friend if it isn't Res6?"

"The crazy cat lady Sister Xelna! There are pictures of them all over the network. Let me go. I have to tell her. She'll want to be here to comfort Electra when she returns."

Sable looks to Res6 for confirmation.

"Absolutely not, Chryl," he says. "This is another secret, for Electra's safety." He mimes zipping his lips like she's prone to do.

Chryl jerks out of Sable's grip. "Very inconsiderate." She spins and storms out the door.

He considers calling security to stop her, but figures that might make things worse. If Electra and the cat lady are photographed all over the network together, it stands to reason she's who Electra's been staying with. That means Sister Xelna probably knows about Electra's nature and will hear about her abduction too. Or he's too tired to fight and no match for Chryl.

When the door closes behind Chryl, Sable takes the cup he's been gripping. "For the love of Zorg, sit."

"I'm not some dog you can just boss around." When her stare doesn't relent, he moves around his desk, plopping into the guest chair since Wanda has taken over his.

Sable's eyes flash. "Good boy."

He rolls his eyes, grumbling, "How is this my life?"

"So what's the deal with Chryl?" Sable asks as Wanda quietly works. "Yes, I'm trying to keep you distracted while we wait."

He explains how Chryl came to be and her brief stint with him. Then how he gave her to Tommy, which is why she's traipsing around his building. He widens his eyes, nodding to Wanda, hoping Sable will understand that there is more to the story that he can't say in front of a NHOS inspector.

Sable's eyes narrow. "I see."

He runs a hand through his hair. "08:25."

"You can stop telling us the time now," Wanda says without looking up. "It worked. They verified it. They're releasing her in a different connected building's lobby in the same quadrant."

"That's a relief." Sable flops down into the chair next to him. "I failed to mention he's MSP's *self-proclaimed* greatest hacker, but now that we know it worked . . ."

He clasps her on the shoulder. "I won't have to murder you and dump your body in a batch of recycling?"

Wanda glances up. "Is that something you've done before?"

He and Sable both break out into peals of laughter, and he feels a little like he's going insane. Must be the sleep deprivation.

"We've got a visual." Wanda shifts the video she is watching onto the large particle pane. They watch as a large man drags Electra by the arm from the bank of ground floor elevators toward the airlock that leads outside. He releases her, picks up an air mask, and throws it at her. It smacks her in the chest, but she catches it and quickly puts it on. He tries to grab her again, but she flings an arm out, sucker-punching him in the neck. He staggers back, hand flying to his throat, and starts sputtering.

"Good Zorg, that was awesome. Maybe I'll be friends with her too," Sable says.

"Just get in the airlock, Electra," he instructs the video.

As if she's heard him, she darts over, cutting in front of the next person waiting. She gives them a little apologetic wave before stepping inside. She turns and watches the doors close and lock. The large man recovers, rushing over to pound on the door with both fists.

"It won't open, will it?" Sable asks. Thankfully, because Res6's heart is caught in his throat.

"I've got a team member overriding the controls," Wanda says.

He breathes a sigh of relief. Electra doesn't know that, but she doesn't look scared either. She raises her hand, holding up her middle finger to the man.

"I take it that is a rude gesture from her time?" Wanda asks.

Curious, he does a quick search. "DumBot says it means *fuck you*," he says.

Both Sable and Wanda chuckle.

Behind Electra, the door slides open. She doesn't hesitate as she runs out into the street, looking both ways before her attention lands on the single SAT hovering on the mag track in the center of the road. It only takes a couple of seconds for three operatives wearing jumpsuits that say Private Extraction Services to fly out of the SAT and surround her. They speak to her for a moment and she nods, looking at them and back at the SAT. A smaller operative, possibly another woman, takes her by the arm and gently guides her around to the front seat, helping her in. The rest of the operatives pile in, and within a moment the SAT carrying the most precious thing in his world is zipping across the city back to him.

Tears well in his eyes and fall unfettered. Sable and Wanda stare at him like they are unsure what to do. "I'm fine," he waves them off. "Just . . . thank you. Thank you."

He excuses himself so he can have a moment alone in his private locker room. He drops onto a bench, leaning back against the wall, letting the horrible events of the last day wash over him. He also carves out space in his mind for one of the most beautiful moments of his life that also happened during the same twenty-four hours. Zorg, he's exhausted.

The prospect of losing her and being a part of the effort to get her back was the hardest thing he's ever experienced. And now that he's moments on the other side of it, he feels like he's been hit by a SAT. He needs to gather himself and set his emotions aside. After what Electra just lived through, she is going to need him more than ever, and he needs to be the man she deserves.

He closes his eyes, taking a few deep breaths to center himself. He remembers her exercise that she uses to ground herself. Just think of three real things.

That's easy.

Electra.

Electra.

Electra.

His phone pings, and he jolts awake. Shit. He glances at the message. It's Sable. *She's on her way up.*

He stuffs his phone in his pocket and runs out of the locker room. His fatigue evaporates the second he sees her walking toward him at the other end of the hall.

"Res6!" she cries.

He sprints for her and doesn't stop until he's scooped her in his arms. She returns the embrace. "Oh Zorg, Electra. You're safe. You're here. I was so worried."

He can barely believe that she's here with him now. He cradles her head, running his hand over her hair.

"Easy, she's injured." Someone tugs on his sleeve. When he releases her, he sees it's the female operative from the video.

He moves away, quickly assessing her. "Did I hurt you?"

"I'm fine. They took a few tissue samples, and I'm a little sore, but . . ." Tears streak down her cheeks, and he takes in the blooming purple bruise there. She holds up her wrists for him to inspect. Stitches zigzag over an almond-shaped cut.

Sable steps up to them, taking Electra's wrist to inspect it. "Fucking bastards."

Electra quickly takes in the other woman. "You're Sable?" she guesses.

"The one and only." She turns to him. "Can you have somebody take me to your medical unit so I can get some equipment to deal with her wounds?"

Just then, Tommy and Chryl rush down the hall, along with a woman dressed in a full leopard bodysuit, complete with fake ears, a tail, and tattooed cat whiskers.

Nothing more than he expects from Chryl, but it reminds him to figure out a permanent solution for her and to make sure the lease term limits got updated as he instructed.

"Oh my God, Electra! I was so worried!" Chryl makes to throw her arms around Electra, but Sable steps in between them.

"No!" she barks. Chryl takes a startled step back. "Better. She's injured." She notes Tommy's presence. "You. Take me to the medical unit now." She turns to Chryl and the cat woman. "You both too. I need you to help . . . carry things." When they look like they're going to argue, she says. "You can visit once she has been debriefed, and I've tended to her wounds."

They don't balk at the command in Sable's voice. Res6 makes a mental note to thank her later.

He leads Electra back to his office, where Wanda is discussing something with one of her team members. They quickly finish the conversation before leaving the three of them alone.

Electra sinks into a chair and yawns big, making everyone else yawn too. "I guess none of us slept," she says from behind her palm.

Wanda chuffs. "I should be dead, considering the amount of coffee I drank."

"Thank you so much for everything—" Electra starts. Then she grins and blinks, attempting to act like a manupartner.

"Don't worry, I know what you are," Wanda says, shaking her head. "No need to thank me. I'm just doing my job."

Wanda takes twenty minutes to debrief her on their side of the operation, then records Electra's testimony of her side of the events of the last twenty-four hours. "And what about Lextr's presence? It appears Res6's former employee was held in the same room with you."

"He was. They're trying to use him to create reincarnates. I promised him I would make sure you knew he wasn't working for them voluntarily. They abducted him too. Since you know their location, can't you raid the building and get him out?"

"If he were in imminent danger, we would, but you said they need his expertise. I'm working under the assumption that they don't plan to kill him. Maybe we can get a message to him so he can help us from the inside. I need to learn their goal. But that isn't anything for you to concern yourself with. Thank you for your testimony."

Electra's brows wrinkle like she isn't pleased with Wanda's plan.

Wanda rises from her chair. "Trust that I have the situation in hand," she says, effectively shutting down the conversation. "I've released control of your system. I'll be in contact with you in a few days to arrange a *legitimate* identification number. Electra, if you think of anything else useful, Res6 has my number."

Electra shoots out of her chair. "I almost forgot." She holds out her hand toward Wanda, wiggling her fingers.

Wanda's brow wrinkles like she's confused, but then she takes Electra's hands, inspecting the gunk beneath her fingernails. "Skin cells! Oh, and there's more." She stuffs her hand into her pocket, pulling out a multicolored wad of hair. "I collected this off the floor. You can use that, right?"

"We can absolutely use it. Excellent work." Wanda pulls out a small container from her satchel. She stares at the hair like she doesn't want to touch it, though.

"It's gross, I know," Electra says, picking it up and setting it inside.

Wanda closes the lid. "This was smart of you to collect. I'm surprised you thought of it after what you went through."

"I'm a writer. What can I say?" Electra shoots him a contagious grin. Being in on the joke makes warmth flow through him.

"I have no idea what that means, but good work. I'm sorry you had to go through that, but this has been an excellent break in our case."

Wanda slips the container back into her satchel and throws it over her shoulder.

Interacting with Electra, when she could be herself, seemed to make Wanda finally believe that reincarnates were real. That bodes well for the individuals still stuck at Camp Reincarnate. Electra will be pleased with that development.

"I'll have one of my team members wait so Sable can collect the samples under your nails. I want it analyzed ASAP. I'll be in touch if I require anything else," Wanda says, rubbing her temples. Right before she closes the door, she pokes her head back in. "Oh, and Electra, welcome to the future."

When she closes the door, Electra leans back in her chair, breaking out into a fit of crazed giggles. He can't do anything except sit and watch, mesmerized. "Are you okay?"

"Not remotely," she says. "Can you believe it? Right before they took me, I told you that everything was going to be perfect. It's so sad, but also too funny. I feel deep empathy for the woman I was yesterday."

He frowns. "That's called irony. It doesn't feel funny at all to me."

"I know, but it is. When I was standing there with those men cutting little footballs in my skin to steal my flesh because I shouldn't even exist, I realized that I never told you I loved you back. I just don't know why all of this has happened and how I ended up dead, then undead. Not like a zombie, though. Sorry. I'm not making any sense. All I know is I'm so grateful to be here with you." She shakes her head as tears well in her eyes. "I'm just so grateful."

He slips out of his chair and kneels before her. "Oh, Electra, don't cry. You don't need to love me back. I love you enough for both of us." He wipes her tears away, being careful about her bruise.

She smacks his shoulder before taking his face in her hands. She leans down so they're eye to eye. "You are seriously the most thick-headed man I've ever met."

"What did I do now?" he asks.

"I don't need you to love me enough for both of us."

"Quickly explain why before I die," he says, feeling rather desperate to hear what he thinks she's about to tell him. Though maybe it's the fatigue warping his mind, or maybe he fell asleep in the locker room and he's dreaming.

"I know this isn't the most romantic setting ever, and I look like a complete disaster. I'm dirty, I stink, and there's blood all over me."

"I don't care. Tell me," he begs.

She grins, and his heart melts a little. "I love you too. I love you so much."

An unbearable warmth blooms in his chest as their lips meet. It's the pain of loving someone. The pain of knowing they could be taken from you at any moment, but choosing to love them anyway for every moment you still have them.

She pulls away, not done with her confession. "I think the part of me that always questions everything and waits for the bad things to happen—I think those people might have killed it. Because I knew you were going to find a way to get me back. I wasn't scared."

He listens eagerly. "You weren't?"

She shrugs. "Well, maybe a little. But I decided to have faith."

Two knocks sound at the door before Sable slips inside. "Hate to interrupt the party, but I'm ready to heal you. Then, your awaiting fans need ten minutes of your time. Then we all desperately need some sleep."

47 – Aftercare

Electra

They get back to Res6's unit by 11:10. She doesn't argue as he strips both their clothes off and pushes her into the shower, following her inside. He runs a warm cloth over her cheek, then down her freshly healed body, so gently it makes her chest feel like an insufficient container for her heart. He washes her hair and towels her off. She even lets him brush out her tangles and carry her to bed.

He makes her drink a VitaShot and a chocolate-flavored protein packet. Then they sleep for twelve hours, tangled in each other's arms.

When she wakes up, he's leaned up on one arm, staring at her. "What?" She pulls the covers over her head, stifling a yawn. He tugs them down.

"Food or sex?"

She grins. "How do I choose between my two favorite things?"

"I thought reading was your favorite thing."

"Fourth, after writing." Her stomach grumbles, making the choice for her.

In the kitchen, they share a few ready-made breakfast meals, even though it's after midnight. She sits on the counter as he rifles through the apartment-sized refrigerator. He pulls out a small package of red fruit. "Berries?"

"Are you fussing?"

"Maybe. Is that a problem?"

"No." She frowns. What story is he concocting in his mind?

"I want to make sure you're okay. What happened to you would reasonably make anyone lose hope."

She shakes her head. "I told you. I knew you would save me. I'm fine. Or fine enough not to lose hope again. I've fought too hard to get here, and I'm determined to be okay. To be happy."

"I believe you," he says, reluctantly enough to make her question whether he's being 100 percent honest. "Are you still hungry?" he counters, changing tact.

"No."

He steps up beside her, sets the container on the counter, and parts her legs to step between them. "You sore?"

Deft fingers run over the barely there evidence of her trauma. The scars that Sable gave her a cream for and said would be gone in a few days' time. "No."

"Tired?"

She sighs. "Nope." It isn't entirely a lie.

"Berries, then." He holds a small red fruit in front of her nose. It lacks the specificity to determine which variety—straw, blue or rasp. Just lab-synthesized red. She opens her mouth. A sweet yet tart flavor bursts across her tongue as she chews. She swallows, licking juice from her lips with intention.

His stare is glued to the motion. He swallows.

She grins. "Not tired," she reminds him.

He kisses her, tasting far better than the berries. She reaches for his T-shirt, but he bats her hands away. "I don't believe you."

"We slept for twelve hours." She groans in frustration as he makes an open-mouthed trail down her neck. Sensing there's no hope of arguing with him until he's certain she's whole and in one piece, she places her hands on the counter behind her and leans back.

He smiles at her acquiescence, biting her nipple through her shirt. The visual of his golden eyes flashing combined with the sharp sensation makes her core pulse.

His hands grip her hips. "Move forward."

He adjusts her so her hips are on the edge of the counter. Anticipation coils in her belly as he drops to his knees and drapes her legs over his shoulders. He pushes up her shirt, exposing the fact that she never put on any panties. Cool air drifts over her bare flesh.

"I need to make you feel good," he says, trailing gentle kisses up the inside of her thigh.

Need to. His breath hitches as his tongue swipes through her center.

Her nerves are alight with a single touch, and all she can say is, "Wow."

She watches as he offers her testing licks, each becoming more insistent, like the act is an aphrodisiac for him, too. Instinctively, she presses her heel into his back, rolling her hips. He groans.

She's only had a few partners go down on her before, and none were as into it as Res6. She wrote about more ravenous men in her books, of course, but they were fiction. "You like this?" she asks.

He pauses, speaking into her pussy as if it were a microphone. "More than you can know. I could drown in your taste."

He dives his tongue in deep for emphasis, drawing out a hiss of pleasure. "I'm so hard right now. I'm aching to be inside you, but not until you come for me."

Her shirt slips down, covering the view of him devouring her.

He tugs the shirt. "Take this off."

She quickly tugs it over her head, tossing it away. "Not entirely fair—ahh!" she cries as his fingers slide inside her, his lips wrapping around her clit. He sucks and her heel digs deeper into his back, the other pressing against the cabinets as her hips climb off the counter. Or they would if his free arm weren't holding her down. The resistance doubles the intensity. A sparkling, throbbing sensation is blooming between her legs, and her inner walls flutter wildly around his plunging fingers.

He must sense she's close because he moans, and the low vibrations send her pleasure cresting. She throws her head back, pleasure crashing over her in wave after wave. She must have left this plane because when she returns, he's standing between her legs again, wiping his grinning mouth on the back of his hand.

"I love making you come almost as much as I love you." He unfastens his pants and pushes them down, his thick erection springing free as he kicks them off. Then he's lining himself up. "Yes?"

"Yes," she moans, boneless and half dazed as he presses inside her.

He wraps her arms around his neck and her legs around his waist. "Hold on."

She squeezes his neck, drawing their bodies flush, which slides him deeper. She hums in pleasure as he grips her thighs and carries her across the room. She thinks he's going back to the bedroom, but he pauses outside the door to the spare room.

"Open it," he commands.

That clears the haze. Even as she's wrapped in his arms, with him buried inside her, nerves dance in her stomach. She reaches down and turns the handle, and the door swings open. He steps into the room, which only heightens her nervous energy. Is there a Jerme manupartner in here who he plans to share her with? No, that's insane.

"You're overthinking." Then all of her worry melts away as he says. "No more locked doors between us. Ever."

He closes the door and presses her back against the cool surface. The symbolism isn't lost on her. "Ever," she agrees.

He rolls his hips, languidly rocking into her.

The boldness of what he did to save her lands in her mind then, and she stares at him in awe. "You put CHOICElover on the line for me."

"I did." His tempo steadily increases, his breathing becoming shallower.

He must sense her questions because he bites out between labored breaths, "No regrets. This is worth it. You're worth it." His eyes flicker down her body, lingering where he's moving inside her. "Touch yourself while I fuck you."

She loosens an arm from around his neck. His stare never wavers as she obeys, running her fingers over her clit, gently at first, then with more intensity. Until her pleasure is building, and the door is rattling with each of his thrusts.

The muscles in his neck tense, veins and tendons popping out, body flexing as he moves. Whoever says women aren't visual creatures too has clearly never been fucked by a man that looks like this. The straining, corded muscles at his hips are what push her to the edge. Or maybe it's his shudders as he clings to control. Maybe it's his gasp as he shouts, "I'm about to—" before he loses control completely, hips thrusting, hitting that deepest part of her, then she's coming.

Pleasure bursts from deep in her core like fireworks. Her mind is too incoherent to form sensible words as she screams. He holds her, swallowing her pants with kisses. She feels so whole, so complete. Relaxed in a way she's never quite felt before.

He disentangles them, gently setting her down. She wobbles, leaning against the wall for support. He quickly rushes to the bathroom and returns with a warm cloth. Once they're cleaned up, he guides her back to bed.

They crawl beneath the pile of blankets, and she curls into his warmth.

"You good?" he asks.

She smiles into his chest as sleep threatens to claim her. There's no hesitation—no other shoe to drop. Confidently, she says, "I've never been better."

48 – The Ultimate Romantic Hero

Res6

January 27, 2391.

"So, these are the two remaining viable samples?" Electra asks, staring at the vials he's set on a silver tray before her.

"Yes," he says, feeling the muscle in his jaw tick.

"And we're going to destroy them?" she asks.

"Yes."

She pauses before stepping into his arms. "We've been through a lot in the past week. If you aren't ready, it would be perfectly understandable."

He shakes his head, swallowing down the lump in his throat. "I can't bring him back. It's time."

"Technically, it still might be possible," Sable says. "I've been doing some research." When neither he nor Electra pays her any heed, she adds, "Only pointing that out."

"I'm officially accepting that he's gone. Someone once told me I can't move on with the future if I'm clinging to the past—which I realize is ironic since I'm standing here literally clinging to someone from the past." He squeezes Electra's hip, earning a chuckle.

Sable studies them. "I suppose that passes the logic check. Since I'm not here to talk you out of it, why did you want me here?"

Electra rolls her eyes. "Because you're his friend, and friends support each other when they're facing life's difficulties."

Sable scratches her head. "I suppose I'll have to read up on that."

"I'll send you a column I wrote about this exact topic," Electra says, laughing.

Wordlessly, he opens the first vial, his breath catching as he tips the contents into a small flask containing the buffer solution. He opens the final vial, taking a few deep breaths as he holds it near the flask's opening. Sable and Electra watch on from either side of him.

"Tread fast into tomorrow's future," Sable says, voice monotone

Electra leans forward, eyeing the other woman. "You're insane."

Sable grins. "Thanks." Suddenly they're all grinning, and he's pouring out his final Jerme sample.

A tear streaks down his cheek. It isn't a sad tear, exactly. Bittersweet. Jerme is gone. But he has Sable and Electra now. Possibly, if Sable's right, even more friends—not *FRIENDS*—await him at the group dinner they're having tonight.

Once complete, he pours the flask into the hydrolysis vat, watching as the liquid is quickly mixed into the greater batch of recycled manu-partners and organic bio-gel substrate. A foot drifts by, floating atop the thick peach-colored sludge.

Electra jumps when she sees it, burying her head in his chest. "Gross!"

He squeezes her shoulders, drawing her away to get a good look at her. "You write about throats getting slit open and green gooey alien blood. How is this gross?"

Sable nods. "Agree. Don't forget that one scene where Analise thrusts her hand into the monster's gaping chest cavity to pull out its heart."

He nods, recalling the exact scene, adding, "Which she promptly offers to the male love interest as a trophy."

Electra slaps her hands over her face. "You have her reading my books, too? I'm going to die of mortification."

Sable pats her on the back. "It's good to know you have a healthy," she clears her throat, "imagination."

"Okay, I'm dead now."

"You can't be dead. Don't you want to give him the present I helped you with?" Sable gestures to a package she brought with her, which she sat on the metal counter when she arrived. He didn't think twice about it, much less suspect it was for him.

He perks up. "A present?" No one's ever given him a present. After all, he can afford anything he wants—and he's never had actual friends.

Electra excitedly hands it to him. He turns it over and shakes it. The intensity of their eyes on him makes him squirm. Fortunately, his curiosity is strong enough to outweigh any feelings of discomfort.

He unseals the envelope flap and slides out the contents. In his hands, he holds a slim book made of real paper. On the cover, there's a beautiful woman on the far side of a thick patch of briars. The man on the opposite side is holding a giant sword in both hands and is depicted mid-slash. On his side, cut briars litter the path he is carving toward the woman. The title is *Once Upon a Dream* by Electra Lynch.

"It's a loose Sleeping Beauty retelling." Electra reaches over and flips open the cover. "Read the dedication."

Both women lean forward, reading with him.

For Jerme. I never got to meet you, but this ridiculous man we both love believes we would have become fast friends.

A lump builds in his throat. "When did you write this?"

Her cheeks turn a delicious shade of pink. "Mid-January."

"That was before we reconciled."

"Before the IdenTECH meeting," she offers.

Sable takes the book and flips through the pages. "Is there sex?"

Electra chuckles. "God no. It's about his brother. A way to memorialize him."

Sable's shoulder slump, and she hands it back to him. "Definitely don't want to read it, then."

He raises a hand. "Hold on. This very specifically says *ridiculous man we both love.* You knew you loved me way back then?"

She bites her lip, nodding.

"And you made me go through that entire meeting—you offered to go to lunch as friends!" he exclaims.

She nods again.

Sable groans. "I think that's my cue to leave."

"I couldn't agree more," Res6 says, and claps her on the shoulder. "Thanks for coming."

Sable nods solemnly. "See you tonight at dinner."

As the three of them leave the recycling station, they part ways with Sable. His private locker room is the closest, so he drags a willing Electra there. When they make it inside, he closes and locks the door. "You are in so much trouble."

Her mischievous grin sends heat straight to his groin. "Good trouble, I hope?"

He sets the book on the counter, then he spins her and bends her over it. "How do you feel about spanking?"

She darts a glance over her shoulder. "Spanking?"

"Yes, it's a sudden, strong urge. Answer me."

Her cheeks are even pinker now. "Curious, I suppose."

"That's good. Because that book is the most thoughtful thing anyone has ever done for me, and I'm going to reward you by spanking your gorgeous ass like you deserve. I'm going to take you like this so I can see my bright red handprint. Then I'm going to spend the rest of our lives being the one giving you the scandalous ideas for those books you write, because believe me, I've been marinating on all the ways I'd like to worship you." He reaches up, taking the band of her leggings in both hands. Her eyes widen as she wets her lower lip and draws it into her mouth. "Sounds like a plan?"

Her pupils dilate. "Wow."

A low chuckle rumbles up his throat. She's clearly intrigued. He seems to be getting the hang of this whole romantic hero thing. She's already wiggling with anticipation as he peels her leggings over the luscious globes of her ass. He runs his hand over one and then the other while palming himself through his jumpsuit.

An accident brought him here to this place with her. This human woman, who he did his best to resist, but who drew him in, broke down his walls, and pierced his heart like the heroine she is.

"Electra," he urges, waiting for her response.

She only wiggles, gripping the edge of the counter, waiting eagerly like she knows it's driving him wild. He raises his hand, preparing to strike. "Do you have any idea how badly I want you?"

A shining smile lights up her beautiful face, like she's been the architect of this entire story. "I think I have an idea."

49 – HEA

Electra

February 26, 2391, a month later.

Electra steps out of their bedroom, and Res6's eyes flick up from the wine glasses he is setting out.

His stare greedily takes her in. "What in Zorg's name are you wearing?"

She shrugs, glancing down at her outfit—a sheer aqua dress covering heart-shaped nipple pasties and a thong—her new friend K8 convinced her is the height of fashion. "K8 took me shopping. This is from Incredible Bill's most recent collection," she says, thinking that based on how much K8 gushed about the designer, Res6 should have some idea of who she's referring to.

"Incredible who?" he asks, stalking toward her.

"Bill. You know, MSP's most famous fashion designer."

His hands wrap around her waist, drawing her into his chest. "Do you want me to walk around with an erection all night in front of our friends?"

She swats him away. "You can control yourself."

He flicks her chest where her nipples are trying to harden under the pasties. "These are giving me ideas."

She snatches his finger. "Behave. Our guests will be here at any moment."

He groans.

"You know, for a hundred and twenty something year old man, you have quite the sexual appetite," she teases.

"Your fault," he says. "And all of your illicit book recommendations."

She glances over at the perfectly set spring-themed kitchen table. "Wait, were you listening to one while you were setting the table?"

He shrugs. "Possibly. Theo had just scented her and was about to chase her through the forest. How could I put it down?"

"I've created a monster!" She clutches her stomach, doubling over with laughter.

"At least you acknowledge that I'm blameless." He holds up a vase containing the real flowers that were a huge splurge. "Where should I put these?"

Res6 said he had plenty of money, so she chose to believe him. Once she made the choice, it was simple, really. With his money and what she's earning from her column, they'll never want for anything. But that's not the point. It's the ease with which she lets herself spend it that's the real difference. Nothing crazy, just some nice things here and there that brighten their world. It's so validating to believe there is more out there waiting for her to claim it.

"Put them in the center of the table," she replies.

He does as she asks and steps behind her. His hand wraps around the base of her neck, and he leans near to whisper in her ear. "I'm proud of you for doing all this. All your effort has really transformed my unit. Everyone is going to love it."

Since she moved back in, they rearranged the furniture, relocating their desks to the spare room, so there would be space for a dining room table. Apparently, most people didn't have those anymore, but she missed sitting around a table drinking wine and chatting with her girlfriends, so when he showed her his bank account and told her to make it happen, she did.

K8 and Sister Xelna, who she learned was also friends with K8, took her shopping in the furniture district. They picked a chunky, rare antique oak table and eight matching chairs, along with a dozen throw pillows to litter his sectional. One could never have too many pillows. It was fun. A blast, even—K8 certainly didn't mind spending the unicoin. So why should she? If Res6 was brave enough to let go of the past and step into the future, she would be, too.

She turns, trying to hold back the tears welling in her eyes. "You think so?"

He gives her a peck, soft enough not to bother her bright pink lipstick. "When have I ever been wrong?"

Her undignified snort catches her off guard. "Hold on. Let me get my tablet. I have a Brain Dump where I keep a tally."

He playfully smacks her ass, and she jumps. Maybe there's time for a quickie. She thinks the command: Time check, still not used to hearing the perfectly human voice in her mind through her new m-volt. 18:58.

Two minutes might be a new record.

The doorbell chimes.

She must slump a little because he takes her by the waist, spinning her in his arms. "Get your mind out of the gutter." He gives her another soft kiss. "Are you ready for our inaugural Fifthday dinner?"

His golden eyes dance in delight as he awaits her answer.

She unleashes her brightest smile upon him. "I can't wait to see what the future holds."

Epilogue – Sable and Alex

Res6

February 26, 2391, earlier that morning.

Res6 glances between the two women engaged in a stare-off from opposite sides of his conference table. "Do I need to play referee between you two?"

"I thought you forgot about our deal," Sable says, crossing her arms defensively. "I messaged multiple times."

"I never forget when someone useful owes me a favor." Inspector Wanda shrugs. "And I've told you multiple times, this is a private NHOS investigation. You were only involved previously because you played a crucial role in that aspect of the investigation."

"I thought we were friends," Sable says, frowning.

Wanda taps her stylus on the table impatiently. "I'm not authorized to share other classified information about an ongoing case with you or any other MSP citizens. I feel like this should be obvious."

"Then what are we here for?" Res6 asks, ready to cut to the chase. More like ready to get back to his unit, which means back to Electra.

"Two reasons. Unfortunately, we couldn't get a match from the hair Electra collected, but we were able to trace two of the DNA samples from under her fingernails. One is the tech at ManuMATE, who we already identified—getting concrete evidence was a huge boon. The other is a sanitary waste technician whose digital traces come up all over BLACKOUT, which led us to an illegal fighting ring. Not Off-the-Books. One called Lights Out, which appears to be a far more exclusive and discreet venue."

"I thought you didn't care about those," Sable says.

"I didn't until I discovered they were keeping a pen of reincarnates to use as fighters. We raided their facility and recovered seven people, plus more evidence. We also arrested the sanitary waste technician who was on guard duty, evidently just a thug for hire. We moved because we thought we'd found the nest, but we discovered nothing concrete that could lead us back to the ManuMATE employee who wasn't there during the raid. It's possible Lights Out was just buying reincarnates for their clients' entertainment. I fear this is bigger than I originally thought. If they are connected to the fighting ring, they'll know we're investigating them, so they'll be more careful covering their tracks."

"I see," Sable says. "So far, we have at least one low-level ManuMATE employee, the woman with the yellow hair who took samples from Electra, and one known criminal you've arrested that may only be a lackey. And what about Lextr?"

"We're still working to get a message to him. No luck yet. We don't want to compromise his safety," Wanda says.

"Where do we fit into this?" Res6 asks impatiently.

Wanda sighs. "My team is suspending GROW's license and shutting them down effectively at midnight tonight until they can show that they can operate without creating any more reincarnates. After discovering more reincarnates, the higher-ups decided it's time to put a stop to this."

"Wow. It sounds like *our evidence* has been really effective for *your team's* investigation. Do you need our help again?" Sable's smile is smug.

Wanda ignores her. "The GROW suspension will give you the perfect excuse to apply at ManuMATE. I need someone on the inside who has a justifiable reason to be there, who can spy on the technician for me."

"Sounds fun. I assume I'll be compensated?" Sable plants her elbows on the table, steepling her fingers. She peers over them, her dark eyes gleaming with intrigue. Something about it reminds him of the female antihero in the last book he read.

"Yes," Wanda agrees. "I'll have my team lead set you up in our system."

"And me?" Res6 asks, hoping it has to do with him and not CHOICElover. Even if he's come to terms with the possibility of something happening to his company, he has thousands of employees to consider.

"We may require the technology in your lab to determine what we're dealing with. Also, we're doing our best to keep this quiet. The nineteen reincarnates in total who we've identified are being housed in a tower in E Quadrant. A few from the fighting pits were in bad shape, so we're running health checks, and providing acclimation training and psychological care. There was one man, however, who we're having a difficult time with."

Res6 and Sable slowly turn, glancing through the glass wall behind them to the man Wanda brought with her. He's slumped in a chair in the hallway with his head buried in his hands.

"His name is Alex Torres. In addition to his forced involvement in the fighting ring, he's battling an illness our medical team lacks the expertise to deal with. We could place him in one of MSP's care facilities, but we're concerned that the public may discover the breadth of our reincarnate problem before we have a better handle on it."

"So you want us to take care of him?" Res6 leans back in his chair, imagining what Electra would do. "I can give Sable full access to our corrections department. Depending on what he's suffering from, I'm sure we can get him taken care of in a matter of hours. Then you can return him to E Quadrant so he can join the acclimation program with the other reincarnates."

Wanda rubs her temples. "That's the problem. He's refusing treatment. He claims he has something called brain cancer, which I tend to believe since he's already had two seizures since he's been in our custody."

Sable's brow wrinkles. "Why doesn't he want to be healed?"

"He claims he's tried everything and there's no hope." Wanda makes air quotes around the words *no hope*.

"Did you inform him that disease has been effectively eradicated in our time?" Res6 asks.

Wanda shakes her head. "We did. He won't listen. I thought since you two had experience with people from his time—he died in 2039—perhaps I could entrust him into your care? My team would be grateful."

Res6 glances at Sable, whose returning stare is pleading. For what, he isn't certain. "I'll gladly commit my resources if it will help. I'd offer to have him come stay with us, but Electra just rearranged the furniture." He turns to Sable. "You have an extra room, right?"

"No," Sable blurts out, bolting up. "Absolutely not. I do not want my free reincarnate with purchase. I will gladly heal him if someone else can convince him to let me, but that is my limit." Sable waves a hand in the general direction of *outside the conference room.* "Don't you have a spare office he can live in?"

Wanda's eyes track the pacing physician. "Please, just consider it."

"Not doing it." Every few steps, Sable steals a glance through the glass at Alex, who is now intently tracking her movements. "I've seen the danger of interacting with the reincarnates—you end up with lovesickness, which I've determined has no cure." She points an accusatory finger at him. "Look at what happened to him. Taking one home is the first step."

Res6 chuckles. "Surely you have more control over your emotions than that? Unless you think you're vulnerable to love . . ." He knows he's goading her, but there is a certain entertainment value to watching her squirm. He can only imagine how fun it would be to watch her fall head over heels for a man from the past.

Sable freezes, crossing her arms. Then she plops back into her seat, scowling. "I'm not remotely vulnerable."

Wanda taps a few things on her tablet before standing up. "Great. It's all settled then. I should introduce you."

"No, I didn't agree—" Sable pauses when she sees the challenge in Wanda's stare. "I don't have a choice, do I?"

"I don't want to make threats about your involvement with Iden-TECH, but I can if needed." This time, it's Wanda's grin that's smug.

Sable groans in resignation. "Fine. I'll deal with this Alex reincarnate, but when he's healed, he's your problem."

"I figured you'd see reason." Wanda pokes her head out the door, calling for Alex.

Res6 watches as the tall, wiry man stands, running a hand through his dark hair. There's a small patch missing on the side of his head—from a scar that must have been from his past life, its epigenetic impact embedded in his DNA sample and expressed in the same way his memories were. Aside from that, the deep purple circles under his sharp blue eyes are the only other notable thing about him.

Beside him, Sable sits motionless as Alex enters the room. He takes a seat across from them, slouching into his chair in a way that suggests he's entirely unaffected about everything he's experiencing.

"This is Alex," Wanda says. "This is Res6, who owns CHOICElover and has kindly offered the use of his medical technology for your benefit. And this is Sable, who will be your physician. Sable will also offer you accommodations throughout the duration of your treatment."

"Hey," Alex says, acknowledging Res6. Then his gaze sweeps over Sable, and it's barely perceptible, but Res6 swears his throat bobs. "Hi." He turns back to Wanda. "I still don't see the need to get other people involved, considering this is pointless." He crosses his arms, mirroring Sable's gesture, but where her back is ramrod straight, his curves into a lazy C.

Wanda pinches the bridge of her nose. "We've been over this. Sable will heal you."

He shakes his head, glancing away. "Do you know how many times I've been told that?" His stare slides back to Sable, who has her arms crossed and might actually be pouting.

"He's all yours," Wanda says, slipping out the door. "My team will prepare Sable's résumé. I'll touch base in the next few days after we've shut down GROW and submitted the résumé to ManuMATE. I'll also send over Alex's initial medical assessment. The physician on our team wanted to make sure you saw he was on a high-powered anticonvulsant that could interact with other pharmacological agents you might administer."

Sable clears her throat. "Noted."

Res6 claps her on the shoulder. "Don't worry, Alex. If anyone can reinstall your hope and heal you, it's Sable."

Alex's eyes narrow. "Considering the way I saw you both look at me, followed by her resounding *No*, I have my doubts."

"This is a bad idea," Sable grumbles.

"Sable, having Alex live with you won't be so bad." Then, because poking at his overly direct friends sounds like a brilliant idea that Electra would appreciate hearing about later, he says, "Alex, you don't have any plans to seduce our dear physician here, do you?"

Alex chuffs. "Why would I do that? I'm dying."

"Which you will no longer be once Sable convinces you to let her heal you." Alex rolls his eyes, but Res6 keeps pushing. "Falling in love with a reincarnate like you is her greatest fear."

Alex must sense what he's doing, because he grins, shaking his head at Res6's antics. "For our short duration, I'll do my best to prevent such a ghastly outcome."

Sable's cheeks darken, and she buries her head in her hands. "Res6, I hate you."

A crazed sense of glee washes over him at disrupting his friend's normally cool façade. He can't wait to tell Electra.

He stands, feeling rather proud of himself. "Off with you two then. The corrections department is waiting." He watches Alex follow her out the door, but just as it's about to close, he catches it, sticking his head out. "Sable!" She turns back, glowering. Watching Sable navigate the next few weeks with her very own reincarnate is going to be highly entertaining.

"What?" she snaps.

"Careful not to trip and fall." *In love* is what he doesn't say, but the implication is clear.

Alex chuckles, and he almost feels sorry for the poor man. He has no idea what's in store for him.

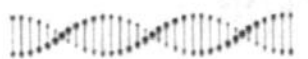

Want to read the rest of Res6 and Electra's little experiment with spanking? Head over to my website to get the full X-rated scene, plus other bonus content: www.jennifermwaldrop.com/choicelover-bon us-scene

I hope you are as excited to read our antihero physician's love story as I was to write it. Sable and Alex are coming up next in Love, Manufactured: Volume 3 – ManuMATE. Find out more on my Amazon author page: https://bit.ly/4l17yjn

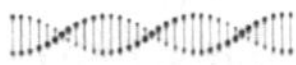

Related Resources:

First Nations' Food Pantry Initiative is a real program for real kids who grew up like Electra. Interested in contributing to their cause? Visit the program here for more information: www.firstnations.org/p rojects/native-food-pantry-initiative/

This book addresses themes related to suicide and mental health. If you or someone you know is experiencing emotional distress or suicidal thoughts, help is available. In the United States, the 988 Suicide & Crisis Lifeline offers free, confidential support 24/7: call or text 988, or chat at 988lifeline.org.

If you're outside the U.S., local crisis lines and health services can offer immediate support; many countries participate in international suicide prevention networks accessible via local health ministries or at https://www.iasp.info/ .

Globally, hundreds of thousands of people die by suicide each year—a stark reminder that community, connection, and timely support can make a life-saving difference.

Acknowledgments

Thank you for continuing this journey with me and for reading *CHOICElover*. If you've made it this far into the *Love, Manufactured* world, I hope you're as invested in these characters and their messy, human (and sometimes not-so-human) choices as I am. Writing this series has been a strange, joyful, deeply satisfying adventure, and I'm grateful you're here for it.

If you enjoyed the book, even a little, I'd be so thankful if you'd consider leaving a review on Amazon or Goodreads. Reviews truly make a difference for indie authors—they help these stories find their readers and keep worlds like this one alive. And if you happen to mention that I made you laugh, all the better. I remain committed to proving—one book at a time—that I am, in fact, funny.

I'm still very much the kind of writer who takes a village, and *CHOICElover* exists because of the continued support, insight, and encouragement of some truly incredible people.

First, to Casey Harris-Parks—the original champion of this strange, delightful idea from the very beginning. You were the first person I pitched this world to, and you didn't just get it—you pushed me to go bigger, weirder, and deeper. Your guidance, especially in the fine-tooth, line-level and developmental work on this book, helped sharpen the story in ways that truly elevated it. Having someone who believes in both the vision *and* the execution is a rare gift, and your impact on this book is woven into every chapter.

To Srishti Rathour—thank you for helping me map this world from the inside out. Your large-scale developmental work—digging into character, motivation, and the broader story architecture—helped shape the emotional and structural backbone of this series. You have a gift for seeing both the forest and the trees, and *CHOICElover* is stronger because of the foundation we built together.

A massive, heartfelt thank-you to Erica Peck, who did an extraordinary amount of heavy lifting in the copyediting phase. Your attention to detail, clarity, patience, and care helped wrangle this story into its cleanest, sharpest form. This book simply would not read the way it does without your work, and I'm deeply appreciative of everything you put into it.

A sincere thank-you as well to The Naughty Nook for proofreading support.

To my amazing street team—thank you for showing up with enthusiasm, creativity, and genuine love for this series. Your posts, messages, encouragement, and willingness to champion these books out in the wild mean more than I can adequately express. This journey is infinitely more fun because of you.

And a very special thank you to @foxysbookshelf (Destin)—my go-to Canva collaborator and all-around force of nature. You have gone so far above and beyond it's honestly hard to keep track. I'm endlessly grateful for you.

Finally, to my husband—my real-life perfect partner. When I said, "I think I want to be an author," you said, "I'm sure you'll be amazing at it." When I said I wanted to learn to sail, you said, "Let's charter boats in the Caribbean." When I said, "Hey, what if we move to Turks and Caicos and try island life?" you packed the bags. And two and a half years later, when I said, "Actually... how about Miami?" you said, "Go find us a condo," and trusted me to set up our next adventure.

You're the rock we've built our wildly adventurous life on—the one who makes the coffee, brings the smoothies, encourages my very K8-like shopping habits, and supports every wild idea I dream up without hesitation. If I could have designed the perfect partner, it would have been you. Thank you for being my constant, my co-conspirator, and my home.

About the Author

Hey, I'm Jennifer. I write stories that explore the human experience—searching for clarity in the chaos, meaning in the unexpected, and connection through the characters we come to love. My work spans from lush fantasy romance to quirky speculative fiction, all rooted in emotional truth, hidden layers, and a touch of the unexpected. Whether I'm exploring love, death, or the weird magic in between, I'm here for readers who crave stories that surprise, resonate, and stay with you long after the final page.

Find me on Instagram @authorjmwaldrop or TikTok @authorjmwaldrop and my website www.jennifermwaldrop.com for: my newsletter sign up, updates on my current WIP, bonus content, and more.

*www.jenniferm
waldrop.com*

Image of the author

*Amazon Author
Page*